Waiting for a
Star to Fall

Waiting for a Star to Fall

Elaine Cremin

ISBN: 1508509727
ISBN 13: 9781508509721
Library of Congress Control Number: 2015902568
CreateSpace Independent Publishing Platform
North Charleston, South Carolina

For Mam and Dad,
Brian, Derek, Orla, Aoife, Killian, Robyn, Andrew and Tom

With special thanks to the following people:

My family, who I dedicate this book to for being supportive of me when I came up with the notion of becoming a writer and writing this novel. It's been a long road, but I got here finally. Thanks for your love, support and encouragement.

Aunty Breda, Derek, Aoife, Orla and Marie (Molls), for reading my manuscript before it went anywhere near an editor! Thank you all for reading it, and for your feedback. It's greatly appreciated and helped me to make it what I hope, is a better read.

My dear friend Giancarlo, for the constant encouragement and support you gave me from start to finish on this book. Thank you, you're a star!

Richéal, thank you for being a fabulous friend and for putting up with me for two weeks in New York, back in September 2014, whilst putting the finishing touches to the book. I had a ball of a time and I'm still laughing!! I'm looking forward to the next visit!

Valentina, Sam and Gabriel for the fun times we had last year as flatmates. Thanks for putting up with my disappearing act for days/evenings on end to edit, edit, edit! Thanks for still talking to me afterwards – not that you really had a choice! Thanks to Valentina who's still putting up with my disappearing act! You're a great friend and flatmate!

Andy Ellis, who was my fiction tutor. You read my manuscript in the early stages and helped me to see what I needed to change. I've learned so much from you, thank you.

Tony Milner, for the wonderful graphics, and producing the cover. Thanks for your hard work and for putting up with my endless emails. I'll bet you're glad to see it's finally finished! Thank you!

To the CreateSpace team, you have been a pleasure to work with. Thank you for your hard work in helping me reach the finish line!

Lastly, to all of my family, and dear friends, too many to list individually, but you all know who you are. Your support over the past few years has been tremendous, and your belief in me has kept me determined to get to this stage. You've all been a part of making my dream come true, so thank you. You are all stars!

Happy reading....

"I've had enough! I'm out!" I shriek.

Jason, my colleague, is looking at me in dismay.

"Crap! What's driven you to that—or should I ask *who*?"

"You'd be correct in thinking the latter, Jason. I can't put up with her anymore. I'm done here. Time to move on."

I grab my things and walk toward the door.

As I glance back, I see that most of my colleagues are wearing confused expressions. Yet, it has never been a secret that I would explode one day.

It was the perfect company for me to work in as far as greeting-card companies go. I could practice my verse writing on the side. Who knew where it would lead to—but now my time has come to an end here. I walk down the stairs and think back to my first day at Dawson Cards.

March 2010

I am sitting quite comfortably at my desk, reading the office manuals, as my new boss, Davina, had instructed me to do. I hear a yell from her office.

"Aly, get in here!"

What have I done? I think. I walk slowly towards her office, dreading what she is going to say. "Hi, Davina, what can I do for you?"

"Plenty! You're sitting on your arse out there, watching the time fly by. You can start by making me tea—white with two sugars!"

"OK," I reply sheepishly. I wasn't expecting to be shouted at for no reason.

I walk towards the kitchen and fill her cup with boiled water and a tea bag. Thoughts of spitting into it and giving it a stir spring to mind. However, I don't, and I rush back as quickly as I can so that she won't jump down my throat again. I return to my desk, hoping she won't come near me again for the rest of the day.

Later that day, I walk home feeling deflated. I relax with my partner, Simon, and sip a glass of wine. He makes me realise that maybe Davina just had a bad day. I agree and decide to forget about it.

The next day I make the journey to the office in a positive frame of mind. Rather than waiting to be summoned, I knock gently on Davina's door and announce my arrival.

"Morning, Davina. How are you today? Do you have anything urgent you would like me to deal with?"

"Please, come in, Aly, and take a seat."

She said "please." That's something I suppose.

"We're expecting new greeting-card verses in for the Christmas season over the coming weeks. They're all regular freelance contributors. I'll give you a list of names. Once you see the emails in my inbox, I want you to print them off and go through them. Ditch the crap ones, and bring the ones that are up to my publishing standards to me."

I dare not ask what might be considered crap, but I have a feeling our tastes are very different.

"Great! I'd love to do that!" I reply.

I walk back to my desk briskly and wait patiently for the emails to come through. It's boring just sitting there, so I start scribbling a few verses. It is one of my favourite things to do in my spare time, and I prefer to look like I'm doing something.

Ping! The first email flashes up forty minutes later. I print it off and glance through the verses. As I do, I hear a thud, like something falling to the floor. I turn around to see Davina standing behind me. I had secretly been hoping she had fallen.

"Acquaint yourself with these!" she says sharply. "You'll be dealing with more cards and verses as you go along. This box of cards will give you an idea of what verses we use."

Before I can thank her, she disappears, muttering under her breath as she walks away.

Jason is sitting next to me. He seems to be a quiet person—at least he was on my first day, because he didn't utter a word.

"Ignore her! She's a bit of a tyrant, not to mention a slag!" he says.

I laugh, as I can't comment on the latter but think it's very funny.

"She shouts at everyone for no reason, but we've learned to ignore her. You'll also learn that she tends to shout mainly at the people who either (a) have refused to sleep with her or (b) are those she sees as prospective mating material. I'm 'a'!" he says, with an air of pride in his Cork accent. "It's better to let you know now. Although you'll be safe enough, I'd say. I've no idea why she shouts at you," he says with a cheeky grin. "I'll go through that box of cards with you and the verses so you'll get a better idea of what she wants."

"Thanks, Jason, I appreciate that."

I'm pleasantly surprised by Jason's wit, and from that moment on, we become good friends.

I learn the ropes reasonably quickly and take on far more responsibility than I should. Once I finish my studies and acquire my diploma in creative marketing and product production, I feel sure I can give much more to the job, and maybe Davina will consider delegating something more challenging my way. She's not aware of my interest in writing verse, and I do not want her to know. She would most likely be cheeky enough to ask if I can contribute for free. Anything to save on company costs! Jason now knows of my pastime of writing and design. He swears he'll never utter a word to Davina because he's aware I'm more interested in climbing to the top of the ladder. I've made a good friend in him.

One year later, and it's a sunny spring day. I'm in the office listening to an old eighties song on the radio, Yazz's "The Only Way Is Up!" I'm daydreaming about what life would be like working in another company and wonder if most offices would be the same as working at Dawson Cards—a witch at the helm of the creative department would be a turnoff to most, I'm sure. It's a shame I didn't know what Davina was like before I started. I turn the radio down. Although I enjoy the song, and it has a happy vibe to it, the atmosphere I work in doesn't.

There's a loud buzzing noise coming from Washington Street, and I can hear the people of Cork chatter as they go about their business. There's a traffic jam outside my window, and car horns are creating disturbance as their impatient drivers all seem to be in a rush. I go to the window to see what the furore is about. I'm no sooner there when I hear, "Aly!"

I make my way hesitantly to her office. One year into the job, and I'm still petrified of her.

"Take a seat. I've got a problem."

"Oh, that sounds serious. I hope it's nothing to do with my work?"

"Why does it always have to be about you, Aly? I'm pretty sure your life is as dull as dishwater. Just take a seat and listen to me!"

"OK!"

I sit nervously, feeling slightly hurt at her comment. I have an exciting life...sometimes.

I stare at her over-Botoxed lips and see that there is something seeping out of the side of her mouth. I feel like puking.

"Right, Aly. What I'm going to tell you is in confidence, so don't breath a word to anyone—and by anyone, I mean *anyone*!"

OK, I think I understand that!

"You know you can trust me to keep my mouth shut," I say.

"Good! Now, Aly, I've met someone."

Not a conversation I was expecting! Since when did we discuss pleasure moments in your office?

"He works here, but that's not the problem. He's married."

OK, I'm not comfortable with this silence. Am I meant to speak now?

"OK, and?" I say.

"And? Is that all you can say to me? You evidently need more to go on if that's your response! His wife is after discovering we're having an affair. I'm terrified she'll hunt me down and start a cat-fight or something. My reputation would be ruined!"

Jesus, I'd say you've managed that already.

I'm trying to stifle a laugh. I know who she is talking about. It's Mattie O'Brien, a big male slut who has aspirations of spreading his seed throughout the country. He's probably impregnated half of Ireland at this stage. How could she even think about looking at him, not to mention anything else?

"Davina, I don't understand why you're telling me this."

"Well, you're my *assistant*, Aly!"

That doesn't mean I want to hear about your twisted love life!

"Yes, I know that, but are you looking for advice from me?" I ask.

"*Yes!* What should I do?"

"Well, end it, of course. Don't even consider going near him again. It's as simple as that."

I wouldn't normally be so blunt, but I'm pissed off at both her shouting and moaning to me each day, and I could certainly have gone without hearing that.

"That's *no* help! *Get out!*"

I retreat to my desk in a lively fashion and manage to stifle the laughter until I reach my seat.

Jason is out, which is probably best, as I'd have found it difficult to keep this new information to myself. He has a persistent way of drawing information from me. Unfortunately for me, Davina continues to tell me her problems in confidence each week thereafter. She pencils me in for a thirty-minute meeting each Thursday, which never seems to be about work. I'll never understand why she chose me as her confidante.

Ten months later, I decide it's time to speak up and change the subject from Davina's love life and sexual exploits to the subject of work.

"Hi, Davina. Is it time for our meeting?" I ask as I stand at her door.

"Yes, yes, come in."

Great, you're in one of your moods. Then again, when aren't you?

"Davina, I was wondering if you could pass a little more responsibility my way. I've acquired my diploma, and I think I'd be very capable of taking on more challenging work. What do you think?"

"What? You might as well be just out of nappies! I'm not passing any important work your way, Aly. If I start doing that, then I might as well give you my job!"

"All I want is the excess work that takes up your time, Davina—the work you'd prefer not to have to deal with. It would be good for me to gain more experience and get to know some of our clients better. To be honest, as my boss, I thought you would be happy to help me out. I've been your assistant for nearly two years now. Surely I deserve your support if I want to make something better of my life. Admittedly, I chose to do the whole college thing a bit later than most, but that doesn't mean I'm not capable of a challenge."

"Deep, Aly, very deep. I think this meeting is over for today."

I sit there waiting for a better response. My focus is on her lips and her forehead. She can barely move either with the overload of Botox. I feel a slight smile creep across my face and know I'm not going to get very far with her. I retreat back to my desk.

Four days pass, and as I'm getting on with my daily duties, I spy Davina approaching me. She seems very sheepish, which makes me think she's after something.

"Can you come into my office for a minute, please? I need to discuss something with you."

"Sure," I say, and I stand up quickly—a little too quickly, because I end up spilling the water I'm holding all over my top.

"Wayhey!" Jason shouts. "We're having a wet T-shirt competition at my side of the office."

My face flushes, and I give Jason the evil eye. The rest of the lads start cheering as my underwear is clearly showing through my top.

"Gobshites!" I shout.

They all laugh.

I enter Davina's office and take a seat.

"Aly, I've informed Tom that you would like more responsibility, and he thinks it's a good idea to pass you some of the backlog sitting on my desk. Are you happy to deal with that?"

"Of course I am. I'd be delighted to!"

"Please realise this is just a trial run. I told him that you got your diploma, and he seems very happy for you to learn the ropes and gain more experience."

"I won't let you down, Davina—or Tom."

"OK, that's it. You can take this lot with you now. The creative budget is something I hate dealing with," she says with a look of satisfaction.

I smile and take the files. I'm not a fan of budgets, but I know I'll never get anywhere if I start moaning to her about that. I pretend I'm thrilled at the prospect of dealing with them.

"I'm very excited about this. Thanks, Davina."

It's not exactly the start I had in mind, but I know her well now, and she'd snatch the opportunity from me again in a shot. I'm even more excited at the prospect of telling my sister. Everything always seems to fall into place for her. She's like the blue-eyed girl everyone loves, and for a change, I'll get the limelight when I tell my parents that the big boss man is happy for me to learn the ropes and make a contribution.

Once I reach home later that evening, I ring my family.

"Mam, I'm so excited. They're passing more responsibility my way at work. The boss is more than happy for me to gain more experience."

"Oh, love, that's great news. You'll be running the company yet!" she exclaims.

"Well, I wouldn't go that far, but it's a good start."

"A great start! Hold on. Vicky's here and wants a word."

Oh crap, just my luck she's there.

"Hey, Alyson, what's happened to make Mum so happy?"

"Hi, sis. Well, they're encouraging me at work to learn the ropes and are giving me more responsibility," I say, full of cheer.

"And?"

"And that's it..." I trail off as she manages to burst my bubble with one word—a conjunction at that!

"Oh. OK, ah, you'll be successful someday. You're only starting out. I gotta go. Tony is picking me up."

Poor Tony. Why he goes out with you is beyond me, especially when you treat him so badly.

"OK, you go. I'll talk to you soon," I say and hang up.

Why can't she ever be happy for me? She will never see me as successful, no matter what I do. I just can't win. I wonder if she would be such a bitch if she hadn't been top of her class in uni and if she wasn't such a successful doctor. It's like she always has to rub it in.

I feel the pressure as the days pass. Each time I walk by Davina's office, she is checking her lips in her pocket mirror. I wonder if I have taken all of her work from her, because she seems incredibly relaxed. I'm starting to feel like her donkey, so I decide to investigate if she does in fact have work to do.

"Hey, Davina."

She looks at me with a startled expression—or as close as she can get to one.

"Oh, hello, come in. I'm just looking at my lips. This is between you and me, Aly. You probably haven't noticed before, but I get Botox injected into my lips and forehead every now and then. I was thinking of having more injected tomorrow. What do you think?"

Oh, Jesus, how do I answer?

"Are you serious? I'd never have thought it, but they look grand. I don't think you need to get them done again."

Are my lies transparent? I never was a good liar. I may have sounded a little too sarcastic even.

"Oh, Aly, that's great to hear. Sometimes when I walk down the street, I feel like people are staring at me, like I'm a freak. I do think they're a bit deflated-looking, though. I might go for it. Was there something you wanted?"

"Yes, I'm almost finished with the budget. I'll drop it into your office in a few minutes."

"Lovely! You can take this lot, then. I'd hate to see you with nothing to do!"

I grin while gritting my teeth. I really want to fire the entire file at her and let her deal with it all herself, but I know I'll just have to put up and shut up.

"Great, thanks, Davina."

I turn on my heels and head for my desk. Jason swings around in his chair.

"Ya fecking idiot! What were you thinking, going in there? Were you looking for more budgetary work?"

"No! I was trying to figure out what her lazy arse was doing!"

"And?"

"Well, she was examining her trout pout, and that was it. Then she informed me of the load of work which still has to be done."

"Oh. Well, that's what you get for spying on the boss," he says with a grin.

I can never get angry with Jason. He always manages to make me laugh or smile, even in the worse situation, so I playfully pretend to throw the stapler at his head.

"Ouch!"

"Sorry! Oh my God, that wasn't supposed to happen. I was only pretending to throw it at you. It slipped!"

"It's OK, no blood—but please be a little more careful?"

"I will. I'm sorry."

For feck sake, what a day! It's just not turning out too good, so I keep my head down and get on with my work for the remainder of it.

The next morning the sun is belting its rays out of the sky, and nobody can upset my mood, not even Davina. As I walk to my desk, I overhear a conversation between Davina and Tom.

"She's just not capable, Tom. She can't tell her arse from her elbow."

Who's she talking about?

"I beg to differ, Davina. I've seen some work Jason passed my way. Her card designs are wonderful, and her verse writing is extremely good. I think it would be a wonderful opportunity for her to progress."

"I disagree; she's barely capable of being my assistant without cocking up."

B-i-t-c-h! She's talking about me!

"Davina, my decision is final. You want the time off, and she runs the show. You know I'm all for people progressing—do not piss me off!"

"Fine!"

I see Tom leave her office.

"Morning, Aly. It's a beautiful morning out there."

"Yes, it is, Tom," I say meekly as he brushes passed me.

I wonder what that was all about? I hope my job isn't in jeopardy—what a horrible cow she is, and after all the crap I've put up with from her.

Davina walks past me and gives me one of her weird nonsmiley smiles. It's probably quite freaky looking to the ordinary person on the street, but I'm used to her, and so I don't take much notice.

"Don't forget the workload on my desk," she says with a smug grin.

"Good morning to you too, Davina," I say as I whisk past her. I wonder if Tom, her boss, is aware of the amount of work she's piled onto me. "I'll collect it when I've made my coffee," I say in a nonchalant voice.

"Good. You seem much more enthusiastic these days, Aly. Shame you weren't like that when you had fewer responsibilities!" she retorts. She turns on her heels and heads for her office.

"Was that just sarcasm I heard on her part?" I ask Jason.

"Yeah, I think so. I did warn you when you started a couple of years ago that she's a pain. Are you only realising it now?"

"No, I realised it from day one, but it's beyond me why I stayed on."

"Aly? Aly, come here for a minute," calls Davina.

"Oh, for goodness' sake, what does she want now? Why do I have to go to her constantly? Why can't she come to me for a change?"

"Perks of the job, Aly. You should know that by now," Jason says.

I walk across the room to her office. It's always been convenient for her to have me within earshot, but it's been close to torture for me.

"Come in, come in," she says with a smile—or grimace; there doesn't seem to be a difference when it comes to Davina.

"I've something to tell you," she continues.

"A little early for our meeting, Davina. It's normally in the afternoon," I say with a tinge of anger.

"Oh, it doesn't matter. We'll have it when I feel like it," she retorts.

Oh no, what the hell is she going to tell me? It's too early for this! She's pregnant! I'll bet that's it. Mattie finally scored a goal.

"I've booked my Botox. Now, the only thing is, they have to operate on my lips before they inject me. They made a botch job of them the last time and need to fix them up. For goodness sake, when I attempt to smile, my lips are so big that sometimes it just looks like I have no teeth and all gums."

"I hadn't noticed," I say with a smirk.

"They said I may have to spend a few weeks out of work, and I'd prefer not to return until the swelling goes down properly. I've had a chat with Tom, and we've both agreed that while I'm gone, it would be good experience for you to do my job as creative director."

Are you having a laugh?

"Well, Aly, don't just stand there like a mannequin. What do you think?"

I shrug my shoulders, still in disbelief, and say, "Sure. I'm up for the challenge." *Obviously, you're very against this idea.* "Davina, are you sure you want to do this? You know that these procedures don't always go to plan."

"Aly, I'm offering you a step up here, and you're criticising what I do in my personal life! I'll take it that you'll do the job as you've been annoying me about it now for some time. Get out!"

"Sorry, yes, I'll do it." I leave in a fairly lively manner. Showing concern for her was the last thing I should have done.

Three weeks later, Davina heads off for her "recuperation period," as she calls it. I'm the only one she told within the creativity department. I'm feeling upbeat, as it's time for me to prove myself to Tom in her absence.

"Good morning, Jason. How do you feel about me being your boss for the next three weeks?"

"What are you talking about, Aly?"

"Davina has gone on leave for a few weeks. She's put me in charge."

"Party, party!"

"Don't get ahead of yourself. I'll be far more relaxed than her, but don't take advantage, either, Jas."

"Ah sure, you know me now. I'm only having the craic with ya. We'll work in the same manner; we wouldn't want you getting into any trouble because of us, Aly."

I smile at him because I know that he and the team won't let me down. In fact, I have a feeling everything will run very smoothly.

Chapter 2

February 2012, Cork, Ireland

I'm feeling happy with myself. It's my final day at the office helm, and for the duration, I've felt like I've been on holiday. I've worked hard, but not having Davina around has been wonderful.

My phone rings.

"Hi, Aly. I'll be back in tomorrow to clear up any mess you've made while I was out."

"Thanks, Davina, but I can assure you there isn't any mess to clear. Everything has been running very smoothly." *Bitch!*

"I'll be the judge of that. I'll see you tomorrow."

I've been expecting that. She rang every day with the exception of the day of her operation and the day after. Each time the conversation was less than two minutes long.

"Was that the witch?" Jason quizzes from his desk.

"Yeah, she's gracing us with her presence tomorrow."

"Party's over, in that case. I might as well get pissed tonight as I'll need to drown out her voice with the aid of a hangover tomorrow," he says in a droll voice.

I snigger to myself. "Truth is, I feel like joining you, but I can't. I know I'll have to be on top form for her majesty's return."

The next morning I'm feeling ill as I approach the office. It feels like everything I've worked so hard for is being stripped from me.

Temptation is there to pull a sickie, but I'll just have to be adult-like and get on with it.

When I enter the office, the first person I see is Jason. He has a head on him like something from a zombie movie.

"Got to bed at five o'clock this morning," he slurs.

I feel oddly proud to see he stuck to his word.

"Nice one, Jas. How are you going to see the day out?"

"Dunno. Feels like I've been here the whole day already, and I only got here ten minutes ago," he mumbles as he walks towards the corridor.

"I'm off to the jacks again," he says loudly.

I giggle. "Thanks for that information."

"*Aly!*"

No! Not now! Why couldn't you come in later?

"Davina, how are you?" I ask. I can't take my gaze away from her humungous lips.

"I'm fine, thank you. What do you think? They look much better, don't they?" she says as she strains a smile.

They are a little better than before but still look ridiculous.

"Lovely job, Davina," is the best I can come up with.

"I've spoken to Tom. It seems you've done a very good job here in my absence." She smiles again, but there's no sign of a thank you. "Now, curiosity is getting the better of me. Who's the new guy in the suit I saw in the corridor?"

"You mean Danny? He's a new PA on the first floor."

"How old is he? Where's he from? Does he smell good?"

Wow, who's dying for a piece of Danny? He's too young for you!

"Davina, he's probably a bit young for you, if that's what you're getting at? He's twenty-five, from Kerry; and I've no idea how he smells, as I haven't been in close enough proximity to decipher that just yet."

"Young, schmung! He's fit, and I'm going to see if I can organise a date with him. I'll wear my short skirt tomorrow, which always works."

I wonder why!

I leave her office, feeling a bit dejected, and return to my old desk next to Jason.

"What the feck has she done to her lips? I thought she was going on holiday. Fishing expedition was it? Caught a few trout, I'd say?"

"Jas, I couldn't tell you. I was sworn to secrecy. She should have known people would notice her lips when she came back. By the way, on another note, poor Danny is on the hit list now."

"I'd better warn him!" Jason says as he removes himself from his seat. The stench of drink leaves with him as he makes his way to the lifts.

Davina is old enough to be Danny's mother—or even his grandmother, if I'm to be cruel. Besides that, she has a thing for wearing short skirts, but when she refers to her "short skirt," she means the one that barely covers her arse.

It's late afternoon, and I haven't seen Jason since earlier. He allegedly has an external meeting, but his diary is empty. If I know Jason, he's taken a diversion to his flat en route to his so-called meeting. It's probably for the best. If Davina saw him in the state he's in, she'd make his life hell. It's been a reasonably peaceful day for me; thankfully, she's kept a very low profile.

The following morning Davina seems very quiet. There's no shouting from the office, which has me somewhat perplexed. I should just enjoy moments like this rather than wonder why.

I spot Danny walking from the lifts. As he passes her office, I watch as the door bursts open and Davina runs from the office, like a dog in heat.

"Ah, Danny, isn't it?" she quizzes in a very posh-sounding voice.

"Who is she kidding with that accent?" Jason says as he swings around to view the spectacle.

"I'm Davina, creative director. Come in and have a cup of coffee with me."

"Oh, poor Danny!" Jason says with a roar of laughter.

He swings around in his chair to face the other lads. "All bets are on. She's closed the blinds. I'll bet ten quid that she's going to go for it in her office."

My stomach churns at the thought of it. Surely she won't seduce him during working hours *and* in her office? There's a small window next to the door, which isn't covered—unfortunately, like most of Davina's private parts today. The lads take advantage and race up and down the corridor like school kids hoping for a glimpse inside. I'm glued to my seat, as I'm afraid of what I might see if I pass by. It's bad enough I'll be subjected to the story in full detail later.

Danny emerges twenty minutes later, looking paler than pale. We sit stony-faced and try to look clueless.

"Ah, Aly," Davina says in a calm manner as she approaches me. "Do come in for a chat later."

I'm unlucky, as it happens to be Thursday.

"OK, Davina," I say with a false smile. I shudder at the thought of what she plans to reveal to me.

"Oh, lovely young fella, that Danny. He smells great, too," she says.

Danny is running at great speed towards the lifts. I glance at Jason, and Jason glances at me; and we both burst out laughing.

Davina turns towards her office and walks away with a swagger, the cheeks of her arse hanging under her skirt.

Nothing she ever says again will shock me, although I was surprised when she asked me if I knew what Danny smelled like. From what I know of her past escapades, she doesn't seem to care about whether her conquests smell good or bad. The nastiest was Mitch. The smell from him was stomach-churning. You could smell him from the second floor—we are based on the fourth. Everyone was polite to him, though, and we all tried our best in a most discreet manner to give him the hint by giving him soaps and such in the secret Santa pool each year. He was a sweet guy—just didn't smell so sweet.

The guys in my team have crowned Davina with the most uncoveted title of "bicycle of the year" each year that I've worked here. I don't really care what she gets up to. It's her business, but I don't want to know about it, either. I know what I'll be subjected to later in the day, and I really don't want to have to deal with it any longer. I need to speak with Tom, so I make my way to the third floor.

"Hi, Tom. I need a word, please," I say as I knock on the door.

"Sure, Aly, come on in. What can I do for you?"

"Well, it's Davina. Tom, I've tried so hard to help her in every way I can, but she just seems to knock my confidence constantly. She roars at me for no reason, and I really can't take it anymore."

"I'm aware of her tendencies to shout at you, Aly. In fact, I think you've handled it all very well. I'm glad I suggested to her that I put you in charge while she was on leave. I don't think it's something she would have suggested herself, but I can see how capable you are of doing the job. However, I'm afraid I can't do much about Davina right now."

"Thank you, by the way, for giving me the opportunity," I say. "I really enjoyed filling in for her."

"I could see both you and the team enjoyed you working at the helm. Look, Davina's father is a massive shareholder in the company. I don't have much of a say when it comes to whether she works here or not."

"Oh, I see. Well, I'm not looking for her to be fired. I just need a break from her. If someone could discreetly point out to her that she's a bit much to deal with at times, that would be good. Maybe ask her to ease off?"

Give me a break from her filthy exploits and non-PC behaviour. That's all I want. A break!

"I'll see what I can do."

"Tom, the only other option I have is to leave. I'm near to that point, to be honest with you, but I know she won't give me a reference."

"Don't worry about that, Aly. I'll be very happy to supply you with an excellent reference if you ever leave. I got to know you quite well while you were covering for Davina. I do hope that thought of leaving will retreat to the back of your mind or even disappear completely though. You're a very valuable member of staff. I don't want to lose you."

I smile. "Thanks, Tom. It's reassuring to know that someone appreciates me."

Tom is a nice man, and I know I can count on him to keep our conversation confidential. Even though I only really got to know him over the three weeks Davina was on leave, I feel he can be trusted. I finally feel appreciated. It makes a nice change.

It's been a long day, and I decide to stop at the off-licence on the way home to pick up a bottle of wine. I feel like unwinding with a drink after being subjected to Davina's lurid activities again.

When I reach the flat, the door is unlocked. Simon must have arrived home early. As I enter, I see the bedroom door is closed. I keep quiet because he may be in bed having a nap. I'm in the kitchen sorting out my bags when I hear mumbling from the bedroom. I wander into the corridor and fling the door open, and there he is, in bed with some floozy.

"Jesus, Aly, I wasn't expecting you so soon. I thought you were going for drinks tonight. That's what your voice message said," he says as he bolts upright in the bed. I'm pretty sure he just injured both himself and his bit on the side.

I'm speechless for a minute.

Breathe; breathe deep breaths, in through the nose, out through the mouth.

"No, my message said I fancied a drink tonight. That didn't mean I was coming home late so you could shag your trollop friend."

"Hi, Aly, I'm Arora. I've heard so much about you!"

"Arora. *Arora*, is it? What kind of a name is that? I'm delighted you've heard so much about me, because I've heard nothing about you!"

"I…I'm sorry, I should go!" she says.

"She's a clever one, Simon," I retort.

She walks to the hallway to get dressed. If she thinks she's getting away that easily, she has another think coming.

I open the door and stand there, looking at her holding her clothing up to hide her nudity.

"Go on, get out," I say in a very calm manner.

She looks at me in surprise. "But I…I need to get dressed!"

"Ah, you're grand. You can do that outside. You've had no problem getting undressed in a stranger's bedroom, so I'm sure you'll have no problem redressing in front of strangers. Now off you go!"

She slowly leaves. I slam the door.

My focus is now back in the bedroom. Simon is sitting on the bed. He's still naked, waiting for me.

"I think you can start getting dressed!" I scream at him.

"Oh, hon, I'm sorry. I made a mistake, that's all. Please forgive me?"

"What kind of a gobshite do you think I am? For the first time ever, you are not going to win this argument!"

"Please, love? I'll be a better man. I promise. I can't lose you! You're the best thing that's ever happened to me!"

That's it. That. Is. It! Those are the words I need to hear to reach boiling point.

"I made a huge mistake going out with you in the first place! For nearly four years, I've had so many doubts about you. You've just proven to me exactly why I've had those doubts! You thought I was going to forgive you just then, didn't you? Just by uttering those words, 'I'll be a better man.' Eejit! Get out of my apartment and get out of my life *now!*"

Simon's hands are trembling. I'm not sure if he is actually scared of me or perhaps of the fact that his manhood is still on display. I take his clothes and throw them at him.

"Go, Simon, go now," I say in a more calm voice. Something has clicked inside of me, and I don't want to shout at him anymore. I just want him gone.

I walk into the kitchen and open the cupboards. I can hear Simon struggling to get his trousers on in the bedroom. I start banging the cupboard doors in a bid to scare him.

As I reach the hallway again, he's standing there waiting, as if he's expecting a goodbye kiss.

"What?" I say when I see him.

"Nothing, I'm going now." He walks to the door, and when I open it for him, Arora is still standing outside like a loyal dog, waiting for him.

"You're still here!" I say.

At least she's managed to put her clothes on. She's very flushed-looking.

She stretches out her hand for Simon to take it, but he edges past her and flees the building as fast as he can. For a split second, I feel sorry for her. Did she really expect so much from him? Did he promise her the world like he promised me? Probably. I've managed to figure out finally what he wants: the happy couple life with extras on the side. Perhaps bachelorhood will suit him better.

In my moment of madness, I give her a sympathetic look and say goodbye. I turn my back and close the door. I walk to the kitchen and take two giant bars of chocolate out of the cupboard, which I was saving for a night in while watching a good movie. Instead, I sit on the sofa and gorge on it while listening to love songs from the eighties. I sob for the entire night as I polish off the wine I brought home with me. The wine I bought to share with Simon.

Chapter 3

I'm not feeling the best, so I'm taking time out for a couple of days. I need the break from Davina, and I need to figure out what I want to do with my life.

I spend four days curled up in my pyjamas listening to big hits from the eighties and crying to any slow ones. I need to talk to someone, so I ring my mother and ask her advice.

"Mam, I've no idea what to do. I just can't take it anymore. My job would actually be really good except for my boss, and now with all this happening with Simon, I don't want to go back. I just want someone to dig me out of this hole."

"I know, love. It will get better, though. Maybe you need to take a break away?"

"All I want right now is a one-way ticket to outer space."

"Well, why not start with a one-way ticket to New York? You were born there, after all. It's not a problem for you to go back whenever you want to. I'm sure you'd find a job no problem there, now that you have your diploma. It could be a nice fresh start for you, and you'd be back with your best friends again. I know how much you miss Karen and Jen, and they miss you."

"Yeah, I'll think about it. Thanks, Mam. It feels good just to get it off my chest."

I hang up. She's planted a seed in my brain. I spend the rest of the day thinking about what a fresh start in New York would be like for me.

I'm sitting watching TV later in the evening when my phone rings.

Oh Christ, it's Vicky. I answer reluctantly.

"Hi, Vicky."

"Hi, Alyson. Are you OK? I was over at Mum's today. She told me about what happened between you and Simon."

"Yes, it's true."

"So, what happened? Did you do something to make him cheat on you?"

"Vicky, why did you ring? To make me feel ten times shittier than I already do? When something good happens to me, you turn it into a negative. When something bad happens, you never offer comforting words. You just twist the knife even more. What is your problem?"

"Oh, Aly, man up. It's not the first or last breakup you'll have… I'm sure! Get over it. We all do."

"You know what, sis? Don't call me again. Why the hell can't you be supportive like our other sisters? That's what I need now. I can't entertain you right now. I'm just not in a good place, and you're not helping. Goodbye." I hang up.

The idea of moving to New York is becoming more appealing by the minute.

I finally snap out of my pathetic state and return to work on the following Wednesday.

"Ah, Aly. Welcome back. What was wrong with you exactly?" Davina asks.

I already informed you I had the flu! Why can't that be enough for you?

"Hi, Davina. Simon and I split up. I wasn't feeling great, so I told you I was ill, but that's the truth."

"Oh, I'm sorry to hear that. He's a fine man, you silly girl."

My eyes are bulging as I try to bite my tongue. It doesn't work. "No, he isn't. You're welcome to him. In fact, you'd make a lovely couple," I say as I walk away from her.

"Right, I'll let you carry on," Davina says and scurries back to her office.

I take a seat at my desk and try to figure out when will be a good time to tell Davina my news. I know I'll have to choose my moment carefully. After spending time thinking about it, I decide to tell Tom first. He's far more approachable.

I remove myself from my chair and go to the third floor. I knock gently on his door.

"Hi, Tom, how are you?"

"Aly! Welcome back. How are you feeling?"

"I'm OK, thanks. Can I come in? I want to talk to you about something."

"My door is always open for you, Aly. Take a seat."

"Simon and I split up. I needed a few days to get my thoughts together to decide what I want to do."

"I'm sorry to hear that, Aly. Anything we can do here to help?"

"Well, you know I've not been very happy here of late. And with all of this mess with Simon, well, I've decided to leave the company and try something else."

"Oh, Aly, I'm sorry to hear that. You are such a valuable member of staff. Davina will be devastated! Have you spoken to her yet?"

My arse she will. If she's devastated, it's because she'll have no one to share her dirty exploits with and shift her workload onto.

"No, I'm trying to pick the right moment. Please don't say anything. I'd like her to hear it from me."

"Of course I won't. Thank you for sharing it with me first—and I'll give you a glowing reference as promised."

"Thanks, Tom. I appreciate that."

"So, what are your plans, or do you know yet? A time out, travel a bit, maybe?"

"I'm thinking of moving to New York. My best friends both live there, so there's a bed waiting for me at least if I decide for definite. Right now I think it could be the right course of action. I need a change," I say with a weak smile. "Thanks for being so understanding, Tom. I don't want to take up any more of your time."

I turn around to leave the office.

"Actually, Aly, before you go, there is one thing I can run by you now. I'm not sure if it will appeal to you, but have a think about it."

"I'm all ears!"

"We have an opening in the New York sister company for a creative director. It could be a good opportunity for you. Jeremy, the creative director, is being promoted, and he'd like to get someone in to learn the ropes from scratch, with a view to them taking over his position. Of course, there would be interviews beforehand, but I'd be pretty certain you'd be the number-one choice when it does come to that time. If suitable, Jeremy would be your boss for the first few months, but you would still carry the title of creative director. I know getting visas to work in the States can take months. I'm not sure how it would work out. I'd be happy to investigate if you are interested. I could find out what timescales we'd be looking at. Now don't get too excited. As I said, this is something random I'm throwing at you. I haven't discussed it with anyone yet, bar you."

"Tom, that would be fantastic! I was actually born in the United States, and my parents moved back to Cork when I was young. I have dual citizenship, so I don't have to go through that malarkey of applying for visas. That's how I was able to make this decision so quickly."

"Brilliant! I'll ring Jeremy Sullivan in New York and find out what the position is with interviews. I'll let you know as soon as I speak with him."

"Thanks so much, Tom. I really appreciate this."

I leave his office feeling very happy. I always knew the day would come when I would need to get some release from that woman.

I return to my desk and sit, doodling. I'm feeling happy that my plan might be coming together effortlessly. I can't concentrate after my discussion with Tom, and Jason isn't in yet to keep me occupied.

I'm just hitting relaxation point when I hear a familiar voice roaring. "Aly, my office, now!"

I sigh and walk towards her office.

"Take a seat. I need to chat to you."

"This sounds serious, Davina. What's up?" *Should I tell you now?*

She's very fidgety and looks to be sitting uncomfortably.

"You probably know Mitch left the company a few weeks back. We had a night out for him, and I ended up with him again. I know now it was the biggest mistake ever."

"Really, why's that? You obviously like him! Was that the second time or third time?"

"Aly, really! You make me sound like a slut! It was the second time. Anyway, as I was saying before you interrupted me, it was a big mistake, as he wants to get serious with me."

"Davina, I don't understand why you are telling me this. You're my boss, and I really don't feel comfortable with you sharing such personal stuff with me. I'm sorry, but you need to sort this one out on your own."

I get up and rush for the door. I'm feeling a little mean, but I have enough of my own problems and can't be dealing with hers too. I return to my desk, and as I spy her from my seat, she's looking very red-faced. I feel a little guilty, but I have had enough of this life and this crap office. I'll inform her later in the day of my departure.

A few hours pass, and I look up to see Tom approaching my desk.

"Aly. I've just spoken to Jeremy. Sorry it took so long—time difference! He'd be delighted to meet with you in relation to the job. There haven't been any interviews yet, but there are four people lined up. He's happy to slot you in for an interview, too. Nothing will be happening for at least another four weeks or so, which gives you time to decide if you are definitely going or not. I explained the situation to him, and he's happy to give you time to make a decision."

"Thanks so much. That's fantastic news. Seems my day is going better than expected."

A shudder of excitement runs through me as I never believed my plans could fall into place so quickly. I've decided for definite I'll make the trip to New York a fixture and not just a thought in my mind.

Work no longer interests me after Tom's visit. I'm too excited and don't feel like doing anything for the afternoon, bar doodling on my notebook. I think back on my chat with Davina earlier, and a wave of relief passes over me, knowing I won't have to put up with her or her sickening chats for much longer. My happy feeling inspires me to write the following:

> *The more I see your face, the more you remind me of a troll.*
> *You are so sad; to find a man, you'd almost sell your soul.*
> *I feel that working with you has been nothing but a farce.*
> *I cannot take it anymore; you're a big pain in my arse.*

Not one of my finer poems, but I've managed to leave off a little steam at least. My phone rings.

"Hey, Aly, it's Danny. I'm stuck on some budgetary thing here for the art department, and I was told you'd be the person to help me. You or Davina, and I'm not going near her."

"Sure, Danny, be there in a minute."

I hang up and go to help him out. On my return, Davina is standing at my desk and snarling at me.

"What's this?" She twirls the sheet of paper from my writing pad in her hand.

Damn, I forgot to bin it.

"That is something I was doing earlier, which wasn't for your review, but was meant to be in the bin by now," I say in a slightly shaky voice.

"My office, now!" She frogmarches me into the office. "How dare you write such a horrid thing! I'm assuming it is about me? I told you about my love life in confidence, and this is how you treat the whole thing, as a joke?"

"Davina, no offence meant. Nobody saw what I wrote. It was in the middle of the writing pad, which I closed. Therefore, you had to be nosing around my desk if you spotted it."

"How dare you speak to me like that, Aly!"

"Davina, I've come into this office every single day and listened to you twitter on about your sexual exploits, and I watch you consistently make a fool of yourself. Any time I want to try to stop you or give my opinion, you kick me out of your office and scream at me. You obviously don't care what people think about you, because if you did, you would have heeded some tiny bit of advice I've given you. I've had enough. I can't take this anymore. I came in here today in the hope that you might be some bit sympathetic to what happened to me, but no. You came out with a snide comment about me letting Simon go, and I'm a silly girl. Well, Davina, I may as well tell you my news now."

"Aly, I didn't say that to you. You're imagining things now. What news are you talking about?"

"I'm tired, Davina. I'm tired of your ways and turning everything around to make it out to be my fault. I'm tired of coming in here every single morning to you snarling at me because you're having a bad day, which seems to be every day!" I sigh. "My news is that I'm moving to New York. I'm out, Davina. I was thinking of being more polite about it, but to be honest, there's no point. It will make no difference to you anyway. I leave in three weeks, and I can't see myself staying here until then."

"Well, I'm disappointed in you. I taught you everything you know in here—how to seduce men, mainly. My skills are second to none, and this is how you repay me?"

I laugh out loud.

"Davina, sorry, but I'm out of here." I turn to walk away.

"Aly, Aly! Come back here!"

I panic for a moment as I realise I need to tell Tom. He told me he'd give me a reference, but he might have a change of mind if I just walk out. I'll go to his office, inform him of my behaviour and just hope for the best. Maybe my honesty will work in my favour.

I spy Tom through the crack in the door, and I knock gently. He swings around in his chair and greets me with a big smile. I feel guilty, and my hands are shaking.

"Tom, I'm sorry to disturb you again. I feel terrible. I've been so awful to Davina, and I told her I'm out! I'm not sure what to do. I'm in a mess. I'm just not thinking straight right now."

"Aly, come in and sit down. You're shaking!"

"I'm sorry. I've had a huge quarrel with Davina just now, and basically, I quit."

"OK, was it so bad that you can't go back and maybe apologise to her?"

"I could, but I really don't want to, Tom. She's made my life hell here, and to top it all off, this morning she made me feel like an idiot over Simon. I felt bad enough, but she just made things a whole lot worse. I'm sorry. I really need a reference, but I don't know if I can put up with her for another three weeks."

"Aly, I know you've had problems with Davina. I think we can sort something out and arrange for you to take your holiday leave rather than quitting. How does that sound? I'll still give that glowing reference I promised you."

"Thank you, I really appreciate that. It's been a tough few days, and to be honest, I could do with another few days off after today's events. I hate leaving you in the lurch, though. You know if you need anything, I'm on my phone, and I'll be happy to give any information you need. Maybe I could work from home for the next three weeks until you find someone?"

"Leave it to me, Aly. I told you, you're one of our best. I'm not going to backtrack on that. I know Davina can be difficult at times, but I think she'll miss you greatly. I'll let her know you're taking leave. You can head home now and leave everything to me. Just be sure to call in to collect that reference before you head off. Jeremy will be in touch with you to arrange that interview. I'll have a word with Davina also. She can't continue treating people like this. She's putting herself in a very dangerous position right now."

"Thanks, Tom."

Back at my desk, I feel I owe a proper explanation to my colleagues, but after my little outburst in front of Jason, I've decided it's best to go. I can meet them at a later stage to tell them what happened. However, Davina's sordid sex life is not something I plan on sharing.

I reach the ground floor, finally, and I'm glad I took the healthy option of the stairwell. A wave of sadness flows over me, as I'm going to miss the friends I've made while working here, especially Jason. I realise I have a major challenge in front of me once again, but at least it's one I can look forward to.

Chapter 4

"Chickie, what's happening with you? I spoke to Jen the other day; she said you're thinking of moving stateside?"

"Karen! Where the hell have you been? I've been ringing for weeks. What have you been up to?"

"Oh, chick, life's been crazy. I'm sorry I'm only contacting you now. So what's happened to say you're coming over to us? Oh, Aly, bring some Taytos with you, please? I'm dying for a taste of home."

"You know, if you came home more often, you wouldn't miss the taste of home so much."

"I know, I know. I have to make more effort. It's just that Dad comes over regularly now, so no real need for me to go. So come on, what's the plan?"

"Yeah, fair enough, but you have other family members and friends who'd love to see you so don't forget them! I'll be over next week. Jen has insisted I bunk in with her. Interview lined up and all."

"Jesus, you're organised, aren't you? Fantastic news. Can't wait to hear about everything. Chickie, gotta go here now. Just going into a meeting. I can't wait to see you. Love you lots. Bye, bye, bye."

"OK, bye, see you soon." I hang up. *Hmmmm, she sounds more hyper than usual.*

Chapter 5

May 2012

Finally, the first day of my new life has arrived.

The drive to the airport is horrible. Nobody is speaking, and I'm choking back the tears as we pass through Cork City.

"Isn't that one of your many drinking haunts over the years?" my father says with a smile.

"Yep, it sure is," I say with great sadness, and I know the tears are going to flow soon. The Grand Parade and South Mall are a gridlock of traffic.

"Look at how calm everyone is. I'll bet if this were New York, the car horns would be blazing at this stage and people shouting abuse at each other," I say.

"Ah what, you know what us Cork people are like—calm to the last, love. Shur isn't this a perfect excuse for having a sing-song? We'll blare up the radio and have one last singalong for you, Aly."

"Jesus, Dad, don't you dare. Don't shame me before I get on the plane." Dad was great for trying to cheer us up but not always the most PC man of our time. However, his comments are some-times so innocent, you can't help but laugh. Once the traffic starts to move, our car returns to silence. We turn onto Washington Street, and a wave of relief passes over me.

"I'll bet you're happy to be leaving this street behind," Mam says.

"Oh yeah, for sure. Especially that nutty bitch Davina," I say with a smirk.

"Aly! Your language!"

"Sorry, Mam," I say and catch Dad's eye in the mirror. The glint in his eye says it all. "Go on, Dad, just laugh if you want to," I say. He turns away, but I know he is still smirking. As we drive past the steps of the courthouse, I smile to myself. It takes me back to the night I met Simon in Reardens pub across the road. Six-inch heels were the problem of the night. I had spoken briefly with Simon in the bar, but when I was leaving, I twisted my ankle and somehow managed to break the heel of my shoe.

"Oh, are you OK?" he said.

"Yeah, I'll be grand, thanks," I replied, quite embarrassed. I started hobbling along, and he grabbed my arm.

"Here, you're looking a little unsteady there. I'll help you across the street. You can sit on the steps to rest up," he said.

"Quite the gent, aren't you?"

"I try," he said with a smile and then with a snigger. "You sound like a horse crossing the street with the clip-clop noise," he said, laughing.

I snigger. "It's true; I do," I admitted.

"Almost there now, horsey, just a few steps to go." *Cheeky fecker.*

"Aly? Aly?" my father says.

"Oh, sorry, Dad. I was miles away, thinking back to some of my nights out here."

"OK, love, traffic is moving fast. We'll be at the airport in no time."

"OK, thanks," I say with a smile. I can feel the lump in my throat growing, and there is no way I'll be able to keep my composure. As we approach the roundabout at Cork airport, I can't take it anymore, and my eyes start streaming. I hate goodbyes. How am I to say goodbye to my entire family...bar Vicky? She never bothered to show.

Chapter 6

I step from the plane and go straight to immigration, which thankfully causes me no problems. I find the guard on duty to be quite charming. Just the right height, and I love his stunning blue eyes and blond hair.

"Ma'am, I need your passport and any documentation you may have, please."

I love it when they call me that. I know Karen and Jen find it insulting, as they say it makes them sound like old women, but I think it's quite sexy. I manage to decipher his accent as being Southern, I think, and he has a cute smile to go with it. Perhaps a little flirtatious smile of my own is in order.

"Here you go," I say with a smile. Our hands touch briefly as I hand the information to him.

He smiles back. "That's a very nice Irish accent you have there!"

I wasn't expecting you to say that. "Well, thank you. You know, you have a very nice accent there yourself!" I reply.

"You hold a US passport. You were born here, I take it?"

"Yes, that's right. I'm making a new life for myself now in New York, where I was born. We moved to Ireland when I was young."

"It also says you're thirty-four years of age here. You look younger! Are you sure you're thirty-four?" He smirks as he quizzes me.

"I am indeed."

"I need you to look right at the camera for me now, sweetie. Great, all done. Welcome to New York, and best of luck." He closes my documentation and returns it to me.

I smile and give him a wink. *Why did I just wink at him?*

I make my way to the baggage area as quickly as possible with a very flushed face. *He must think I'm a pure gobshite for winking at him.*

I sit on the edge of the carousel, waiting for my bags to make an appearance. Thoughts of all that's happened to me in the past couple of years at home are flooding back to me, and I'm starting to get upset. What upsets me most is what Simon did to me. I know it's time for me to move on, though, and as thoughts of one lot of baggage disappear from my mind, I spot my other baggage on the carousel. My red bags stand out more than any others do, and I grab them and place them on a trolley as quickly as I can. I know Jen and Karen are waiting at the other side of the exit doors, and I can't wait to see them.

As I push my trolley along into the arrivals hallway, I can see my best friends waiting for me. Karen is the wild one—always out late partying and drinking until the early hours. Jen is a bit more civilised and tends to be on time for everything. She looks immaculate and groomed to the last, always.

I move closer to the girls, and I detect the pungent smell of alcohol in the air. I know the source of the smell, and as I approach Karen to hug her, I hold my nose.

"Cheeky! I don't smell that bad, do I?" she quizzes.

"Honestly? Yes, you do," I say and laugh heartily. "You're on your way home, aren't you, Karen? If I know you, you've been out partying all night. Am I right?"

Her hair is tossed, her mascara dried into her eyelids, and her eyeballs are almost to the point of hanging out of their sockets.

She laughs. "Of course I was, chick! This is New York, baby!"

I look at Jen, who greets me with one of her great hugs and smiles. "Welcome to New York. It's great to have you here, especially now that us three are back together again. It just makes a change for us all to be together in New York rather than Cork now. It's time to celebrate, I think!"

"Sounds good to me, but I think we should get Karen to bed first. She can't go on for another day and night like this."

"Don't worry. Give her another hour, and she'll be crashed out. We can let her sleep while we catch up over lunch if you want?" Jen suggests.

"Hey, hey, what's all this about lunch and me crashing out?" Karen booms out. "I'm coming, too."

I know that Karen will be out like a light within five minutes of sitting on a sofa. A yellow taxi pulls up, and before we even leave for Jen's apartment, Karen is snoring. It's a beautiful day, and as we drive from JFK airport to Manhattan, the skyline looks spectacular, with the sun almost blinding us with the reflection from the buildings. My heart starts thumping with excitement, and a shiver travels down my spine. I know I've made the right decision moving here. As I look ahead, I see streams of cars, mainly bright yellow taxis. "Traffic is a bit crazy today!" I say to the taxi driver.

"Oh, sweetheart, this ain't nothing. Give it another hour, and we'd be completely stopped. This will move along fairly quickly."

Once we arrive in the West Village, I step from the taxi and breathe in the New York air. It isn't fresh air, but it smells of the local bakery, which is starting to make me hungry. It feels good to be back again, only this time to live for a while—or perhaps forever.

My first challenge is ahead of me as Jen and I look at each other and then look at Karen in the back of the taxi.

"There's a touch of déjà vu about this scene," I say to Jen.

I bend down and put my arm on Karen's shoulder, shaking her lightly.

"Karen. Karen, wake up. We're here at Jen's apartment."

She snorts.

"Ladies, I think I'll deal with this." The taxi driver muscles his way past us and starts to shake Karen vigorously.

"Leave me alone, I'm sleeping," Karen slurs.

"I ain't leaving you asleep in my taxi, lady. Get out, or I'll have to push you out from the other side!"

I catch Jen's eye, and we both snigger. He seemed like such a polite man for the entire journey, but I can see why he might be angry.

"Lady, move it or I'll charge you for every minute you sleep here, and looking at the state of you, I'd say I'll be parked here all day!"

Jen decides to try to nudge her out from the other side. Karen will freak out if the taxi driver goes anywhere near her again.

We finally manage to wake her out of her drunken stupor, and she puts up a struggle as we manoeuvre her out.

As we stand outside Jen's building, I look up and congratulate her on her apartment find. It's an old brownstone building set in the West Village, and I've always fancied living in a building just like it. She hasn't been in her new home very long, but she loves it, and the West Village is a vibrant, fun place.

We finally reach the top of the building, struggling with my bags.

"Did they ever hear of lifts—or elevators, as they call them here?" I quiz.

"Let me guess what's in the bags to make them so heavy," Karen slurs. "You've got your 'I-won't-go-anywhere-in-the-world-without-my-eighties-hits' collection, your collection of underwear and those astrology books you take with you every—*hic*—where. Aren't I right?"

"Well done, Karen. You know me well," I say as I glance at Jen.

"I think she's been so excited about you coming over to live here that she went a bit crazy on the drink last night," Jen says.

"I know. No worries. Let's get her inside. Maybe we'll just relax for a while ourselves and let Karen get some sleep. We can all go for something to eat later. What do you think?"

"Sounds like a good idea. You must be pretty shattered yourself after the journey," Jen says.

"Yeah, so don't be blaming me. I know you're tired too and need sleep, but it's always easier to blame the drunken person," Karen says.

Strangely enough, I'm not tired. I'd like to go out on a big trek of New York for the hundredth time, I'm feeling so lively.

Within five minutes, Karen is snoring again, and Jen and I go to the kitchen for a coffee and a catch-up.

Two hours later, Karen wakes. "Aw, for fuck's sake!" The loud smack of Karen's head on one of the low beams that runs across the apartment must have been what prompted that. It must have hurt considerably as she's clutching her head and expelling a torrent of expletives.

"I need aspirin or something. My head hurts."

"Is that a hangover headache or one from the knock you just gave your head?" I ask.

"Not sure."

I produce some fast-acting paracetamol from my handbag, which Karen gratefully takes.

"OK, let's go out and have some fun!" Karen says.

Both Jen and I stare at her in shock. I know they are fast-acting, but they can't work that quickly.

"What? Come on, I don't want you two wasting your day over me. It was self-inflicted, and I have to suffer the consequences. However, I may not manage to stay out with you all night. I just want to make sure you know that before we go out."

I stop her from saying anything else. "Karen, seriously, stay in bed. You're not well. You won't be missing out on anything, I promise. We'll probably just go for something to eat and chill out. We won't be partying heavily tonight because I'll be exhausted by then."

"Are you sure?" She throws me a puppy-dog face.

"Go back to bed," I say with a smile.

Karen smiles and heads towards the bedroom again.

Jen and I leave the apartment and wander up through the West Village. I adore the designer boutiques, and as I walk by the local bakery, the waft of fresh cupcakes makes my mouth water.

"Oh my God! Look at those cupcakes, Jen. Let's go in. Come on."

"I'd prefer not to, Aly, if you don't mind. I need something a bit more substantial and healthy now. If I eat one of them, I won't have a proper lunch."

"OK, no problem. However, we do have to call here on our way back. You're right. I need something healthier than a cupcake right now—something like fast food!" I say with a smirk.

"I like that you haven't lost that sarcastic sense of humour of yours. I've got somewhere nice in mind."

"Great, you've saved me from making myself look like a hound, so I'm eternally grateful. Salad would be nice, actually. I'd love some beetroot. I had a craving for the entire plane journey, and when I asked the air stewardess if they had any beetroot, she looked at me like I was from another planet. Surely she, being from the Kingdom of Skinny, should have known what I wanted."

"What did she say?"

"Nothing. I think she thought I was taking the piss out of her. I told her forget it and took the chicken dish she gave me. It was grand, but you know plane food. It's like fast food; it fills you for an hour, and then you're starving again."

"I know. Well, they have a great menu where I'm planning on taking you. Oh, Aly, I've missed you. It'll be like old times with the three of us now, just based in New York rather than at home in

Cork. I'm so happy you've decided to make this move," Jen says as she puts her arm around me.

"Me too, hon, me too. Now that I'm free and single, I plan on having a good time while I'm here, Jen. I want to see you both as often as possible, and I want plenty of girlie shopping days and hanging-out time. Men are the last thing on my agenda right now. At least until the first hunk comes my way," I say, laughing.

"Great! Well, speaking of shopping. You have your interview coming up in a few days. How about we go buy you a nice suit to wear before then?"

"Sounds like a plan. Let's do it."

Washington Square has always been a favourite spot of mine. As we enter, it's thronged with people, and the sound of buskers playing guitar and singing fills the air. It's a very warm early spring day, and the sun is at its peak. We decide it would be best to get some shade as my skin, being pale and freckly, would be likely to sizzle, even in the mild spring sunshine. I remove the factor fifty from my bag and start to apply it vigorously, just in case.

Jen laughs at me as she claims I won't burn in the sun because it's too mild. I assure her that her laughter will not deter me, as I know myself, and I could blister just as easily in the mild heat. We're a short distance from Union Square, and I'm slightly excited, as I love that area, especially if the farmer's market is there complete with its local New Yorkers. We mooch around for a short while, and I soak up the aroma of freshly made hotdogs, pretzels, and cakes on the various stalls. "Oh, Jen, look!" I say as I point to the Chrysler Building in the background. "I love that building so much. It's so beautiful," I say as I stand there, staring up at it. Jen smiles but doesn't utter a word. I appreciate her letting me soak the moment up. My stomach suddenly starts churning out weird grumbling noises, which are quite loud.

"Belly rumbling, need food," I say in a caveman voice.

Jen laughs. "Let's go in here." She gestures at the small restaurant on the corner.

The lunch rush has just finished, and it isn't too crowded.

"Let's sit here by the window," I say, full of glee.

"Of course. I know how much you love to people watch."

We glance at the menu, and there are many options, as Jen had said.

"Well, what do you fancy?" Jen asks.

"You know, Jen, if we are out later tonight for dinner, I think I'll be good and opt for a salad. It's buffet, so at least I can eat as much as I want, and it won't be too heavy."

"I'm with you on the salad, but I'll have a small one. I had a good breakfast this morning."

I glance at Jen's frame, which seems far slimmer than the last time I saw her. I'm slightly concerned about her. Usually when we pass a cake shop at home in Cork, she's the first one in. Today she shunned it as if it were evil. I hope she's not dieting.

"Jen, don't turn into a stick insect, please," I say. "There are enough of them in the world already!"

"Don't worry. I'm just watching what I eat. I tend to eat a bit more healthily these days. I'm not dieting."

I believe her, as she has always been the sensible one of the group.

"So how does it feel to be back—but back for good, maybe?" Jen asks.

"Well, it feels good so far. I felt very sad and lonely leaving my family, as I really don't know when I'll be home again, but knowing I was coming over to both you and Karen made me perk up. I really missed you both when you left Cork. It's good, girl; it's good to be back!"

I can see from Jen's expression that she is happy to have me around. Though I can sometimes be as wild as Karen can, Jen knows I have a more sensible side also.

"I'm so glad you've come over. I really missed our nights out and our girlie chats. You're like a sister to me. Karen is, too, but you know it's not the same looking after Karen on my own." She giggles. "She's great, but she gets so out of control sometimes, and I really don't know what to do with her. I don't want to mother her, but I do worry."

"She's grand; she's always been like this, Jen."

"You're right, Aly. I think she might feel lonely sometimes, though."

"Well, we'll try and get her to feel loved and wanted between both of us, Jen. Don't worry; she's fine."

We decide to make our way to the buffet cart. Jen insists I go first in case someone takes our seat by the window.

As I wander back to our table laden with beetroot salad, I collide with the most handsome man I've ever laid eyes on. He slips on the floor and takes me with him on impact. I go arse to floor direction, my beetroot salad goes plate to chest direction, and he somehow manages to be back on his feet within two seconds of falling. Miraculously, I don't break anything, and I save my salad, but my pride is very much dented and my face is slowly changing to not quite beetroot colour but more of a nice tomato shade.

"Are you OK?" he exclaims. "Damn, I'm so sorry! I have no idea how that happened, but it's entirely my fault. Can you move?"

Yes, but my arse hurts like hell! "I'm grand. No problems, no broken bones, and I managed to save my food!" I blurt out.

Cringe!

"OK. It does look like you might have done some damage to that lovely cream blouse of yours, though. Let me help you up."

As I glance downward, all I can see are two purple rings strategically placed around my boob region. I'm feeling very humiliated.

I give him my arm, and he hoists me up like I weigh nothing more than a bag of sugar. Not that I have ever been overweight, but I am considerably heavier than most of the long strings of misery that are feeding on salad in the restaurant.

"Thank you," I say. *Think of something else to say, you idiot. He's gorgeous!*

"No problem. Now let me at least pay for you and your friend's lunch as an apology. If it wasn't for my stupidity of not looking where I was going, I wouldn't have caused you this embarrassment."

"No, really, it's not your fault. It could happen to anyone. Besides, I'm used to silly things happening to me from time to time. Really, it's fine, but thanks for the offer."

"I insist, and I also want to pay for the dry cleaning of that blouse of yours," he says.

"No, really, it's fine. Don't worry about it, thank you. It gives me the excuse to go shopping for a new top now," I say with a smile.

You're hot! Ask me on a date, please? Go on, ask me out!

He gives me a very nice smile, and I love his perfect, pearly white teeth. I smile back at him and make my way back to the table to Jen as quickly as possible.

"Stop with the laughing, Jen," I say. "It's not funny."

"Sorry, Aly, I really am—but it's been so long since I've witnessed you get into one of your awkward situations, and that was very funny. At least you didn't hurt yourself."

"No, but my arse does ache. I could hardly tell him that, though. How hot is he? I certainly pick them, don't I?"

"Don't you know who he is?" she asks.

"No; should I?"

"It's Jack Morgan! He's a very well-known actor here. I don't think he's as well-known overseas, but the ladies swoon over him, girl. You certainly do pick them!"

"Wow! I'm not even here a few hours and I manage to make a fool out of myself in front of a famous actor who's hot tottie. That's the best one to date. Wait until we tell Karen! In the meantime,

I think I need to go shopping. Somehow, I don't think beetroot boobs will start a new fashion craze here in New York."

"You'd be surprised. For now though, I think you might be right. Let's get you sorted out when we finish up here."

Jen looks at me and goes back to laughing hysterically. Although I've made a fool of myself, I'm already enjoying my time in New York. I stuff the remnants of my mushed beetroot salad into my mouth. I grin at Jen, and for the first time in a long time, I feel oddly happy.

Chapter 7

I 've overspent slightly. My first day in New York, and I've been a little overenthusiastic in relation to shopping. I've bought a few new blouses and a new interview suit. However, I do need a new suit and at least one new blouse after the kerfuffle in the restaurant.

Karen is bounding around like a hyperactive puppy when we open the front door of Jen's apartment.

"Welcome back, ladies! I'm feeling much better. Had five hours of sleep, and now I'm ready to hit the town."

"Great, Karen. That sounds good, but we did say we'd take it easy tonight, so it will be an early one, OK? I'm actually quite shattered now, and I'm going to get some sleep for a while. I'll want to go out to eat later and maybe go for one drink, but really it can't be a heavy one for me tonight."

"Me too!" Jen pipes up.

"Sure, that's no problem. I'm sure I'll feel exhausted again later. I've just got a second wind now, girls. I'll go home and freshen up, and both of you take a nap. We can meet back here at, say, nine o'clock?" Karen says with a big, happy grin on her face.

"That sounds good to me!" I say.

"Oh, and, honey, it's great to see you back with us, and I love that you brought your big CD collection with you. We've missed you," Karen says.

"Thanks; I've missed you both too. I've no doubt, though, that you'll be cursing my collection again when you have to help me take it down the stairs once I find my own apartment," I say with a cheeky grin.

"You know, you could invest in an MP3 player with a docking station," she replies as she heads towards the door. "OK, I'm out of here, girls. I'm starving. I'll grab a snack on the way home, I think. See ya later!"

Once Karen leaves, I go straight to bed and drift off to sleep in a matter of seconds.

When the alarm clock rings, I manage to scrape myself out of the bed, but I'd be just as happy to stay there. My stomach is rumbling, and I can't ignore the food call. I proceed to the living area where Jen is sitting.

"You're ready this early?" I say.

"Yep; said I may as well. I've only one bathroom working at the moment as I have problems with the en suite. At least this way you have all the space that you need to get ready."

"Good thinking! You look amazing as always, by the way! Are you on the prowl tonight?" I ask.

"Let's just say if a nice man comes my way, I'd be happy to have a drink with him," she replies.

Jen is always such a lady. She's very demure; oozes sophistication; and is tall, elegant, and incredibly pretty. I sometimes wish I could carry myself as well as she does.

"I want all the gossip tonight on what's been happening on the man front for both of you!" I say as I leave the room. I head back to the bedroom where my suitcase is still unopened.

When it comes to choosing what to wear, I have options for a change. I open the suitcase and take out the new skirt and top I bought before I left Ireland. I think the attire is appropriate after seeing Jen wearing a very expensive-looking dress.

I spruce myself up, and while I'm applying make-up, I hear the doorbell. I run to open it. Karen is standing there with two bottles of champagne in her hand.

"And here I was thinking you were taking it easy tonight," I say.

Karen ignores my monotonous tone. "Yeah, yeah, life is short, and the champagne may run out at some stage. Better to get as much in as possible in one lifetime."

I like her seize-the-day attitude and the fact that she can still manage to party so hard.

Astute as ever, Jen must have heard the word "champagne" as I hear the clinking of glasses being placed on the table before Karen even gets past the front door. Karen walks into the living area where Jen is sitting. This is probably a routine for them on a night out.

"I think drinking champagne is something I'll have to get used to," I say. "I don't tend to drink it too often at home, girls. The bubbles go straight to my head."

"I'd doubt it's the bubbles, love," Karen says with a wink and a smirk.

"I'm sure it's something I'll become accustomed to. Bring it on!"

Karen pours the bubbly drink into a crystal champagne flute. It overflows slightly onto my hands and wrist and then trickles onto the table.

"Anyone got a straw?" Karen roars.

"Please tell me you're joking!" I say, laughing.

"'Course I am, chick. You know me; I love a good laugh. Although I have been known to try sucking it up with a straw before. I was drunk, though. I also drank it out of my shoe once—I was very drunk then. Tasted even better than I thought it would."

I grimace at the thought of it. I take my glass and raise it as the girls take theirs.

"To my best friends. Thanks for your support, girls. To good friends and good times!"

We clink our glasses together and take a sip.

"That was nice, Aly. I wish I could make toasts like that. I'm normally too drunk," Karen says with a peal of laughter.

I smile at them as they start talking, but my mind wanders back to the life I left behind. My normal routine for a night out during the last three weeks of being at home in Ireland entailed me sitting in front of the TV with one of the girls. We'd share a pizza and some wine. It was all very exciting. I didn't like going out much at home, not since the Simon fiasco. The idea of any form of confrontation with him horrified me, and so I thought it best to stay indoors. I realise now, seeing my friends again that it was incredibly silly of me, and that it's time I move on. I now have a new start, which I plan on making the most of.

Jen has booked Buddakan for dinner, where the waiters are very dishy. The food is good, too.

"You know, Aly, we never go to Buddakan unless you're with us. It just doesn't seem right without you."

"And here I was thinking that you go there every week."

"We'd love to, but what Jen said is true," says Karen. "It's not the same without you. It seems to be our restaurant, and it wouldn't be the same going there with anyone else, I think. I have to go for luncheons with work every now and then, but that's definitely not the same!"

"Aw, girls, that's lovely to hear. I'm so glad I made this move. We have so much to catch up on. Let's go. Will we get the subway or grab a taxi? I'm starving—and a little drunk already after the bubbles."

"Oh, let's take the subway. Once we reach the nearest stop to Buddakan, we can take a taxi from there so we don't have to walk too far in our heels," Karen says.

"Good thinking, lady!" I exclaim.

The subway is hot and sweaty, and I feel a little uncomfortable. "I wasn't expecting it to be so warm so early in the year," I say.

"Yeah, it's been pretty warm for the past few days. You'll be grand. We'll be getting out shortly, and we can walk to Buddakan if you prefer. It's not that far," Jen says.

As we exit the subway, people swarm onto the streets. It's incredible; there's a feel of summer creeping in as people walk past in short sleeves and bright colours with jackets thrown over their arms just in case. The loud roars of laughter from people enjoying themselves reverberate through the streets, and the queues to enter some of the bars are starting already.

"Let's hop into a taxi, if we can get one," I suggest.

"Sure, there are generally plenty around this area at this time," Karen says. We manage to flag one within two minutes. Karen is in very high spirits, probably due to downing so many. She's the life and soul of the place.

"Jesus, wouldn't the lights almost blind you here sometimes and the smell of stale ciggies in the taxis make you puke," Karen says, not caring that the taxi driver gave her a filthy look.

"Sure, Karen, but it's all part of the big smoke. All part of my new life, chick, and I intend on embracing it, both good and bad sides. Now, enough about that as I can see one of its really good points coming into view now—and just in time, as I'm starving," I say, rubbing my stomach.

Time seems to pass very swiftly, and as it's getting late, we decide to go home and end the night on a high note.

"Girls, I have to be up early in the morning. Apartment hunting isn't my favourite thing to do, and I don't want to make any mistakes when it comes to where I'm going to live."

"Sure, let's go, Aly. I'm bushed anyway, need my bed," Jen says.

"I'm da same," Karen says as she lets a huge yawn escape.

The next day, I'm finding it difficult to remove myself from the bed. Jet lag has set in, and I just want to sleep. However, I force myself to get up, and I trudge to the kitchen to make some breakfast. There's a note on the table from Jen.

Hello, miss. I hope you slept OK. I'm not trying to get you out in a rush, hon, you are welcome to stay as long as you want, but I know you are anxious to get your own spot also. This paper is great for buildings in the local area.

Needless to say, I'm thrilled to accept any help given. I glance through the paper, and there are many very stylish apartments for rent, but all of them are extremely pricey. I haven't even secured a job yet, so I decide to tame my tastes a little and go for something a bit less expensive and not as sophisticated as I'd like.

Once I've eaten, I head out and into the wonderful West Village for a stroll. I mooch around the shops for a little while and check out some of the café windows to see if there are any advertisements on display. Unfortunately, I don't have much luck. I keep wandering around and come across the local bakery with its lovely cupcakes again. Jen and I never did return for one yesterday. I decide to treat myself.

"What can I get ya, sweetheart?" asks the man behind the counter.

"Oh, I'll have one of those lovely chocolatey cupcakes, please. I've been dreaming of it since I saw them when I passed yesterday."

"They're our most popular. Sold out by one o'clock most days. Johnny in the back gets peeved because he always has to make a fresh batch as he's about to go home. Business is business, though. So, I'm guessing you're just visiting with that lovely accent of yours?"

"No, I've just moved here, new to the area. I've a big job of apartment hunting today and thought I'd pop in here to fuel up for the big challenge ahead of me."

"Good choice. Nothing like a nice cupcake with your cooiiffee. Old DeAngelo on Charles Street has some apartments going. The rent is low as it's a bit dilapidated, but you could ask him. I think it's to be refurbished soon. No harm in asking."

"Sure, I'll do that. That's only across the street. Nothing to lose by asking."

"Here ya go, one extra chocolately fudge cupcake, chock full of calories, but so damn tasty I have to eat one each day. And I wonder why I can't lose weight," he says with a peal of laughter.

"Well, I don't count calories. You know what? I'll take four, please. They're not all for me, by the way. I'll treat my friends."

"Sure, sure. That's what they all say. Here ya go. It's hot out there today. You might want to put these in the fridge pretty quick. The frosting melts fast, and you don't wanna look like a two-year-old eatin' them," he says with a smile.

I take the box. "I certainly don't, thank you. I'm looking forward to sampling them at last. What's your name?"

"Oh, I'm Harvey. Nice to meet you." He removes the plastic glove from his hand and shakes mine.

"Good to meet you, Harvey. I'm Aly. I'm sure I'll be a regular customer if I manage to find a spot to live in the area."

"We'll look forward to seeing you again, Aly. Good luck. OK, who's next?"

I smile and wave goodbye as I make my way back to Jen's. Once the cakes are in their safe haven in the fridge, I grab my bag and leave, turning left up Charles Street in the direction of the flats Harvey told me about.

I knock on the main door of the building, but there is no reply. I contemplate ringing all the doorbells. I figure at least one person will·answer if I do, so I proceed with my plan. An old man peers through his window. I wonder if he's the owner of the building.

When he opens the door, I have a proper look at him. He's frail and has a few greying hairs left on his head. He walks with a slight stoop but looks really sweet, and my first instinct is actually to give him a hug. However, I stop myself from doing something so irrational. I'm sure if I hug him, he'll have the cops on my arse in two minutes, thinking I'm some sort of weirdo.

"Yes, can I help you, young lady?" he quizzes.

"I'm looking for the landlord or owner of this building."

"Sure, I'm the landlord and owner."

"Hi, I'm Aly. I need to find a new apartment. I've just moved here from Ireland, and I'm staying with friends at the moment, but I'd like to get my own place as soon as possible. I just got chatting to Harvey from the bakery, and he told me you had some apartments for rent here. Is that true?"

"Sure, come on in. I warn you though; the building is being renovated soon. You'll only be able to have the place for a short while. All tenants will have to find temporary accommodation while the renovation takes place, and then the rent goes up once it's complete. Right now, it doesn't look like much. I'm only letting the ground-floor apartments as it doesn't make sense to make people climb all those stairs with furniture and belongings when they'd have to move again shortly."

"How shortly is shortly?" I ask.

"Well, if you're lucky, you'll get four or maybe five months outta the place. However, they told me recently it might start sooner than that, so I can't give you a definite answer. Here you are—flat two, opposite mine, is free. Whaddaya think?"

If nothing else, he's a straight-to-the point, no-nonsense New Yorker. I love his quirky accent and the way he does business.

I look around, but the apartment is pretty sparse.

"What are the chances of getting some furniture, or would that be asking a lot?"

"Well, I got some bits lying around that I could put in there. They're nothing fancy, you understand, just some old stuff, but it would do for the time you'd be staying here I'm sure. You'd have to get a bed yourself. I don't have any spare beds. Oh, and you'll have to fork out for a few kitchen utensils, too." He starts laughing. "Geddit?" he asks.

It takes a few minutes for me to cop on to his "fork out for a few kitchen utensils" joke. I blame it on the jetlag and give him a polite smile, no matter how corny I think it is.

"So, you in or out?"

Wow, you're impatient!

"Can I think about it for a couple of days?"

"Sure, but someone else might come this way like you did and take it. Don't take too long. Rent is low—a hundred dollars per week. Let me know within forty-eight hours."

"OK. I'll get back to you shortly," I say, feeling pressured.

That evening I sit down with Jen, and we discuss the pros and cons of it. It's so close to where Jen lives on Charles Street. I decide I have to take it. Sure, it's a bit dark, murky, and dirty, but I'm used to cleaning up after Simon, so cleaning this place will be a doddle.

The following morning, I don't waste any time. I go back to the beautiful brownstone building. I ring the bell, and there is no answer. I ring again.

The landlord sticks his head out of the window and roars, "Ha, I thought it was you. I was waiting for you to ring all the bells again. The old guy in apartment four would have had a stroke had you disturbed him. I was hoping you would. I might finally get rid of him from the building. He's a pain in the ass. I'll let you in now."

It makes me laugh that the landlord was calling the guy in apartment four old. *Am I moving into a building of geriatrics?* The lock clicks, and the landlord opens the door to let me enter.

"You're taking it, ain't ya?"

"How did you know?" I reply.

"Ah, I knew you wanted some place quick, and this old place ain't bad. Sure it needs an overhaul, but at a hundred dollars a week, I think you'd be crazy not to take it."

"Well, yes, I weighed up the options last night, and it's situated in a great area for me, so I've decided I'll take it. My friend lives at the top of the street, and it's very convenient for everything."

"Yes, great, but remember that you might be moving out again soon, so don't get too attached!"

He's a bit scary at times, but I know he means well.

"I'll have the rent for this month and deposit before the end of the day," I say.

"OK, sweetheart. I know you'll get it to me. I hope you enjoy the space, even though it won't be for long. By the way, I never did give my name. I'm Paul DeAngelo."

"I'm Aly Hughes."

He shakes my hand, and I leave feeling very contented. I feel like I've made my first new friend in New York, although maybe it's best for me not to confuse friendship with what might be an overzealous attitude to money, seeing as I don't really know him.

I return to Jen's place and start making my plans for the big move. I know that I really need to secure that job I'm going for; otherwise, my apartment plan may not work out in the optimistic way I'm hoping it will. I wonder what Jeremy Sullivan will be like. I'll have to make a good impression. I sit down to prepare myself for my interview before Jen gets back from work and Karen calls looking to go on a drinking fest. I'm hoping I might escape a night out tonight.

Chapter 8

I wake with a start.

I have to be up early today. I did set my alarm last night, but it hasn't rung! I stretch my hand out in a bid to pull the clock nearer to my face so I can see what time it is. Thankfully, I'm safe; it's only 7:30 a.m.

I decide to make a special effort and don my new suit, which I bought on my first day in New York. I feel quite confident in it, and I certainly need confidence going to my job interview. I'm not sure if I should wear my Louboutins; they're my favourite shoes and make my legs look ridiculously long. However, the six-inch heels on them may cause problems walking on the uneven surfaces of the New York City sidewalks. I decide against them. I tie my shoulder-length brown hair back in a bun and spot a few stray grey hairs in the process. *Time to break out the hair dye again.* I've kept my eye make-up simple with black mascara as my blue eyes stand out with black.

I enjoy my walk through the village and hop on the subway at Washington Square. When I reach Lexington Avenue, I feel a rush of adrenaline. The company offices are facing me, and I'm amazed at the size of the building, which stretches what seems to be almost past the clouds. It's chaos, and between the noise and the rank smell of rubbish in the air, I'm finding it tough going. The smell is exaggerated by the heat, and although I know it's trash collection day (as I spot all the bags nearby piled for collection), it doesn't help the fact that I now feel like I smell of rubbish. I pull my perfume from my bag and give myself a spray. I enter via the large, glass double doors and sign in with security.

"Second floor, ma'am," the security guard informs me when I ask where Lexington Cards is based. Once I reach the second floor, I turn the corner, where a set of large, glass double doors greet me again. I push my way beyond the doors, and immediately I'm greeted by a tall, rather handsome-looking man.

"Hi, Aly?"

"Yes, I'm Aly."

"Jeremy. I'm delighted to meet you."

Not bad at all. Nice eyes and smile. Stop it! Stop it! Stop it! He's your prospective new boss, and you have an interview to get through!

I quickly snap out of my daze and take his hand, giving it a good, firm shake. I have always believed a firm handshake tells a lot about a person. Thus, I'm disappointed to find that he has quite a limp shake, which makes me wonder if he can be trusted.

"This will be very informal, Aly. It's just me doing the interview, and I feel I know you already after the glowing reference Tom has given you. Take a seat, please."

"Thanks. Yes, well, Tom is a great man. He's been so supportive of everything I've done while working at Dawson Cards."

"There is one thing I need to ask you about, though. I've spoken to Davina. She was your boss there, wasn't she?"

"Yes, she was," I say with confidence, as I know that Tom's reference will counteract anything bad Davina might say about me.

"She tells me you left in a rather abrupt manner. Can you enlighten me about the situation?"

"Well, Jeremy, I'll be honest. I had a lot of personal things going on at the time, which caused me a great deal of upset. I decided I was going to leave the company when I went to work that day and had thoughts of coming to New York. I just wasn't in a great place at the time, and Tom had agreed that I could take a few weeks of my leave rather than work notice. I didn't want to leave in that way, but because of the circumstances, they made an allowance for me."

"Sure, I understand. I've heard on the grapevine that Davina is a real nightmare to work with, though, and that you've been a saint for putting up with her tantrums." He laughs. "I shouldn't really have said that, so let's keep it between us. I have to say, though, she's always been nothing but nice to me."

I wonder why!

I smile and take the compliment that obviously everyone in the Cork office was on my side.

"She is a lovely woman," I say. *Lies; she's a right bitch.*

"Great; glad we have that out of the way. I've been looking at the budget figures you've done over the year, and it's quite impressive. Also, the input you've had on client accounts is very interesting, Aly, not to mention your input on designs. Tom told me you did a great job for the three weeks you covered for Davina."

"Thank you. I was anxious to learn the ropes. Once I attained my diploma, I wanted to get as much experience as possible so I could aim higher."

"We like go-getters, Aly. I'm just wondering, do you see yourself living here short or long-term?"

"Long-term. I have no plans to go back for a long time. I need to take a new path in my life and to give it a good go. I'll need to stay here for at least five years, I think. Who knows after that. I may stay forever!"

"Good. I need to know that you'd be willing to stay on long-term. We've had a tremendous year, and it's getting busier. The situation is that I'm anxious to spread my wings a little. I'm considering my own business; it's just a thought for now, though. I've been promoted recently, and right now I'd like to get someone who can fill my shoes and learn the ropes quickly. I think you'd do a great job from the feedback I got. As I said, this is just an informal interview. You seem very competent, Aly, and I'm happy if you are."

"Wow, I'd normally say I'd like to think about it, but I'm in. I've been hoping this past week that I'd get the job, and if I did, I knew I'd definitely take it. I wasn't expecting to hear so soon, though. I thought it would be a few days before I'd be informed."

"Normally that is the case, Aly, but I interviewed the other candidates last week, and I can say that your experience is far superior to any of theirs. Also, you show great enthusiasm, which is something I look for in a candidate. I'm not going to take the risk of letting you slip away to another company by leaving it a few days."

"Well, I'm in. Thanks so much, Jeremy."

He's sticking his hand out again, and I'm dreading that limp shake, but for the duration of time I've spent talking to him, he seems like a very nice person. I decide I have to put the limp handshake business to the back of my mind and concentrate on the fact that he is now my new boss. I'll work hard to impress him and make him realise he hasn't made a mistake in hiring me.

As I exit the building, I feel relief wash over me. Jen is at home eagerly awaiting the news of how I got on, so I rush back.

I turn the corner of Ninety-Sixth Street. In my rush to the subway, I can sense someone staring at me. I turn sharply to see the lovely, handsome Jack Morgan standing at the lights, waiting to cross the street. He smiles and waves at me. I'm content with that, but he has to go the extra mile and shout, "No beetroot for lunch today?"

Thankfully not!

I feel an air of pride flush through me as my suit is looking as immaculate as it was when I left the apartment. I do pride myself on my style; I spend enough money on my clothes each month to look as stylish as I do look. I gesture to it and shout back, "Doesn't look like it."

I smile at him, wave and continue on my journey back to Jen's. *Why can't I be a bigger flirt? I'm too embarrassed even to try after my last encounter with him. It's weird to see him again in such a short space of time—and in such a big city, too. Perhaps it's a sign.*

When I open the front door of Jen's apartment, she's nearly on top of me.

"Well, how did it go? When will you know?"

"Sweetest Jesus, you frightened the life out of me!"

"Ah, sorry, sorry, just excited. Dying to know how you got on."

"Well, I know already, Jen. I got the job. You're now looking at the new creative director at Lexington Cards."

"What? How did they tell you so soon? That's fantastic, congratulations! You deserve it so much, Aly."

"Thanks! Apparently, Tom's reference was a glowing one. Bit of an awkward moment all right when he asked me about the day I left. Davina had told him I left 'abruptly.' I lied, though, and painted her as a lovely woman."

"Best thing to do. I'm sure he'd feel sorry for you if he really knew what you put up with."

"I'm sure he would, too, but I couldn't paint her in a bad light. He might only see negativity in me then. He also said the other candidates didn't have enough experience, so I'm quite happy with that. I suppose that because I worked so closely with Davina, I ended up doing her job for her most of the time. I'd imagine Tom had a lot to do with me getting it, though."

"Good for you. Don't put yourself down! I'm sure Tom gave you a glowing reference, but it was that wonderful brain of yours that won him over. I got a bottle of bubbly—just in case."

The doorbell rings. I run to answer it, knowing Karen will be dying to know the news also. When I open it, I'm surprised to see that she's standing there looking stunning and very well-groomed, almost as if she has slept.

"Looking good, lady! No party last night?"

"No…well, actually yes, but I didn't go. I thought I'd make the effort and look good today for a change. Ah, I don't party every night, Aly. I know my job permits me to, as it's all part of the fashion industry, and I do get invited to lots of parties, but I just wasn't in the mood last night. I wanted an early night, and look at me today: bright and full of energy. Real energy for a change and not from those drinks you can buy. Now, enough about me; how did you get on?"

"Good for you, Karen. You look great. Perhaps you should stick to this little routine now and just party at the weekends."

"Yeah, yeah, how did it go? Come on, Aly, tell me."

"It went really well. I got the job!"

"That's great! Well done, chick. I knew you could do it! And let's not get ahead of ourselves now in relation to the no partying. One day at a time," she says with a smile as Jen pops open the champagne.

Chapter 9

I turn the key in the lock and push the door open. The place looks dull and a bit sad when I enter, but Mr. DeAngelo has left a few plants outside the door for me with a little note. As I start to move them to various locations, I hear a knock on the door.

"Hey, I hope you like the little gift I left for you. I had a few too many in my apartment, so I thought you might like some to make the place look more cheery."

"Hi, Mr. DeAngelo. Thanks so much. They're beautiful and will brighten the place up nicely. It's very kind of you."

"There's a lot of cleaning up to do in there, so I won't keep you. I just wanted to welcome you, really. So, welcome to the building. I hope you enjoy your stay here. Please try not to make too much noise as I'm a light sleeper. No three o'clock in the morning parties, at least not with more than four people; and if you have to have them, whisper."

"Don't worry; I won't be having any parties here. I might just have the girls around every now and then, but we'll keep the noise down."

"Sure. Well, I hope you settle in OK. As I said, the place is being renovated soon, so I dunno how you feel about staying here after, but you can let me know nearer the time."

"Great, thanks. I'll do my best to be a good tenant."

"Good, I like the sound of that," he says as he chuckles to himself and walks across the hallway.

I like Mr. DeAngelo. I think we'll get along just fine.

My new abode needs a good clean, so I close the door and start scrubbing the place from top to bottom. I venture out fairly early in the day to buy some white paint to give it a fresh coat and to brighten it up a little. Grey walls were never my thing. By the end of the day, it's looking spotless.

Just as I finish up for the day, I hear a knock on the outside door. It's Jen, and I run to let her in.

"Come in, come in. I'm so happy, Jen."

"Hey, girl. Wow, look at this place. You've worked wonders here."

"It's amazing what a lick of paint and a good clean can do. Mr. DeAngelo is giving me some furniture until the renovations take place, and I can decide what I want to do then. I'm pleasantly surprised, actually. The stuff he's offered me is quite modern."

"Great," she says. "You'll be sorted in no time at this rate."

"Jen, thanks for letting me stay at yours. It'll only be for another three nights or so, as I can't move in tonight or tomorrow with the paint fumes—and I have no bed yet anyway."

"Aly, you know you are welcome to stay for as long as you want. That's why I have a spare room!"

"I know, and thanks," I say. "I think now that I have this job, I should move on with everything and get my life into shape finally."

"OK, up to you. You're welcome at mine anytime, though. How about we call it a night and head back there now? We can grab a takeaway on the way and stuff our faces with that for the night."

"That sounds like a plan. Did you hear from Karen today?"

"She's on her way as we speak. I told her earlier we'd be back by nineish, and we'd grab the takeaway on our way back. She'll bring the drink."

"How did I guess? She's such a party animal."

I leave feeling contented with my day's work. We slowly walk down the steps, and I can see Mr. DeAngelo looking out of his window.

He waves and smiles at us as we turn to look at the building when we reach the last step.

"How cute is he?" Jen whispers.

"Pervert! He's old," I say with a snigger.

"You know what I mean!"

"Yeah, I know. He's great. He's been so helpful. On my initial meeting with him, I wasn't expecting him to be so nice. I've been lucky, Jen. Things are falling into place nicely for me right now."

"Yes, they are. I can't believe you're only here a week, and you've got your job and your apartment. Things never happen that easily for me."

I realise how lucky I really am when I hear Jen saying that. It is true; she's had a tough time for the past few years. The only thing that keeps her going is her job working as a Personal Assistant to a designer. She is spoiled rotten by them—freebies every week. However, her life outside the job hasn't been so good. Her last relationship, which lasted three years, was very turbulent; and her boyfriend turned violent once or twice. He damaged her confidence so much that after she split from him, she used to call me every second night in Ireland, crying down the phone, telling me she'd never meet anyone again as she felt she was getting old. Thankfully, for the past three or four months, she's been far better and is now starting to gain a little confidence back. I think my move to New York is also helping her.

"Great. There's Risotteria!" she says. "Let's get takeaway from there."

"Italian! Good choice," I reply.

I place an order for pizza, risotto and salad. We sit and wait, watching the many fine males who pass by.

"Check him out. Bit of a hottie," I say as I nudge Jen and nod my head in the direction of a tall, dark-haired man.

"Just my type. He's gorgeous," Jen replies.

I try to encourage her to approach him until a small blonde comes from the ladies' room and throws her arms around him.

"Oh, sweetie, did you miss me?" she asks him.

I nudge Jen. "Sweetest Jesus, how long was she in the toilet to ask him that?" I say with a snigger. Jen erupts into laughter. "Oh well, not to worry, plenty of them out there, Jen."

"Not worried at all. I've started to believe that the right man will come my way when it's meant to be," Jen says.

"Well, good for you. I think I've started thinking that way myself, too. I forgot to tell you this, though. I saw that Jack Morgan guy again on my way back from the interview the other day."

"What? And you're only telling me now? Aly, that's strange. I mean, Jack Morgan? I've lived here years, and that day you had your little food incident with him was the first time I've ever seen him in New York. Now you're telling me that you've seen him twice in one week. Maybe it's fate, Aly."

"Hmmm, not sure about that. I do fancy him, though."

"O'Donnell? We have an order for O'Donnell," yells the man behind the counter.

"Oh, that's me," Jen pipes up.

We head back to Jen's. Karen arrives shortly after us, laden down with enough booze for a party of ten people. We just laugh when we see her and don't pass any comments. We all sit down and pig out on the food from Risotteria and the copious bottles of drink Karen has brought with her. I can't think of a better way to end my day than to spend it in their company.

$\mathcal{M}$ ake-up—check.
Handbag—check.

Right, time to go. I step out from my new apartment. The sun is penetrating, and the smell of rubbish is rank as I walk in the direction of the subway. The long line of yellow taxis seems to go on for miles, and the constant blowing of car horns is starting to grate on my nerves. I reach the subway and carefully walk down the steps. I'm wearing my new heels, which in reality are far too high to wear tottering around New York City. I am, however, determined to make an effort, and I've somehow managed to convince myself that they will be worth the pain.

I board my train, and as we pull onto Fourteenth Street, I spot the lovely Jack Morgan. He speedily makes his way through the carriage to reach me.

Oh, feck! He's seen me! Oh Jesus, is that sweat I feel on my forehead? This is too much for me today. Deep breaths, Aly. Act cool, ya Muppet!

"Hey, we have to stop meeting like this!" he says when he reaches me.

Corny line, but an icebreaker at least, I'll have to give you that.

"Indeed, that's three times in one week," I blurt out. So much for me acting cool.

"Wow, are you counting? So what does that mean, do you think? It's pretty awesome, huh?"

I can feel my face flushing. "I have no idea. That we met three times in a week, I suppose, and no, I'm not counting. It just happens that my brain is very functional and calculates things very quickly, that's all. I can't help it. I'm very intelligent," I say.

"I'll bet you are. So did you calculate that you would strategically place two rings of beetroot on your blouse also on that first day we bumped into each other?"

Smartarse! Don't turn me off you!

"Ha! Funny man! No, I didn't, and I might add it was you who bumped into me."

"You're right, it was. How is that blouse? Did you get it cleaned? I really would like to pay for it. I feel really bad, and it was such a nice blouse," he says with a nonchalant tone.

"No, I didn't. I binned it. It was one of my favourites, but it doesn't matter now. It gave me the excuse to go shopping anyway for mooooooooooooooooore—" The train jolts, and I am pushed forward against Jack. I can feel his warm hand across my back in a bid to save me. *My hero!* I'm even more self-conscious now but want him to keep his hand there. It feels right. I look up, and his gorgeous face is so close to mine. His sexy eyes are enough to send me into a trance.

"You OK? Sorry, I didn't want to manhandle you in any way. I hope you understand I was just trying to save you from injury."

"Yeah, I'm fine. Thanks. That woman looks hurt. Maybe you should help her?" I suggest. *What did I say that for? I want him to hold onto me!*

"Ouch, that does look like a nasty cut. No, I'm not letting go of you that easily. Besides, there are three people helping her, and you're my priority."

Result!

Oh, Jack, I love your smile. If this were a great romantic movie, it would be a perfect scenario for you to grab me and kiss me. Although, why should I wait for you? Kiss him. Go on, kiss him. You've nothing to lose.

For some odd reason, my brain malfunctions, and I find myself locking my lips with his. When I pull away from Jack's lips, I realise what I've done and feel like a pure gobshite.

"Oh, Jesus!" I exclaim. "I'm sorry. I've no idea what came over me there."

Oh my God! What the hell have I just done?

There's no going back now. I have officially screwed any chance of a date with him. I'm panicking. Jack is grinning from ear to ear.

"I'm sorry, this is my stop. I've got to go. Nice seeing you again, and sorry. Sorry!" I say as I shake my head.

I run from the train as quickly as my five-inch heels will carry me. I twist my right ankle in the process. It's at least six stops from work yet and a long walk, but I can't stay on the train now. I need air. Oddly enough, I'm not feeling any pain. No pain could be as bad as the embarrassment I've just caused myself. My heart is pounding, and I'm not sure if it's with shame or love!

The train is pulling out of the station again, and I can see Jack looking through the window. He has the most wonderful smile etched across his face. Maybe he enjoyed the kiss? I don't know, but what I do know is that this is not the start I was looking for on the first day of my new job. I walk up the stairs to exit the station and decide to walk to work in my bare feet if necessary. I need fresh air.

I reach the office thirty minutes later, and my feet are in agony. I've just about managed to avoid cutting my feet to shreds on shards of glass scattered around the streets, but I'm glad that I made the decision to leave the train in such a rushed manner. I've reached the conclusion that I'll just have to forget about Jack. Chances are that I may not bump into him again for a long time, if ever. Then again, I'm not sure I want to after pouncing on him like some primate.

"Aly, welcome to your new job." Jeremy approaches me with an outstretched hand and eyes me up and down.

I shake his hand firmly, and I think I've just seen him grimace. *Did I hurt you? Man up, for God's sake!*

"You're shaking. Are you OK?" he asks.

"Yeah, I'm fine, thanks. There was just a little jam on the brakes incident on the train this morning, but I'm fine. Someone managed to grab hold of me before I went flying to the other end of the carriage."

I get a warm feeling as I think of Jack's manly hand across my back when he saved me from falling, which brings a smile to my face.

"Oh no, anyone injured? I'm glad to see you can still manage to smile at least."

"Well, there was one woman close to me who struck her head on the door, but she was OK. No harm done, or so she said to those around her. I could do with a cup of tea, though. Would stop the shaking, I'm sure."

"Sure, come into my office. We'll get some tea, and you can relax a bit before we get down to business. Today won't be the most stressful day for you, anyway. We'll ease you into it."

"Great. Thanks, Jeremy. I don't mind. I like to be busy."

We adjourn to his office, and I sit down to take the weight off my feet. I so want to kick my damn shoes off, but although Jeremy comes across to me as being quite casual, I'm not sure how that would look, especially on my first day. Besides, I already made one impulsive decision on the train.

"So, Aly, are you settling into New York OK?"

"Yeah, thanks. It's all going well so far. Got my apartment sorted and feeling quite happy."

"Good, good. It's a big change from Cork. I love Cork. I spent a lot of time there when I was in university. Great university it is, too. Happy days they were, Aly, I can tell you."

"Hahaha, oh, I know. UCC is amazing. I guess we've all had fun times in university, though."

"Yeah. I still have a great friend there, actually, Sarah Jacobs. She's more of an old flame, really, but we've stayed in touch over the years."

"She's not from Bishopstown, is she?"

"Ah, Jesus, you're joking. Surely you don't know her?"

"Went to school with her, Jeremy."

"That's just crazy. Cork is a small place, even if it is the biggest county, Aly."

"Oh, you dropped that in well. You know us Corkonians and how we love our county."

"I do—and don't start now, please. You'll give me a pain in my brain," he says with a smirk.

It's nice to share a little information about each other. I feel I'm getting to know my new boss and someone who could potentially be a new friend.

He shows me around the office and introduces me to the team. They seem friendly, and I have a good feeling that I will settle in nicely.

Later in the day, Jeremy approaches me.

"Aly, I'm sure your first day has been long enough. Office manuals are never that much fun to have to read, so you head off early."

"Thanks, Jeremy. I'll take you up on that. I've read these manuals already in the Cork office. They're more or less the same policies—nothing different, from what I recall."

"I know, boring stuff. Go home and relax. We'll have you on board properly tomorrow."

"Cheers. Have a good evening, Jeremy. I'll see you tomorrow."

On my way home, I purchase a pair of pumps as my feet just can't take any more pain. Travelling will be made easier now. I've no intention of wearing five-inch heels for the journey to work again. I've learned a valuable lesson.

I return to my apartment, and Mr. DeAngelo is there to greet me. "Hey, it's my lovely Irish neighbour. How you doin'? Settling in OK?"

"Mr. DeAngelo, it's lovely to see you. Yes, I'm good, thanks. I started my new job today. All's good. I'm really pleased with the apartment, too. It feels like home already."

"Good, good. How did the new job go for ya?"

"Great, thanks. Early days yet, but they are a friendly bunch. I'm looking forward to getting to know them."

"Good for you. OK, I'm off for my cards night. Have a good evening."

"Enjoy yourself. Oh, by the way, my friends are calling over this evening. A first-day celebration kind of thing. I promise we won't be too noisy, though."

"That's fine. I'm out anyway. You girls have fun, and I'll see you tomorrow or the day after, I'm sure."

"Thanks. Night, Mr. DeAngelo. Have a good one."

"I will, thanks. As long as I beat that Pete Cusamano tonight, I'll be happy."

He turns and chuckles to himself as he ventures down the steps.

I close my door and kick my shoes off, literally. I break a lamp in the process, but I don't care. I make my way to the bedroom, unhook my bra, remove it, and fire it across the room. Time to let my hair down and let it all hang loose. As I glance around my bedroom, I realise how untidy I've become since arriving in New York. I keep forgetting to buy a laundry basket. *Buy a bloody laundry basket, woman!* The girls are due to call around, and I want to shower and chill out a little before they do. I just won't let them near the bedroom.

At 8:00 p.m. sharp, my doorbell rings. I jump as I haven't heard it ring yet, and it's loud when it works. I usher the girls into the lounge quickly because I'm dying to tell them my story of shame from this morning.

"Hey, girl, how are you? Well, how was the first day?" Jen asks with fervour.

"It's a bit dark in here; you could do with a few lamps! How did you get on, chick?" Karen asks.

"Ladies, enter, please. The lack of lighting is a story I'll get to. Day at work went great, barring the incident that happened in the morning."

"What happened?" they say in unison.

"It can't be too bad. You're laughing!" Karen says.

"Well, it is, and it isn't. Take a seat, and I'll tell you."

As I unfold my tale of woe to the girls, they fall around the place, laughing. I can see the funny side of it, and Jack might never have asked me out anyway, but I'm definitely after blowing any chances with him now.

"Aly, that's so funny. It's so like something you'd do," Jen remarks.

She's right. It is typical of me to do or say something without thinking.

"Yet, slightly romantic," Karen adds.

"Romantic? You think that was romantic?"

"Yes. Think about it. You obviously were so caught up in the moment that your instinct told you it was a romantic situation, and you took advantage of it. Isn't it weird how you've bumped into him three times already in one week? Third time lucky, they say," Karen says with a grin.

"Well, yes, I did let the romantic side get the better of me. And yes, it is strange that I bumped into him again. In fact, he did tease me about that as I mentioned it was the third time."

"*No!* You didn't. Please tell me you didn't? Don't you know the first rule when you like someone is to act cool, like you don't care?" Karen says.

"Yes, I know that's rule number one for us, but he was just so charming—and that smile. Oh God, how could I have messed up so badly?"

"Girl, relax. I think you two are meant to be together if you meet again. Did you check your astrology books to see if you would be compatible?" Jen quizzes.

"I did not. I don't know his star sign. In fact, I don't know anything about him, except that he's around six feet tall and has luscious green eyes, blond hair, and a beautiful smile. He's exactly the kind of guy I go for, but of course I've messed up."

"Google him!" I hear Karen roar from the kitchen.

"Yes, go on, Google him. You'll get the info you need then."

"No, no, I can't. I'd be like a stalker then. I'd know all about him, and he'd know nothing about me. No, we'll just let it be now. Besides, I might never see him again."

"Here, drink this back. It'll soften the blow," Karen says as she hands me a giant glass of wine. Though it certainly tastes good, I don't think anything can soften the blow that I may never see Jack Morgan again. Even if I do, I'll probably have to run in the opposite direction.

Chapter 11

June 2012

few weeks have passed, and I have settled into my job nicely. Jeremy is what I can only describe as the perfect boss. He explains everything in great detail so I can learn the ropes properly and from scratch. It's a far cry from working with Davina, and I'm really starting to enjoy it.

I'm lucky enough to share a bit of banter with him from time to time also. If it isn't some joke between us about home, it'll be something else. We've managed to form a good working relationship.

It's Thursday afternoon, and I'm just on my way out the door to lunch when I see Jeremy approaching me.

"Hey, I'm heading to lunch. Want to join me? There are a few things I want to run past you," he suggests.

"OK, sounds good. I don't have any plans."

It's a very relaxed lunch meeting, and Jeremy orders wine. I hadn't planned on drinking, but if the boss is, then I'll join him and have a small glass. We chat about various procedures, and then he makes a proposal (not that kind of proposal!).

"Aly, I'd like you to take over some accounts, if you don't mind. Just to take on a bit more responsibility as I'm pretty swamped at the moment."

"I'd be delighted to. You just need to run through the procedure with me."

I'm smiling at him and acting interested, but I'm really starting to get bored. If I have to sit here for the rest of lunch listening to him going through the entire workload, I'll nod off. I now know I shouldn't have had a glass of wine. He's stopped talking; perhaps he realises that he's boring me.

"Let's give the shop talk a skip for the rest of lunch. What do you think?" he says.

It only took you forty minutes to realise you're boring me!

"I don't mind, really, Jeremy. If it's something we need to do, then I'm happy to do it."

Oh, that was a bad lie. You've definitely seen through that. Or else you realise the glass of wine is going to my head.

"No, let's get to know each other," he says.

Are you cracking onto me? Oh my God, awkward!

I can feel my face flush, and I reach for my bag as if to search for something inside. Anything so I don't have to look him in the eye.

"So, what music do you like? I only ask because I have some tickets for the Bon Jovi concert, which I can't attend now. I'm trying to find someone who might be interested in taking them off my hands. I'd hate to see them go to waste."

My ears prick up like a dog's, and my boredom has suddenly disappeared. I realise now he's just making small talk, but I can feel my face getting a deeper shade of red—not from embarrassment but excitement. *Did he say Bon Jovi?*

"Did you just say Bon Jovi? I adore them. I'll take them off your hands if you like. How much are you looking for them—face value, I hope?"

"Oh no, I don't want any money for them. I just want to know that they are going to someone who will appreciate them. I hate to see good tickets go to waste just because I can no longer go. It's actually a buddy of mine who loves them. She's a fanatic. However, there's some family gig this weekend, and she's distraught that she has to go to that instead. I insisted I'd find someone who would appreciate them, and I'd get her tickets for the next time they play here instead."

"I'm sorry to hear that. I know I'd be gutted if I had them and couldn't go. Luckily, I can, and if you are happy for me to use them, I know I'll enjoy every minute of it."

I smile and thank him. I shake his hand vigorously—a little too vigorously. I notice it's purple when I let it go. I keep forgetting he's not a fan of strong handshakes.

"OK, well, let's finish this bottle and head back to the office," he says as he gulps down the remnants of the bottle.

The journey back to the office is nice. We both seem very relaxed after the wine, and we are spotting the silliest of things to laugh at. I feel slightly guilty for drinking as I know the afternoon won't be very productive on my part. However, it'll be even less productive for Jeremy, I imagine. He guzzled back most of the bottle and seems very merry.

Once we reach the office, I sit and daydream for a while. The thought of seeing Bon Jovi playing live in New York has me on a high, and I can't concentrate on work. I have a tough decision to make: whom do I invite to the concert? I think I'll opt for Jen. Karen would get up on stage if possible and do her best to seduce Jon Bon Jovi. Jen is a safe bet.

Finally, it's home time. I rush for the door but then double back because I realise it would be rude not to say goodbye to Jeremy. He has been so kind, offering me the tickets.

"Have a good evening, Jeremy, I'll see you tomorrow," I say as I tap on the door.

"Hey, you too, Aly. I'll bring those tickets with me in the morning. The concert is on Saturday, by the way, so I hope you've got someone to take with you on short notice."

"Oh, I've one or two people in mind. I'm pretty sure I'll have someone to take. Thanks again, Jeremy. See you tomorrow."

I'm feeling a little drained, and my day hasn't been the most productive.

When I reach home, I throw off my shoes and turn up the volume on my stereo. Bon Jovi, of course, is the music of choice for the evening. "Someday I'll Be Saturday Night" is blaring as I'm dialling Jen's number on my phone, and the excitement is killing me. I scream when she answers, "You're not going to believe what happened today!"

"You didn't get fired, did you?"

"Thanks for the vote of confidence. No, I didn't, but I did get my hands on two free tickets to Bon Jovi on Saturday night. You will come with me, won't you?"

"Wow! How did you swing that, then?" she exclaims. "I'd love to come. What about Karen, though? Any chance we can get a ticket for her?"

"I'll call her and see if she is interested. I really don't want her to feel left out in any way."

"This is great. I'm excited now. Is that Bon Jovi I hear in the background?"

"Yes, it is. I'm bloody excited now! I'm going to hang up, Jen. I'll give Karen a call to see if she wants to come with us."

"OK, you go, and I'll talk to you later. Thanks for the ticket. Can't wait!"

"No problem, chat to you later."

I hang up feeling super happy that Jen can come with me. However, I'm not sure what to do if Karen wants to come along. I only have one spare ticket, and even if I buy one for Karen, it will be in a different location than ours. We have VIP tickets, whatever that means! I decide to just bite the bullet and call her. I can deal with any circumstances later.

"Hey, loser, how are you?" she answers.

"Nice! Thanks, oh good friend. I'm fine, thanks. How're you? Drunk again?"

"That's an even nicer reply! I'm good, thanks. What's happening? You're never ringing me to go partying with you on a week night, are you?" she asks.

"Listen, I was wondering what you are doing Saturday night."

"I'm going to dinner. Would you believe I have a hot date? He's involved in the music industry, a big name apparently. I've never heard of him myself, but I met him last night at a party. We clicked, and he invited me to dinner on Saturday. I'll do my best to keep my undies on!"

"That was a lot of information in one go—just trying to process it all here. He sounds interesting. Yes, please, just let him chase you for a bit before you go losing the undies."

"Thanks! I can see your humour is still intact. I've missed having that around for the past few years. Glad you're back on board, Hughes! So you think I should wait then?"

"Yes. I think you should, but I don't think you will."

"OK, I'll bet you five bucks that I will make him wait."

"For how long? Twelve hours?"

"No. How about three weeks?"

"You'll never last. If he's that hot, you'll jump him within twelve minutes. I know you, Karen." I chuckle.

"OK, you know me well, but I want to change, so let's have a bet: twenty bucks that I'll keep him at bay for three weeks or more. If I last up until the stroke of midnight at the end of the third week, then I win. I will have permission to do whatever I wish after that, though."

"Poor guy. I can't believe we are betting on him, but go for it. I'm in. Twenty bucks says that you won't last."

"Deal! Sorry, I got a little sidetracked there. What are you up to Saturday night? Or were you requesting the pleasure of my company as you had nothing planned yet?"

"I'm going to Bon Jovi with Jen. Was wondering if you fancied coming with us."

"Aren't I lucky I have that date? If I had to sit or stand next to you and listen to you belting out your version of Bon Jovi hits live, I'd end up in a coma from the drink. Thanks for asking, but no. I'll stick with the date, I think. You have a fun time, though!"

"Oh smart! It wouldn't be me belting them out. It would be Bon Jovi."

"I know. I might actually enjoy seeing them, but I know you'd be next to me singing to Jon at the top of your voice, completely out of tune and crying. I wouldn't be able for it."

I can't help but laugh. "Karen, you know I wouldn't be like that. I like them, but I'm not obsessed, cheeky! Anyway, you too. Remember to keep your knickers on—and no cheating by not wearing any to begin with!"

"I will keep them firmly on. I might even use masking tape to make sure. See you soon and have fun!"

I hang up. A wave of both relief and sadness passes over me. I feel bad for not having invited Karen first, as she is as good a friend as Jen, but I am relieved that I don't have to fork out for a ticket as I'm not very flush on the money front just yet. I'm pleased for Karen, though. Normally when she'd go on a date, it seemed to be with undesirable men—usually because of the wine goggles she wears. However, this time, maybe, just maybe, she's growing up and actually really likes this guy.

The next day is a nice, warm day. The subway journey is a pleasure. For some reason, it's sparsely occupied, and I manage to get a seat. When I reach the office, I sit comfortably at my desk and start going through my new accounts. Jeremy's secretary approaches me later in the morning.

"Hey, Aly, Jeremy is out for the day at meetings. He left this envelope on my desk for you."

"Cheers, Sam."

I open the envelope, and I'm ecstatic to see he has remembered to leave the tickets for me. The excitement for the concert is building, but the day seems to be dragging. It's not long to go until the day finishes, and I'm getting prepared to exit the building as quickly as possible.

By five o'clock, I'm tired of waiting around, and I'm not being very productive. I decide to go home. I'm heading towards the door when my mobile phone rings.

"How're ya? It's Karen. Fancy a drink?"

"You read my mind. Is the West Village good?"

"Woman, I think you know me by now. Anywhere is good as long as there is drink available!"

"There in twenty minutes."

I enter the bar and spot Karen straight away. She looks fantastic.

"Look at you," I exclaim. "I've never seen you with your hair swept back like that, and that dress is amazing. It really shows your figure off."

"Thanks! I feel like shit, though. My clothes are getting too tight. Think I'll have to join a gym."

"Karen, seriously, you look great. You OK? You sounded like you really needed to get out."

"I'm nervous, Aly," she says. "I've not been on a date for months, and the last guy I went on one with, well, he scared me a little."

"What do you mean exactly?"

"Well, he freaked me out. The way he was talking. It just re-minded me of Jen's ex and how he treated her. It made me think that all men out there are violent. It scared me. That's why I've been partying so hard and not really meeting any men."

"God, Karen. I hope you didn't let him get away with anything."

"What, you mean like my knickers? Nah, I'm more careful these days. Besides, with the expensive knickers I buy these days, I'd sue him if he even attempted to get anywhere near them. I'm choosy about my guys as I'm getting older. Some might call it be-ing sensible...believe it or not."

"Good for you; glad to hear it. I know what you mean about the underwear. I've got such a thing for expensive underwear of late. In fact, I saw this gorgeous bra and knickers set for five hundred dollars the other day. When I get my first paycheque, I'm contemplating buying them."

"Go for it, girl. Nothing like a nice pair!" she says with a grin.

Time seems to be slipping by quickly, and the laughter and catch up we're having are great. However, I've unintentionally steered Karen away from the men subject and her fear of them. I broach the subject again, and she's talking more about her experience. It's been a long time since she's opened up to me like this, and I'm starting to realise that she's been through some tough, scary times in recent years.

"Aly, I haven't told Jen any of this as she's such a worrier. I know I can trust you not to say it to anyone, but I think above all I just needed encouragement, which I knew I'd get from you. You're Miss Motivator, after all."

"Aw, you know I won't say anything, Karen. Anything that's said in confidence stays that way. Don't worry. Call me if you feel you're in any danger or you just need me to come get you, OK?"

"Thanks, chick, I will. Oh, I've missed you so much." I hug Karen and assure her she will be fine. It's time to go home as we are both tired. When I reach home, I lie in my bed for most of the night, thinking about our conversation and about how my funny, energetic friend is in fact hiding behind a mask in a world of fear and low self-esteem.

Chapter 12

"*Y*ou ready to party, chick?" I ask when I open the door to Jen. "Absolutely! I can't believe we have VIP tickets!"

"I know! Good on Jeremy for giving them to me. Looking good, girl; love the skinnies and T-shirt. You've great legs!" I tell her.

"Hello? Look who's talking. Yours are up to your armpits! And I love that T-shirt."

"Vintage, I call it. I bought it back in the eighties when I first saw Bon Jovi live. Surprised it's not threadbare at this stage," I reply.

"So what's on the agenda?" Jen asks.

"Well, I was thinking we go straight to the stadium and then for food. To be honest, I have no idea what being a VIP involves, but it sounds good."

"Excellent. Let's treat ourselves, OK?"

"Yep, sounds like a plan."

It sounds great, but I'm exhausted. I didn't drink much with Karen last night, but I couldn't sleep properly after what she told me. I decide not to mention to Jen that we were out without her, though. I realise Karen needs to confide in me from time to time, and what she told me is something I want to keep to myself.

When Jen and I reach the stadium, we are led to a backstage area where we can get food and drink. We stuff our faces and wash it down with a beer. When we're ready to be seated, we're escorted to a corporate box, which is situated to the side of the stage. We have a very close view of the band. The time speedily passes, and

I'm feeling hoarse because I can never resist singing along to a Bon Jovi number. The concert finale is "Bed of Roses." Jen and I sing along, as if singing to Jon himself, and we cry like two lunatics. We're lucky Karen isn't here, or she'd never let us live it down. When the concert finishes, we both leave, swooning over Jon Bon Jovi.

"I'm pretty sure he smiled at me at one point, Jen."

"Nah, that was at me."

"Nope, definitely me. He saw me looking sexy in my vintage T-shirt and said to himself, 'She's a right piece of hot tottie.'"

It's quite a clear sky, and I can't help but notice how fantastic the skyline looks tonight. Since I arrived, I haven't had time to notice the bright lights, but tonight they really stand out. We both laugh our way through the streets of New York as we stagger home. We didn't realise being a VIP meant free drink all night, and we took advantage of it. I suggest to Jen that she stay in mine so we can discuss the day's events.

I check my phone when I get home, and there is a message on the machine. "Hiya, just Karen checking in. Thanks for last night. It was a relief to tell somebody. Date went well, and he didn't try any funny business. I'm feeling happy. Hope you had a great night. Byeeeee."

"What's that about?" Jen asks.

"Oh, nothing. She just asked if she could borrow a skirt from me for tonight. I dropped it over to her last night, and we had a quick chat about her date."

"Ah, OK."

I feel so guilty, lying to Jen, but Karen confided in me, and I can't let her down.

I decide to go to bed. I'm both relieved and happy for Karen. I fall into a deep slumber while thinking of Jon Bon Jovi and the great day out Jen and I have spent together. I spend all day Sunday chilling out on the couch to prepare me for the week ahead.

Monday mornings I generally find it difficult to get energetic and enthusiastic, but after such a great Saturday, I surprise myself. I'm bouncing with energy and looking forward to work.

"Als, how are you? How did the concert go?" Jeremy quizzes when I walk into the office.

Als! That's a bit familiar.

"Great, thanks, Jeremy. It was amazing. Thanks so much for the tickets."

"No problem. Can you come into my office for a minute, please?" He sounds serious. "Aly, there's an office night out this Friday. It was organised before you started, so you may not have been included in the email. I just wanted to let you know as you are, after all, part of the team."

"I hadn't heard anything about it. Thanks for letting me know. Are you going?"

"But of course. I never miss a good auld piss up. I'll introduce you to more people too. I think it'll be a great opportunity for you to get to know some people in the other departments."

"Great, count me in. Thanks, Jeremy."

I leave the office in good form, knowing that I have another event in my calendar for the following Friday. I think it's a little strange that Jeremy called me into his office to tell me this, though.

The week passes quickly, and on Friday afternoon, things start to wind down in a lively fashion in the office. People are cracking open bottles of champagne, wine, and beer. I'm used to the wine and beer being opened in the Cork office, but never champagne unless it was a special occasion. Thankfully, they have more of a work-hard-play-hard ethic in this office. I know most of the other companies in New York don't tend to wind down so early on a Friday—and not in this fashion, either.

"It's the normal thing for us to do here if we're having a work night out. You'll get used to it," Jeremy says with a smile.

I can't help but feel a slight attraction for him. *I have to stop thinking like this. It's just wrong to fancy your boss.*

"Well, I look forward to many more of these then!" I say to him.

He hands me a large glass of champagne, and I savour every minute of it. I really need to drink less tonight, though. I feel I've been partying and drinking far too much since I arrived. When the booze supply runs out, we decide to go to one of the bars in the locality. I'm enjoying myself, and I feel that Jeremy and I have formed a close working relationship that feels like it's bordering on a good friendship. He is more relaxed, and I am, too, outside of the workplace.

"I love this place. Reminds me of home."

"Really?" I ask.

"Yeah, it's the music. I love live music. Sometimes it makes me feel a bit lonesome, though."

"Aw, poor Jeremy," I say and pull a puppy-dog face.

"You shouldn't pull that face too often. You look too cute."

Are you flirting with me, Jeremy Sullivan? You're my boss; that's not allowed. However, tonight I'm in the mood myself for a little flirting.

"Are you trying to tell me you think I'm cute, Jeremy?"

He smiles and puts his arm around me. "Here, your fortieth glass of champagne tonight, Ms. Hughes," he says, handing me an oversized glass.

"Avoiding the question, Sullivan? Don't exaggerate; it's number thirty-nine!"

"Not at all. I think you're super cute and have from the first time I saw you."

Most of the other people from the office are on the dance floor, throwing weird shapes to the music that is playing. I have a feeling Jeremy is going to put the moves on me, and before I can say anything, he leans in to steal a kiss from me. I'm more than happy to oblige.

"What do you say we get out of here, Als?"

I take a moment to soak up what has actually happened, and it feels all wrong. "Um, no, I don't think so, Jeremy. I'm sorry, but this shouldn't have happened."

I grab my coat and leave as fast as I can.

Fecking gobshite! What are you thinking, getting involved with the boss?

I contemplate what happened on the entire journey home. I can feel the tears welling up inside, but I don't want anyone seeing me like this. I wait until I manage to close my apartment door and let it all out.

I feel frustrated and cheated to a certain degree. What am I to do when I meet a man whom I have a very obvious attraction to and I can't do anything about it? It's like Jack Morgan, whom, incidentally, I haven't seen since the subway. I'm going to bed to get some sleep—if I can, that is. I have the weekend to mull over my actions. I'm really not looking forward to going to work on Monday morning.

Chapter 13

*S*adly, Monday morning arrives a little too soon for me. I'm dreading going to work. I feel like I've really cocked things up for myself. Everything was coming together for me, and then I had to go and kiss the boss.

I walk into the office, and the first person I see is Jeremy.

"Hi, Aly."

"Hi," I say as I stare at the ground.

I walk on. I can't do anything else or even think of something to say to him. There's tension in the air, and I know he'll have to call me into his office in relation to work at some point. Thankfully, he waits until later in the day.

"Aly, can you come in to discuss this account please?"

My face flushes. "Yes, of course."

I traipse into the office, and the nearer I get, the more I can feel my face burning up.

"Close the door, please, and take a seat."

Oh, please don't fire me.

"I'm going to be honest with you," he begins. "I don't need to chat to you about the account. I want to talk about the other night."

"OK."

"I'm sorry, Aly. I shouldn't have put you in that position. I'm your boss, and I should have kept it professional. We can just forget about it all now and carry on as normal. I hope you can do that."

"Look, it wasn't your entire fault," I tell him. "You kissed me, and I kissed you back. I shouldn't have encouraged you. Yes, that's fine, let's forget it and move on."

"So back to friends and work colleagues, then?"

"Sure, Jeremy."

I smile at him but feel very awkward. I'm not sure things can or will go back to the way they were.

A few days later, I discover Jeremy has a casual partner, which I'm not very happy about. He shouldn't have made a move on me if he's with someone. *Is he a bit of a love rat?* We built up a great bond over the few weeks I've worked in New York, and all it took was one small kiss to ruin it. However, I'm determined not to let it ruin my work life.

A few weeks pass, and Jeremy and I avoid each other as much as possible, until one of the office Friday nights out. It's noisy, but I'm standing close enough to hear Jeremy and Debs chatting.

"What's up with you and pretty girl?" Debs asks.

"What are you talking about?" Jeremy replies.

"Well, you've been eyeing each other up for the past few weeks. Would you just do it and get it over with?"

"Debs, I'd prefer if you'd keep your nose out of my business, please, and for the record, we've been doing no such thing."

"Oh, whatever, Jeremy. I know what I see."

Oh, sweetest Jesus, they all saw what happened. They must have!

Jeremy walks towards me, and I feel like running, but I can't. It would be obvious that I overheard and would give Deborah the opportunity to spread gossip as it's what she does best. Thankfully, this time we chat quite civilly again, and it's far more relaxed. We manage to stick to the chatting and avoid kissing and flirting. It's an enjoyable night out, and I'm starting to feel like I'm getting back on track. Maybe we can remain as good friends and colleagues without any awkward feelings. The following weeks prove me right.

As time progresses, and many work nights out follow, we both manage to contain ourselves. The attraction we once seemed to have for each other has waned. Party night is due again, and I'm in the mood for finding a man (someone who doesn't work in the office). It's time for me to see if there is someone out in this big city for me. There are always plenty of good-looking men around when we go to the pub. It's high time I meet one.

I jump in the shower and make a quick change into my new minidress and new super-high Louboutin shoes. I'm not one for designer wear normally, but since I moved from home, the girls have had an effect on me and the type of clothing and footwear I buy.

I emerge from the changing room to find Jeremy is waiting to escort me.

"The others went ahead. I know this place can be a bit creepy when you're here on your own, so I said I'd wait for you. Jaysus, are you on the prowl tonight?"

"I am not! I felt like dressing up for a change. So many of the other girls dress up when they go out from work, and I thought I'd do the same tonight. I'm tired of wearing a suit every week; I feel more like me in this. Thanks for waiting, by the way."

It's none of your damn business to know that yes, I am "on the prowl" as you put it.

I can feel him staring at me, and I'm starting to wonder if I look tarty or something. "Why are you staring?" I ask. "Is my make-up Oompa Loompaish? Dress too short? Do I look like a hooker? Should I change back into my suit?"

"No, Aly, you look amazing. I've just never seen you in something as glamorous as what you're wearing. Don't change. If you're on the prowl, you'll definitely pull with the way you look."

"I'm not on the prowl, I told you!" *Lies.* "And what do you mean by 'the way I look?'"

"I mean, you look…sexy, OK?" he says. "I didn't want to say it, as I thought you'd think I was coming onto you again, and we'd be back to square one. I don't want that, so if you think you should change back into your suit, then do. I'm not telling you to, though. I was just trying to be polite by saying how nice you look."

"Oh, OK. Thanks. Don't worry, now that I know in what context you meant what you said, it's fine. I haven't had a nice compliment like that in a long time, Jeremy, so thank you."

My heart is racing so fast, and I know the attraction for him is still there. I have to persuade myself to forget about it; even though I feel so good in his presence, I'm very aware that nothing can happen between us.

We reach the pub ten minutes later.

"What do you fancy?" Jeremy asks.

How about you, ya big sexy beast?

"Um, vodka and Coke, please," I reply.

"You sure? You normally drink wine, don't you?"

"Yeah, just fancy something different tonight."

"OK, as long as you don't get too drunk and start coming onto me again," he says with a smirk.

"You wish, Jeremy Sullivan!" *Cheeky fecker.*

Once we get our drinks, we make our way around the crowds, which seem to have grown in the five minutes we were waiting to be served. There are over five levels in the pub, and it takes us the best part of thirty minutes to get to the top level. Unfortunately, we can't find anyone from the office. "Try calling Deborah. She always has her phone on," I suggest. I'm not her biggest fan, but as she's the office party animal, she is a sure bet.

"I've tried calling a few of the crew already, but while it's showing that there's coverage here, I can't get through. I get cut off each time I try. I think we should just park ourselves here, Aly, and wait to see if the others find us. What do you think?"

"Good thinking. Looks like they're leaving," I say, pointing to the couple in the corner. I quickly grab the spot in the corner before someone else comes along.

"My round!" I pipe up.

"You're a fast drinker, aren't you?" Jeremy says.

"Sure, this doesn't really last too long. I'm hitting the cocktails I think. Been a heavy week; could do with a good party night tonight."

"OK, maybe I'll join you then. Get me a man's one, though, not one of those pink girlie cocktails—and no umbrellas or streamers hanging from it, please."

"What do you want, then? Something with a lash of whisky in it?"

"That sounds good."

I return with a tray of two cocktails each. It is such a trial to be served at the bar, particularly when they don't know you.

"Who's trying to get me drunk tonight?" Jeremy quizzes.

I laugh. "I'm not; I just think we need a good party night. Come on, get those down you. I'll be finished before you again, probably."

"You're some woman for the drink, aren't ya?"

"Not really. I only go mad every now and then, Jeremy, but when I do, I have a good session."

I feel him move a little closer. I should feel uncomfortable, but for some reason, I don't.

He moves towards me and presses his lips to mine. I don't hesitate in reciprocating. I come up for air after a couple of minutes.

"Jeremy, I need to know something."

"What's that?"

"I heard recently on the office grapevine that you're in a casual relationship."

"Jesus, Aly, don't bring that up now."

"Well, I don't feel comfortable about this if you are with someone."

"OK, I was, the last time we kissed. I'm not anymore. Besides, it was casual. Casual means casual. We were allowed to do our own thing. We were both in agreement."

"So you're not with anyone now?"

"No, only you right now. Now come here and let me continue that kiss. You're a great kisser."

Relief! He's not cheating on anyone. I let him move closer again.

Four hours later, I find myself fumbling for my keys in my coat pocket.

"They're here somewhere, Jeremy. I know I had them in my pocket."

"Come on, will ya? I'm dying for a piss."

"OK. Ah, here we go; they were in the mobile make-up unit."

"Huh? Where?"

"The MMU. My handbag."

"Ah, right, that's a good name for it."

"Thanks. It's my friend who calls it that. Years ago I used to take a huge bag out with me and had copious amounts of make-up in it. It then was nicknamed the MMU. I only take a small bag now but still call it that. Just thought I'd enlighten you with that interesting piece of information," I slur.

"That's great, Aly, thanks, very interesting. Key into keyhole, please, or I'll have to go on the street."

"Don't do that! This is a respectable neighbourhood. Hic! Right, here we go. Now I just need to figure out which key is my apartment one."

"Aly!"

"I'm only joking, hic! Go on in, and it's the first door on the right."

He runs past me. I'm making tea in the kitchen when he returns a few minutes later, looking happier. At least that's how he seems.

"OK, come here to me, Aly Hughes. Where's the bedroom?"

"Split level apartment. Upstairs."

He grabs me up in his arms and makes his way towards the stairs. Sadly, I only stay in his arms for two seconds. He trips, and we both land on the hard wooden floor.

"Any need for an ambulance?" he quizzes amid a roar of laughter.

"I don't think so. No bones broken on me. What were you trying to achieve exactly?" I ask with a giggle.

"I was trying to be romantic."

"I know. I'm kidding. Come on, let's walk up."

On entering my room, Jeremy spots my CD collection and browses through it. "Aly, you've some collection here. I don't believe it; I haven't heard this in years," he slurs.

I've no idea what he is referring to until I hear the familiar beats of Faithless's "Insomnia" blaring. He's chosen from the few nineties hits among my ridiculously large eighties-hits collection.

"Turn it down! You'll wake my landlord."

"Oh, sorry. Love this song," he whispers as if it's his voice that needs to be muted. Jeremy proceeds to throw some odd shapes as he dances his way towards me.

"Aly Hughes, what *big*…eyes you have," he says with a chuckle. "I know you thought I was going to say something else there." He moves in to kiss me.

"Well, if you had, I'd say you need a trip to Specsavers!"

We both laugh, but I laugh even harder when Jeremy continues to dance around the room. I'm waiting patiently for the grand finale of the night. I've stripped down to my new $500 matching bra and knickers, and finally he moves towards me again.

He's belting out the words of the song at the top of his voice.

Oh shit! Please don't say he's going to act out the words.

The next line in the song has something to do with using his teeth to tear tights off. I'm not wearing tights. The only thing he can tear off with his teeth is my $200 dollar knickers!

He gets a firm grip on them with his teeth; I jump and squeal, "Not my designer knickers!"

"Aw fuck!"

"Jesus, Jeremy, what's wrong?"

"*Ouch!* Aly, you've yanked my tooth out!"

As I look down, all I can see are my beautiful new designer satin knickers ruined. The lace edge has come away with the aid of Jeremy's tooth getting stuck in them. Then I see the flow of blood streaming down his face, and I start to panic.

"Oh, my God! Jeremy, what just happened?"

"You fucking yanked my tooth out! I was trying to be romantic and sexy for you, but you moved and yanked my tooth out! I need to get to a hospital, now!"

I want to shout back at him that if he wasn't being so silly trying to tear my knickers (which should be tights) off, it wouldn't have happened, but I don't have the heart to shout. Although my undies are ruined, I feel bad for him, especially as there is no sign of the bleeding stopping.

"OK, I'll hail a taxi. Here, put your coat on."

I grab my mac and rush outside.

"Taxi," I say in a slightly meek voice. I'm still not used to shouting at the top of my voice for taxis. I'm not yet a proper New Yorker. Luckily, a taxi stops within minutes. It must be the bit of leg that's flashing through my mac that made him stop.

I run inside.

"You, OK? The taxi's outside now. Come on, let's get going."

"No, I'm not OK. I'm actually feeling very weak. Can you help me?"

"Oh, Jeremy, I'm sorry. Here, lean on me."

It seems like a lifetime to take the usual ten-minute journey to the hospital. The traffic is chaotic, and the stream of yellow taxis in front of us seems never-ending. To top it all off, it's started raining, and the normally beautiful lights of NYC look dull and dismal.

Each time the taxi stops at traffic lights, I'm seeing a homeless person shuffle further in off the street in the hope of keeping his or her home for the night dry. Thirty minutes later, we arrive at St. Vincent's hospital. I hold a towel to his face and rush him inside. A nurse approaches.

"OK, honey, what's happened here?"

How do I explain this to you?

"Bit of a long story. Didn't involve any violence, I just want to clarify that. It was just a very simple accident."

Think fast, or she won't believe you!

"Basically, he was being all romantic, taking me upstairs to bed, and he fell, dropped me and somehow smashed or yanked his tooth out."

That's believable enough and almost true.

"OK, sir, are you feeling nauseous, faint or dizzy?"

"All of the above."

"Honey, we'll take it from here. Do you want to go get yourself a cup of coffee?"

"Sure. Thanks."

Temptation is there to go home. I realise, though, that with just a mac on and underwear underneath, they may think I'm a woman of the night. At least if I stay, it will look like I care about him and that I'm probably "with" him. I do care about him.

I sit in the corridor and wait patiently for some news. My head is spinning, and the smell of drink wafting from me is strong enough to knock a horse.

Finally, Jeremy emerges.

"Thanks very much. I'll arrange an appointment first thing tomorrow morning," he says to the nurse through his very swollen mouth and face.

"You do that. In the meantime, the painkillers should do the trick. No more strip routines and trying to rip off young ladies' underwear, you hear?" the nurse says.

Sweetest Jesus, he told the nurse! I can only imagine how she'll perceive me now.

"And you, young lady. Don't go wearing two-hundred-dollar underwear anymore on a night out—or at least not with this man," she says with a smile.

Cringe!

"I won't; don't worry," I say with a smile, like butter wouldn't melt.

I turn to Jeremy and throw him a withering look. I want to reprimand him for what he has done. However, I can't. He's been through enough for one night, and so I call a taxi and help to get him home.

We reach his flat, and I go inside with him to ensure he's OK. I tuck him into bed as pangs of guilt wash over me. When did I become such a bitch? Why was I worrying more about underwear than the pain Jeremy was suffering? I feel so bad.

"Jeremy, can I stay tonight? I mean, like, in the spare room? I'm just a bit worried about you."

"Als, it's OK, I'm fine. I don't want you losing any sleep over me, but if you want to stay, please do. I feel pretty bad myself, as you must be exhausted. Thanks for all of the waiting around. Any other woman probably wouldn't have. I knew there was something special about you."

"Hey, I'm not special. The thought of leaving did run through my mind, but I couldn't do that to you. You're a good guy and my best male friend here, Jeremy—actually, my only male friend here, as well as being my boss. I mean, how would that look, not staying with my boss to look after him?"

"Yeah, especially when he was trying to get into your knickers," he says, laughing.

"Good to see the sense of humour didn't get damaged."

"Never. Sure, isn't that how I reeled you in, Hughes? You couldn't resist me that day at the interview. I could see you eyeing me up and down and thinking to yourself, 'I want a piece of him.'"

"OK, you're delusional now," I say. "I think it's time you get some sleep."

His eyes are already closing, and it looks like he'll be snoring within seconds. I bend down, kiss his cheek, and whisper, "I hope you feel better tomorrow, Jeremy. I'll be here in the morning to make sure you're OK."

He grins and slurs something along the lines of "I'd give you my last Rolo any day, Aly."

Oh, bless you, Jeremy, you're out of your mind.

I walk across the hallway to the spare room. I grab the quilt from there and decide to rest on the small couch that is in Jeremy's bedroom, just in case.

The next morning, I feel something brushing against my cheek. It's the back of Jeremy's hand. It feels soft, and the instinct I have is to hold onto it and keep it pressed to my cheek.

"Hey, Aly, I'm off to the dentist now. It's nine o'clock. Hop into my bed and get some sleep. Did you stay here on the couch all night?"

"Hmmm? Oh, yeah. I'm feeling it now, too."

"Thanks, that was really sweet. And thanks for looking after me last night."

"No problem. Listen, I think I might head home and sleep there. No offence meant. I am pretty tired, though."

"Sure, do what's right for you. I'm going to be out of it for most of the day anyway, so maybe you're better off."

"Well, I could stay, if you want me to look after you."

"No, that's not necessary. Thanks, though. Well, I guess I better get going now. I'll see you Monday?"

I feel sad, but I'm not sure why. "Yeah, sure. See you Monday. Good luck with the dentist, and don't be afraid to call if you need anything."

"Cheers."

"Oh, and Jeremy, I'm sorry about the way everything worked out last night."

"Me too, Als. That's me and my drunken stupidity."

I smile. "I think we were both pretty drunk and stupid."

He turns and winks at me. "See ya."

I really want to run after him and give him a big smacker on the lips to make him want me, but I know it's the wrong thing to do. He's still in agony, and a kiss from me is probably the last thing he wants.

I drag myself from the couch, take my mac and my MMU, and stroll home.

Chapter 14

I'm having a quiet weekend, and as Monday creeps closer, I really want to ring Jeremy and see how he is. I pick the phone up a few times and dial all but one of the digits. I then place the phone back on its cradle. I just can't do it.

It's a sunny Sunday; the summer evenings are amazing and seem to last forever. I don't really want to be on my own, so I call Jen, as she lives nearest to me. I need to talk to someone.

"Hey, Jen, how are ya?" I say in a tired and emotional-sounding voice.

"Hey, honey, what're you up to? I'm great, thanks. I haven't heard from you all weekend. Bit unusual for you. Is everything OK?"

"Not really. Can you come around, please?"

"Sure, give me ten minutes and I'll be there! I take it by your tone of voice we're not going anywhere? I'm wearing my sweat-pants and top. I'm only dressed for running from A to B right now."

"I've no plans for doing anything, hon. Come on over. I'm in my PJs still."

"OK. See you soon."

I feel better already, knowing I can get what happened with Jeremy off my chest.

When Jen arrives, she looks amazing as always, wearing a figure-hugging velour tracksuit that accentuates her slim figure.

Her brown hair is swept back into a ponytail, which she has even gone to the trouble of curling, and her blue eyes look bright and alert.

I, on the other hand, look like crap. I've been in my pyjamas since I got back from Jeremy's on Saturday. I have no interest in getting dressed, never mind go running, go to the gym or anything else that involves removing myself from the couch or bed.

I'm greeted with a big hug. "Thanks. I needed that."

"What's happened to you? You seemed so chirpy and upbeat last week, and now you look so down and sound so sad. Are you homesick or something?"

"No, Jen. I've cocked up again."

"Why, love, what did you do?"

"Jeremy. Although I didn't actually but nearly did."

"What? I thought you guys had sorted that out. All chummy, but that was it, no love affair as he's involved and because you have a strict rule of not getting into office relationships!"

"I know, but Friday night we somehow managed to be left alone in the pub, and, well, it started with a kiss."

"Wait, you're not going to burst into song now, are you?"

I start laughing. "No, I'm not. Good song, though."

"OK, I agree; yes, good song, but let's not get sidetracked."

"Right. Well, we ended up back here, and we were both very inebriated. One thing led to another, and then his tooth was yanked out by some lace on my knickers. We ended up in hospital, him in excruciating pain and me in my undies, which were nearly falling down as he tore the elastic too, and my mac."

Jen is laughing hysterically. "I'm sorry, I'm...Hang on, I've got to catch my breath. That's so funny."

"It's OK; I knew you would laugh. I suppose it is funny, but I feel so nervous and awkward about work tomorrow."

"Well, how did it all end with Jeremy? Did you leave him there at the hospital or what?"

"No, I stayed. I even went home with him and tucked him in. Yes, I know he's not a child before you say anything! I stayed by his side all night in case anything went wrong. He even told me to stay in his bed that morning while he went to the dentist, as he was worried I didn't get any sleep."

"So, it all sounds OK to me. You didn't fight or anything before you left, did you?"

"No, thankfully, there were no disagreements. I just feel so awkward. I think it would be different had I seen him after he got back from the dentist yesterday. I opted to come home, though."

"Well, why don't you ring him? Arrange to meet him this evening or tonight before you go back to work."

"I've tried, and I end up hanging up before I dial the last digit."

"OK, miss. You need to pull yourself together. You're overanalysing the whole situation here. Call him and talk to him. You know he's probably thinking the same thing right now. You are probably both feeling stupid because you were drunk. A simple phone call could clear it all up."

"You're right, I suppose. I'll call him later. OK, enough about me. How're you doing? Have you lost weight?"

"You noticed! Hurrah! Yes, I'm on this fitness regime at the moment. I want to lose a bit of weight as I'm applying for a PA position in a modelling agency. I know they are quite picky about how their staff look as well as their models, so I just need to lose a few pounds."

"Jen, seriously, you're very tall. What are you, five-nine? You need to be in proportion weight-wise. Please don't lose any more, or you'll turn into one of those stick insects."

"Don't worry. I've got it under control."

"OK. I can tell you want to change the subject. Are you heading out tonight?"

"Not tonight. Karen rang earlier; she wants to party. She always wants to party, but particularly on a Sunday night. I told her I had something else on because I'm just tired. I want to get to work fresh-faced tomorrow and not exhausted-looking. She said she was ringing you, too, so if you want a night out, she's your woman."

"I don't think so. Look at the state of me. Besides, if I go out with her, I know I won't get home until dawn. I'll have to skip it tonight. What about this guy she met? She sounded happy."

"Oh, he's blown her off twice now. I think maybe she's acting too keen."

"She hasn't done anything with him yet, I hope, has she?" I ask.

"No, she hasn't had the chance as she rang him four times in a bid to set up another date, but nothing has materialised. I've told her to just forget him, but she won't give up."

"That's disappointing for her. I can't go with her tonight, though. I think I'm still in hangover central since Friday night."

"Don't worry; she'll find someone in the 'industry' to go party with. She always does. Aly, I'm thinking of going to the gym for a while; fancy joining me? It might help you get out of this low mood you've got yourself into."

"No thanks. I'm good. I've got to figure out what I'm going to say to Jeremy when I call him."

"OK. You can always call to practice on me beforehand if you want," she says with a grin.

"I'm not that pathetic, Jen. My situation, I'll sort it out; but thanks for listening to me. It helps to get stuff like this off the chest, especially as it might stop me overanalysing now."

"OK, let me know how it all goes, and good luck at work tomorrow. You know, Aly, I promised myself I wouldn't say this, but I'm going to because I worry about you. I think you need to get out and about a bit more, not just with the work people. If you get involved with Jeremy, it might end in tears. I don't want to interfere, as it's your life, and God knows you need to have a bit of fun with a man, but just don't get too attached to him. If he's into casual affairs, it might be all he wants with you, too."

"I know. That's the part I can't seem to accept for some reason. I do need a little fun, though, so I'll see what happens."

"Hey, before I go, I've been meaning to ask, have you seen Jack Morgan around since you forced yourself on him?"

"Oh God, Jen, please don't bring him up. No, I haven't. I'm sure he must have only been around for a week or so as it must be more than six weeks since I last saw him. Not that I want to, even if he is a sexy beast."

"That's a pity. I was convinced for a while you were meant to be. Three times in one week to meet someone like that in New York is a rarity. Anyway, I'll let you get on. Good luck. Talk to you tomorrow."

"Thanks for calling around, Jen."

I'm standing on the steps of the brownstone building I live in as I watch Jen jog up the street. I take a deep breath and return indoors. I pick up the phone and dial Jeremy's number.

"Hi, Jeremy, it's Aly."

"Hey, Als, are ya all right, girl?"

"Yeah, I'm grand, thanks. Um, how are you?"

"All good, Aly. I'm high as a kite from the painkillers, but I've not a bother on me."

"Ah, that's good. No bothers due to painkillers, I assume?"

"Hahaha, yeah, that's it. Are you OK?"

"Yeah, I've just been feeling a bit awkward as I wasn't sure how we left things yesterday, Jeremy."

"I know; I'm the same, to be honest. I should have called last night but wasn't sure if you'd want to chat, so I left it."

"Jeremy, have we made a mistake here? I mean, we work together, and I really don't like getting involved with people from the office. It makes life awkward, and you're my boss!"

"I know. Look, I've no problem with it, Aly, but if you want to cool it, we can. We could be discreet, but I don't want to pressure you, either."

"I just don't think it's good timing, Jeremy. I fancy you, but I've always had a thing about not getting involved with colleagues."

"First time for everything, Als."

"Ha! Yes, there is, but now's not the time. I'm not long in the job, and I don't know, it just doesn't feel right. Sorry."

"Don't be sorry. It's fine, Als. We can go back to normality to-morrow. However, I'm going to come up with a good excuse for this swollen face," he says, chuckling.

"I'm sure we or you will think of something. Thanks for under-standing. I hope you feel better about it all."

"Yeah, Als. Seriously, I think we both just felt a little awkward, but there's no need really. We'll put it behind us and move on."

"OK, I'll see you tomorrow. Thanks, Jeremy. Have a good rest tonight."

"Sound, Als, I'll do that. You too. See you tomorrow. Good-night."

I put the phone down on the worktop.

Phew! That went better than I thought. Now, an early night for me, I think.

Chapter 15

On Monday morning, I reach the office early and Jeremy greets me with a smile of sorts. However, his face is so swollen, I'm trying to figure out if it actually is a smile. Without waiting to be called, I make my way into his office and close the door behind me.

"Hey, how are you doing? That looks a bit painful still."

"Hurts like hell, but what can I do? I just have to be a man about it and put up with it."

I feel a smile spread across my face. I know he really wants to have a whinge about it, but maybe he feels he's blamed me enough already.

"You should go home if you don't feel up to being here."

"I'll see how I go. Thanks for coming in to see how I'm doing. As you can imagine, they're all asking questions as to how it happened."

"And what did you tell them? Not the truth, I hope, like that nurse you told the other night. That was kind of embarrassing for me."

"And it wasn't for me? Thought there was no point in lying. Besides, I was too tired and weak that night to know what I was saying to her. I just told them I was playing a round of golf at the weekend and there was a little accident. That was it. They're all wondering what happened now, but leave them off. They aren't going to get the real story."

I hope not—ever!

"Good. Well, I'll just pretend you told me the same and that I haven't seen you until now," I say.

"Thanks for calling last night, by the way. It cheered me up as I thought we had left things a little casual on Saturday. You were great to look after me that night, staying there in the room while I slept."

"Ah, it was nothing. I was worried about you, and it is kind of my fault that you're now lacking a front tooth."

"Let's not start blaming now. It's no one's fault. It was an accident that happened, and we need to forget about it as soon as I'm no longer toothless and swollen."

"OK. You know, you look good like that. Maybe I should try it again sometime," I say with a giggle.

"Very funny. Remember, I'm still your boss." He chuckles as he opens the door in a gentlemanly fashion to let me return to my office.

"I know you are," I reply in a flirtatious manner as I push my office door open.

The following Friday, Jeremy approaches me.

"Hey, fancy a drink after work?"

I thought we weren't doing this again. Hmmm, maybe it's just a friendship thing. It won't hurt me to say yes.

"Yeah, sure, why not!"

"Great. There's a small place just off Lexington so we can have a chat and avoid this lot."

"Sounds good."

I have an odd feeling about the whole situation, though. Time passes quickly, and before I know it, it's 12:30 a.m.

"Let's go back to yours and make some magic tonight, baby," Jeremy slurs.

"Sweetest Jesus, Jeremy," I say as I laugh out loud.

"What? Aren't I being romantic enough for you?" he says with a peal of laughter and pulls me close. "I know we said no to this, but I can't stay away from you, Als."

I smile. "I know; I'm the same. This whole avoidance thing and staying clear of each other isn't working for me."

We make our way back to my apartment and manage to avoid any accidents this time. We both wake up the next morning in one piece and feeling very happy. I bounce out of the bed when I hear a knock on the door. It's Jen.

"Hey, you! I thought I'd hear from you yesterday. Are we on for dinner or lunch over the weekend? Bit late for you to still be in bed!"

"Hiya," I whisper.

"Oh, have you got a man in there? It's not Jeremy, is it?"

"Yes, it is," I squeal.

"Ah, OK. I'll leave you alone, then. Give me a shout tomorrow if you want to do lunch, OK?"

"OK. Sorry, I'd invite you in, but…"

"Stop! It's fine. Go enjoy yourself. Just be careful."

"I will. Thanks, Jen. I'll ring you later."

I head back to the bedroom, where I see Jeremy rushing to get his trousers on.

"Oh, sorry, did I wake you?"

"No, no, I'm late for an appointment. Sorry, I need to go. Thanks for last night. I really enjoyed myself."

"Me too. So I'll see you at work on Monday?" I ask, hoping he'll say he'd like to see me later today or this evening.

"Yep, see you then. Thanks again. Sorry for rushing out so quickly."

He kisses my forehead and leaves.

I close the door behind him and start beating myself up for being so stupid. He's my boss, a man who only seems to want casual flings and nothing serious. If I'm to be involved with him, then this is all I can expect.

I head for the shower, and once I cry my eyes out over being so silly and wash the tears away, I get dressed, ring Jen, and apologise to her. Jen, being Jen, is as forgiving as ever and decides I need cheering up. She says she'll call over in thirty minutes.

True to her word, I hear my temperamental doorbell ring thirty minutes later. I open the door to one of Jen's bear hugs.

"OK, Hughes, it's been a while since we had a proper girlie day, so today is the day. I've been in contact with Karen; she's up for it, too."

"Great! Any ideas of what we should do?"

"Yep," she says. "Let's start off with a lunch at the Boat House. We haven't been since you arrived here, and we've had some great lunches there in the past when you were here on holiday. Karen's going to meet us there. We can have a big conference then about your situation with Jeremy."

"This is one of the many reasons I've missed you both so much," I tell her. "You always run to my rescue when I'm feeling down. The Boat House is a great idea. I haven't been to Central Park since I arrived, not to mention the Boat House."

"Glad you are in agreement. I've booked it already, so they are expecting us at midday. That's not too early, is it?"

"Not for me. I'm ready to go now. Although, it might be early for Karen."

"Surprisingly, our dear friend is up early today. She didn't even party yet this weekend and decided to stay in last Sunday too," Jen states.

"I have to admit, I was surprised I didn't hear from her last week, especially after you told me she wanted someone to go out with her."

"She actually sounds in good form, so I'm hopeful that she is getting a bit sensible finally."

"Good for her. Let's go now and take a nice long walk on the way," I say.

I grab my jacket, and we both make our way down the steps and up Charles Street. I love where I live. It's such a vibrant area, and having Jen at the top of the street makes it even better. It's like another world when I step outside—the noise, the smells, and the chaos are all very different from my safe, noise-free abode. Still, the West Village is nowhere near as noisy as uptown.

We eventually arrive in Central Park and take a seat at our table while we wait for Karen to arrive. "Where is she? She's twenty minutes late," Jen says.

Karen rocks up and is in very chirpy form. "Ladies, how are we?"

"Great, thanks. You're in flying form. What's happened?" I ask.

"I've had a good night's sleep, and I've got two dates lined up for this week."

"No wonder you're grinning from ear to ear. Who with? The no-sex-for-three-weeks guy?"

"No, I've cast him aside like a pair of smelly auld knickers. These guys are gorgeous, and I think one of them might actually have a personality."

Jen pipes up, "Only one of them has a personality? What about the other?"

"Nah, he'll be handy for a night, but he's a bit dull."

We both laugh.

"So what's the plan of action for today, ladies?" Karen asks. "Are we hitting the town after this big feed?"

"I don't know really, Karen," I say. "I'm feeling a bit low so we'll see."

"Why? What happened?"

Jen just has to get in before me. "One word: Jeremy."

"Oh no! You didn't, did you?"

"Oh yes, I did." I explain the situation, and as I haven't seen Karen in nearly ten days, I tell her the entire story.

Naturally, she reacts as I thought she would. She laughs hysterically over our first attempt at a night of passion, and now she's lecturing me for the actions of last night.

"Aly, I thought you were more sensible than me! Why did you go there, him being your boss and all? You always had a rule about no relationships with people from work. Why now?"

"Karen, if only I could tell you. I have no idea. All I know is that I've been really attracted to him from the first day I saw him. Now I'm kind of hooked."

"Was he good in the sack?"

"Karen!" Jen shouts.

"What? Well, it does make a difference!"

"Yes," I say sheepishly. "I'm half regretting it now, yet I still feel there could be something good between us."

"Well, go with your gut instinct," Karen says. "I always say that."

"Problem is, Karen, so do I—but this time, while my gut instinct told me it was right, today I'm not so sure."

"You know, what you need is a good girlie night out. Meet someone new, someone who doesn't work with you."

"How true, if only I could meet more men," I reply.

"Girls, I say we eat a light lunch and go to Buddakan tonight, to be followed by drinks in the Spring Lounge. We're bound to get chatting to some guys there," Karen exclaims with enthusiasm.

I hesitate, but before I know it, the words "Let's do it" are expelled from my mouth.

Jen seems keen, too. Seeing as we haven't had a proper night out together in a while, we agree to treat ourselves.

We enjoy a lovely lunch in the Boat House. It's not as busy as usual, or perhaps it's just Karen's loudness that turns people off.

Once we finish, we go to Soho for a manicure and pedicure. It's jam-packed with tourists; the majority seem to be heading in the direction of Canal Street in search of imitation handbags, I expect.

We find ourselves with some spare time on our hands afterwards, so we wander in the direction of the restaurant. We pop into a little bar nearby and treat ourselves to a bottle of champagne. When we arrive at the restaurant, we still have time before being taken to our table, so we order some of their speciality cocktails, Charm cocktails. Rather than stick to one, Karen, as per usual, drinks a considerable amount more than we do.

"Ladies, your table awaits you," the waiter says in a lovely Southern accent.

"Thank you," both Jen and I reply. Karen winks and says nothing.

"I see you've already studied the menu. Would you like me to take your order now, or do you need a few more minutes?"

"No, we're ready, thanks," I say.

We all order our respective dishes and a bottle of Sauvignon blanc to wash it down.

When the waiter turns to walk away, all I see is Karen's hand appearing from nowhere, and she pinches his arse.

"Jesus, Karen, are you trying to get us kicked out?" I'm furious. Sure, it's a little funny, admittedly, but it's also embarrassing. She really can't control herself with drink.

"Very pert," she says with a serious face.

It's no surprise to me that we have a different waiter when our meals arrive. Karen looks disgusted, and I just look at him and smile.

"Don't you go pinching my fine ass now, you hear?" he says to Karen in a strong southern accent as he walks to the table next to us.

Karen evidently doesn't fancy him as much as the other guy, as she's keeping her hands to herself. He makes an appearance again within two minutes.

"Ladies, the gents at the table next to you would like to buy you all a cocktail of your choice."

We all look at each other in shock. "Um, OK, thanks. I'll have a Charm again, please," I say with delight.

"And you, ladies?"

"I'll have the same please," Jen says with a grin.

"And me!" Karen squeals with delight.

I glance over to catch a glimpse of the men at the table.

"Jesus, girls, yer man looks like Boris Becker, the tennis player," I say. We all laugh.

"You know, you're not wrong there, Aly. He does look like him. I think I'd fancy this guy more, though," Jen says.

Karen just can't stop laughing. She can't get any words out.

"Thank you," I say with a smile to the men at the other table.

The men smile back. "You're welcome, ladies."

"We don't have to ask them to join us, do we?" Jen whispers. "I'd like to enjoy my dinner as it's a girlie night out."

"I don't think they would join us, to be honest, Jen," I say. "Boris looks a bit on the shy side. He wasn't overly confident when we thanked him."

"Ah, feck that for a story. We'll eat our dinner, and they can join us later if they want. Just because they bought us a cocktail doesn't give them permission to come and join the party," Karen says, deciding for all of us.

When the waiter reappears with the cocktails, we raise our glasses to Boris and his friends. "Thank you and cheers."

They go one step further as one of them approaches. "Hey, ladies, we won't interrupt your night any more. We just wanted to say hi and cheers."

"Well, thank you, and thank you for the drink. That's very kind of you," I say with a smile.

As he walks away, Karen nudges me. "He's mine. You and Jen can fight over Boris." Thankfully, she whispered.

After a fairly large and exquisite dinner, we're ready to hit the town. As we prepare ourselves for leaving the restaurant, we turn to thank the guys again, but they ignore us. "Oops! Are they pissed off with us because we didn't ask them to join us?" I ask.

Jen whispers, "I think maybe we're a little too tipsy for them now."

We leave in as dignified a manner as we can, except for Karen. "Night, Boris and Co. Thanks very mush for the drink again," she slurs.

I grab her arm and try to veer her towards the door as quickly as possible.

"Where do we go now? We're all still in good form, I think?" asks Karen.

"Pubbing?" I say hesitantly. *Why didn't I suggest going home?*

"That's the spirit! Let's go on to the Spotted Pig for cocktails."

"Sounds good to me," I murmur in a non-eager manner.

There's a queue starting to form outside the bar when we reach it. I really want to go home. I know I can't leave Jen on her own with Karen when she's in such a drunken state, and neither of us wants to leave Karen on her own.

We're finally inside, and Karen is chatting to people she knows. She starts dancing in the middle of the floor, and Jen and I stay by the bar, observing everything and sipping on a mineral in a bid to keep ourselves sane and sober. We are midconversation when we both spot a handsome man strolling into the bar.

"Oh my God! Aly, look at him. He's handsome."

"Too right he is. Jen, he's walking in this direction, so smiley face! And he's looking at you, I might add."

"Is he?" she asks. "I thought he was just checking out the bar."

"Nope, looks like it's you he's checking out. This place is small, and he's looking right at you. I'm off to the ladies. Enjoy."

"What? Don't leave me here on my own!"

"You're fine. He's fine. Go for it. Besides, you're not on your own." I gaze over to where Karen is dancing seductively by herself. "Make the most of the time you have on your own with him."

"OK, thanks," Jen replies.

I glance back on my way to the ladies to see him approaching Jen. She looks beautiful, and it's no wonder he's spotted her.

When I return, Karen is dancing with a very good-looking stranger. I really want to go home, but I can't leave her on her own here, just on the off chance the stranger she's dancing with is a psycho. I decide to stay, so I grab a bar stool not too far from where Jen is sitting.

Jen catches sight of me and beckons me over.

"This is my friend, Aly. Aly, this is Tommy."

"Hi, Aly, lovely to meet you."

"Likewise, Tommy. And where do you hail from?" *What the fuck did I just say? Where do you hail from? I've never used that expression in my life; I really must be picking up my father's sayings.*

"I'm from Long Island, Irish descent, though. I'm very proud of my Irish roots."

"Sure, who isn't Irish here, Tommy?"

"Very true. Would you like a drink? I'm just going to order."

"Very kind of you. I'll have a Nightingale cocktail, please."

"Sure. So that's two cocktails, one Cosmo and one Nightingale cocktail, and a pint of the black stuff for me."

"You know, you don't have to drink the black stuff on our account," I say, smiling.

"Oh, I love it. Makes me the strong man that I am," he says jokingly. He smiles at both of us as he makes his way to the bar.

"Good catch, Jen. He seems lovely. So what does he do?"

"Lawyer," she says with a big grin.

"Nice! Listen, when he gets back, I'm going to go for a wander around. It's pretty full here now. I can check out the guys. I want to give you more time on your own, get to know him a little."

"You don't have to do that, Aly."

"I know, but I want to. This guy seems really nice. In fact, he's the first guy you've ever introduced me to that I get a good gut instinct about from the minute I met him. He could be good for you, and I don't want to mess that up by being the friend glued to your hip. Now, here he comes."

"Here you go, Aly, one Nightingale, and Jen, one Cosmo. Cheers, ladies."

"Cheers, Tommy. Thank you."

I wait a few minutes before going walkabout, as I don't want to seem rude.

"Listen, I'm going have a walk around. I've spotted someone I know. Sorry, I'm not being rude. I'll be back again. I just want to say hi before they leave."

"Sure, that's no problem. We'll be here," Tommy says in a happy tone.

I'm lucky there are so many people here. I lied, as I don't know anyone here, but I had to come up with some excuse so Jen could be on her own with him. I take a seat towards the back of the bar and start playing with my phone. I really want to ring Jeremy.

I can't; I'm a little tipsy. It's a bad idea, so I sit, stirring my drink instead. When I look up, I spy a familiar face smiling at me.

It can't be, surely!

The light is quite dim, but it looks like Jack Morgan. I'm not going to wander in his direction since the last time I saw him, I lunged for him and disgraced myself. He raises his glass and smiles. *Is that an invitation to join you?* I smile back and raise my glass. I place my drink back on the bar and start stirring it vigorously with the stirrer—anything to avoid looking directly at him.

"You know, if you stir it any faster, you're likely to send that glass flying across the bar."

I look up and smile as he stands next to me.

"Hi, um, yeah, I like to mix my drink well."

"I see. How are you doing? It's been a long time since I've seen you."

"I'm good, thanks. It has been. How are you?"

"Wow, aren't you going to tell me how long it's been? Last time you told me you're very intelligent and you can calculate things quite quickly. I'm great, thanks—even better for seeing you."

I'm not sure what to say to him. I'm still cringing with embarrassment from the last time I saw him.

"Thank you. I…I'm feeling a little awkward here," I stutter.

"I know; you don't even know my name, after all," he says with a smirk.

"I do, actually. I know your name is Jack Morgan!" I say in an angry tone.

"Wow, you fall into my traps every time. OK so, you know who I am, but you, my beautiful Irish friend who has an accent I could listen to all night, you have yet to disclose your name to me. By the way, does that mean you've Googled me?"

I grin.

"Thanks. My name is Aly, Aly Hughes. No, I have not Googled you. I only know your name because my friend recognised you that day—the day you pulled me to the ground and disgraced me in the restaurant. She told me who you were, and while I might have been tempted to Google you, I didn't. I didn't see the point, and just for the record, I have never been classified as a stalker before."

"Well, Ms. Hughes, are you telling me you had no idea who I was? I'm glad I pulled you to the ground," he says with a cheeky grin.

"No, I didn't know who you were. Sure, no one knows you in Europe, and even though my friend told me who you are, I've still not seen you star in anything on TV."

He looks hurt.

"I'm sorry; I didn't mean to upset you in any way," I say.

"I've caught you again. You make me smile, Aly. Each time I've met you so far, you get agitated so easily and do things to make your life complicated. I find you funny. Come on, you know I want to get to know you better. Why can't you let me in? I'm kidding around with you. Since the first day I saw you, I was mesmerised by you. Those blue eyes just had me, even more than your beetroot boobs. And then there was that unexpected kiss in the train. It was so spontaneous. You drove me crazy that day. Then you left, and I'll bet it wasn't even your stop."

"No, it wasn't my stop," I say as I look at him sheepishly. "I'm sorry I've been rude to you. It's just that I feel so awkward and embarrassed about that whole situation. My gut told me to act on impulse that day, and I did. And while I'm embarrassed, I definitely don't regret it."

"Good, because neither do I. How about we start from the beginning and get to know each other? What's that you're drinking?"

"Nightingale."

"OK, one Nightingale coming up. Try not to spill it on yourself."

I give him a wry smile. "I won't. I never fancied a Nightingale on my boobs. Thanks."

I glance towards the top of the bar but can't see Jen anywhere. I feel a tap on my shoulder. It's Jen. "Hey, you, so he's the person you spotted."

"No, I didn't realise he was here until I sat down and felt someone staring at me, I swear."

"Chill out, Aly; it's great. Could do a lot worse than him, I'll bet."

"Yeah, I guess so. He's just buying me a drink so we can 'start from scratch,' getting to know each other. He's actually kind of funny, and he seems to be a gentleman, so I really should give him a chance."

"I told you. You met him three times in a week; that has to be some sort of sign. Listen, I'm heading home. I'll say hi to him before I go," Jen says.

"OK, is Karen all right?"

"She's fine; she's glued to some guy at the top of the bar. A different guy since you last saw her."

"Oh no, she's in dire condition. I should take her home, really," I say.

"Don't be silly! Stay and at least have one drink with him. He's gorgeous!"

Jack returns with two cocktails.

"Jack, this is my friend Jen. She was with me the day of the beetroot fiasco."

"Ah yes, I remember you were with someone. Hi, Jen, I'm Jack. It's a pleasure meeting you."

"Likewise, Jack. Not to be rude, but I'm just leaving. I just wanted to pop over and let Aly know—and, of course, to say hello to you."

"Well, I'll make sure she gets home safely."

"If only it were that simple," I say. "Jack, see the lovely drunken soul at the other side of the bar?" I point in Karen's direction. "That's our friend Karen, and I have to ensure she gets home safely."

"Aly, she'll be fine. She does this all the time," Jen says convincingly, but I want to be sure.

"No, I want to ensure she's safe."

"I promise I will get both of you home safely. How does that sound?" Jack asks.

Chivalrous!

"Thanks, Jack. That's really sweet. I hope I'll get to see you again soon," Jen says as she throws a sly wink in my direction.

"I hope so too, Jen. I need to butter your friend up a little here first, though. She's a tough cookie to impress."

"Don't I know it!" Jen nudges me playfully and turns to walk away.

"You two have fun. Aly, I'll call you tomorrow. Night, Jack, look after her."

"Night, Jen. Oh, I will, if she'll let me."

"Bye, Jen, talk tomorrow," I shout as she walks away.

She smiles and waves. I turn my attention back to Jack. "Thanks for the cocktail, Mr. Morgan."

"Very welcome, Ms. Hughes. So let's start from the beginning. This is going to seem stupid, but we might as well do it," he says.

"Do what?"

"I'll get up now, walk over there, and pretend that we've never met."

I start laughing.

"Then I'll pretend I've seen you for the first time, make my way over, and introduce myself. We can chat, like you didn't bump into me initially and you never lunged at me and stuck your tongue down my throat in the train."

"Jack, I didn't stick my tongue down your throat. I simply pursed my lips and kissed you."

"OK, slight exaggeration. Right, I'm going over there now."

I snigger.

"Are you ready?" he shouts from a few feet away. I can barely hear him with the music, but I manage to decipher what he says by lip reading.

"OK, here I come. Hi, how are you? I'm Jack."

"Hi there, I'm Aly."

"It's lovely to meet you, Aly. I'm sorry, I normally don't come up to people in bars, but I spotted you earlier in the night, and I have to say you are incredibly attractive. I'd love to buy you a drink and get to know you."

"Jack, that's corny."

"Come on, just play along. We can get to the getting-to-know-each-other bit later."

"OK, that would be nice. Sure, take a seat."

"Great, what would you like to drink?"

"You're not buying me another drink. You just got me one."

"Wow, you're really not very good at this. Pretend, Aly, pretend. You'd make a really bad actress."

I laugh. "OK, thanks." I pretend to accept a drink.

"Great, so, Aly, where are you from?"

"I'm from Cork, in Ireland."

"Wow, beautiful part of Ireland. I was there once on vacation. West Cork has such beautiful scenery."

"Oh, I love West Cork. And you, Jack, where are you from?"

"I was born and raised here. I was born into a family of actors, so I guess it was expected that I'd become one. I live in LA now, but I miss this city so much. New York is so awesome—such a great vibe here."

"Oh really? It must have been exciting growing up here. It's such a vibrant city. I was born here myself, but we moved to Ireland when I was young, so I don't recall the early years here."

"Just to let you know, you're getting the hang of this. Well done. So, yeah, it was OK. Sometimes I crave a bit of a quieter lifestyle, though."

"Like West Cork?" I say, smiling.

"Yeah, like West Cork. Bit far away, but you'd never know, I might buy a cottage there one day. Now, more about you, Aly. Any siblings?"

"I have three sisters and one brother, all younger than me. Both parents still alive, thankfully. I miss them some days when I'm alone and have time to think," I say.

"I'll bet you do. I was never fortunate enough to have any siblings. Must be fun, I'd imagine."

"It's fun, but not when we disagree about something. I get to ask the next question."

"Sure, it's your turn anyway," he says.

"What star sign are you, Jack?"

"Huh? Why ask me a question like that?"

"Curious. Remember, this is a get-to-know-you chat."

"Hmmm, you're intriguing, Aly. I'm a Scorpio. Fourth of November, 1974."

"Interesting."

"Why?"

"I'm a Taurus."

"I'm not very good at this astrology thing, but I'm guessing Taurus and Scorpio are either (a) meant to hate each other and are totally incompatible or (b) are a perfect match and sparks will fly—in a good way, of course."

"Could be either; bit like marmite. We'd either love or hate each other."

"OK, I'm interested in learning more about this."

"I'll bet you are. You'll have to wait!"

"So what date is your birthday?"

"Eleventh of May, 1978. I have to admit, Jack, this was a good idea. I'm enjoying myself."

"So am I, Aly. I'm curious to know what you work at, actually."

"I'm the creative director at Lexington Cards."

"That's interesting. Bit of a creative lady, then?"

"I try. I got my diploma in Ireland and worked in Lexington's sister company before I moved to New York. I know I'm not meant to bring this up, as we're meant to be meeting for the first time tonight, but those first three times I met you were during my first week here."

"Really? You had a look of confidence about you, as if you knew where you were going every time I saw you—except the first day, that is. Oh, and the day you kissed me." He smiles.

"Nope, I'm just here six months now. I love it."

Jack and I continue our conversation, and I'm really enjoying getting to know him. It feels like we have been chatting for some time, though. I look at my watch, and it's getting very late. I've enjoyed myself so much with Jack that I've forgotten completely about Karen.

"Look at the time! We've been chatting for nearly four hours, Jack."

"I know. Don't panic. I've had my eye on Karen from here. I guess I should get you ladies home, though. It'll be sunrise soon, and I'm pretty beat."

"You don't have to do that, Jack. I'll take Karen home to my place. I don't want to put you to any trouble."

"No trouble at all, and besides, I did promise Jen I'd get you both home safely."

I stand up from the barstool, and he grabs my hand and leads me to the opposite end of the bar, where Karen is now chatting up the barman. I tap her on the shoulder, and she acts like she hasn't even been out with me.

"Aly, how are you? I didn't know you were coming here tonight!"

"Um, Karen, we arrived together. Remember, we've been out all day, the Boat House, Buddakan, and then we came here?"

"Oh!" Karen says and then pauses as if to recap. "Yes, that's right, I must be so pissed I forgot. I feel sober, though. Is it possible to drink yourself sober? I feel sober. Who's the lasher next to you?"

"No, I think you're still under the influence a little, Karen. This is Jack, a friend of mine."

"Lasher? What's that?" Jack whispers into my ear.

"It's Cork slang for a good-looking guy."

He smiles, looking very pleased with himself, but right now I don't care if he is the most gorgeous guy in the world. I know I have a challenge ahead of me in getting Karen home.

"Come on, Karen. Home time."

"OK, Mam, I'm coming."

"Don't be like that. We've been out all night. You need sleep."

"I know, I know. I love you, Aly. You're the bestest friend in the whole wide world."

Jack smiles. "I'll bet she is."

Jack and I look at each other, and for a split second it feels like a real moment between us. No jokes, just us staring into each other's eyes, and I feel quivery inside.

"Oops!" Karen says as she slides off the stool and onto the floor, nearly pulling me with her.

Jack picks her up and helps me carry her outside. I'm trying desperately to hail a taxi, but it seems none of them wants to stop when they see the state Karen is in.

"He's a right sexy beast, Aly. Where did you find him?" Karen quizzes, trying to whisper but just a little too loud.

"I'll tell you tomorrow, Karen."

I can see by Jack's face that he's lapping up the compliments, and while I agree with Karen, I don't want him thinking he's going to win me over that easily. If I'm to be honest, though, I'm more like putty in his hands already.

"Jack, have you seen…Jack is your name, isn't it?" Karen slurs.

"Yes, that's me, Jack."

"Have you seen Aly's CD collection of eighties music yet? It's rocking, but she takes it everywhere. It nearly broke my back trying to take it up the stairs of Jen's place when she arrived."

"No, I haven't, but I'd love to see it sometime. I'm a big fan of that era. There were some great tunes back then."

I wasn't expecting that! A taxi finally comes to a halt next to us. We manage to bundle Karen into the car and reach our destination within a few minutes.

"Charles Street, lovely place to live. I lived here for a short stint two years ago," Jack says.

"It seems we have something in common, Jack Morgan."

"I told you. And you laughed over me setting the scenario of first meeting tonight."

"I know," I say. "I'm sorry."

I open the door of the taxi and step onto the kerb. Jack runs around to my side of the car and helps me lift Karen out of the cab. Once she steps onto the pavement, she slurs a little, but we can't figure out what she is saying.

"I'm going to…"

"You're going where, Karen?"

"Does she always get this plastered?" Jack asks.

"Not this bad, to the best of my knowledge anyway," I reply.

Before I know it, both my new Louboutins and Jack's shoes are covered in Karen's puke. Not exactly the finish to my nice night out I was expecting.

Jack looks at me and then at Karen. All I can see is an unimpressed face.

"Jack, I'm so sorry. I can't believe she's done this."

"Jack, I'm sorry I puked on you. It won't happen again. Next time I'll do it into my handbag," Karen says with sincerity.

We both manage a laugh. I get her indoors with Jack's help, and I sit her on the couch so she can sleep the drink and looming hangover off.

"I should get going," he says.

"I'll walk you to the door," I say. "Jack, I'm really sorry about Karen. I hope…"

He presses his index finger to my lips.

"That's not your fault, Aly. Besides, it happens to the best of us. I'm just glad it was Karen in that state and not you."

"I still feel bad, though. Look at your shoes!" I turn my gaze downward to see his shoes covered in what looks like lumps of carrot. It's disgusting, and yet while I feel bad, I can't help but start laughing hysterically.

"It's laughable, Aly. Go ahead."

"I'm sorry, I'm sorry," I manage to expel between bursts of laughter. He gives in and also laughs.

"It's OK. I'll dump these later, but I need to wear something for the journey to the hotel. I wonder if the taxi driver will allow me to travel now."

"He's still waiting. Hop in while you can. He won't get the smell for a few minutes. You'll almost be at your hotel by then."

"True. Aly, can I have your number? I'd really like to see you again—only next time for a proper date."

"Sure."

I give my number to him, and I cheekily ask for his, which to my surprise he hands to me on a piece of paper.

"So do I need to contact your PA or assistant before I manage to get through to you?" I ask.

"Oh no, I don't have a PA, Aly. I like to organise myself," he says with a smile. "OK, Aly Hughes, I'll be in touch very soon," he says as he moves towards me and kisses my cheek.

"OK, talk to you soon, Jack."

I retreat into my apartment, and the feeling in the pit of my stomach is one I haven't experienced in a long time: butterflies.

Chapter 16

"Karen, Karen, wake up."

"Leave me to rot in peace, please."

I snigger as I manage to pull the cover from over her head.

"Seriously, Aly, you don't want to see me. I know I must look like a rotting spud. I'm probably covered in spots and have massive black circles under my eyes."

She isn't wrong.

"Go into my bed. You'll be in agony with the way you've been sleeping on the couch."

"OK."

She attempts to get up, but when she manages to straighten herself upright, she falls back onto the couch again.

"I can't move. I feel like someone's trampled on my head. Did someone trample on my head? Is that why I feel like this? Where am I, anyway?"

"Karen, you're in my place. No, thankfully, nobody trampled on you, but you drank a ridiculous amount of alcohol yesterday. Come on, I'll try and help you to the bedroom."

I finally manage to get her into the bedroom, where she literally collapses into the bed. I grab some clean clothes for myself and leave her to sleep it off.

I think I got enough sleep, but I'm still a little groggy. I need food. I stand in my small galley kitchen, whisking some eggs for breakfast and thinking about the wonderful time I had with Jack Morgan.

I seriously consider calling him but decide not to. I need to step back and let him do the chasing.

The phone rings. My heart thumps. *Oh my God, is that him?*

"Hey, lady. Well, how did the rest of your night go?"

"Jen! Well, I think I should ask you that!"

"Oh, Aly, Tommy is fantastic! He's such a lovely guy. He walked me home, and there was no hint of expectation from him. He's a rare find, I'd say."

"Lucky you! I hope something great comes of this, Jen. You deserve it, especially after the last few creeps you've been with."

"Yes, I know. I think this time around I'm more careful, too. I'm not rushing into anything, and the fact that he respects that is making me fall for him already. I need to curb my enthusiasm a little, though. I don't want to turn him off."

"Jen, I've a feeling he's very into you. Don't curb it too much, either, or he might think you're not interested. Just be yourself. So did you get a number?"

"Yes, I did. He took mine, and we've already arranged the next date: tonight!"

"Nice! Not rushing?"

"I know, but it's just dinner. He knows that's all it is."

"I'm only kidding. I have to say, he seemed really nice last night. I hope it all goes well."

"Thanks, Aly. Here's me blabbing on. Jack Morgan! Tell me!"

"Well, we chatted for four hours after you left, would you believe?"

"Great, and…"

"And then he took myself and Karen home—after some effort, as no taxi would stop. I reckon because Karen was in such a state."

"Oh no! So what happened?"

"Well, we managed to get one eventually. Here's the funnyish part. I'm angry but can't stay angry at Karen, as it was funny."

"Come on, tell me!"

"Karen got out of the taxi and puked on my Louboutins and on Jack's shoes. I've no idea what his were, but they looked expensive, too."

"Jesus, she didn't, did she?" exclaims Jen. "That's hilarious."

"It is now. I think my shoes will smell of puke for a while, though. I actually cleaned them when I got in, as I didn't want it sticking to them. I think I need something stronger to remove the bad odour, though."

"We'll get you new shoes. Don't worry about them. What about Jack? Was he angry?"

"He didn't look too impressed, but in the end he laughed it off."

"Did he stay over?"

"No, he went home, but he did take my number, and he was very sweet and complimentary to me. I really like him, Jen."

"Hurrah! Great, now maybe you'll forget about Jeremy and meet up with Jack more regularly."

"Well, I'd like to, but how realistic is it? I mean, he's an actor who spends half of his time in LA."

"I know, the location might be a bit of an issue, but go with the flow. If he likes you, and you like him, it will sort itself out."

"Yeah, true, I guess. Let's hope he calls after all this. Oh, he's so lovely. I felt butterflies, Jen—butterflies! The last time I felt them I think I was in my teens."

"He'd be mad not to call. I'm sure he will. I felt a little flutter myself with Tommy. So after all that excitement...where's Karen?"

"She's in bed. She looks dreadful today. She thought someone had trampled on her head, it's so sore. I'm going to let her sleep it off for whatever length of time it takes, though. She needs a good rest."

"You're right. Better to let her get it out of her system. OK, hon, I'm going to hang up now as I need to decide what to wear tonight. I'm so excited."

"You have a great night out. Tell Tommy I said hi, and good luck to you."

"Thanks, Aly. Hope Jack calls tonight."

"I do, too. I don't think he will, though. Have fun, Jen, and talk tomorrow."

I hang up. I'm staring at the phone. The not-so-sensible side of me is taking over again, wanting me to pick up the phone and call Jack. I take the piece of paper from my jacket pocket and look at it. I really want to call him, but I don't want to annoy him, either. I should probably let him do the chasing, and so I punch the number into my phone and press the save button instead. At least that way I know I'm not at risk of losing it—unless I lose my phone, that is.

I decide to chill out for the afternoon. I go to the corner store and buy a few necessities like Coke, chocolate, and crisps; they are my very bad but very effective hangover cure. I think it would be good for Karen to have something salty when she gets up, so I remove some bacon and sausages from the freezer.

Four hours later Karen rises from the bed.

"Hi, Aly, how are you?"

"How am I? I'm grand; it's you I should be asking that question to."

"I'm better now. I had a good deep sleep there but would mangle something salty."

"I read your mind. There are sausages and rashers from home there. I'll put them on now."

"Excellent," she says. "Are you on for another mad night out tonight?"

"Please tell me you're joking."

"Nope, course not. Come on, we're only young once, girl."

"Karen," I say, "at the rate you've been drinking lately, you won't be with us for much longer, never mind be young."

"Hey, that's a bit harsh. I'm only having fun. You don't want to come, obviously."

"Sorry, but no, I'm not going out tonight. Last night and Friday night were enough for this weekend."

"OK. There's a funny smell in here like puke or something."

"Funny you should say that."

I produce my shoes, and she sniffs them. "Urgh, what the hell happened to them?" she exclaims.

"You puked on them when you got out of the car last night, remember?"

"Oh my God! I vaguely remember. I'm so sorry; they're your Louboutins! I'll get you another pair; don't worry. The same ones, and I might even get you a spare pair too. Hang on, wasn't there someone else with us? A guy, from what I remember. He looked like that actor guy, Jack...what's his name, Jack Morgan, that's it!"

I smile. "Yep, there was a guy, and yes, he looked like that ac-tor guy because he *is* that actor guy. He didn't escape your insides, either."

"Jack Morgan? You were with Jack Morgan last night? Is he still here?"

"No, he didn't stay. He was such a gent. He helped me get you into the apartment, and then he left but not before kissing me on the cheek, giving me his number, and taking mine."

"Excited! I can't believe you bagged yourself Jack Morgan. He's so hot. Well, I can believe it because you're gorgeous, but things like that never happen to us. Well done, Aly. He must think I'm such a lush though, does he?"

"Well, hang on now; we swapped numbers, and he did sug-gest us going on a proper date next time, but it doesn't mean I've 'bagged him.' In relation to you, no, he doesn't think that. His words were something along the lines of 'It happens to the best of us, Aly, but I'm just glad it wasn't you in that state.'"

"OK, he must be interested in you if he asked for your number. You go, girl. So he wasn't too mad, then?"

"No, not mad, just a bit perplexed, I'd say, by the whole situation. I'd imagine he hadn't planned on someone puking on his shoes at the end of his night out." I burst into laughter. "To be honest, he found it amusing in the end. He's a nice guy, and I think we got off to the wrong start initially due to my paranoia and impulsiveness, but apparently he likes that in me. How many sausages and rashers do you want?"

"Oh, four of each, please. I'm starving. Maybe you'll forget this thing with Jeremy now, seeing as you have a new distraction."

I plate up her hangover cure and hand it to her with a cup of strong coffee.

"Yeah, maybe I will. We'll see what happens."

"Oh, girl, you've been worrying too long about finding a man. You know the expression, for every teapot there's a lid? Well, it looks like you have two right now. You just need to choose which lid fits best. I know which one I'd choose," Karen says.

I can't help but erupt into laughter. She's right, and I know which lid I'd choose, too. I just hope the lid fits this teapot.

Karen wolfs her food back and leaves shortly afterwards. Thankfully, she seems pretty sober. I sit on the couch for what's left of the day, treat myself to some munchies, and watch TV for a full-on relaxation session.

The next day I get up early, and I feel good. I've convinced myself that I will no longer look at Jeremy "in that way" and tell him that I want us to be just friends. I think it's the sensible thing to do. Jack Morgan has been a good distraction for me, but I hope in my heart that he will be more than that.

I reach the office a little later than anticipated as I've walked part of the journey to work.

"Hey, Als. You're a little late today. Everything OK?" Jeremy quizzes.

"Yep, everything is great, thanks, Jeremy. I walked part of the way and miscalculated how much time I'd need."

"Ah, OK. Everything good after, you know, the other night?" he whispers.

"I'm grand, thanks. And you?" I whisper back. "You know, if we whisper, we look like we're guilty or hiding something, Jeremy."

"You're right. I can't really broadcast it, though. Let's go into your office or mine or somewhere quiet so we can have a chat."

We are nearer my office, so I go in before him and take a seat at my desk.

"So what's up? You sound like you need to talk to me urgently or something."

"Well, I do. I think I left a bit abruptly the other day, and I wanted to apologise to you. I had a fantastic night with you, Aly, and I should have let you know that I had an appointment with my dentist the following morning."

"Honestly, Jeremy, at the time I was a bit annoyed and hurt that you left so suddenly, but I'm well over it now. Seriously, I know you're just looking for a bit of fun, but I really think we need to put a stop to it as I'm looking for something more than fun right now, I think."

"Oh, I wasn't expecting that from you. OK, if that's what you want, let's just be friends. Although we did agree on that already a few weeks back, and we still ended up together last Friday night."

"I know, but I'm looking at the bigger picture now, and it's really not going to work, is it?"

"If that's what you think. I'll leave you to it," he says with a slight tone of sadness in his voice. I wonder if that is for my benefit or if it's genuine.

I get on with my workload. When Jeremy or I pass each other for the rest of the day, we just smile cordially at each other. It's as if nothing has happened. I'm glad I made the decision to end it, but I also regret it slightly. However, I think I've pinned all my hopes on Jack Morgan's phone call, which I still haven't received. I can't string Jeremy along, though; it wouldn't be fair.

It's Friday evening, and I'm leaving the office. My phone vibrates in my pocket.

"Hello, Jennifer!" I answer.

"Hey, you. What's happening? Do you fancy going for drinks or coffee tomorrow with Tommy and me? It will give you a chance to get to know him better. I'll ask Karen, too, or maybe you'd like to bring Mr. Morgan with you?"

"That sounds like a plan," I say. "I'd love to get to know Tommy better. Seems like a sweetie. I'd say Mr. Morgan won't be coming, though. He never called, Jen."

"Oh, Aly, I'm sorry. Still, it's early days. Maybe he had to go back to LA. Did he actually state he would call you this week?"

"No, he didn't, and maybe you're right. I probably just got it into my head that he would. Anyway, not to worry, I'm definitely on for tomorrow night."

"Great," she says. "Are you heading out with the work crowd tonight?"

"No plans to. I've just left the office, but I wouldn't mind a bit of social activity this evening. Maybe I'll join them for one or two."

"Social activity? I hope that's not what I think it means."

"No, it's not. I'm going to be a good girl tonight."

"Good for you. I'll see you tomorrow night. Be good and have a nice evening."

"Cheers. You too, hon. Talk tomorrow."

I hang up, and within five seconds of doing so, the phone rings again.

"Als, it's Jeremy. Where have you gone? Don't tell me you're not coming out with us tonight?"

"Hi, Jeremy. Well, I wasn't going to, but I've changed my mind. I'll see you all in five minutes."

"Great, see you then."

I stroll down to the pub, which is a great attraction on Fridays due to the live music. It's like a taste of home, and I really enjoy it there. The first person I spy when I get there is Jeremy. He's looking very smiley and finally has a new tooth in place of the old one. It makes all the difference to his appearance.

"Hey, I took the liberty of getting you a cocktail. I hope that's what you want."

"Thanks, Jeremy. I was actually going to hit the wine tonight as I'm not staying long, but you know what, a cocktail sounds delicious. That's very kind of you."

Idiot! You don't have to sound so formal!

"Aly, I've been thinking about what you said earlier in the week. I really like you, and although I'm not really one for relationships, I would like to give this a go with you."

"Jeremy, can we talk about something else, please? I'm not in the mood for this conversation tonight."

I'm still thinking about Jack Morgan and if he will call. Where would I be then, stuck between two men and fancying both of them? I've never been in that situation before and don't want to experience it. I wouldn't know how to handle it.

"Sure, if that's what you want," he says sulkily.

We stand in silence. It's the most awkward ten minutes of my week, and then Deborah approaches us.

"What's wrong with you two? You look like you both ate a bag of nails!" she says with a roar of laughter.

"Nothing, Deborah. Aly and I were just discussing the accounts from the office. We're both a bit tired from working on them all week, and I guess you just caught us as we finished our conversation."

"Shop talk—I've no interest in it. So, Jeremy, are you coming clubbing with us tonight?" she quizzes in a very flirtatious manner.

"No, Deborah, not tonight. I'm going home to get some much-needed rest."

"I wonder why you're so tired?" She sniggers and walks away.

Oh my God! Does she know that Jeremy and I slept together? What else could she mean by that? She probably thinks we've been at it all week!

"Jeremy, did you tell that motormouth that we slept together?" I whisper.

"I did not! What kind of eejit do you think I am?"

"OK, sorry; maybe I'm being paranoid."

"Yes, you are. I've had enough for tonight. I'm out of here."

I sense that he is upset and feel bad for shouting at him, and so I follow him.

"Jeremy, wait please." I manage to catch up to him.

"What, Aly?"

"I'm sorry," I say. "I shouldn't have treated you in that way to-night. You don't deserve it."

"You've treated me like that all week, Aly."

"I know, and I'm sorry. It's just…I feel it would be so complicated if there was an 'us' in the workplace. It makes life difficult, especially with busybodies like Deborah hanging around."

"Yes, I can see your point, but I think we could be throwing something good away here. Why waste something good?"

"True."

"How about we walk and talk about it? I'll walk you home," he says.

"OK."

We walk right across the city. It's a good walk, but the air is crisp and the sky clear. It's romantic, bar the screaming sirens. When we reach my flat, I invite Jeremy in for a glass of wine and some dinner. It seems like the right thing to do, as we are both starving.

I wake the next morning, and this time Jeremy lies there in deep slumber next to me. Although I did promise myself I wouldn't get involved with him again, I also realise what he said the night before was true, about us throwing something good away. So I decide to take a chance and go with the flow.

"Morning, gorgeous," he utters. I'm in deep thought, looking at his very handsome face.

"Morning, boss. Sleep OK?"

"Yep, slept like a log. What's the plan of action today?"

"Nothing. I'm going out with Jen tonight, but that's it."

Should I invite him? Maybe it's too soon.

"Right, so no lunch plans?" he asks.

"No. Why?"

"I'm going to treat you to a lovely, leisurely lunch today."

"Nice. To what do I owe that?" I ask.

"Nothing. I'd like to treat you. I think it would be nice to spend more time together today. You don't have to if you don't want to."

"No, I think I'm good for that."

We walk into the village. Jeremy treats me to a lovely lunch at the Spotted Pig. There's a great feeling around the West Village. Everyone looks happy. The humidity is high, and there's a strong summer vibe. I feel contented as I get the impression from him that he finally wants something more than just a casual fling with me. He hasn't actually stated that though, not properly. We part ways at the end of the lunch, and this time he gives me more than just a kiss on the forehead, unlike the previous week.

"Als, I could spend the whole day with you today, but I know you have other plans. Maybe next weekend we can do something together for the whole weekend. What do you think?"

Don't give in. Don't give in…Keep him on a string. Remember, he has a reputation with the ladies. Why the hell do you have to fancy him out of all the eligible men in New York?

"I can't give you a definite on that yet, Jeremy. There might be something in the pipeline for next weekend as I've a provisional booking, but I'll know later in the week. Is that OK? If something else comes up for you, go for it, as I don't want you to be hanging around waiting for an answer from me."

"Well, the offer is there. If something does crop up, I'll let you know."

"Great. Thanks," I say. "I had a really nice time with you, both last night and today. It's good we're getting to know each other better."

"It is, Aly," he says. "This is strange for me, you know? I never want to commit or spend too much time with one person normally, but you're that little bit different."

He used the word "commit"!

I blush. "Thanks, Jeremy. That's really sweet."

"OK, better go. I'll call you over the weekend."

"See ya." I glance back at him as I stroll away, and he winks at me and flashes one of his cute smiles, the one that attracted me to him in the first place.

Later I get ready and go out on the town with Jen and Tommy. Karen shows her face for about ten minutes and then leaves again. She's going on a second date with one of the guys she met earlier in the week—the guy with "a nice personality and nice face," to use her words.

Jen, Tommy, and I spend the evening discussing everything from court cases and fashion to the greeting-card industry. Jack Morgan even crops up in conversation. It's a fun night, and I'm glad I have the opportunity to meet Jen's new man. They seem very in tune and are perfect for each other astrologically. I really need to talk to Jen alone, though, and I only manage it during Tommy's toilet breaks.

"Jen, I've something to tell you."

"Oh, he rang, didn't he?"

"Who? Oh Jack, no, sadly, he didn't. I had a bit of a discussion with Jeremy last night, and he walked me home. Don't worry; we only had around half a cocktail each so it wasn't drunken. Basically, we got to my place, and we were both starving, and so I invited him in to cook for him. One thing led to another, and, well, I'll leave the rest to your imagination."

"Aly, you didn't! Not again! I thought you were going to stay clear of him. You said he has a reputation of being a ladies' man. Surely you don't want to get involved with someone like that after Simon cheating on you?"

"Well, no, I don't, but we had a chat, and I get the feeling that he wants something more from this. Not just a casual fling."

"Hmmm, I'm not convinced. Look, I warned you. Be it on your own head."

I sit in silence. She's fuming, and I don't blame her. I know she's only looking out for me.

"It's OK. I'm playing a chase game with him. He won't get me that easily. He wants to spend the whole weekend with me next weekend, but I told him I've something provisionally booked in. I don't but thought it would be good to keep him on the long finger."

"Good. Well, that's something I suppose. Why the hell didn't that Jack Morgan ring you? I'm angry at him more than anyone, I think."

"Jen, he's an actor. I wanted to believe he would, but let's face it: he probably has women falling all over him in both New York, LA, and any other state he might visit in the United States. Why would I even stand a slight chance of him fancying me? He obviously doesn't as he didn't call."

"Not true. He looked very interested that night, Aly. Don't put yourself down. You're as good as any of those women—in fact, you're better. You're not all Botox and plastic boobs! You're real, and I think that's one of the qualities he likes in you. There has to be a good explanation for all of this. There has to be."

"Look, let's forget about it now. Tommy is coming back, and I don't want him thinking we're arguing over something silly."

"OK. Sorry, you know I'm just looking out for you, Aly."

"I know, hon; don't worry. I've learned my lesson. I won't let Jeremy hurt me."

It's getting late, and we decide to go home. I need time alone to think, and so I wander home through the village and soak up the party atmosphere that surrounds me. I love being in New York, but there's just one thing missing from my life: a true romance, something real, with someone I can rely on. I keep thinking of Jeremy and wonder if it really would be that bad having a relationship of sorts with him.

Chapter 17

ℱour weeks have passed. It's a Thursday afternoon, and I'm sitting in my office, trying to decide on some new designs the team came up with. My phone rings.

"Hey, beautiful, how are you?"

"Who's this?" I quiz. *Feck you anyway, Jack Morgan, ringing me four weeks later. Who do you think you are?*

"It's Jack, Jack Morgan. Listen, before you berate me, I'm really, really sorry. Something came up unexpectedly in LA, and I had no choice but to go. I was meant to stay in New York for a few days but couldn't."

"I wasn't going to berate you," I mutter in a joking manner, but in reality, I want to scream down the phone at him. *Four fecking weeks, Jack! Four fecking weeks!*

"Ah good, nice to see you're an understanding woman. So I was wondering if you'd like to go out for dinner with me. How about Monday night?"

"Hmmm, Monday's not really good for me. I could do Thursday."

"Sure, I'm around from Monday until Friday, and then I'm off again for a few weeks to LA."

"Ah, OK." *Well shit, anyway! I could have a whole week of dates with Jack if I didn't open my big mouth. I need to find a way to backtrack and change the plan back to earlier in the week.* "Well, actually, I'm just checking my diary," I say. "I might be able to do Tuesday, if that's any good?"

"No, Thursday is fine. I've got a business meeting on Tuesday night, unfortunately."

Shit! "OK, Thursday it is."

"Great. I'll pick you up. Eight thirty OK for you?"

"You know the address? Oh, of course you do. It was where your lovely shoes were ruined. That time suits nicely."

"Indeed it was. Don't worry about them. So see you on Thursday night. I'm really psyched about seeing you again, Aly. Sorry to rush; I'm just heading into a meeting. This is the first chance I got to call you."

"That's fine, Jack; I'll see you then, and thanks for calling." I hang up. *Aggghhhhh, he called! He called!* Why the hell didn't he call sooner? He couldn't use the old "they have no phones in LA yet" excuse.

There's a knock on my door.

"Hey, Als. Saw you doing a little dance there. Something good happening?"

Fuck! What do I tell him? I have to think fast!

"Yeah, yeah, one of my friends from home just called to tell me she had a baby girl this morning. I'm just so excited for her."

"Lovely. Bet she must be a little cutie. So I was thinking, how about we go to the cinema or something light this weekend? We haven't spent as much time together as I would have liked over the last couple of weekends."

Yes, Jeremy, that's right. We haven't. You've been working all the time. Weekend is for fun, remember?

"That's fine with me. Don't worry; you know we don't have to be in each other's pockets. We see one another every day, Jeremy."

"I know, but I'd like to see more of you."

"Tell you what. Why don't we go back to yours for a change this weekend? Every weekend so far when you've not been working, it's been the same story: pub after work then back to mine. Always promises of spending more time with me, and it never happens.

It would mean a lot to me if you invited me around to your place every now and then, Jeremy. I feel like you're hiding something from me sometimes. You talk about wanting something more serious, but then you have your guard up when I suggest something like that. I mean, we really are very casual right now."

"I know, and I'm sorry. It's just, you know, it's been a busy month, and I have to get the accounts in shape and make sure everything is up to date. One of our biggest freelancers pulled out and went to another company because they pay more. This could cause a massive loss for us. He wrote some great verse, Aly."

"Yes, I know. But you need to chill out and relax, too. You can't work all of the time. I really do think that it would be nice to stay somewhere other than my apartment some night. I'd like to see yours properly—get to know the real Jeremy."

"We'll do it soon, I promise." He walks back to his office.

Yet another promise.

I won't tell him that I am going on a date the following Thursday with Jack Morgan. Maybe I should. He might finally cop himself on and treat me with more respect. I don't even know where I really stand with Jeremy right now.

Later that day, I get a call from Jen.

"Aly, remember that job I applied for with the modelling agency? Well, I got it!"

"Jen, I'm so pleased for you! That's fantastic news."

"Yeah, I just told Tommy. He's spoiling me tonight."

"That's lovely! What a lovely guy. Congratulations, Jen; you deserve it."

"Thanks. Have to go now again. I haven't told my boss I'm leaving yet. Going to miss this place. They've been so good to me, but I need to try something different."

"They'll understand, and they will miss you. Go, before they fire you."

"OK, thanks, Aly. Talk to you soon."

"Bye."

I'm very pleased for Jen. I want to tell her that I have a date with Jack next Thursday night but don't want to spoil her new-job buzz. I'll tell her another time, maybe after it happens.

Jeremy is passing in and out of my office all week, and although I like his company and presence, it's just a little too smothering at times. I try my best to avoid him, but there isn't really any avoidance happening, as his office is situated right next to mine.

Thursday comes around quickly, and I'm so excited about my date with Jack. Unfortunately, Jeremy seems to spot my excitement a mile off.

"You're very chirpy today. Is there something happening?"

"Nope, just in good form."

"Good for you. You look great. Are we good for tomorrow night?"

"Hmm, yeah, I think so. I'd prefer it wasn't a late night, though. I've had too many late nights recently. I've been out with Karen a few nights, and she can be a handful to look after."

"Aly, she's thirty-something. She doesn't need looking after."

"I'm one of her best friends, Jeremy. Of course I'm going to make sure she gets home safely, whether she does it on a regular basis on her own or not. When she's out with me, I have to know she's home safe."

"OK, well, let's not argue over Karen," he says. "We don't have to do anything if you don't want. Skip a weekend or just mooch at your place on the couch."

"We'll see. Let's decide tomorrow night."

"Sure. Keep smiling. You look very hot today, by the way."

"Thanks. Close the door after you, please. I'm busy," I say with a sultry smile.

I'm not really busy—well, I am, but not with work. I'm trying to piece together my outfit in my head for my night out with Jack.

When it's time to go home, I head for the door in a very speedy manner and escape the building before Jeremy can catch up with me.

When I reach home, I ring Karen.

"Hey, I need to borrow some shoes," I tell her.

"No borrowing necessary. I got those Louboutins for you today, and the latest fashion trend, too. Gorgeous—you're going to die when you see them."

"Nice. Thanks, Karen. I owe you one."

"No, you don't," she says. "Remember, I ruined your shoes a few weeks back, chick. I owe you, so this is repayment. I'll drop them over tomorrow."

"Thanks! One pair would have been enough, but I won't say no to them. You know me when it comes to shoes!"

"Yep, and underwear, but we won't mention that fiasco again."

"No, please don't; it's better forgotten. I need the shoes tonight though, Karen."

"Oh, hot date with Jeremy? OK, I'm on my way home in five minutes. I'll drop them off on the way."

"You star! Hmmm, yeah, hot date with Jeremy."

I don't want to lie, but I know how excited she would be if I told her the truth, and I have no idea what will happen on the date with Jack. What if he changes his mind about me after the date? I'll just keep it to myself for now.

"See you shortly then." She hangs up.

Those butterflies are fluttering around in my stomach again. I'm pleased I have two whole hours to get ready. The dress I chose already, but I have to make sure the shoes are right with it. I have another outfit on standby just in case.

I run a bath because I know it will take an hour before Karen will reach me.

Thirty minutes later, there's a knock on the door. I didn't expect her to be so fast. I grab my robe and run to open the door.

"You got here very quickly! Jeremy…Hi, what a pleasant *[is it?]* surprise!"

"Hi, thought I'd surprise you with a bottle of wine. Got the time?"

"I'm sorry, Jeremy, I actually have plans tonight."

"You never said."

"Well, we are just casual, aren't we? I mean, we aren't committed fully or anything. It's just with Karen, don't worry." *Lies!*

"It's OK. I should have checked with you first. I suck at this relationship thing. It's been too long since I've been in a proper one, so I guess you'll have to teach me."

I just smile. I'm such a thundering bitch for lying to him. I wonder if this brands me as a man-iser?

"It's no problem. We can do something tomorrow night like we said earlier," I say.

"OK, have a good night with Karen. Don't get too drunk. I know what a night out with her can end up like."

Oh, you have no idea!

"I won't. It always ends up with me babysitting. I don't intend on having too much anyway, school night and all that."

"OK, see you tomorrow," he says as he flashes me his cute smile and kisses me. As if I don't feel bad enough.

Karen arrives on the doorstep twenty minutes later. I'm lucky she hasn't met Jeremy or there could have been major confusion. Lies and deceit are not my thing, and after this night, I know that two-timing anyone is a bad idea. I still don't feel like I'm totally betraying Jeremy, though. Yes, he mentioned commitment a few weeks back, but I've not seen any signs of it. Besides, it's just dinner with a friend—an incredibly handsome and sexy friend.

I try on the new shoes and opt for the leopard-print ones with five-inch heels. They're perfect with my red dress.

"Sexy lady!" Karen roars. "You look smoking hot, girl. You won't even get past the door tonight, I'd say."

"Thanks. I feel good, I have to say. I'm starving, so we better get past the door!"

"You have a good night, hon. I'm off home. No parties to go to tonight, and I feel I could do with a rest."

"Not like you. Are you ill?"

"No, just don't have a party to go to, which is unusual. I normally find one to crash, but there doesn't seem to be anything happening in my circle tonight. A night off won't do any harm."

"True. Be good, and thanks for the shoes. They're amazing."

"Very welcome. It was the least I could do. Enjoy your night and hi to Jeremy. When are we going to meet him?"

"Soon, very soon." I smile and wave goodbye.

The clock is ticking at what seems like a very slow pace. *Will the next half hour ever pass?* I'm drained, and my excitement is waning slightly. I hear Jack knocking on the door, and I quickly snap out of my dozy mode. I run to open the door as fast as I can.

"Mr. Morgan. It's lovely to see you. Are you coming in?"

"Are you ready? If so, we'll go straight there."

"OK, let's go. Wow, swish car."

"Yeah, they're nice wheels—that's just to impress you," he says with a snigger.

"Right, I've changed my mind," I say. "I'm not going out."

"Oh come on, you know I'm kidding. You look stunning, by the way. Red suits you, and I'm wondering, are those new Louboutins you're wearing?"

"You know your stuff, Jack! I'm impressed. Thanks; I said I'd make some bit of an effort for you. It took a lot of thought to decide whether I would or not, but I opted to make the effort in the end." I look at him and wink. "Karen got me the shoes to make up for her ruining the others."

"Nice of her."

"Yes. In fact, she asked me a few weeks back if you had contacted me so she could get you a pair of shoes, too."

"Well, I don't look so good in heels, Aly, but thank her for the offer. No, seriously, there's no need. As I said, it could happen to anyone. She doesn't need to worry about me. Tell her chill. I'm totally cool about it all."

"I'll let her know."

"Le Bernardin, please, Brad."

Oh lovely!

He holds the door open for me and closes it once I'm settled. He then proceeds to the other side of the car.

"You have your own driver?"

"No, not always. Brad drives me around when I'm in New York, but normally I don't have a driver in LA. I just couldn't be bothered hiring a car here. I never know how long I'll be staying, so it's easier for me to call Brad. You know how difficult it is to get a taxi here when you really need one!"

"And he gives me work, so I don't complain," Brad says.

"Good, well, I'll have to ensure he carries on doing that then, Brad."

"So how's life been treating you? Any new guy since I was last here?" Jack asks.

"Well, no, not really. I've been saving myself for you, Jack," I say in a sarcastic tone.

"I'll bet you have, and I don't blame you," he says. I love his smart comments, especially when they come with that luscious smile.

"I must apologise to you, Aly," he says after a moment. "I should have called sooner. I had some problems in LA, and they were dragging me down a little. To be honest, I think you would have picked me up had I called, but I didn't want to burden you with my problems."

"What? You should have called. Jack, I thought you didn't want to contact me or you were playing it cool."

"Nope; just didn't want to hassle you. Well, I'm here now, and I know it's not for long as I have to go back tomorrow, but let's make the most of tonight."

I smile. *I really want to grab your face and kiss your beautiful lips, but I have to control myself and learn not to be so impulsive.*

We pull up outside the restaurant on West Fifty-First Street. Once we are seated, I gaze at the menu and just want one of everything, as the choice is so amazing. We spend hours talking over fine wine and food, and I enjoy every moment of it. As a special surprise, Jack has organised for us to take in the view from the Empire State Building by night. I love a bit of romance. It's bitterly cold at the top, but the view that surrounds us makes up for it—even more so when Jack puts his arms around me to keep me warm. The sky is clear, and I feel like I can almost touch the stars because I'm so high up. As we glance downward, the cars look smaller than ants, and the city's lights make it look spectacular. I so want Jack to kiss me. It's the perfect setting for a kiss, but he's such a gent that he doesn't. It's getting late, so Jack drops me home, and I am very tempted to ask him to come in, but I decide against it. Instead, I keep him lingering on at the front door of the building.

"So?"

"So, Hughes. Did you have a good night?"

I like when he calls me that.

"I had a wonderful night. Thank you, Jack."

"I'm glad. So did I. You are amazing—great conversation, and you look stunning, my lady in red."

"Thanks—just don't sing it, please."

I don't believe it. He's singing the lyrics—the opposite of what I ask. I should have known.

"Jack, stop, please." I start giggling. I'm actually cringing. Corny song, it bugs me.

He grabs me close and starts slow dancing with me while humming the rest of the song.

"You know what? I'm allergic to that song," I say.

He laughs. "The one song I choose, and you don't like it. But it's from the eighties; you love that era."

"Not in its entirety, but you get kudos for the romantic side, and you can actually sing, sort of. You might even make me like the song after this."

"Good. I love that song, and it's given me the excuse to pull you closer to me for that good-night kiss."

I gaze into his eyes. He leans forward and gently kisses me on the lips. I feel like my head is spinning. I really want to invite him in, but I keep reminding myself that I need to make him wait. He pulls away from me and stares at me for a few minutes. It's the most comfortable silence I've ever experienced. I hold his gaze for as long as I can, and then he starts to walk down the steps. Still holding my hand, he turns to me and says, "Good night, Aly Hughes. Thank you for a wonderful night, and I promise I'll ring you on schedule next time. Damn, you're beautiful."

"Thank you, Jack, I had an amazing night. I'll expect your call."

I smile and watch the car drive away at a snail's pace with Jack staring out of the window at me. He's smiling and looks really happy. I wave, smile and enter the building.

"Aly!" I hear.

Sweetest Jesus, don't let that be Jeremy, please?

All I'd need is for him to be waiting for me like a stalker. I turn to see Mr. DeAngelo smiling at me. I exhale a sigh of relief. "Mr. DeAngelo, how are you? I haven't seen you in a while. Is everything OK with you?"

"Oh, I'm fine, Aly. I was in hospital for a few days and stayed at my sister's afterwards, but I'm fine now. Speaking of fine, you're looking very fine tonight. Hot date?"

He makes me smile. If it was any other man, I'd be thinking *pervert!* However, Mr. DeAngelo is a sweet old man whom I get along well with.

"Very hot date. He's an absolute gentleman, and I had a fantastic night, Mr. De, thanks."

"Well, he's certainly put a beautiful smile across that pretty face of yours. He's a lucky guy. You're a special girl, Aly. I hope he realises that."

"Aw, thanks, Mr. De. You call my cell if you need anything, OK? If you're not feeling well, I want to know if I can help you."

"I will, thanks," he says with a broad smile.

I open the door of my apartment, and once I close it, I let out a slight shriek. I can't recall ever enjoying myself so much on a date. I want to call Jen and Karen, but it's too late, and I don't think they'll appreciate me calling at this hour. Instead, I sit on the couch for a few moments and enjoy the same feeling I experienced the previous time I met Jack Morgan: butterflies.

Chapter 18

*I*t's early, and I wake to the sound of the birds chirping outside my window. I still have that nice feeling after my night out with Jack and wish that it wouldn't fade. I hope he calls.

I make my way to work, and when I get there, everyone seems very lively, and Jeremy is very dressed up. He always dresses well, but there is something different about him this morning.

"Looking very snazzy today, Jeremy," I say as I walk past his office.

"I told him he should get a bedhead look to his hair and that a blue shirt would suit him," Deborah says as she strolls past.

Interesting! How do Deborah and Jeremy have that kind of relationship? He never speaks of her in a very respectful manner, and I've never seen them chatting in the office.

"Ah, yeah, she suggested it one night when we were all in the pub. Said I'd try it out as I've been trying to sort my hair out for a long time. I never seem to find a style that suits me," he says.

He seems slightly perturbed.

"Well, she's right; it does suit you. Looking good!" I say as I head straight for my office.

I close the door and hope he won't come in. A little daydreaming time is in order for me to reminisce over my date with Jack. I also need to figure out how to finish this thing with Jeremy. I just know for sure he's not for me. When I'm with him, I don't feel like I do with Jack. It's just all wrong.

At 11:00 a.m. my phone rings.

"Hello."

"Hi, Aly, it's Jack."

My heart is thumping and my face is flushed, and I just want to scream down the phone, I'm so happy.

"I'm just about to board my plane now and thought I'd give you a call before I do. I wanted to thank you for a lovely time last night. I don't think I've ever met anyone quite like you, to be honest, and I don't want to lose you too easily, either; hence the call. I hope I haven't caught you at a bad time?"

"Jack, it's lovely to hear from you. I was just thinking about you, actually."

Idiot, shut up! Don't give the game away that you are nuts about him.

"Oh, really?"

"Uh, yeah, I was thinking of the night Karen destroyed both our shoes."

He's not going to believe that!

"Ah, OK. You weren't thinking of me in a romantic way then."

"Well, no, not really, sorry. But, just so you know, I really loved our date last night. You're a very nice guy, Jack, and I'm happy you called."

Oh God, that was too nonchalant of me. I really want to tell you that I'm falling in love with you!

"Good! I was worried for a second that I was the only one who enjoyed it. So I have to go soon. I'll call you in the next day or two, sweetheart. How does that sound?"

"So soon?" I say. "I mean, you have to go so soon? I wasn't complaining about you wanting to ring in the next day or two."

"Sadly, I have to. They've just called the flight to board. I'd like to chat with you longer, Aly."

"That's OK. Do you think you might drop me a text tonight when you get there? Just so I know you arrived in one piece?"

I can almost feel his smile through the phone. "Sure I will. That's super cute, Aly. I'm glad I called. Just hearing your voice has put a smile on my face. Text you later."

"I'm glad you called too. Have a safe flight, and I'll look forward to hearing from you later. Thanks for calling. Oh, and Jack..."

"Yep."

"I was actually thinking about you. I was trying to play it cool, telling you I was thinking of shoe-gate. You've put a huge smile on my face by ringing me today."

"I knew you were," he says. "I know you, Hughes, better than you realise, and after only eight or ten hours of chat. You're a keeper, and I'm going to do my best to do just that: keep you."

I think I'm having some sort of attack. My heart is thumping so loudly he must be able to hear it. I wonder if his is too. "Aw, Jack, thank you. You take care, and safe journey."

"Thanks, Aly. Bye."

I hang up the phone, and for a moment, I feel like bursting into tears—tears of joy. I so want to relive our date. I'm swinging around in my chair like a five-year-old child playing, and the grin on my face must be huge.

A loud knock on the door quickly snaps me out of my daydream.

"Hey, have you thought about what you want to do tonight, Aly?" Jeremy asks.

I haven't, but right now, I fancy a trip to the pub as the idea of spending any more time on my own with Jeremy is wrecking my head. I have to finish it with him.

"Yeah, you know what, why don't we go to the pub like we usually do with everyone from the office? I'm in the mood for a drink after all."

"OK. You're a difficult one to figure out sometimes, Aly," he says with a smirk as he leaves my office.

Oh good, now at least I can chat to others from the office. I can keep him at arm's length and maybe finish with him later. Oh God, what's happening to me of late? I hate treating people like crap, and I know he's been making a great effort. He seems keen to be in a proper relationship with me, but there's something that just doesn't feel right.

As the day drifts by, I keep checking my watch, trying to estimate what time Jack will land in LA. I wonder if he'll text me like he said. I really have to stop this. I'm turning into an obsessive.

Later in the day, I suggest we leave the office early. The evenings are closing in fast, and none of us seems to want to work too late. I always feel like hibernating in October, to be honest. Thankfully, Jeremy is in agreement that we go early. Any excuse for a party.

"Let the party begin!" I shout.

"Aly, what's come over you today? You're acting very strange," Jeremy says.

"Sorry, I'm just in the mood for partying. I love a good party."

"You're just dying for a piss up, aren't ya?"

"Oh, that's it, Jeremy, I'm gagging for a pint. So come on, let's go."

"I was thinking, how about you come back to mine tonight, Als?"

Oh dear God, please just let a massive hole appear right now and swallow me up.

"Right, that's fine with me," I blurt out. *Jesus, woman, shut up. You're digging yourself in deeper.*

Numerous drinks later, Jeremy and I are the only two left from the office. I'm stalling for as long as I can, and I'm hopeful that if I get drunk enough, he might get pissed off at me, give up, and go home...alone.

"OK, you ready to head back to mine?" he slurs.

"Sure, let's go," I say with a sigh. I give up instead. He seems drunker than I am, so he'll just keep going now until I stop. I decide I'll go home with him and have a chat with him in the morning. I don't want to upset him with alcohol in his system.

When we reach his apartment, I'm very impressed. It's very clean and tidy, and it's very modern. I didn't take much notice of what it was like the last time I was here. After all, I was still very drunk and nursing Jeremy for the night. I was too exhausted the next morning to take any notice. I'm very impressed at how contemporary and funky it looks.

"Nice space, Jeremy. I wasn't expecting it to be like this."

"And what were you expecting, Als?" he says as he grabs me close.

I know there's no point in trying to talk to him at this stage, and I surrender. I am, after all, getting my own way by finally seeing his apartment properly, but I can't carry on like this.

I can't sleep, and I'm tossing and turning, wondering how I'll break up with him in the morning. *Shit! I never checked to see if Jack called. Aw damn! Two texts and a missed call.*

Somehow, I eventually manage to drift off to sleep, and when I wake again, it's 12:30 p.m. I wasn't planning to stay here this late. Jeremy is no longer in the bed, and I can hear the shower running. I wander into the living room, where I see his computer is switched on. *Excellent, I can check my mails while he's in the shower.*

His email account is open, and while I would never do this normally, I have the urge to give a quick flit through his mails. *Hmmm, it can't hurt to have a sneaky peek surely. Oh God, what am I thinking? That's just wrong. I'll just log out so I can log into my own account. I'll feel guilty if I...*

"What the fuck?" I open the email quickly.

"Debs, I'm sorry, you can't come around tonight. I'm heading to Aly's place. I'm sorry, another night, OK?"

Reply: "Oh lovely. What am I, your bit on the side? I thought that's all she was. We were having a nice fling, and then she came along. I only see you now when you're not seeing her! I think you should change your plans, or I'm out of this farcical situation."

I note the date on the email: October 6, Thursday—the night I had my date with Jack, the night Jeremy came around with the bottle of wine! I click out of the email and into another one. It is dated the same date; it was later in the evening, after he was knocked back by me.

"Debs, I'm sorry, I've changed my plans so you can come around. I've bought a really good bottle of wine for us to share. Come over when you can, if you get this email."

Reply: "Glad you came to your senses. I'll be there in an hour."

Has he been seeing Debs all this time that we've been together? Right, that's it! Here I sit feeling guilty like some gobshite because I went for dinner with Jack, and why? I wait for him to get out of the shower. I can't believe he's been leading me on to make me think that he is trying to form a proper relationship with me, while he is poking "Debs" behind my back—and I'm not talking Facebook poking! No wonder she seemed so smug about his hair and look that day.

I hear the shower stop, and Jeremy walks into the living room, towel-drying his new "hairdo."

"Hey, Als. Nice night last night. I hope you enjoyed it as much as I did."

"Really? Are you sure you enjoyed it? Because part of me thinks that maybe it would have been better as a threesome."

He sniggers, and I can feel my face reddening with anger, like I'm going to explode.

"Wow, well, if that's what you fancy, then we can arrange that, I'm sure."

"Yeah, let's do that, and I've got the perfect person in mind."

He looks at me warily. I know he has finally sensed the hostility in my voice and that I am being sarcastic.

"OK, who's that?"

"How about Debs? Debs would be amazing in the sack, I'm sure, although no better person to let me know that than you! My God, I was iffy about getting involved with you from the start, and your emails have just proven to me that I was right. I should have stuck to my gut instinct of not getting with the boss, but instead I ignored it. I mean…"

"Hold up, Als, let me get a word in."

"No! You'll have your turn when I say so! You have been leading me to believe you wanted a proper relationship with me, Jeremy. What was all of that about inviting me back last night? You really want to have your cake and eat it, don't you? Well, you cannot have it or eat it!"

"Als, wait. Why were you reading my emails in the first place? That's my private account."

"I was reading your emails because while you were in the shower, I decided I'd have a quick look at my own. Your account was opened because obviously you didn't expect me to be up and about when you got out of the shower, and you didn't sign out. I was curious when I saw Debs's name in your personal inbox. I'm fecking glad I read them because at least now I know what a lying, cheating knob you really are!"

"Als, I'm sorry. I really wanted to give it a go with you, but I guess I'm not ready to settle down yet. I don't know if I'll ever be ready."

"So what are you saying? You expect me to hang around for you? Jeremy, you know my past. You know I've had a lying, cheating arsehole boyfriend before. Why on earth did you think I'd want another one? Look, I'm not wasting any more time on this. We're through."

"Als, wait!"

"It's not 'Als!' My name is Alyson—Aly for short—and stop shortening it again to Als! I hate when you call me that!"

"Sorry."

I've silenced him. I really don't want to hear another word from him. I know I've been out with Jack on one date, and we kissed, but this liar has been carrying on with Debs and who knows how many others since we started seeing each other. He swore he wasn't with anyone else, and during that time Deborah was with him, probably more often than I was.

I hail a cab. Once I get back to my flat and close the door, the tears start to flow. It's something I need to get out of my system. I'm upset that Jack is gone, and I'm upset now that yet another man has made a fool of me. I take my phone off the hook and spend the day relaxing on the couch.

Karen and Jen call over.

"I don't know what to say," mutters Karen. "I can't believe you didn't shag Jack the other night. Are you crazy?"

"Karen, shagging Jack would be nice, but I want to take it slow. Besides, he's in LA, so I might need to forget about him."

"Nooooo! You can't forget about him," Jen pipes up. "He texted you, woman, and he rang. Did you respond, by the way?"

"Not yet. I'm not sure what to do. I mean, right now I feel like a horrible person. I feel bad."

"Why?" Karen blurts out.

"Because while I know Jeremy was cheating on me that night, I too was cheating on him, and I gave him a hard time today. You know me, girls. The last thing I'd want to do is upset or hurt him in any way. I hate fighting or ill feeling with anyone. I don't know what even possessed me to go on the date with Jack while I was seeing someone else."

"There's a big difference, Aly. He's been cheating on you since you started seeing him. He was constantly telling you that he wanted a more serious relationship and that he wasn't with anyone else. Even if you didn't want that with him, and you were heading for break-up anyway, he was wrong. Give yourself a break, girl. I know it mightn't have been right going out with Jack the other night, but you didn't do anything wrong, particularly knowing that Jeremy had the office slut in his bed while you just had dinner and a small kiss with Jack," Jen says.

"She's right," Karen butts in. "Not only that, but, hon, you needed to go out with Jack the other night. Your gut instinct made you do it.

Maybe you knew deep down that Jeremy has been cheating on you all along. You obviously had some reservations about him. You wouldn't have gone out otherwise. I think you did the right thing. Besides, who in their right mind would turn Jack Morgan down for dinner?"

"It's still cheating, and I feel like crap. I feel bad for Jack, too. I really like him, and it seems that he likes me. How do I ignore him now after him texting and calling me? I lied to him, too."

"Jack will be fine. Honey, you have to contact him. He's good for you, and, damn, you looked so good when you went out with him the other night. You were radiant, and if that's what he does to you, then you need to contact him."

"Thanks, Karen. You're right. He does make me feel good, and he was good enough to text and call."

When the girls leave, I pick up my phone and text Jack: "Hey, Mr. Morgan. How are you? I'm so sorry I'm only getting back to you now. Something came up last night, and I left my phone at home. It was late when I got your message and missed call (sorry). I hope you can forgive me for the late reply. A. XX."

One or two kisses? Am I looking too interested? Oh, who cares? I am interested, and I can't afford to cock this up.

I'm sitting comfortably and watching TV when my phone beeps. It's Jack: "Hi, Aly. I'm glad you texted me. I thought that maybe you didn't want to hear from me and that I misunderstood you completely. Glad all is OK, though. Got back in one piece, and my complicated life here just gets more and more complicated. I think I need to move somewhere more free-flowing like New York. Miss you already, Aly. J. XX."

Sweet! He misses me.

"Miss you too, Jack. Maybe that move might be a good idea? I certainly wouldn't complain. I'm off to bed now, had an exhausting day. I'll tell you about it sometime. Hope you have a good weekend. Night-night. A. XX."

"It is something I'm thinking very seriously about, Aly. I'll talk to you more about it soon. You get a good sleep and have sweet dreams. Night, Ms. Hughes. Jack XX."

I place my phone on the bedside locker and pull my duvet up around me. I close my eyes and imagine Jack lying there next to me. When I open my eyes again, it's ten thirty Sunday morning, and I'm full of beans after a decent night's sleep.

The girls are calling around to ensure I'm OK. I'll have to analyse the situation with them. How else am I going to face Jeremy at work tomorrow? I need to figure out what to say to him or what to do. I'm not looking forward to it, but I created the situation, and I'll have to deal with it.

Chapter 19

*I*t's four weeks after the Jeremy saga, and I haven't uttered a word to him yet. He often approaches me in my office, asking for things, and I always somehow manage to avoid speaking for more than two seconds. Yes and no answers are all I can muster.

It's Friday evening, and there's a knock on the door. I peer up to see Jeremy standing there with a slight smile. I'm allergic to him.

"Hi, Aly, can I talk to you for a minute?"

I normally ignore him, but this time I choose to be adult-like and speak to him properly for the first time in weeks.

"Hi, yep, come in."

"Aly, I'm really sorry, but I'd like to try and put this behind us. It's awkward when my number one isn't talking to me. I need to get your input. That brain of yours is fantastic, and I could really do with your help on a project right now."

"Jeremy, I know I haven't made life easy for you of late, and because I don't want to be unprofessional, for the sake of the business and because you need my fantastic brain, I'll be willing to make amends."

"Great, I…"

"However! Do not make any passes at me, do not even attempt to come around the other side of my desk, and never sit anywhere near me in meetings or such. We need to keep our distance, Jeremy. I'm really annoyed at you."

"I know you are, and I don't blame you. I'm sorry."

"Well, apology accepted." I sigh as I realise I need to clear my own conscience.

"Look, I need to be honest because I've been feeling pretty bad. Something has been niggling at me that I wanted to tell you about for the past few weeks," I blurt out.

"Sure, go ahead."

"Remember that night you called around with the bottle of wine, and I was all dolled up? I told you I was meeting Karen for a night out."

"I do. You shunned me out the door."

"Well, I wasn't meeting Karen. I was actually going on a date with someone else. I had planned to break up with you anyway. I didn't see us going anywhere. I just needed to pick the right moment. I was furious to see that you had been pretending for so long that you wanted some form of a more serious relationship with me, especially when you were with Deborah behind my back. I wanted to split from you even more then, obviously."

"Well, aren't the tables turning now? So you were cheating on me that night?"

"Not really…well, sort of. We had dinner, and he did kiss me at the end of the night, and I didn't stop him. However, it was nothing like what you've done, Jeremy. Anyway, that's it. I wanted to get it off my chest more than anything. I'm sorry. I didn't want to hurt you, and I went out that night with the intention of dinner only. The kiss was an unexpected ending to the night. You know me. It's not my thing to cheat. Anyway, that's it, and I'm sorry. However, I still think it's best for us to keep our distance now."

"It's still cheating, Aly. I've been feeling like such an arse for the past four weeks, and now you tell me this!"

"Well, you are an arse. You were cheating on me from the minute we started dating—with Deborah, I might add. Talk about shitting on your own doorstep!"

"Debs is all right."

"'Debs,' as you call her, has always had a bit of a name for herself, from what I hear, Jeremy. I might not have been here even a year yet, but I remember you calling her something along the lines of 'slag' once or twice."

"Well, maybe my feelings have changed."

"Good. Well, I hope you and Debs will be very happy, then. Good luck to you."

"OK, look, I didn't come here for an argument, Aly. I just want us to try and communicate somehow in a professional manner."

"That's fine with me. I can do that."

"Great. Now, it's Friday evening, and I'm heading to the pub. I don't suppose you want to join us?"

I just smile. *You really are thick.* "No thanks, Jeremy. I'll be skipping the Friday pub drinks from now on I'd say. Enjoy yourself, and see you on Monday."

"OK. See you Monday. Have a good weekend."

He leaves the office, but within two minutes, I hear a knock again.

"Hi, sorry to interrupt you again. I'm just curious. Did you meet this guy again?"

"Not since. We're on the phone most evenings. He lives in LA, but he should be here shortly for a visit."

"Wow, LA! OK, well, I hope he's worth having to wait weeks on end before you see him," he says with a smug look on his face.

"He's well worth it, Jeremy. Well worth it," I say with a large smile.

He looks slightly upset at that remark. He walks out of the office.

I decide to work late as I have some bits to tidy up on the client accounts. I stay until I have everything finished, just for my own satisfaction. I'm just leaving the office, and my phone rings.

"Hey, you. How's my favourite Irish woman tonight?"

"Hey, yourself," I say. "I'm good, thanks. How are you doing?"

"Great, thanks. I said I'd call and give you a heads up that I'm coming to New York at the end of next week. I hope you can find some time to meet me?"

I squeal with joy. I cover the phone first in case he hears my enthusiasm.

"Jack, that's great. Of course I'll find time to meet you. Actually, I was thinking to take a few days off over the next week. I could do with a break from the office."

"Sounds good. Maybe I can take you to my new beach house in the Hamptons."

"Nice! When did you buy that?"

"Last week. I sent a few people down to take some pictures of it and a surveyor to give it the once-over. It seems great. I'm not going to lie to you, Aly. I was there last week, but it was literally for one hour to check the place out and make my final decision. I didn't want to call you in case you thought I could meet up and I was making excuses not to. I flew back the same day. Craziness on my part as it's too much flying for one day, really."

"Oh, OK. That's a shame but not to worry. You'll be here soon enough! How much time should I book off?"

"Well, I'll be there for seven nights. So if you want to book that time off, then great," he says.

"I'll arrange it on Monday. So how have you been keeping? I was going to ring you tonight. You normally ring me at some point during the week, but I was worried when I hadn't heard," I utter.

"Yeah, a few problems arose here in LA. I need to tell you a lot about my life here, Aly. It's complicated, and for me, New York is a massive escape."

"OK, sounds like you're under a lot of stress there."

"Yeah, you could say that. I'll save it for another time, though. Listen, I have to go again. I have a dinner meeting with some TV producers tonight. Would love if you were here. You'd lighten the serious mood of these business meetings."

"Aw, thanks. Well, one day maybe. Thanks for calling, Jack. I'm looking forward to seeing you next week. I'll let you know once I sort out the holidays."

"Great. Sorry for the short notice. I hope it won't be a problem for you."

"No, I've been slaving away for months without taking any break, so I don't think they will have any grounds to say no to me."

"I'm sure they won't. Don't work too hard. I'll talk to you again soon. Miss you."

"I won't, and that goes for you, too. Don't work too hard. Miss you too."

"I won't. Bye, Aly."

"Bye, Jack."

I press the red button and sigh—a sigh of joy, relief, and just general happiness. What a productive day it's been! Not just work-wise but also managing to tell Jeremy about my kiss with Jack is a massive relief. When Jack called, it was the perfect ending to my day. Things might finally be getting back on track after a long month.

I'm meeting Jen tonight. I haven't seen her in a few weeks, because she's been busy in the new job and is very loved up with Tommy.

When I rock up to the Spotted Pig restaurant, I can't see her anywhere. I approach the waiter.

"Hello, I've a table booked in the surname Hughes?"

"Sure, your guest is here already. Just follow me, please."

There must be some mistake. I can't see Jen anywhere.

"Here we are, Ms. Hughes," he says.

"Thank you," I say as I take a seat.

I wait for him to leave before I give Jen a hug. *Jesus! Where have you disappeared to, Jen?* "Hey, Jen, how are you?"

"I'm OK, thanks, Aly. I'm so happy to see you tonight."

"Me too. Jen, what's wrong with you? Are you ill?"

"No, I've just lost a little weight."

"A little? Jen, it looks like you've lost half your body weight. I can feel your ribs through the dress."

"I'm fine, really. I've been working all hours of late. It's been hectic, and then the whole diet goes up in the air—eating some meals, no time for others."

"Jen, really, you can't lose anymore. It's not healthy for you. You're so pale, and that beautiful dress was so perfect on you before. Now it's hanging off of you."

"Yeah, I know, but that will all change now soon. I have big news," she says with a smile.

You're not pregnant, anyway, not with that frame.

"Tommy has asked me to move in with him."

"Jen, that's fantastic. Oh, I'm so pleased for you both. That's really great news. I knew he was the right one for you."

"Well, let's not get ahead of ourselves now, Aly. We are moving in, but we're not getting married—not yet, anyway. It's all happening really quickly. We've only been together around two months, but it just feels right. I won't be moving for a few weeks yet."

"I know, but you will get married. I know you will. He's so right for you. I've never seen you smile as much as you do when you're with him."

"Now, that is true. He definitely makes me feel really happy, and I do hope we'll get married one day. This is definitely a step in the right direction for us," Jen states.

We spend the evening catching up on the past month, and Jen informs me of her and Tommy's plans for the big move. Tommy has bought a house not too far from where she lives on Charles Street, and she's planning to rent out her apartment. She'll move into his flat for a few months until the house is ready. I feel so happy for her, but I really worry about her very scrawny frame and question if I should contact Tommy for a chat.

I return home that night and meet the lovely Mr. DeAngelo when I arrive inside the building.

"Hey, Aly, how are ya, sweetheart? Are you working all hours, or what? I haven't seen you in a long time."

"Hi. Mr. De. I've been pretty busy with work of late. I've been skipping the nights out, too. This is the first night out I've had in ages. I just needed a break."

"I know; sometimes you do, Aly. It's good to relax every now and then. I'm glad you got the sense to do that. You ain't been working late every day, have ya?"

"No, not every day. I generally finish around nine o'clock if I do work late. I just had a few things to sort out in my life, and throwing myself into work was the best way to deal with it. I'm easing off now, though."

"Good, good. Listen, Aly, remember I told you the building wasn't getting renovated for a few more months the last time I spoke to you?"

I don't like the sound of this. I understand before he says anything that my time is ending in this old building.

"Well, I'm sorry to tell ya, I managed to secure the guys to sort it out in four weeks' time. I know it's not masses of notice, but if I don't get them in now, we could be waiting another four or five months. You know what they're like—a big pain in my ass."

He makes me laugh. "Mr. De, I'm going to miss you. Is there any way they can skip my old apartment? I actually like it the way it is."

"Honey, I can't let them do that. Part of the structure of the building ain't safe. I need them to get it sorted sooner rather than later, or we might fall with the building, if ya get my drift?"

"Sure, I understand. I'll start looking tomorrow, Mr. De. Thanks for letting me know."

"No problem, and Aly, you know you're welcome to come back here when it's all finished. It's a pleasure having you around here. I'll miss you greatly."

"Thanks. Well, you know, I'll come visit you anyway even if I do have to leave, Mr. De."

"Aw, thanks, sweetheart. You're a lovely kid. Night, Aly."

"Night, Mr. De."

I feel sad at the thought of leaving my apartment. Even though I didn't splash out on anything new bar a few lamps and things, which would be easy to move, I love this place.

It's a cold Saturday morning, and the idea of having to move as winter approaches isn't appealing to me. I run out to the corner store and buy all the newspapers and magazines where I'm likely to find somewhere new to live. I glance through each one carefully so as not to miss anything. When I finish four hours later, I have ring-marked only six apartments.

I'm tired and need a pick-me-up, and so I get dolled up and call around to Karen. I know that in all her madness she will cheer me up somehow.

"Come in, come in. I'm not long here."

"You're kidding me! You've been out partying all night until now?" I enquire.

"No, I was at the bakery. I needed something sweet today. I'm becoming addicted to sweet things, I think. I was out last night but not too late. I had a few bottles of wine here when I got home and watched a DVD."

"Drinking alone? A few bottles of wine?"

"Yeah, you know me. One is never enough. I had two and half, to be precise. I might finish the other one later. I don't like when it's hanging around too long. It just doesn't taste the same, Aly."

"Right. And did you have drink while you were out, too?"

"Yeah, had a few glasses, but I'm fine. I've put on a few pounds all right of late—probably all the sweet things I've been eating, though."

"Are you sure? Karen, drink puts mountains of weight on a person, especially at our age. Maybe you should cut back on the drink."

"Aly, please don't lecture. Now here, have a cupcake. They're fresh from the Sweet Corner Bakeshop near where you live."

"Oh, what a great place. It's so tempting, just walking past it each day. I can see why you might be addicted to their stuff," I say, and I take a large mouthful.

"Yeah, it's definitely my love of sweet things in general that's putting the weight on," Karen says.

"So I haven't seen you in a while, Karen. How's life treating you?"

"Yeah, where have you been? It's like you've been in hiding since the J and J fiasco," she says jokingly.

I laugh. "J and J fiasco—I take it you mean Jeremy and Jack?"

"Indeed. So what's happening on that front?"

"Well, I'm heading to Jack's new summer home in the Hamptons with him next week. It's not quite summer weather, but I'm pretty sure he's invested in heating. At least I hope he has."

"What? Well done, you! Glad you got in contact with him that night."

"Yeah, so am I. I also cleared my guilty conscience with Jeremy. Of course, he pulled the 'you-cheated-on-me-and-then-made-me-feel-guilty' line. I think I won that one, though, when I pointed out he'd been seeing Debs, as he calls her, from the start, if not before the start, of our little romance."

"Good for you. Delighted you sorted it all out."

"So what have you been up to? Partying like an animal? Mingling with the stars?"

"No, not really. I've been very quiet of late, to be honest with you, Aly. Jen is all loved up and moving in with Tommy. I presume you know about that?"

"Yeah, I met her last night. She's super thin, though. I'm worried about her."

"She'll be fine. I think she's been working very hard of late. Besides that, I've a feeling they may be putting pressure on her at work to be thinner than she already is. Those damn modelling agencies. I wouldn't mind, but half of them are far from thin. It's disgraceful."

"I did wonder if work had something to do with it," I say.

"Imagine if I rocked up with my newly formed muffin top hanging out and caused a scene if they wouldn't accept me. Maybe I should do it for the laugh," Karen says with a peal of laughter.

I burst out laughing. Karen's muffin top is a new accessory she's carrying, and I'm very surprised to see how much weight she actually has gained in a month.

"Karen, it's not that bad. Besides, if you give up the drink and the sweet things, you'll be back to your slimmer figure again. I think you look fine like that. You look healthy, at least. Please don't go starving yourself. I can't deal with two skinny best friends and me the pudgy one in the middle."

"You're not pudgy. You look just right, Aly. I'm telling you, it's not the drink. It's the cakes."

"OK. So you haven't told me what you've been up to for the past month. How's work going? Why no partying?"

"Well, work is going OK. Although I've had a couple of warnings because of turning up late due to late-night partying. Not good. So I decided I'd be a good girl and just party on the weekends instead. I've now become accustomed to sitting down most nights with a bottle or two of wine and chilling out watching DVDs. Even at the weekend, it seems like an effort now to go out on the town, especially on the cold nights."

It's a bit of a shock for me to see that Karen has turned into a hermit, drinking alone most nights. Her liver must be in dire condition. Her drinking habit has become far worse than I thought.

"OK, Karen, this isn't you. I'm going to swear solemnly to go out with you at least three times per week or more from here on in. It's not healthy for you to be at home drinking alone."

"I'm fine, seriously, Aly. It's done me good as I go to bed early and get into work early."

"No, look, I'm not happy about the fact that I've been such a hermit myself for the past month, either. So starting tonight, we are hitting the town. We need to take it easy on the drink, though. We always had a laugh years ago without the aid of alcohol. I'll ring Jen and see if she's free, but I'd doubt it. She seems pretty busy with organising her move to Tommy's."

Karen's face lights up. *This will probably be an experience I'll regret, but you're my friend, after all. I want to try and get you back on track,* I think. I smile back at her.

"Well, OK then. But Jack is around next week, Aly, so I don't expect you to give up your time with him. Maybe I'll get to meet him properly, though, so I can apologise for shoe-gate."

"I might be a little less available next week, but we'll deal with that when the time comes. Don't worry about apologising. He's forgotten that, hon. I'd like you to meet him properly, though, see what a gent he is."

"That sounds good," she says. "Well, how about we start getting ready to hit the town now? Let's go from here. You can borrow something from me."

I'm done with my make-up already, but my clothes do look a little casual. "Will I fit into anything of yours?" I ask.

"Aly, trust me, you're more likely to fit into my clothes these days than I am. I need to find a muffin-top-friendly dress or top for myself."

We both erupt into hysterical laughter. I love Karen; she has such a great sense of humour, even if she is sometimes a bit loud and brash. She always stands by me no matter what, and now it's time for me to repay her when she needs someone. I realize how lonely she really is here. None of her "friends" in New York can be considered real friends, apart from myself and Jen.

We rifle through her humungous wardrobe of designer labels. She has some of the most amazing outfits I have ever seen.

"It's the perk of the job, Aly. They send me loads of samples to try and see if I think they will sell. It's a great job in that respect, but the designers can be so demanding at times."

"I'm sure it must be exhausting, but for these clothes, it must be worth it. I mean, have you even worn this yet?" I ask. I point to a Diane von Furstenberg dress, which still has the tags on it.

"No, but I'm keeping that for something special. It's a special dress for a special occasion."

"True; I'd be afraid to wear something so chic and beautiful on a normal night out. Some eejit would probably spill drink all over it," I say.

"Exactly! And that eejit would probably be me! I think that dress would be more for a wedding. It is very classy. It fits perfectly, too—that is, when I don't have a muffin top."

"Oh, Karen, it's not that bad. Come on, try some stuff on, and I'll tell you honestly what it's like."

"OK, I'll try these two tops and those trousers."

She opts for one strappy top, very flashy but not over the top, and a pair of trousers. They are very classy-looking.

"I told you," she says as she leaves the dressing room. "My belly is hanging out. They are too low-rise."

"OK, I agree, they are a bit low. Try the others."

This time she appears looking amazing. She's wearing a cerise pink top with the leather skinny trousers.

"Wow, now you look hot in that, Karen."

"Yeah, not too bad. I haven't worn these yet. They've been in there for over six months."

"I'm sure you don't even know what clothes you have. The selection in your wardrobe is so vast."

"You probably have a point there. Here, I chose this for you. It's sexy, and I haven't worn it yet. Try it on, Aly."

"What size is it? It looks small."

"US size four. It'll fit; you're slim."

"Karen, I'm a US four to six, and this looks tiny."

"Try it. It'll fit; I know it will," she says.

I take the dress from her and head to her dressing room. Karen loves the finer things in life, and she's on a big, fat salary. Mine is big but not in comparison to what Karen earns. She treated herself to many things in her home when she moved in, including her walk-in wardrobe with dressing room, something I've always dreamed of having.

"What do ya think?"

"You look stunning. First go, Aly, and you get something to fit you. You look amazing in that."

"OK, let's go with this. What time do you want to go out? We must ring Jen!"

"Give her a call and see what she's up to, and we'll gauge it then on what time she can meet us—if she's coming, that is."

"Good idea."

I pick up my phone and dial Jen's number.

"Aly! How are you?"

"Great, thanks. Karen and I have a great idea…well, not great. It's not any master plan or anything, but we are going to hit the town tonight. Can you come?"

"Hang on." I can hear her discussing with Tommy in the background.

"Tell the girls I said hi and enjoy yourselves," I can hear him shout.

"Aly, yep, I'm in. We were going to go for dinner, but Tommy insists I go with you both as we haven't had one of our nights out in so long."

"Fantastic; how much time do you need?" I ask. "We're in Karen's now. It's a last-minute thing, so I'm getting ready here and borrowing something from her. Is it easier for you to meet here, or will we pick a place and meet you there?"

"No, you go ahead. I'll make it in around nineish or thereabouts. Just text me when you settle on a place."

"Great! See you there later, then."

"I'll see you both later! Thanks, Aly."

She hangs up. I wander back into the dressing room to Karen.

"Well, Jen, is on for a night out. We haven't done this in so long."

"Excellent!" she says. "It's going to be a good one, Aly."

Karen and I head into the city centre. It's a busy night and difficult to hail a cab. Karen makes a bid to stop one by pulling at the dress I'm wearing and hoisting it up. I'm just about to scream at her to stop when a taxi pulls up. *Pervert.* However, he seems to be our only chance of getting anywhere, so I don't berate her, but I avoid all eye contact with the driver.

"Where to, ladies?"

"Buddakan, please," Karen states.

"Karen, we don't have a reservation," I say.

"I know; it's fine. I know them well in there as I've been on business lunches where we spend ridiculous amounts of money. They'll find a place for us."

"And there I was thinking it was 'our spot.'"

"It is! It's just not the same for business lunches."

I decide to text Jen and let her know where we'll be. I imagine it will still take some time for us to get a table, and we can have a Charm cocktail while we wait.

Jen arrives, looking pretty but gaunt. Tonight will be a good time to make sure she eats plenty in front of us. We enjoy the meal immensely, and even Jen eats like she normally would, if not more.

"So, Aly, what's the update on your apartment? Are they ever going to renovate the building?" Jen asks.

"Well, now that you mention it, it's been stressing me out all day. I've a month. Mr. DeAngelo told me last night. I spent four hours trawling the papers today for a new place to live. I've circled a few, but I think they might be a bit out of my price range."

"A month isn't very long, is it?" Karen says.

"No, but he can't do anything about it. The builders cancelled last time, and when he called them for an update, they fixed the date. Otherwise, he'd be waiting another three months."

"Crazy. We'll help you look for places, anyway. Don't worry, hon," Jen replies.

"Thanks, girls."

I quickly try to forget about the dilemma that faces me, and I concentrate more on the girls telling me about any updates they have. The night passes very quickly, and much to my surprise, Karen is the first to fade.

"Oh, Jesus, 'tis midnight, girls. I'm exhausted. Time to go home, I think," Karen declares.

"Are you feeling OK?" I ask.

"Yeah, just been a long day. Could do with my bed."

"I'm with you there, to be honest. I'm shattered," Jen says.

"Well, I'm not going to sit here alone, girls, so let's go. I'm pretty tired myself too," I say.

"Aly, why don't you stay in mine? It's not far from here, at least," Karen says.

"Sure, why not? Thanks, lady." I'm happy to accept, as I know trying to hail a cab on my own at that hour might not be too easy.

We reach Karen's, and once I make myself comfortable in her spare room, I fall into a deep slumber.

Chapter 20

I'm gazing around the room and have no idea where I am. I look down to see that I'm wearing a beautiful pair of new silk pyjamas, which I can't recall owning. It takes a few minutes for me to realise I'm in Karen's. I wander to the kitchen and throw a few slices of toast into the toaster. Karen's bedroom door is open, and I can only see the tip of her head peeking out over the duvet. I don't want to disturb her, as she is the one who suggested going home early last night, which led me to believe that she needed a good sleep.

My stomach starts rumbling, and I spot the four cupcakes that Karen bought yesterday, which are sitting in the fridge. It would be healthier for me to eat at least the toast before hounding into a cupcake though. One of them will definitely be consumed later; I have no doubt about that. I click the kettle to the on position and wait patiently for it to boil. My head is a bit groggy, but it's not the worst hangover I've had from a night out with the girls. I'm quite pleased by that. I didn't drink too much. I glance around the kitchen and spot one empty wine bottle and a half-full one on the countertop. They certainly weren't there when we arrived last night. I decide not to dwell on it and sit at the counter.

"Good morning, Aly!" comes the thundering voice of Karen from the bedroom.

"Good morning, yourself! I'm in here, in the kitchen. Want a cuppa?"

"Oh yes, please," she says as she enters the kitchen. "In the meantime, I'll just finish off this bottle."

"Karen, it's eight thirty in the morning!"

"So? You know I hate to leave it lying around. It never tastes as good if it's left lingering for too long."

"And how long has it been lingering now?" I question.

"A few hours; I opened those when I got in last night. I thought you were going to join me when I opened one of them. When I went to call you, you had already passed out on the bed. I decided it would be a shame to waste it, so I drank it myself."

"What about the other bottle?"

"Yep, I also drank the half bottle. I didn't have too much in the restaurant, really. None of us did."

"Karen, we had three bottles. That's a bottle each!"

"Did we? It felt like I only had a glass. Oh well. I'm fine, look at me. Aren't I out of the bed nice and early, Aly?"

I watch her guzzle the remainder of the bottle. I feel very angry with her for taking advantage of her health, for getting into such states, and for letting both Jen and myself down.

"Here, eat this," I say with discontentment as I push the plate of toast towards her.

"OK, sergeant!"

"Look, Karen, I'm not going to fight with you. Maybe I should go home. I can see I'm not really getting through to you right now. I'm just concerned that you could be causing major health problems for yourself."

"I'm fine, Aly, really. Sorry I snapped. I suppose I'm not used to having someone watch me as carefully as you've been doing since you arrived here. I missed not having you around all those years. Jen's been great, but she'd never say anything to me like you just did. I think she's too quiet and doesn't want to interfere."

"Unlike me, the interfering friend?"

"No, I don't mean it like that. I mean that she just acts different towards me than you do, and I want you around to give me that kick up the arse I need every now and then. Just sometimes I feel claustrophobic if you keep harping on at me."

"OK, point taken. I'll not mention your drinking again. However, if you do hear it from Jen at some point, then you know you have to get help, Karen." I only say this to shut her up. It is clear to me now that her drinking problem is spiralling out of control, and I have to help her somehow. "I'm going to head home, Karen. Can I take one of these cupcakes with me to munch on?"

"Sure, knock yourself out, girl."

"I take it you don't mean that literally?" I say with a grin.

"Hardly. Oh, do you like the PJs I gave you last night?"

"Yes, I do. I had no idea where I was when I woke, and I didn't recognise the PJs. They're amazing and comfy."

"And expensive," she says. "They're yours. New and don't fit me right now, so keep them."

"Thanks, Karen, that's very generous. I have to stay here more often. Free PJs and takeaway cupcakes. What more could a girl ask for?"

She gives me a hug as I leave, and it makes me feel a little better. She's forgiven me for tackling her over the drink. I walk home with cupcake in hand. I contemplate what to do about what very obviously seems to be a drink problem, which Karen has. Jen and Tommy will need to be told as I'll need some support, and somehow we'll have to come to a solution together. I think I'll take a timeout for the rest of the day to prepare for the week ahead of me.

The following day on my way to work, I receive a call from Tommy. "Hi, Aly. Sorry to disturb you, as you must be pretty busy."

"Tommy, you know you never disturb me," I say. "What can I do for you?"

"Well, I'm worried about Jen."

"That makes two of us."

"She came home last night and vomited everything she ate. I mean she made herself ill. That's the first time I've heard or seen her do that. I was in bed, and I got up to see her in the bathroom with her fingers down her throat. When I tried to question her about it, she got annoyed with me and told me I don't understand what pressure she's under from work. I'm at my wits' end now, Aly. I knew she was getting thinner, but I had no idea she had an eating disorder!"

"Tommy, I'm so sorry to hear you had to go through that. I did mention it to her on Friday when I saw her. I told her she doesn't need to lose any more weight. If anything, she needs to put it on. I was going to call you later in the week anyway in relation to another topic, but that will wait for now. Do you want me to talk to her and see if I can help her in some way?"

"That would be great, Aly. She doesn't seem to want to open up to me about this for some reason."

"It's OK, Tommy. I'll meet with her tonight or tomorrow and talk it through with her. I'll see if I can persuade her to get help for this."

"Thank you, Aly; that means a great deal to me. Maybe we can both do it together, but I think if you manage to get her to open up a little first, that would be a massive help."

"Sure. Thanks for calling and letting me know, Tommy. And don't worry, we'll get her sorted."

I hang up and want to tear my hair out. *How have my two best friends let themselves go like this? How can they do this to me on the week Jack is coming to New York? Oh damn, I'm being selfish now.* I have to cast my thoughts to one side for now as I'm entering the office building, and I'm going straight to Jeremy's office to ask for time off.

"Knock, knock. Can I come in?"

"Yep, come on in, Aly. What can I do for you?"

Not a so-called sexy dance to "Insomnia," that's for sure! Why do these thoughts come into my mind at the wrong moment?

"You look happy, Aly."

"No, not really."

"Care to share?"

"No, it's not important. Anyway, I'll cut to the chase. I need time off, please, from Thursday this week until the end of next week. That OK?"

You're not really in a position to say no to me Jeremy, not after what you did. Be nice for once.

"Hmmm, I'm not sure. You're not really giving much notice, are you, Aly?"

"No, maybe not, but Jeremy, I've been here over nine months, and in that time I haven't had more than two days of leave. I think to be fair, I've worked my arse off and would like to take the time that I have coming to me now. It's seven working days, not a month. Besides, my fantastic brain needs a rest."

"True, you have worked very hard here. I can't deny you that. Leave it with me."

"Sure. Can you let me know before the end of the day, please? I am due to go on vacation, and my friend is waiting to hear before booking it."

"OK, Aly. Will do."

I want a yes answer right now, not "leave it with me!"

I walk, or more like storm, out of his office. I slam the door of my office and plonk myself down in my chair. As I sit contemplating what an arsehole Jeremy is, I hear a knock on the door. I swing around in my chair and see him peering through the blinds. *Hmmm, feeling guilty, are we, Jeremy?*

"Come in."

"Hi. Sorry, I just wanted to see you squirm a little rather than tell you straight out that you can have the time. I couldn't resist."

"Aren't you the right funny man? Well, thanks. You can go now again, and don't forget to close my door behind you."

"Oh, touchy. Who's boss here? Me or you, Aly?" he says with a very sarcastic tone as he closes the door. "Oh, and by the way, you can pay me back sometime," he says with a wink.

I know I have to watch my step. My mouth rules me sometimes, and it could have caused serious trouble for me just now. I choose to keep a low profile for the rest of the day and avoid Jeremy at all costs. *What the hell did he mean by that, though?*

In the afternoon, I manage to get in touch with Jen on the phone.

"Hi, Jen, it's me. I need a chat. Can you meet me later this evening for a quick bite to eat?"

"Well, I told Tommy I'd be home early, but if it's urgent, sure. I'll let him know."

"Great, thanks. Where's good for you, Jen?"

"How about I meet you at your offices, and we can go from there?"

"Sounds good," I say. "Great, see you later."

"See you then."

She sounds exhausted, not her usual happy self that she has been since she met Tommy. I know I'll have to do my best to get her to spill it out this evening.

At the end of the day, I'm just about to leave the office when I hear, "Grump, are you off home?"

I turn to see Jeremy standing behind me.

"Yes, I am. Why?"

"No reason. I'm just checking to see if you are still talking to me after making you stew a little today."

"Yes, I am. I'm rushing now so have to go."

"OK, have a good evening. Don't come in with a hangover tomorrow. We have to meet with some new clients!"

"I won't."

I run from the building as fast as I can in case someone else nabs me. I'm nervous about meeting Jen, as I still haven't really figured out how to broach the subject of her eating disorder. She's waiting patiently with a big smile across her face, but I can tell she doesn't feel like smiling. It looks forced, and she looks like she is ready to burst into tears.

"How are you?" I ask.

"I'm OK, I've been better."

"What's up, Jen? Don't fob me off. You're not yourself."

"This is about you tonight," she says. "You have the problem you need to talk about, remember?"

"Yes, OK. Let's go in here." I point to the local pub that I've had many a drunken night in, which led to Jeremy and me having our "thing."

Once we're comfortable, I take the food menu in hand and glance at it. Jen's face drops. "I'm going for the burger and chips. I haven't had a feed of rubbishy food in a while," I say.

"I'm OK for now," Jen replies.

"No, you're not. You're going to order food, or I'm going to force-feed my burger and chips to you."

"What? Oh, Aly, stop. Come on now, tell me what's up."

"Jen, you're what's up."

"What do you mean?"

"I think you know. I know you've got an eating disorder."

She starts crying. "It was Tommy who told you, wasn't it?"

"Well, I think I actually figured it out for myself when I saw you on Friday night. You lost half your body weight in a month, Jen. That's not normal. What set you off on this dieting fad?"

"Well, I'd been trying to lose a few pounds when you came over earlier in the year."

"Yes, I know, but at least you ate something back then. It was healthy food, and you ate enough to keep you sustained. Now you don't eat, and if you do, you make yourself sick. Honey, we need to get help for you. Please say you'll go see someone."

"Aly, it's easy for you to say that. In my new job, there's so much pressure for me to stay thin or get thinner than I am. On my first day, the photographer said to me that I had such a pretty face, but with the extra weight I'm carrying, I'd never get in front of the camera lens. Not that I want to, but I'm fat. He told me so, Aly."

"Jen, please tell me you didn't take that seriously. Surely he was joking."

"No, he wasn't. Most of the girls in the agency are even skinnier than I am now, Aly. I'm like a big fatty next to them."

"Jesus, that bastard has some cheek, I can tell you. Jen, you have to leave that job. You're too good for them. We need to get you back to full health."

She stops crying. I give her a huge hug. "We're all here for you, hon. You just need to trust in us."

"It's not that easy. I had a fight with Tommy the other morning. I've been snapping at him, and I don't even know if he wants us to move into the house any longer."

"Of course he does. Look, I spoke to Tommy today. He's really worried about you. He asked me to meet you, Jen, because he's at his wits' end and doesn't know how to help you. Don't give him grief over that. The guy was close to tears on the phone."

"OK, I won't. Oh God, I'm making his life so miserable," she says as the tears start to flow again.

"Come on, love. Let's get you home."

"It's too far for you, Aly. I'll make my way home myself."

"No, you won't. We can all sit down and chat about this once we get back to Tommy's place. Tommy needs to hear it too, OK?"

She nods. She looks scared.

We arrive back considerably earlier than I thought we would. Tommy greets both of us with a big smile and a huge hug for Jen.

"I've been so worried about you, baby. I hope chatting with Aly has helped you."

Jen is sobbing again but nodding her head as if the chat has relieved her of her secret. "Tommy, I'm so sorry. I've been terrible to you. I'm so sorry."

"Shhh, stop crying, Jen. It's OK. I know you weren't yourself. We'll get this thing sorted. Don't you worry."

I sit in the living room with Jen as Tommy goes to make some dinner in the kitchen.

"Thanks, Aly. It's strange how just telling someone can help."

"Jen, you're my best friend. Of course I'm here to help you."

I really want to talk to them about Karen but know that now isn't the best time. However, I can't let Karen carry on in her current phase for too long.

Tommy returns with a glass of wine for me and dinner for all of us. I must look like I need it. Jen starts eating the dinner but slowly. We all sit in the living room for two hours and talk about her eating disorder in detail. She initially denies having a problem. However, she finally gives in and admits that her behaviour is not normal but insists that she can sort it out herself. She doesn't want to go for any kind of therapy or professional help. We are to be the ones who get her through it.

"Oh, Jen, that's not going to be possible as neither of us is qualified, but we'll help you in any way we can." I take her hand before I leave the house. "You've got to promise me you'll make an effort, Jen, and please keep what you've eaten in tonight."

She smiles. "I promise. Thanks for your help, Aly."

I squeeze her hand and smile at her.

Tommy calls a taxi for me, and he is quick to pay the taxi driver before I even get into the car.

I see the light shining outside my apartment block as we turn onto Charles Street. *Home, sweet home.* It's late, and I'm exhausted.

It's Tuesday morning, and I don't even remember turning the light out last night. It takes great effort for me to get up, but I manage eventually and saunter into work.

Karen keeps fluttering in and out of my mind throughout the day, and I feel guilty because I didn't spot that her problem was serious at an earlier stage. However, I can't enlist Jen and Tommy to help until I'm sure Jen is OK.

Lunchtime approaches, and I can hear the familiar buzzing of my phone from my bag.

"Hi, Aly. It's Jack."

"Hi there! I'm delighted to hear from you. Listen, I got the time off. My boss was messing me about a bit at first, but I managed to secure it."

"Well, that's what I wanted to talk to you about. I've been drafted into a new TV show, and the producers want to meet with me on Thursday and Friday of this week to discuss contracts. They want me in a trial run next week to see how it goes. It's sort of an audition but a weeklong one. Aly, I'm so sorry. I can't say no to this. It's a big show, and it could be great for my career."

"Oh, Jack."

I'm so disappointed, but it's his career, so I have to snap out of this and reassure him he's doing the right thing.

"It's OK, really. I can cancel the holidays, and we can do it another time. Your career is more important than holidays, after all."

"Well, normally I'd say they would have to wait, but this is so big I really can't say no to it. I'm sorry, really sorry. I was hoping to see you this weekend."

"Honestly, Jack, it's OK. Don't worry about it. I have to go here; big meeting just starting."

"OK, Aly, I'll call you at the weekend, OK?"

"Sure, Jack. Bye."

I hang up as quickly as I can. I want to cry. *What the hell is happening to my life? The first man I met when I moved here cheated on me, and the second one is devoted to work. One best friend with an eating disorder and another with a drink problem. Why me? Maybe I shouldn't have left home after all!* I sit at my desk with my face in my hands and sob until I don't have any more tears to cry. Of course, perfect timing as always, Jeremy sticks his head around the door.

"Hey, Aly. Jesus, what's wrong? You look like you've been crying for hours!"

"Thanks, Jeremy. That makes me feel really good. You're always great for compliments."

"Hey, come on. It's not my fault you're crying, is it?"

"Don't flatter yourself. No, it's not. My holiday has been cancelled. I'm still going to take those holidays though, I feel I need a break."

"Sorry to hear that. Of course, take the holidays. Want an ear to bend?"

I smile. "Thanks, but I don't know if I would be bending the right ear."

"You could always bend the left one. I'm easy in that respect. My ears don't seem to mind, either."

I start laughing. "No, Jeremy, it's fine. Thank you though," I say with a smile.

"You know, Aly, don't think I'm offering because I want to get into your undies again. But if you want to be a bitch about it, I can be a pure prick, too." He turns and leaves the office.

What the fuck is wrong with everyone today?

Chapter 21

A couple of days have passed, and I haven't really heard from anyone. I decide to meet Tommy for lunch to discuss how Jen is doing.

"Do we need to send her to a shrink? God, I hate that word. It's so American! No offence meant," I say.

"None taken. I can't stand it myself. Naaahhhh. I asked her to tell me the truth about what she's eating and if she's keeping it down. I believe her when she tells me, but sometimes I think that she might be keeping things from me."

"I know what you mean, and that's very tough for you. You can't accuse her of lying or making things up as it will only lead to arguments. To be honest, I've been thinking about going to see someone myself of late, just to get over all that crap I dealt with at home from Simon and then here with Jeremy. I feel weird doing that, but you know, it might help me to move on properly."

I don't want to tell him that I haven't a clue how to deal with both of my best friends' problems, especially when he doesn't know what I witnessed in Karen's apartment.

"Well, most people I know in New York do attend one. It can help with issues that just keep circling in your mind. I went to one once or twice myself, generally when I had a heavy caseload and just needed to get some form of release from it all. It helped greatly. I found myself pouring my heart out to someone I didn't even know. Stuff came out that I had never told anyone, and I felt like a load had been lifted. I really think Jen should see someone, too," he says.

"Why don't I make an appointment for myself, and then I can recommend that Jen go? At least if she thinks I went before her and know what it's like, she might consider it."

"Good thinking. We can talk to her about it. On another note, do you think her old job might take her back? They keep ringing, looking for her and asking her where things are while she's at work."

"I think it would be the best thing ever if they did. She's miserable in that agency, and that gobshite photographer should be fired," I say.

"Yeah, well, I've had my own thoughts on how to deal with him. Not nice thoughts, but obviously I have to keep a clean sheet. I ought to have words with him at least."

"I know I'd love to boot him up the arse with the pointiest shoe I possess!" I say.

We both laugh.

"So what else is happening in the world of Aly?" he asks.

"I'll be homeless in three weeks if I don't get my arse into gear and find myself a new apartment. Jeremy's been acting weird, and Jack had to cancel our mini break to the Hamptons, but I'm still taking time off."

"That's a shame. Sounds like things are piling up on you a bit, but you know how Jen and I are buying a house? We're signing the contracts tomorrow. She's holding onto her apartment but wants to rent it out. She'll be moving her stuff into my apartment for the time being, as the house won't be ready for a while, but she's leaving all the furniture."

I can see where he is going with this, and the idea of renting Jen's apartment hadn't even occurred to me, probably because I've been so caught up in her and Karen.

"Yes, she did mention that, but the rent she'll be looking for will probably be more than I can afford, Tommy."

"Look, how about I talk to her and see what she's looking for? I'm sure she'll be in contact with you anyway over the coming days. It would be great if you could rent it. It would save her so much trouble, and she'd know you would keep it in perfect condition."

"Sure, mention it to her, but I don't want to put her under any pressure."

"Don't worry, Aly. I've a feeling she'll jump at the idea."

The lunch hour flies by, and it's great to catch up with Tommy. He's got such gentlemanly qualities, and I'm so glad for Jen that she has finally found her man.

Back at the office, I sit and think. Even though Jen hasn't suggested it to me yet, I won't take her apartment if she offers it. It's a bad idea, and I'd hate if anything went wrong with it while I was there as her tenant. I know I'll find something I can afford. I pick up the papers I collected on my way back to the office and start my search again.

I spend the afternoon shuffling paper and checking the papers intermittently. Eventually, I decide to try to deal with some figures on the computer. Jeremy pops his head around the door.

"Hi, I need you in a meeting now."

"Jaysus, no please or thanks or even asking?"

"Don't get smart, Aly. The boardroom, now!"

I get up from my seat, feeling flushed and confused. *I thought we were going to stay friends. What's with the mood change?*

As I sit in the meeting and give my input on our lack of verse writers, Jeremy is giving me daggers across the table. I look at him as if to say, "What?" He looks away.

"I'd be happy to contribute if needs be. If we have a lack of writers, then why not? I'm not particularly looking for extra work, but I could find a spare hour in the day to scribble a few verses."

"What a great idea, Aly. I wasn't aware you were a keen verse writer," Vincent, our chairman, announces.

"Oh, Vincent, it's just something I do in my spare time, as a hobby really, you could say. It can help to get rid of any sadness or anger, or even if you're happy, it's a good way of expressing it."

"Yeah, I can imagine how good they are!" Jeremy butts in with an air of sarcasm.

"OK, problem solved. Aly, let's go with your idea for now as your workload will be increasing soon anyway. Christmas has to be dealt with shortly. Let's make it short-term for now—and depending on what you write, of course."

"Sure!" I say with a smile, which turns to the death stare as I turn my gaze to Jeremy.

I leave the boardroom and head back to my office. Tired of Jeremy being a gobshite, I sit at my desk and decide to do something I swore I wouldn't do: I click into Google, and my fingers start typing the name "Jack Morgan" into the search box. A rush of guilt flows over me when I find a few interesting articles. Even though I am guilt-ridden, I proceed and click into one site in particular that gives me plenty of information on him. However, the only part I'm interested in is the bit about his girlfriend. *Aghhhhhhhhh, why did I do that? Bloody eejit, I knew I'd find something I wouldn't like if I Googled him!* Nonetheless, I have done the deed, and as I have the information in front of me, I'm curious. It appears that she is a well-known model. "She's most infamous for her wild parties and her jealous ways when boyfriend—or ex-boyfriend, some say—Jack Morgan is seen out and about," it says.

Jesus! This is what I'd have to contend with. Is she his girlfriend or not? This is confusing. How do I approach him about this without sounding like I've been spying on him?

I quickly close the website and turn back to my pending workload.

It looks like a late night is required of me in the office to get through this lot, and I've no one to blame but myself.

I end up working late for the rest of the week. Friday evening, I feel I deserve a drink in the pub with everyone else, but I opt not to go. Instead, I go directly back to my apartment with the idea of having a nice, relaxing night.

I'm enjoying cooking a nice meal for myself when I hear a knock on my door. I can see Jen's little face beaming in through the panes of glass on the building door.

"Hi, Aly. How are you?"

"I'm fine, thanks, Jen. How are you doing? Come in! Are you feeling any better?"

"Actually, I was thinking about your apartment situation."

I get it; you don't want to talk about your problem.

"Oh yeah? What about it?"

"Tommy and I have more or less moved in together at this stage, and we'll be moving to the new house in a few months. We signed the contract the other day and got the keys. So I was wondering if you'd be interested in renting my apartment. It would take a huge amount of pressure off you and me. What do you think?"

"That's a fantastic idea, but I'm going to say no, Jen. Thank you so much though. I'd just be worried if something went wrong while I'm living there. It would be on my conscience. Tommy mentioned it the other night, and I have thought about it, but I'm definitely going to say no."

"Oh, that's a shame," she says. "I know you'd look after it, and it would make life easier on all of us."

"I know, lovey, but as I said, if something went wrong, I'd feel bad forevermore. It's probably better, too, not to have your best friend as your landlady—who knows what disputes may arise."

"Hmm, true, I hadn't looked at it from that point of view. OK, let's let it go for now then. In other news—and this will cheer you up—Tommy has somehow managed to persuade me to go to counselling for my eating disorder. Wow, that's weird; it's the first time I've called it that! I'm going next week, but I'm scared, Aly."

"Jen, that's great news. I'm so happy to hear that. I was so worried that what we said might not have got through, and I didn't want to pester you about it, either. Well, you know if you want someone to go along and hold your hand, I'd be happy to go. There's no need for you to be scared, love. This is going to help you. Actually, while we're on the subject, I've been thinking about seeing someone myself."

"Why?"

"Well, I never really spoke to anyone in great detail about my breakup with Simon—or Jeremy for that matter—and I think it might help me a little, or even a lot."

"It might not be a bad idea. You know Karen and I are always here for you, Aly."

"I know, hon, and thanks, but I think maybe I'd blurt more out if I was to talk to a stranger who knows nothing about me."

"Sure, I understand. Have a think about it. So what are you up to tonight? I don't want to disturb you, as you nearly always have plans on a Friday night. I'm just popping in on my way back to my place. I need to collect more of my stuff."

"Zero plans, would you believe? A nice bath, maybe. I'm just after making some noodles and stir-fry. Want to stay and help me out with them?"

"Aly, you're not checking up on me again, are you?" she asks.

"No! God, no, Jen. I'm just asking. I've made too much so there's plenty there if you fancy it. I never was very good with gauging how many noodles and veg I should use. Weighing scales don't come into the equation with me. I suppose I should invest in one, though. I could call Karen and see what she's up to, or Tommy, if you prefer," I say.

"OK, let's call Karen."

Karen's phone rings out. I'm guessing she's partying or else has drunk herself into an oblivious state again. I'll try again later.

"You know, if you want that bath, go for it, Aly. I can sit here and try Karen again while you relax for a while."

"OK, thanks." I head for the bath. Once finished, I'm incredibly relaxed and head back into the living room to Jen.

"That was amazing," I say.

"I'll bet. There are times when nothing but a good bubble bath will do. I've managed to speak to Karen. She's out, hammered, and slurring badly."

"Oh, no. Jen, I've no idea what to do with her. I've something to tell you over dinner."

As I plate up the vegetable stir-fry and noodles, I'm thrilled to see Jen eating a little. It's not much, and she's eating slowly but eating nonetheless. I disclose what happened in Karen's place the week before, and Jen doesn't seem in the slightest bit surprised.

"Aly, she's been out of control for too long," she says. "We need to get some form of help for her."

"I know."

"About three months before you arrived, I noticed that she seemed to be in a constantly inebriated state. I hadn't a clue what to do. Then she eased off, and that day you arrived was the first time in months I'd seen her like that. I was so delighted when you decided to give New York a try. You were always sensible and are always the problem solver. But when you hadn't said anything to me about Karen, apart from the odd comment, I assumed that maybe you thought she was OK and that I'd been overreacting."

"No, I've noticed it since I arrived here, but I thought she was just partying like she's always done. I realise now that she's out at least five nights per week and must lash back on average three bottles of wine or champagne per night. I think last weekend was the final straw for me, though."

"I've had discussions with Tommy about it, but he says we can't really do anything until she comes to us for help. I can't watch her like this anymore, Aly. Her poor dad would be in an awful state if he saw her like this."

"OK, do you think if we talk to Tommy again, he might be able to get some advice or numbers that we could discretely leave on her kitchen table or something?"

"I'll ask him. Two or three heads are definitely better than one in this situation."

"Well, I'll tell you what. How about you get yourself better first? I don't want you worrying about anything else right now. You've got enough on your plate. I can chat to Tommy some evening, and then when you feel up to it, we'll all discuss it. What do you think?"

"Ah, I'm fine, Aly. In fact, focussing on Karen would take my mind off my own problems. This is a great meal, by the way."

I hug her tightly. It's great to see her smile. It's as if she genuinely is enjoying it. I take the dishes to the kitchen, and as I do, Jen's phone rings. I return from the kitchen.

"That was Tommy. He's collecting me later, and we'll stay here on Charles Street tonight."

"Ahh, so in lurve," I say with a smile. I know he suggested picking her up to keep an eye on her so she won't try to bring her food back up. That's clever of him, as I too am worried that she might try.

"So what else is new?" she asks.

"Well, remember I was meant to be in the Hamptons this weekend?"

"Aly! I forgot completely. What happened?"

"Jack rang earlier in the week. He was really sorry, but he wouldn't make it due to getting a job on a new TV show that could make his career skyrocket. They expect it to be a hit in Europe, too. He had to meet with the producers and sign contracts yesterday and today. Next week he has to work on the show or something like that. I was so close to crying, I hardly remember what excuse he gave me."

"Oh, pet, I'm so sorry to hear that. Did he say he'd make it up to you, or did he just leave it?"

"He did say he would make it up to me, but each time he talks to me, he mentions how complicated his life in LA is. I can never understand how it can be. OK, he's an actor, but it's like there's something he needs to tell me."

"What do you think it is? A secret life? A wife and kids?"

"I hope not! Well, I had forgotten about it most of this week until today."

"What did you do? Were you totally distracted at work?"

"Yeah, I cried my eyes out when I hung up. Of course, Jeremy saw me crying as he peeked into the office. I have to admit though, he's been a real dick lately, and I've no idea why!"

"Oh, Aly, no, please don't go there. You know he's probably jealous of Jack; that's why!"

"No, don't worry, I won't. He's really making me feel uncomfortable, like he's got some hold over me if I don't do what he asks or says. It's weird, and while I know we weren't together that long, it seems out of character for him. Work is a terrible environment to be in now."

"Hmm, be careful of that. Maybe it's a good thing, in a way, as you won't be tempted again. Please, I'm begging you, don't go back to him."

"Not a chance, girl."

"You mentioned a few minutes ago that you had forgotten about Jack until today. What happened today?"

"Ah, yes. I know I said I wouldn't—and don't ridicule me, please? I was just dying to see a photo of him today, just to remind me of him. It's been a few weeks, and even though we speak regularly on the phone, it's nice to see the face, too."

Jen starts sniggering. "You Googled him, didn't you?"

I hang my head in shame. "Yes. I know I shouldn't have, and I'm officially a stalker now."

"Ah, would you stop? You're grand; you were in need of seeing his gorgeous face! Besides, I think you're amazing for not Googling him sooner. If it was Karen or me, we'd have been on the Internet the first day."

I smile. "Thanks. I don't feel so bad now. The thing is, though, I found a site which had a huge amount of information on him, and when I clicked into it, there was something about his girlfriend! Now, it mentioned that some say she's his ex, but no one seems to know."

"Do you know her name?"

"Some model. I don't recall her name."

"Ah yes, I remember he was going out with a model, but that was over a year ago, Aly. I don't think he's with her anymore."

"I don't know, Jen. It just pissed me right off to see that today. I knew I shouldn't have gone near that damn Internet."

"I'm sure there's an explanation. Jack seems like a decent guy."

I wonder if he really is. That stupid Internet site has planted a small seed of doubt in my mind, and I hate it. There's a loud knock on the door, and we both jump.

"That sounds like Tommy," says Jen.

I giggle. "How can you tell if that's him?"

"I'm just guessing. He's got a strong, loud knock."

"Jen, the things you come out with sometimes."

I open the door to Tommy. "Come on in, Tom. Have you eaten? There's still some left. I can heat it up for you."

"Nope, I haven't, and that sounds good to me. Sorry, hope I'm not interrupting anything."

"Course not; you're very welcome to join us."

We sit and chat while Tommy wolfs down the food I give him. I watch him and Jen as they converse and laugh. They just look generally happy. I wonder if I'll ever find that happiness with someone—with Jack, maybe. I'll have to think about something else, though, as I don't know when Jack will saunter back into my life, if ever.

Jen and Tommy leave for her apartment later. I am absolutely exhausted and go straight to bed. I'm in bed five minutes when my phone beeps. I glance to see who it is, and I'm surprised to see Jack's name flashing on the screen.

"Sorry, did I wake you?"

"No, no, I'm just after getting into bed."

"Oh, saucy; let's FaceTime," he says.

I laugh. I'm certainly not trying to be saucy, and if he could see the state of me in my penguin pyjamas, he wouldn't think that way, either.

"No, let's not! How are you?" I ask.

"OK, I'm just feeling a bit crappy that I had to cancel this weekend with you, I feel I've screwed up big time."

"I'm sorry you had to cancel, too, but there's not much we can do about it now, Jack. There'll be another weekend and week, I'm sure. How did the contract signing go? That was today, wasn't it?"

"Yep, all signed and sealed. I'm quite happy about it, actually. They're offering me a great deal. However, not wanting to change the subject, I'll make it up to you, Aly. I promise."

"No worries, Jack. Look, we've only gone out twice, and one of those times, it was a case of us bumping into eachother. In fact, we don't even know each other apart from our telephone conversations, which admittedly last for over two hours sometimes."

"I feel I know you pretty well. In fact, I feel I've gotten to know you very well through our phone conversations," he says.

"Actually, Jack, there's something I want to ask you about."

"Oh, you better get that."

"What?"

"The door. Did someone just knock on your door?"

"I didn't hear it."

With that, I hear a loud knock. It must be Jen and Tommy after forgetting something.

"Just heard it now. How on earth did you hear it?"

"I've great ears."

"Give me two minutes. It's probably Jen after forgetting something."

"OK."

I'm running to the door but can't see who is there. All I can see is someone holding a bunch of red roses up to his or her face. Must be the wrong apartment. Being polite, I open the door to redirect whoever it is.

"Hi, I think you have the wrong…"

"Hi!"

I can't believe my eyes when I see Jack standing there smiling as he lowers the roses from in front of his face.

I'm overwhelmed with emotion. I'm hugging him tightly when I realise I'm in my penguin pyjamas. My hair is greasy and smells of stir-fried noodles, and I don't have any make-up on!

"Hmmm, you smell nice," he says. "Some sort of fried dish for dinner?"

"Jack! Stop, I feel embarrassed enough looking like this."

"I know, Aly. I just can't help myself. You look beautiful as always, penguins and all."

I laugh. "Come in. You've really taken me by surprise!"

"I know. I would imagine if you were expecting me, you wouldn't be wearing penguin pyjamas, although they are very cute and suit you. The food smell is the best part, though."

"Jack, stop it, please," I plead as I laugh. I can feel my face flushing with embarrassment.

"So are you happy to see me?"

"Of course I am! I'm a bit gobsmacked, to be honest. I thought it was some dude who had the wrong address—and how did you know my favourite flowers are roses?"

"I do my research. Not just a pretty face, you know?"

"They're beautiful. Take a seat, Jack. I'll get changed."

"Do not! You look gorgeous—nice and snug. Honestly, I'll be annoyed if you change."

"OK. So do you have somewhere to stay tonight?"

"Nah, I'll probably book into a nearby hotel. I'm taking you to the Hamptons tomorrow, and it's better to be nearby so I can pick you up early. Any chance you can take that week off still? I know this is a stupid stunt to pull as you're not prepared now."

"No, it's fine. I decided to take the week off anyway. I need a break. I've been working nonstop since I got here. It's not a stupid stunt; it's the most bloody romantic thing any man has ever done for me." I lean towards him and kiss him on the cheek. "Thank you, Jack Morgan."

He takes my hand and pulls me down on top of him on the couch.

Nice! Now please kiss me, Jack, kiss me!

He moves nearer to me, places his lips closer to mine, and goes for a full-on passion-filled kiss. I really don't want to move from this spot right now. It's the most perfect moment.

"So I thought you had to stay in LA all week?" I quiz.

"Nope. I knew I had to sign the contracts yesterday and today, but I had this great brainwave to come to New York to surprise you and whisk you away anyway."

"Nice surprise. It was lucky I didn't cancel my days off."

"You're telling me. I knew I was taking a risk—a big risk."

"You know, Jack, you can stay here tonight if you want. No funny business, mind you. I'll decide when the show begins."

He's laughing. "The show?"

"Yeah, you know what I mean."

"Sure I do. I'd love to stay and snuggle up to you all night, but I think by the look of it, you were ready for a nice night sprawled out in your bed before I came along and ruined it. So I'm going to go to a hotel. I'll be around early, and I want you to get a good sleep. Besides, if I stay, you might be tempted to let 'the show' begin."

For a split second, I wonder if I've been a bit too pushy. Then I realise he's just being himself, gentlemanly in every way. Jack Morgan, the perfect gentleman—*my* perfect gentleman.

We sit, chat, and kiss for another half hour or so.

"Nice soft lips you have," he says.

I suppose that's romantic, but I'm never very good with accepting compliments. "What's next, what nice big eyes I have? Where's your red cape?" I say.

"Aly, you are funny, but you just spoiled the moment."

"No, I didn't. You can start again like we pretended we met for the first time in that bar."

"We could, but it's getting late. I'm gonna split as I'm beat. I had a long flight today. It's taking its toll on me."

"I can imagine. Are you sure you don't want to stay here? If you don't want to share the bed, I can make up the sofa bed for you."

I feel weird saying that to him. After all, I've a feeling that things are going to heat up over the weekend in the Hamptons anyway.

"No, I'll go, my sweet. I think we both need a good sleep. I promise I'll be around early in the morning."

"OK, I'll look forward to it. Jack, thanks for the roses and for travelling here to see me."

"My pleasure."

Not yet it's not, but it will be tomorrow night, Jack Morgan!

I smile at him and walk him to the door. I peek out to see Brad waiting outside patiently. "Good evening, Aly," he calls out. "It's nice to see you again."

"Likewise, Brad."

"Jack, I got a hotel booking for you," he continues. "The Trump Soho."

"Perfect. Thanks, Brad."

"So, Aly, I'll see you in the morning," he says as he leans in to give me that last good-night kiss. "You sleep well and sweet dreams," he whispers in my ear.

I can feel goose bumps rising on every element of my body.

"Good-night, Jack. Thank you, and see you tomorrow."

I wave them goodbye and retreat back into my apartment. I go to bed and lie there thinking about him. I feel myself drifting off into a welcome deep sleep.

Chapter 22

*I*t's Saturday morning, and I'm super excited about our break. Jack arrives on my doorstep at nine o'clock.

"Hi, gorgeous. I'm sorry; I'm actually later than planned. I had the idea of collecting you really early to go for breakfast somewhere nice and make a full day of it, but I slept in."

"No problem. I only got up an hour ago myself. It was an exhausting week, and I must have drifted off into a very deep sleep last night when you left. Anyway, we have the whole week! Are you coming in for a few minutes?"

"Sure, I know what you gals are like. You probably aren't even fully packed yet."

"Well, as a big surprise to you, Jack, I am…almost. Just one or two small things to fit into the case, and I'm ready then. Make yourself at home. Did you eat? There's plenty of food in my kitchen if you want to eat something."

My mother always told me the way to a man's heart is through his stomach!

"No thanks. I grabbed something quick as I left the hotel. Besides, we might have a nice big lunch instead later."

"OK, but lunch is a few hours away yet. I don't want you starving, and I've enough to contend with one of my friends currently putting herself through that."

"Don't worry. I had enough to keep me going. Who are you talking about?"

"Oh, it doesn't matter," I say. "I might tell you later. You'll probably guess when you see her anyway."

"All right. Go, go, get ready, chatterbox," he says with a smile.

I hurry to the hallway where my suitcase is almost ready, and I'm just about managing to squeeze another pair of shoes into it. Now that's sorted, I feel ready to go. I walk back to the lounge.

"OK, ready."

He bursts into laughter. "Aly, are you coming for a week or a month?"

"There's not that much there. One suitcase and a weekend bag. I need my girly things, Jack."

"I know; I know what you ladies are like. I might wear this, I might wear that. Forty pairs of shoes, am I right? You must have been up since five o'clock to say you packed this morning."

"Not quite. Ten pairs of shoes. I like to prepare for all eventualities. OK, I lied about my start this morning. I've been up since six o'clock. I woke after a deep sleep and couldn't sleep any longer, so I thought I might as well pack all I need."

"OK, let me take that."

He lifts the case to the door.

"What is in here? It's definitely more than twenty kilos! You'd be charged if you were getting on a plane!"

"Well, we aren't getting on a plane, are we?"

"No, not this time, anyway. But remember, if we holiday anywhere outside of the country or anywhere that needs to be reached by air, twenty kilos max allowance."

"OK, no need to lecture me now. Come on, chop chop, you're a bit slow at moving it. I'd have been faster myself," I say with a snigger.

He glances at me, and I can tell by the grin on his face that he's trying hard to come up with something smart to say back to me but isn't successful. I'll say nothing and just enjoy the moment.

We reach Jack's new house, and I'm in complete awe of the place. It's a seven-bedroom villa with swimming pool and gym. It even has a cinema.

"Can I ask you something, Jack?"

"Shoot."

"Why would you buy a seven-bedroom house for one person?"

"For when I have guests staying over, like you. This is your room."

I must look perplexed. Jack seems interested in me, but if he's offering me my own room, then he obviously hasn't planned any seduction technique for this evening—or any other evening.

"Oh, thanks; it's beautiful. I'll just unpack my things, then."

"Are you OK? You sound a little upset, Aly."

"No, no, I'm fine. This is perfect, Jack; thanks. I'm really looking forward to us spending this time together."

"Me too. Come down when you're ready, and we can go for lunch."

I watch him close the door. I feel like crying. What was all that about last night? It was as if he couldn't get enough of me—kissing me and flirting. I sit there sighing to myself when I hear the door open again.

"Gotcha! You'll be sleeping over here with me," he says as he pulls me up from the bed and holds me in his arms. "Sorry, I couldn't resist, Aly. Your cute face just looked so sad when you saw we were going to have separate rooms."

I playfully punch his shoulder. "Don't do things like that to me. I was getting really upset there. I thought you were just acting with me and that you didn't like me at all," I say in a playful manner.

"Nah, I just couldn't resist. There's no pressure on you in relation to 'the show,' by the way."

My face has to be puce right now. Why did I refer to it as "the show?"

"You can let me know when you're ready in your own time, OK?" he says.

"Thanks. Very gentlemanly of you. I wish you would stop referring to it as 'the show,' though."

"I didn't; you did. I'm just mimicking what you said."

"I know, and don't I regret it. It was a spur-of-the-moment comment that I will live to regret forever, I'm sure."

"Hmmm, forever? I like the way you're thinking, Aly. So you think I'll be around forever to mock you over this?"

"Aghhhh, you're doing it again. Stop."

"OK."

He faces me again and kisses me softly. The butterflies in my stomach are nearly coming up my throat because I'm so excited and happy to be around him. At least I hope it's butterflies. However, I'm not ready just yet, and I don't want to give him the impression that I am some sort of floozy, either. Although we have met properly a few times, and we have exchanged numerous phone calls, I need to clarify what his love life situation is before I get in too deep.

"Let's go for lunch," I suggest with a big smile across my face.

"Sure, let's go, honey."

The lunch is spectacular. I'm sipping on fine wine and eating fresh seafood just caught this morning—or at least that's what the waiter told us. I really want to ask Jack about the information I found on Google yesterday. I have no idea how to raise the matter without actually disclosing that I performed an Internet search on him.

"Aly, there's something I wanted to talk to you about."

Oh, maybe I don't have to ask him!

"I live a pretty complicated life in LA. Not the job side of it—except the paparazzi drive me crazy sometimes, but thankfully they are reasonably respectable towards me. I was in a relationship with someone up until September last year, about six months before you arrived here. We were together three years, and the relation-ship was, let's just say, interesting."

"OK, where is this heading?" I interject. "Are you getting back with her? Just tell me if you are."

"No way! Stop jumping ahead of yourself. Basically, she's a very jealous character, and since we broke up, she's been making my life hell. Before I met you, I used to see other women in LA. Not many; just one or two dates. If I was seen out on the town with a woman, even if she was just a friend, my ex used to go ballistic and spread all sorts of rumours about me. I got back with her briefly about three months after we split, and it was the last straw for me when she interrupted a very important black-tie event that I at-tended. I hadn't invited her as she was meant to be on a photo shoot in Antigua."

"Sounds like a psycho bitch from hell."

"She is. That's a good name for her. May I use that?"

"Sure, at no cost."

"Thanks. Anyway, I was in the middle of giving a speech at this event when she burst in the door of the main hall and started screaming and shouting at me. She accused me of being there with a woman who is actually married with three children, which caused a major scandal in LA. I was there alone because I didn't feel the need to bring someone with me that night. To a certain degree, I felt free of all the things that had been troubling me for so long, namely her."

"That sounds terrible. It must have been so humiliating for you."

"It was. She was very drunk and paranoid, and I basically took her gently by the elbow and escorted her from the building. I told her to never come anywhere near me again. That was how we split for the second time."

"Poor you. She sounds like a nightmare. Freak of nature girl-friend was on the loose, then? Has she found someone since?"

"I'll get to that. She's like a freaking stalker, and I've even had injunctions placed against her. That is why I sometimes might not be myself. I have to treat her delicately to some extent, as she is crazy, Aly. I've been afraid of what she might do."

"I can understand that," I say.

He looks like he needs to smile; I might try lightening the mood.

"You know, you can always send her in my direction. I've some great shoes at home that are really fantastic for arse kicking—grand pointy toes on them."

It's worked; he's laughing and smiling. Phew, that could have gone either way!

"You'd be some match for her. If it were a battle of words, you'd win hands down. However, she's known to have pulled a few hair extensions off of unsuspecting girls—and over something very trivial. I can't condone that behaviour. I want to be with someone who's sensitive and can make me laugh. I want to be with a lady—in other words, you, Aly."

"Aw, Jack, that's so sweet. Are you telling me I'm your ideal woman, then?"

"In one word, yes."

"Well, to repay the compliment, likewise," I say.

"I'm your ideal woman? Thanks. I always thought I was quite manly."

"You know what I mean. I think we make a good team, Jack."

"Me too, Aly. Now, that's my tale of woe."

"And now what's the story? Because that was well over nine months ago, if I'm working this out correctly."

"Yes, but she's been pestering me for the past six or seven months. I keep telling her I'm not interested in her selfish ways and her bully tactics. I reached the point of no return around five weeks ago. I told her never to try any of her antics again, and I really don't care what happens to her. I didn't mean that I don't care, though; she pushed me to say it. I was very upset that night,

Aly. I really wanted to call you, but I couldn't bother you with that. What would you have thought of me back then? You were just getting to know me."

"You know, you should have. I could have maybe come to LA to see you."

"God, no!" he exclaims. "She would have flipped if she saw you in my company. You're too pretty, Aly. She'd make straight for you on a night out. Anyway, to cut a long story short, she called my agent last week."

"Why?" I ask.

"Because I've barred all her calls so she can't call me directly. She asked my agent to let me know that she won't be bothering me again because she's found a man, a real man."

"God love the poor bastard!"

"My sentiments exactly. I actually felt so relieved to know that. I felt free for the first time in two years. I can't say the entire relationship was bad, because the first two years were great. However, she's someone else's responsibility now, and I am so happy to be rid of her. I know that probably sounds heartless, but you've no idea what she's capable of."

"No, it doesn't sound heartless. I really feel for you. She wasn't your responsibility anyway, but I get that she obviously made you feel guilty at every opportunity she possibly could. It must be a massive relief for you."

"Yes, it is. That's what I wanted to talk to you about whenever I mentioned that I had something to tell you. However, I wasn't expecting that the next time I'd see you, I'd be free from her clutches. It feels great being able to tell you and not being afraid to bring you to LA now."

"Oh, so you want to bring me to LA?" I ask with a smile.

"Well, if it comes to the stage where we are apart too much and I can't get to you, then I'd have no problem flying you to LA to be with me—if you're free, of course. I would never expect you to rush there on my account. It's only if you want to."

"I'm sure I wouldn't turn the offer down. I like this connection we have, Jack." *I love it. Oh, I think I love you!*

We spend the day lounging around the house. It's very relaxing and just what I need. Being in Jack's company is invigorating, and as the time progresses, we are learning more about each other and our likes and dislikes. We have quite a lot in common, really, apart from him loving the song "Lady in Red."

In the late afternoon, I find his stash of vinyl records, which I'm blown away by. He has a massive collection of eighties and nineties singles and albums. Jack insists that I play some of them, even the cheesy ones; and as we consume more champagne, we end up dancing around his lounge in a very drunken state and performing what can only be classed as bad wedding dancing.

As darkness falls, Jack takes my hand and leads me out towards the swimming pool.

"Where are you taking me? You're not going to drown me, are you?" I snigger.

"No chance of that. There's something else I want to show you out here."

"Jack, you dirty lad. You don't have to take me out here to show me that. Besides, it's freezing!"

"Aly! You're the dirty one. I'm trying to be all chivalrous, and you're dropping your ladylike status. I've knocked two points off your status now. I'll be deducting more if you keep this up."

"OK, sir, I'll stop now. Look at you, trying to be all serious when you love it."

"I hold my hands up, Aly, and admit it, honey."

"Admit what?" I ask.

He opens a gate, which I hadn't noticed earlier, which is situated just beyond the swimming pool. It opens out onto the beach.

It's a cold night, but there's a clear sky, and the stars can be seen quite clearly.

"Jack, it's beautiful here. I never realised the house backed onto the beach."

"Glad you like it. Romantic, isn't it?" he says.

"Very!"

He pulls me closer and before he presses his lips against mine, he utters, "As I was saying, I hold my hands up and admit that I love you, Aly."

I could scream, I'm so damn excited! I really want to reply back that I love him too, but before I can get the words out, he's kissing me, and I'm so swept up in the kiss that I don't get the chance to tell him. When we stop, the moment has gone, and I can't say it now. It would seem like really crap timing on my part, like an afterthought. He doesn't seem to mind, though. *I'll tell you later, Jack.*

We walk along the beach for an hour or so, arms wrapped around each other; and when we return, we're both well and truly exhausted.

We head for bed, and although I didn't plan to give into temptation tonight, I just can't resist. I'm in love with Jack Morgan, and it seems as good a time as any to show him how I feel.

The following morning when I wake, Jack isn't in the bed; and I figure either he's not impressed with the night before and can't wait to get away from me, or he's just an early bird who can't stay in bed once he wakes. I prefer to think it's the latter. A waft of bacon and sausages is slowly reaching my nostrils. It reminds me of home and the ridiculous breakfast my mother used make us eat before we went out to school. No wonder I was more than pudgy as a child.

I can hear footsteps approaching, and I fix my hair to try and make myself look a bit more respectable. Jack pushes the door open.

"Hi," he says with a sexy glint in his eye.

"Hi," I reply with a broad smile.

"I made you breakfast."

"It smells totally delicious. Thank you."

"I had these flown over especially: Clonakilty black pudding, sausages and rashers."

"You're kidding me. OK, you can go now and leave the entire lot for me," I say as I erupt into laughter. "I can't believe you got them especially for our trip here. Thank you so much. I haven't had a taste of home in so long."

"I thought you'd enjoy them. I hope not as much as last night, though."

"Oh, the rashers and sausages win hands down, Jack, sorry." A smile creeps across my face. "Jack, I loved last night, and while I didn't tell you when we were on the beach as the moment had kind of passed, well, I love you, Jack."

"I love you too, Aly. Without wanting to sound stalker-like myself, I don't think I've ever felt this attached to someone so quickly, especially considering the distance between us."

"Isn't it funny how we met? We really were two of the most unlikely people to bond, a clumsy Irish woman and a handsome actor from LA. We do have the stalker tag in common though," I say.

"Well, clumsy and stalker-like as we are, it was meant to be," he replies with a grin. "I think I was the clumsy one, by the way. I pulled you to the ground."

"Jen keeps saying that we are meant to be. Not wanting to change the subject, but this breakfast is divine. You get brownie points for this, you know."

He laughs out loud. I continue to stuff my face. I seem to have a massive appetite this morning.

After breakfast, we get ready and head into town. It's so picturesque. There are people pointing and staring at us as we walk by, but no one has approached us yet, thankfully.

"I'm so glad I can get away from it all here. No one ever disturbs me," Jack utters in a very happy tone.

"I know, but they must be wondering who the woman with you is. 'Plain auld thing, isn't she?' I'll bet that's what they're saying," I say.

"Are you fishing for compliments, Aly?" he says. "You're not going to get any from me this time."

"Ah, you do know me well, don't you?" I say with a smile.

We carry on walking with our arms wrapped around each other. I know this is going to be a week I'll enjoy immensely and a week we both deserve so much.

As the days pass, I disclose Karen's drinking problem and Jen's eating disorder to Jack. He is very empathetic in relation to both and promises me if I need anything, he will be there to help. I feel like a weight has been lifted off my shoulders, as I know he is probably the best person to help with Karen, especially after he informed me that his ex-girlfriend had been in rehab a few times.

It's Friday evening when we return to Manhattan, and sadness takes over on our journey back. We reach my apartment, and as Jack removes my bags from the car, I have to ask, "So are you going to stay with me tonight, or are you heading back to the hotel?"

"What do you think? I'm spending every second I can with you, Aly. I don't fly out until tomorrow, and if it means following you around your apartment for every move you make, then I'll do it... unless you want me to stay at the hotel?"

"Sweet. Of course I want you to stay with me. Maybe I can cook something for you. You've not tasted my wonderful culinary delights yet."

"Sure, would love you to cook for me tonight. Do I get 'the show' afterwards?"

"Jack!"

"I'm sorry, I know I promised I wouldn't bring it up again," he says with a smirk.

"OK, just don't go blurting it out in front of others," I say, red-faced.

We settle down for a cosy night in my apartment, and we share even more stories about ourselves. When bedtime comes, I know my time with Jack is almost over, and I dread the thought of not having him around the next day.

Chapter 23

"Hi, sexy, how are ya?"

"Hello yourself. You OK? You seem a bit agitated lately. I hope it's not because you're still after Aly."

"Jesus, no; that bitch will suffer now. You offer help or just want to be friends, and she ignores you. No, definitely not her."

"Yeah, she's a bit too goody two-shoes for you, Jeremy. You're a bit of a bad boy and need a bad girl."

"Oh, is that right, Debs?"

Ugggghhhhhh, I can't believe what I'm hearing! This is not what I need on a Monday morning: Jeremy slobbering all over his slut. Hmmm, I'm going to eavesdrop just a little more, though. At least I've an idea as to what his problem is now.

"She's not that good a girl at all, Debs, but she's messing with the wrong man, that's for sure."

"Oh, Jeremy, I love it when you're angry like this. It's very manly. It really turns me on."

Enough! I want to puke!

I walk to my office and see Jeremy has spotted me. At that moment, he grabs Debs and starts to kiss her as he eyeballs me passing.

Sweetest Jesus, get over it, Jeremy!

Within five minutes, he's at my door. "I need your input on something."

"Good morning to you too, Jeremy!"

"My office, now!"

"OK! Jesus, Jeremy, what's wrong with you?"

"Just come into my office, Aly!"

I walk in, and he shows me some design layouts on his desk. "Which of these works for the Christmas project that's coming up?" he asks.

"Um, this one, in my opinion," I say as I glance at him.

As I do, I feel him grab my arse and push me onto the desk. "Jesus, Aly, I still want you so much. You're driving me crazy."

"Fuck! Jeremy, get off me, you fecking oaf! I'm not interested! How many times do we have to have this conversation?"

"Aly, come on. I know you want me, too. We're good together."

Enough! On instinct, I raise my knee, and he bends over in pain. "Don't you ever try that again, Jeremy, or I'll have you up in court!" I roar.

"No witnesses, you bitch," he shouts back as I run from his office.

He is right. It is only 7:30 a.m., and no one else from our floor has reached the office. Debs has returned to her desk on the floor beneath us. I feel ill for the rest of the day and decide to finish up early. I wander home, shaking, and en route call to see Jen.

What a horrendous start to my week. I am literally pining for Jack's company already. I reach Jen's apartment.

"Hey, lovey, how are you feeling today?" she says as she opens her arms wide to give me one of her bear hugs.

"I needed one of your hugs, Jen," I say. "I'm OK."

"We've all been worried about you. Hey, why are you home so early today? Are you OK? You're shaking, Aly."

"I know I sound really pathetic, but I miss Jack terribly. I'm like a teenager, the way I'm acting, but I really can't help myself. I'm just feeling a bit ill, so I left early." *I can't tell her what happened.*

"Well, I was going to call over anyway to see you as I'm having a wardrobe clear-out tonight, and as you know, I have masses of stuff, some of which I haven't even worn. At this stage, it's not likely that I'll wear any of them, so why don't you have a look and see if you want to take any of it off my hands? I called Karen earlier, and she's coming, too."

"Oh, I don't know, Jen. I'm exhausted and just want my bed."

"I was being polite, just asking, but I'm not taking no for an answer. I know you don't feel well, but you're probably just love-sick. Besides, I think tonight might be a good time for us to chat to Karen. What do you think?"

I let out a sigh. "OK, I'm in."

"We can have a chat about you and Jack, and I can get started on the food."

"OK, let's do it."

"So have you been sleeping? You look like crap," Jen says.

"Wow, that's a fine compliment, thanks. No, I haven't. I'm wondering, Jen, what if I'm getting in too deep with Jack? I mean, we've both used the 'L' word already! That's not me normally. Am I really over everything that's happened to me? I'm so scared that the same thing might happen with Jack, even though, to be fair, he seems a pretty honest and decent guy."

"Aly, listen, men don't throw the 'L' word around so easily. I believe Jack, and at least he's been honest enough to explain the situation with his ex. If he was hiding something and didn't tell you, I'd say you'd have something to be worried about then. But the guy is in the public eye, and if he wants this to work, he knows he has to be honest. From what I'm hearing, he's smitten with you, and why wouldn't he be? You're beautiful, intelligent and have the best sense of humour. Everyone really likes you."

"Thanks. Yeah, you're right about Jack. Am I overanalysing again?"

"Yes. That's something you're going to have to stop doing— and stop being paranoid. I know you've met cheating, lying bastards in the past, haven't we all? But they aren't all like that, Aly. Have you thought anymore about seeing a shrink?"

"No, not since I told you. Speaking of which, did you have your first appointment yet?" I ask.

"I've had two, believe it or not! I'm finding it weird, but I think it's helping a little bit. It's good to have someone who just listens constantly and asks the right questions. Each time I've left so far, I feel like I've left my troubles locked up in her office. Maybe you should give it a try."

"Maybe I will. I'll have a think about it, thanks. So has she managed to change your attitude about food already?"

"No, but that's going to be a long, slow process. I am picking more at food, though, and I've been thinking for the last two weeks that I might give them a call at my old job and see if they've filled it yet. Tommy thinks they want me back as they keep ringing, looking for things."

"That's great, Jen. So when did you come up with the idea of leaving, or has Tommy been putting pressure on you?"

"No, he's mentioned it, but I never really thought about it until I was in therapy yesterday. I started talking about how much I loved my old job and how I took this job on as I thought it would be a challenge. However, the bottom line is, I've been miserable since I started it. When I got back to Tommy's last night, I discussed it with him and asked what he thought. Needless to say, he was delighted that I'd even considered going back—if there's still a position there, that is."

"Ring them tomorrow, Jen. I think it could be the best decision you'll make in a long time."

"I will. I think I'm already sold on that idea. Now, more importantly, going back to Jack; did you hear from him?"

"Not really. He did call when he arrived back in LA. We were on Skype for three hours."

"Three hours? What were you talking about for that length of time?"

"We spoke about everything. Remember when I used to call you when I was in Ireland? We used to have those long conversations about everything. Well, it was just like that. Even though we spent a whole week together, we still had so much to talk about."

"Aly, that's great. It's a good start for you both. He's like your best friend. That doesn't happen to many people. It's exactly how it was for Tommy and me. We had so much to talk about; we still do."

"Well, if Jack and I end up like you and Tommy, I'll be very pleased."

"Didn't that tarot card reader you went to before you left Ireland predict you'd meet someone with his initials?"

"Hmm, I can't remember, to be honest. You've got a good memory, Jen."

"Don't you think it is strange, though, that most of what she said has happened?"

"You know, Jen, I didn't even think any more about what she said. I told you on the phone that night when I was in Cork, but I completely forgot about it after that. Thinking back now, most of what she predicted has happened. I have the piece of paper somewhere with all the information written down as she made a recording of it. I took note of the major stuff she told me. I must find it."

"Well, that will keep you going tomorrow, then. Let me know what it says."

"Oh, I will!" I shriek in a slightly overenthusiastic tone, which makes Jen laugh. I'm determined to find that A4 page that I wrote all the details on and will go over it with a fine-tooth comb, if necessary. From memory though, most of what the tarot reader told me has happened.

I hear Jen's doorbell ring.

"Ding-dong, ding-dong," Karen laughs down the intercom when I answer.

"Hey, slacker, come on up. Jen is making a massive feed for us."

"Great, I'm starving."

Karen arrives at the front door ten minutes later. I've no idea why it took her so long to reach the apartment. "Hey, girl, how are you?" I ask with open arms.

"Great, honey, and you? Are you feeling a bit better?"

"Yeah, I've had Jen cheering me up, so it's all good. However, I was waiting for you to arrive to add the final touches to the cheering-up session. You've arrived in one piece, I'm glad to see."

"Indeed, and I'm raring to go. Champagne, ladies?"

"Give us a hug first," Jen pipes up.

"I'll get the champagne flutes from the kitchen," Karen adds after Jen gives her the customary hug.

"You haven't brought too much I hope, have you, Karen? I ask."

"Well, it's probably too much to you, but to me it's normal for a group of three people. Six bottles—not too much, not too little. I've left them just outside the door. I thought I'd say hello first."

Jen and I glance at each other. I understand why it took her so long to get upstairs now.

"How did you manage to carry them?" Jen asks.

"Don't know, to be honest," she says cheerfully. "Full of adrenaline, I am. Had a great workout earlier; buzzing since then."

"OK, well, how about you sit down there and rest up after carrying that amount of alcohol all the way up here, and I'll take these to the kitchen and get the flutes," I say.

"That sounds good, Aly. Thanks. I could do with a nice crisp glass of champers now."

I walk to the kitchen briskly with the box of champagne. Jen walks ahead of me to hold the door.

"How the hell did she carry these up the stairs herself?" I ask Jen.

"No idea. I'd say she locked onto some hot guy and asked for his help. They're really heavy."

"I could barely lift them from the door to the kitchen. Should we hide some of them? We can't let her get off her face tonight. We need to talk to her, seriously."

"Yeah, I'll leave two out and hide the other four. Put them in the cupboard over there. Thanks, Aly."

I return to the lounge with two glasses and leave one for Jen to sip on in the kitchen.

"Ah, thanks, Aly. This is lovely," Karen says as she takes a large sip from the glass.

"Nice. Thank you, Karen. How can you afford to buy this so regularly?"

"I get it at a cheap price. I mean, I'm on a great salary, but I couldn't be buying it so often if it wasn't for the discount. So what's been happening? Has Jack called?"

"He called last week when he got back, but I haven't really heard from him since. The odd text message here and there each day but no calls. We were just talking about that before you arrived, actually."

"I wouldn't worry. He's probably busy, Aly. Besides, remember that he's only got eyes for you."

"I hope so! We were talking about a time I went to a tarot reader in Cork before I arrived here and how most of what she told me has actually happened. I can't remember if I told you."

"Think you did, but you know me; I don't believe in all of that."

"Yes, but I have everything she told me written on an A-four page in my apartment. I think I know where I put it, so I'll have to dig it out."

"Hmmm, I'm intrigued. Well, if there is something on there that has happened, I might not be so sceptical anymore."

"Girls, dinner's almost ready. We can go through the clothes later and maybe watch a DVD. What do you think?" Jen shouts from the kitchen.

"That's fine, as long as we can keep drinking, too!" Karen has to have the last word.

We sit and chat about our week and eat Jen's wonderful home cooking. As the meal progresses and both champagne bottles empty, Karen scurries to the kitchen in search of more. "Where's the champagne, girls?"

I glance at Jen. "Is now the time to broach the subject?"

"I think so. Karen, can you come here a minute please?"

Karen ventures as far as the door of the kitchen. "Yep, what's up?"

"Here, take a seat, love. We need to talk to you," Jen says in a concerned tone.

"Don't like the sound of this," says Karen. "Is there something wrong?"

"Look, we're both extremely worried about you. You've been drinking ridiculous amounts of alcohol for well over a year now."

"Ah, sorry, but who's counting what I'm drinking?" she asks.

"Well, we both are, now," I say.

"What's the problem? I'm having a fun time. It's not interfering with anyone, and besides, I don't drink that much."

"Karen, you have a problem. Whether you want to admit it or not, you do."

"I do not!" she exclaims. "I go out, have a few drinks, and go home. Admittedly, with a man from time to time, but that doesn't mean I have a problem."

"Since I moved to New York, Karen, you've spent most of your time out on the party circuit. When I hear from you or see you after a night out, you're hung over. You've told me recently that after partying, you continue to drink at home alone. It's not healthy, and we can't continue to let you harm yourself like this."

Jen slips into the kitchen. I can't believe she's bottled out and is leaving me to deal with this alone. Karen goes off on a tirade of expletives while I stare at the glass kitchen door. I can see Jen is on the phone to someone. I can't be sure, but I assume she's calling Tommy to see if he can come over. When she returns from the kitchen, Karen is banging her empty glass on the table, and I'm quite scared of her.

"Why the fuck can't I have another drink? I bought it, after all! Is that what you two are doing, stashing the drink so you can have it when I'm gone? Some friends you are!"

"Karen, please calm down. We're only trying to help you."

"Calm down? I'll fucking calm down when I can get a drink—the drink that I brought with me!"

"OK, look, we'll give you a drink. Jen, can you show me where you put the drink in the kitchen, please?"

Jen returns to the kitchen, and I follow.

"I wasn't expecting her to get so agitated with us," whispers Jen.

"Tell me about it," I say. "Sure, I expected her to throw a few expletives into every sentence, but nothing like this."

"Tommy is on his way over. We'll see if he can talk some sense into her."

"I don't want to sound like a broken record, but I wish Jack was here, too. He was telling me he could give me some information on good rehab clinics as his ex was there a few times. If there was someone here who had knowledge of them, she might be more willing to accept it and give it a go."

"To be honest, neither of us knows much about alcoholism, Aly, but what I do know is that she seems to be showing some traits of it. Hang on, Tommy's outside. He's just texted. He has a key, so there won't be any surprise bursts for the door from Karen."

"What are you two whispering about in there? Where's my champagne? This lovely dinner you cooked is getting cold. I was enjoying it until you both jumped on me."

I grab the new bottle and open it quickly. I don't know what else to do. I fill her glass but place the bottle back in the kitchen.

I certainly don't want any more, especially after seeing Karen's reaction.

Tommy enters the apartment in his usual manner, always smiling and looking contented with life.

"Ladies, how are we all doing tonight? Looks like you're enjoying yourselves."

"Hi, Tommy, you're such a lovely man. Pull up a seat as it will be nice to talk to someone who's not going to jump down my throat over every sip of champagne I take," Karen says.

"Hi, Karen. Lovely to see you." He bends down and kisses her cheek and then mine. "Aly, how are you doing? Heard you had a tough week."

"Tough?" exclaims Karen. "She doesn't know the meaning of the word! Aly flew in from Cork ten months ago, and her life has been plain sailing, with everything falling into place as usual. She has a lovely man who's not only famous, but absolutely adores her, and if he doesn't call in a week, she gets depressed. She has a great job where the people are friendly, and she has made plenty of new friends in this big, lonely city. Aly is fine!"

Tears are forming in my eyes. I can't look at anyone, particularly Karen. I have never seen her behave like this before. Jen holds my arm, and I can see she, too, is upset. Tommy pulls a chair up next to Karen.

"Karen, honey, this isn't about Aly. It's about you. The girls aren't ganging up on you tonight, nor am I, but it's obvious you need help. While you seem to think it's normal to go around partying and drinking as much as you do, it's not. You're doing serious harm to your body, and we'd just like you to get help and get yourself sorted out."

"Oh, and I have Dr Phil sitting next to me now. How do you know so much about me? Are you and Jen having little chit-chats about me over dinner?"

"Karen, come on, please. We're all here to help. Please don't be like that with us. We're your friends, and we are all worried about you. We can't make you go to a rehab clinic. We want you to make the decision yourself, but if it comes to it, then someone will have to take a stand, as we can't carry on seeing you like this," Tommy states.

"Haven't you got enough to deal with, like your super-scrawny girlfriend there? How about getting her better before you start thinking about me?" Karen snaps.

That is the last straw for all of us. Jen is in tears.

"She doesn't mean it, Jen," I say, trying to convince her.

Tommy backs away and takes Jen into the kitchen.

"Well, look at that. Aren't I the right bitch in all of this now? Jen is crying because Karen said something nasty. Boohoo. It's about time you all grow up and realise that I can live my life the way I want to. I've had enough of this. Thanks for the dinner, Jen, but I'm out of here."

"Karen, no one is thinking like that. Come on, sit back down, please?" I beg.

She approaches me, wagging her finger into my face. "Aly, above all, I'm most surprised at you. You were always fun; what the hell happened to you?"

"I still am, Karen, but I guess I've just grown up a bit faster than you."

She looks at me, and I see tears forming in her eyes. I don't want to make her cry, but maybe the tears are a sign we're getting through to her.

"Don't bother calling me again, Aly. Goodbye."

Karen leaves, but not before slamming every door as she exits.

I sit on the chair and stare into space. I can feel my phone vibrate in my pocket. I glance at the screen, and Jack's name is flashing up.

Oh, Jack, you have some timing. I'm near to crying, and I can't talk to him when I'm like this.

Jen and Tommy return from the kitchen. "Honey, you OK?" Tommy asks.

"Not really. Have we made a mistake, guys?" I ask.

"No, Aly, we haven't," says Jen. "For too long Karen has been behaving like this, and she needs someone to put her in her place. What she said to all of us tonight was wrong."

"Yeah, maybe, Jen, but she's walked out now and just told me never to call her again. I can't live like that. We've all known each other since we were knee-high. Our friendship can't end like this."

"Don't worry, girls," says Tommy. "She'll come around eventually. She'd be too lonely without you both. We'll persuade her somehow, but in the meantime, give her some distance. Give her time to digest what we've all said to her tonight, OK?"

"You think, Tommy?"

"Yep, she needs space after that. Think about it; if someone blurted all that at you right now, you wouldn't be feeling pleased with them, would you? You'd probably want a lot of space. She might not realise it now, but being on her own for a while might do her good."

"Or bad! I'm afraid; what if she does something stupid now?" I exclaim.

"She's crazy, but not that crazy, Aly. She won't do anything stupid," Jen states.

I sit back and stare at the table. I hope I haven't just watched one of my best friends walk out of my life for good.

As our wardrobe-clearance night has been cut short, I decide to head home.

"Want us to walk over with you?" Jen asks.

"No, chick, thanks. I just need to soak up some fresh air now and stroll home. Besides, I'm only up the street."

"OK. You never got to check out the wardrobe. Call around tomorrow, and we'll do it then. I need to get the place cleared for my new tenants next week."

"Thanks, Jen; will do. Right now I'm just thinking of my bed, and hopefully we'll all get a bit of sleep tonight."

I kiss them both on the cheek and give Jen a big hug.

"See you tomorrow."

"Yep. She'll come around, Aly, you'll see. I did," Jen says.

"Yeah, true, but you didn't fly off the handle like she did, and it was a different issue."

"Yes, but we all have to swallow our pride every now and then. You get some sleep."

I stroll down the steps of Jen's building, feeling so sad over what has just happened in her apartment. I take a few breaths of crisp, cold air and start walking home. The stars are shining, and it's such a beautiful night. I veer a little off course as I want to enjoy the fresh air for a while longer, and so I saunter up Perry Street. I reach the top of the street and turn the corner onto Hudson Street. It feels so romantic; the old street lights almost make me feel like I've stepped back in time. I can see the lights are on in the Sweet Corner Bake Shop still, and I take a chance to see if any of their delicious sea-salt-and-chocolate-chip cookies are left. I wonder, if I call over to Karen's with some, will she forgive me? The likelihood is that she's propping up a bar somewhere. As I enter the bakery, I spy a cupcake sitting behind the counter.

"Hi, is that plain chocolate?"

"Oh, that's chocolate fudge cake. It's delicious. You want to buy it?"

"Yes, please." It doesn't take long for me to change my mind when I spot four of their amazing sea-salt-and-chocolate-chip cookies behind the counter. "Actually, I'll have those four cookies to go, please." I dare not tell her they are just for me.

I exit the shop, and the smell of the cookies is driving me crazy. I feel like opening the box and devouring them en route, but I don't want to look like a savage in public.

I lay the box on my kitchen table and remove one cookie. I eat it like someone who has never tasted cookies before and proceed to eat a second one. I'm sitting in the kitchen, stuffing my face, and analysing the evening's events and the situation we have now found ourselves in. However, I can't class Karen as a situation. She is one of my best friends, and it tears me apart to see her like that. After a while, I realise there are only so many cookies I can eat, and they aren't going to take away the upset caused after our argument. Instead, I take my phone from my pocket and listen to the message Jack left.

"Hi, sweetheart, it's Jack. I'm sorry I didn't get to call you all week except for the odd text. It's been pretty hectic as filming for that pilot started, and I've been working pretty long hours. It's seven thirty here now. Give me a call if you aren't out with the girls and get back early enough. Thanks. Love you."

My heart is racing, and it's so nice to hear Jack's voice after all that has happened this evening. I return his call immediately.

"Hey, it's me," I say.

"Hi, Aly. Sorry, I probably sound sleepy. How are you, sweetheart? I take it you didn't go out, then?"

"No, it's been a bit of an exhausting day and evening, to be honest. I'm quite drained, but then I got your message and that put a smile back on my face. Sorry I'm wittering on. How are you, love?"

"Yeah, I'm good," he says. "Had an exhausting week, too. So much so that each night when I got home, it was too late to call you, and it was too hectic during the day while we were filming."

"I know; don't worry about that," I say. "Sorry for waking you up."

"No really, I'm delighted to hear from you. So what happened this evening?"

"Well, you mean apart from me stuffing myself with three huge cookies?"

"Wow, must be pretty bad if you did that. I know you hate overindulging."

"Yep, well, we spoke to Karen tonight about her drinking. She went ballistic and started insulting all of us, including Tommy, who thought he might get through to her as she doesn't know him all that well yet."

"Oh, dear. Well, that's a pretty normal reaction, Aly. She probably felt that you were ganging up on her. Was she drunk at the time, or is that a stupid question?"

"Merry. We had to give her some drink, though; she brought six bottles of champagne with her. If we didn't give her any, she would have walked out the door before we even sat down to eat."

"True. Still, it's better to say these things to her when she's sober. From the sound of it, that's a rare occasion, though."

"Exactly; these days, it is a rarity. Anyway, look, I don't want to take up all of our time talking about what happened with Karen. The bottom line is that she stormed out and told me never to call her again, which is the part that's upsetting me most."

"I wish I was there with you. Look, Aly, she's going to wake up tomorrow and hopefully not be too hung over to actually remember some of what you said. If it sinks in, she might be back sooner than you think."

"I hope so, Jack; I really do."

I can tell he's sleepy, so I dare not mention what happened with Jeremy. We finish our conversation, as it's late, and I hang up. I feel a bit more relieved after talking to him, but I still feel a bit empty after what happened with Karen. I glance over to the last cookie sitting on the table, and not an ounce of guilt sweeps over me as I shove the entire thing into my mouth. Not one of my better ideas.

My greed almost causes me to choke on the crumbs as I cough and splutter. However, after removing some of the contents, I manage to chew what's left without any problems, and savour every bit of it. I feel sleepy, but there's one thing that's niggling at me since Jen brought it up tonight. I have to find that A4 sheet of paper and see what the tarot card reader predicted.

I search high and low in the bedroom for the sheet of paper. *Where the hell did I put it?* I open my handbag and remove my wallet. I'm going through each scrap of paper, and I finally see the A4 sheet with luminous green writing on the outside. "Do Not Throw Out" is scrawled in capital letters across the folded sheet.

Slowly I unfold it and study the first few lines, but I can feel my eyes closing. *Hmm, this will have to wait until tomorrow.*

Chapter 24

$\mathcal{T}$he next day, I'm up early to view three apartments. The first one I see is on Hudson Street. Jen comes with me.

"Jesus, this smells rank. Is there something dead in here?" I ask the estate agent.

"Ma'am, I assure you, we don't show apartments that have anything dead inside."

"OK, at least not that you know of…" I say with a smile. Jen giggles. "I think I'll let this one go," I say. "Thanks for showing it to me. What's up next, please?"

"I've two more, one on Perry Street and another nearer to the Flat Iron building."

"Oh, the Flat Iron one sounds interesting. However, let's go see Perry Street. Ideally, I'd like to stay around this area if possible."

"Sure, no problem."

We walk onto Perry Street. As I walk up the steps, I get a gut instinct that I'll really like the apartment, and I'm not wrong.

"Now, this is what I'm talking about. I like!"

"It is lovely, Aly—very you," Jen says with an air of excitement.

"OK, well, here you've got the bedroom, walk-in wardrobe, and en-suite bathroom. It's quite a large apartment for a one-bedroom in this area. This is the living area with separate kitchen. You've also got storage in the hallway."

"It's perfect!"

"Maybe you should see the Flat Iron one first?" Jens asks.

"No, no, no…Gut instinct says this is the one," I shriek with excitement.

"OK, shall we start drawing up the paperwork?" the estate agent asks.

"Yes," I say with a very wide smile.

As I walk home, Jen walks with me as it's wardrobe-clearance day.

"I'll be over shortly. I need to collect something here before I do," I say to Jen.

"OK, just call over when you're ready. See you later," she says with a smile.

"Thanks, Jen, for everything. I'll see you in a while."

As I enter my apartment, Jack calls. "Hey, sweetie, how are you?"

"Hey, lover boy, delighted to hear from you again today," I say.

"You sound happy! Everything sorted out with Karen, I take it?"

"No, no noise from her. I got my new apartment sorted today, though, which has cheered me up."

"Aw, that's great news. So have you taken time off for packing your stuff away this week?"

"Oh, Christ on a bike! I forgot about that."

Suddenly, thoughts of Jeremy come into my head, and I feel ill. So much happened this weekend, I managed to put him to the back of my mind.

"Aly, are you there?"

"Sorry, yeah, I am. I just forgot that I need time off to pack and move. I'm not sure they'll be so kind as to give it to me."

"What? Your boss has given you time off before. I'm sure he will. He seems an OK guy."

"I'm not so sure, Jack…I'm not so sure."

"Listen, I know you're busy today as you're going to Jen's, right? I might call again later tonight, as I don't want to interrupt your day too much, sweetheart."

"OK, thanks for calling, Jack. Speak later. Love you."

"I love you too, sweetie."

I race up the steps, grab the piece of paper from the bed, and make my way over to Jen's.

I ring the bell of Jen's apartment and wait.

"Is that you, Aly? Come on up!" she calls out.

"Yep, it's me."

I race up the stairs as fast as I can. I'm dying to read what's written on the paper but want Jen to read it out to me as it's too exciting.

"You OK, Jen?"

"Yep, just a bit tired. The apartment hunt took my mind off the Karen situation this morning, but I had a bit of a sleepless night. Everything going through my head about us losing Karen as a friend; it just really upset me."

"I know. It upset me too, but I had a chat with Jack last night, and it gave me a little hope that something might have struck a chord with her."

"Jack? Did you ring him or did he ring you?"

"He actually rang while I was here, but I couldn't talk to him at the time as Karen had just left, and I was in a daze as to what had just gone on. I let it ring out. I called him when I got home, but it was after I savaged three of those delicious sea-salt-and-chocolate-chip cookies from the bakery."

"Aly, you didn't, did you? You make me laugh, girl. Were you ill afterwards? They are pretty large."

"I felt very full but proceeded to eat a fourth after I got off the phone from Jack. I feel very guilty today."

"Self-inflicted; however, they are delicious! So what's the story with the lovely Jack?"

"Well, he's been working hard on the pilot of the new series all week, so he didn't get a great deal of spare time. In the evenings he thought it too late to ring because of the three-hour difference. I believe him. I'm not going to be paranoid this time. I don't think he'd have stayed on the phone to me for so long if he wasn't interested, as I woke him up when I called."

"Aw, bless him," says Jen. "He's so sweet."

"And the best thing of all, when I was heading to bed, I found my A4 sheet of paper with all the predictions," I say as I wave it in the air.

"Oh, I think we'll need some brekkie and a coffee to wash this down," Jen says.

We sit ourselves comfortably on the high stools in the kitchen, and Jen pours me a cup of strong coffee. It's just what I need.

"I've got Clonakilty sausages and rashers from home. You want some?" she asks.

"Let's wait a while. I'm not that hungry, especially after what I ate lastnight. Those sausages and rashers are to be savoured girl, we can tuck into them later. Here, I want you to read this."

Jen takes the paper and unfolds it gently, as if something is going to pop out and scare her.

"Hmmm, this is very interesting. Oh my God, Aly!" she exclaims.

"Jen, I want you to read it out loud, not to yourself! I haven't read it yet as I thought it would be more fun to share it with you."

"OK, get ready for this!" she says excitedly. "I see you moving overseas. It's because of a man. By that, I mean you want to escape from a man." Jen looks at me with huge eyes.

"I guess that means escaping Simon?"

"The country you go to won't be in Europe; it could be the United States."

"Yep, I remember her saying that," I interject. "I hadn't a clue what she was ranting about when she said that about me escaping a man, and I didn't think anything of it at the time. Thought it was a holiday she was referring to or something."

"When you go to this country, you will come in contact with two men in the first few weeks. One will bounce in and out of your life very briefly in the first month. You will be very attracted to him. The other man will feature more prominently. You may have an affair with him, but a word of warning: he has similar characteristics to the man you are escaping." Jen pauses and looks up. "Oh, my God! So Jack must have been the man who bounced in and out for the first month and then Jeremy the other. Wow, Aly, this woman is amazing! You completely forgot about all of this, didn't you?"

"Of course I did. It was so long ago, and it was literally four days before I walked in on Simon and that trollop. I've pushed most of what happened in those weeks to the back of my mind. It's a bit weird how accurate she was, though."

"Yep, but wait—this is the best and funniest part!"

"Oh no, what is it?" I exclaim.

"I see some connection with this man who keeps bouncing in and out of your life. It's something to do with beetroot," Jen says as she bursts into laughter.

"Liar! That's not in there, is it? No, that would be too freaky!"

"No, it isn't, but it did get a smile out of you. That *would* be a little too freaky, Aly. It's very interesting as she goes on to say that your fling with, we'll say Jeremy, will come to an abrupt end, and you will feel hurt again. Then she mentions that the man who comes in and out of your life is your soulmate. You will keep meeting him until you finally come together and accept that you were meant to be together. Aly, this is so accurate. 'A close friend will fight a battle with some form of substance abuse.'"

"Wow! I wonder if Karen would have believed it if we read it to her?" I muse. "She's so sceptical about these things, she'd probably think I went home and wrote it out myself last night. But, girl, that's enough to put a smile on anyone's face. Well, bar poor Karen's, that is."

"True," says Jen. "Think she'll come back to us?"

"I don't know. We can only hope; but as Tommy suggested, I'm going to stay clear for a while now, as I really don't want to push her too far, either. I might end up pushing her away from us rather than bringing her closer."

"Yeah, I know what you mean. Let's hope she does come back. I'm excited for you after reading that, Aly. Come on, let's go through that wardrobe of mine and see if there's anything there you like."

"I'm there before you, girl. I love a good shop, and if it's a free one, even better!"

We walk through the glass doors that open into Jen's bedroom.

"Jen, please don't tell me you're getting rid of those Jimmy Choos?" I say.

"Too small. They were a gift. Gorgeous, aren't they? I should have got rid of them a long time ago, but they were so pretty, I had to keep them and just look at them every now and then. What size are you?"

"UK six. What's that, a US eight?"

"Yep. Fine, they're yours. Enjoy, and yes, I'm jealous that you can wear them and I never got to, but I'd prefer you to get a good wear out of them. I can still admire them at least," Jen says with a smile. "So when's Jack coming to visit again?"

"Not sure. I don't want to put pressure on him now, as I know he's filming. I do hope I'll see him soon, though. Would it be a bit premature of me to ask him to come to Ireland with me for Christmas?"

"I don't know. Nice idea, and it would be lovely for you to spend Christmas together. It would be a big change from last year when you were with Simon!"

"How true that is. Little did I know that I'd be living in New York and dating an actor—a sexy beast of an actor, at that."

"You deserve it, Aly. Just enjoy every moment, girl. Here, what do you think of this dress? Never wore it as they more or less gave me a wardrobe full of stuff that month. It's a beautiful dress though."

"Don't think that would fit me."

"Try it. You never know until you try. Here, try these too." Jen hands me the skinniest pair of skinny jeans I've ever seen. I know they won't fit me, but I'll try them anyway, and she can have a laugh.

First up are the skinny jeans. I manage to get them over my thighs, but they are overstretched across the tummy. I walk over to Jen holding my breath so the button won't pop and wear my new Jimmy Choos.

"What ya think, love?"

Jen bursts into hysterical laughter. I can't resist laughing either. Once I do, the button pops and my belly is hanging out and not looking very attractive. It took me five minutes to get them on but twenty-five to get them back off over my thighs.

"Did these actually fit you once?" I ask.

"Yeah, but only barely," she says. "They were even a little tight on me—probably too big now, though."

Oh, what do I say to that? Ignore it?

"OK, I'll try that dress and give you another giggle," I say.

I rush to get it on, and strangely enough, the dress fits beautifully.

"Gorgeous," exclaims Jen. "This would be perfect for your next date with Jack. Wear your hair up and some nice jewellery with those shoes. You'll be simply stunning. I really didn't want to have to give this stuff away to just anyone, especially when they haven't even been worn."

"Well, I'm happy to take them off your hands, hon. Thank you."

Jen rummages through the wardrobes and pulls out numerous tops, trousers, skirts, dresses, and even some new gym clothes. I try everything on, and I'm delighted to see most of the items fit nicely. It's also given me an indication of how much weight she has lost. The day flies by. Jen has a date night later with Tommy, and I am happy to return to my abode and sit and watch a few DVDs for the night.

I wake on Monday morning to a worrying thought. *How do I approach Jeremy?* I make my way to the office, take a deep breath, and decide to get it over with.

"Jeremy, sorry to interrupt. I'm in a state of panic."

"Aw, poor Als. What's wrong with the little girl?"

I give him a dirty look. "I'm moving to my new apartment on Saturday. You know, because they are renovating my building now."

"So?"

"I have five days to pack up, and I haven't even started! Can I take Thursday and Friday off, please, and Monday and Tuesday?"

"Hang on, I thought you might want a couple of days at the end of the week, but next week too?"

"Yeah, I did, but then as an afterthought, I said I'd ask for Monday and Tuesday, too, just so I can relax and get organised a little."

"What if I say no, Aly?"

"I just won't be very productive at work, I guess," I say with a grin.

He smirks.

Give in, you prick; you know what you did last week was wrong!

He sighs. "OK, you can have the days," he says.

"Right, I'll get back to work then. Thanks." I'm glad that's over. I feel ill looking at him now. Creep.

When I get home later that evening, I start working in a lively fashion and fill some of the empty boxes which were being dumped from the office. I am pleasantly surprised by the amount of stuff I've managed to squeeze into the boxes. The lounge is practically packed up, bar the TV and the lamps, which I need until I actually move. I've decided that I'll do a little bit each day, and by Friday, I'll be well and truly ready for my new abode.

Chapter 25

Thursday morning I have a lie-in, and it's one of the biggest thrills I've experienced in ages. I have a tough job ahead of me, moving box after box from my street, to the next street over, so I take my time getting up and then finish what remains of the packing.

It's early morning when the outside doorbell rings. I peek through the blinds of the lounge window and see a very pleasant surprise awaiting me. Jack is standing at the door, looking very casual, wearing old baggy jeans and work boots.

I squeal like a child when I see him. I rush to the door to let him in. "What are you doing here?" I ask with a big grin across my face.

"Well, that's a nice welcome," he says. "No, 'Oh, Jack, my hero, coming all the way from LA to help me move.'"

I look at him with my mouth open. "Are you serious? You've come all the way here to help me move this weekend?"

"Sure! You're the lady in my life, aren't you? I'm not going to have you carting boxes up and down stairs for the entire weekend by yourself. You'd be dead by the end of it, and there's no way I'd want that to happen. I came down late yesterday evening. I wanted to surprise you this morning, so I called you from the hotel last night."

"Jack, you're the best! I can't believe you've done this! Thank you, thank you, thank you!" I throw my arms around him and hug him tightly. "By the way, you look hot in those work boots. A dark-blue overall is all you need, and I'd be drooling."

"Yeah, and if I stoop low enough, I've got a fine builder's crack sticking out in these jeans. Wanna see?"

I push him playfully. "I'll skip on that, thanks."

We relax for an hour and have a catch up before we start packing everything else away.

"No news from Karen, I take it?" he asks.

"Nothing. I'm really tempted to call her or turn up at her apartment. I've been so busy with packing all week, though, that I haven't actually had a proper chance to consider the idea. It's probably for the best."

"She'll come around in her own time. I brought a list of brochures with me, by the way. Rehab ones. Thought you might like to have a look at them at least and see if it's something she might go for when she does give in."

"Thanks for those," I say. "I'll glance through them with Jen one day when this move is over. You seem pretty sure Karen will give in."

"She will; they always do in the end. My ex was in rehab three times. Drugs the first time, drink the other two times. Sometimes I think she just needed a time out and wanted to go there for a break from it all, which isn't a bad thing either, I guess. She'd always disappear for a few days or weeks before she'd come crawling back asking for my help. It's sad to see people you love in such a state, Aly, so I know exactly what you're all feeling right now. For now we're going to make this whole packing and unpacking business as pleasant as we can, and I'm here to help take your mind off Karen and help you relax."

"Oh, and how do you plan on doing that, hmmm?" I ask.

"I'm not so sure yet, but let's start with a little kiss here."

Jack nibbles my neck, and I give in immediately. I am bloody crazy about him, and there is no denying it. The feeling I get when

I'm around him is nothing like what I felt with previous boyfriends. Jack is different in every way.

It's early afternoon before we start working, and he's shocked to see how much packing I've managed to complete already in the week. There isn't too much left to pack, and so after filling another few boxes, we take a break and go for something to eat. On our return, we call to Jen's apartment to say hi and see how organised she is.

"Jennifer, it's your best friend and her lovely man from LA," I announce.

"Oh, come up, come up," she squeals into the intercom, nearly deafening us.

I know she wants to meet Jack properly, as the last time she saw him was the night she first met Tommy.

"Aly! Jack! I'm delighted you called in. Jack, I didn't know you were coming down this weekend. How are you? Aly, how are you, hon? All packed? Sorry, too many questions, super excited!"

I can tell she's excited both because Jack is here and because of her big move. I'm excited myself as she will finally have a proper chat with him, and he'll finally meet Tommy also.

"Hey, Aly!" Tommy comes towards me and hugs me.

"Tommy, this is Jack. Jen, you've met briefly a couple of times before."

After pleasantries are exchanged, we all sit down and have a chat and a cup of tea. I'm delighted my friends finally have the opportunity to get to know my man. I can finally say that: *my* man!

Jen looks highly organised as all her boxes are labelled and ready to move.

We spend an hour chatting to them, but I know she's under pressure, so Jack and I leave them to get on with it. As we stroll back to my apartment, we take a short detour. It's been a while since Jack took a walk in his old neighbourhood.

"I loved that café. Ever go there?" he asks.

"No; what's so special about it?" I ask.

"Early morning pancakes. Out of this world; and seeing as I'm on vacation, sort of, for a few days, I suggest we go there tomorrow morning. You'll see what I'm talking about."

"I'm not going to say no. You know me for cakes, pastries, and anything that's bad for me."

"Isn't that your favourite bakery there? Want to buy another four of your favourite cookies for yourself tonight?"

I snigger. "That was a one-off. We could buy one, and I'll give you a piece of it! At least that way you can't accuse me of eating the whole thing."

"I'd hate to deprive you of it, Aly. How about I buy you two, and then at least you'd get one whole one for yourself plus another three-quarters on top of it?"

"Hilarious, Jack. I do fancy one now, though, from all this chat about them."

"OK, then, let's get you one later. Not wanting to change subjects, but I was wondering if you're planning on going home for Christmas this year or hanging out in New York. I know it's a while away yet, but I just thought I'd ask early enough to see what you're doing."

"Yeah; I won't have seen my family in ten months. I'm dying to see them. Why? Did you want to come with me or something?"

"Wow! I wasn't expecting that, but that would be really nice—if you'd like me to come, that is. I feel honoured you'd want to introduce me to your family. It would be nice to spend Christmas and New Year together too. I'm sure it will be great 'craic,' as you say."

"It will be great craic, and I promise you, you'll not want to leave."

"Maybe," he says. "You know how much I do love Ireland. Check it out at home first, as I don't want to impose or anything."

"Jack, they'll be thrilled at the thought of me bringing some-one home. I know my family. I will ask them, though, for the sake of being polite."

"Great. That was sweet of you to offer; thank you."

"Well, Morgan, if I didn't, we'd both be wondering what the other was doing over Christmas as I know you're far too nice and gentlemanly in your ways to invite yourself."

"Maybe you're right. Come on, let's go back and relax for the night."

"I won't argue with that idea."

We head back to my apartment and light the few candles that are left lying around. It looks bare and gloomy, but I know that I can always come back one day if I want to. I feel a little sad at the thought of leaving it as so much has happened while I've lived here. At least I'll have the memory of my first kiss with Jack on the steps while he sang that song to me. I can't deny it, though; it was definitely romantic, and that will be one memory that will stick with me forever.

Chapter 26

It's Monday morning, and Jack is having a lie-in, so I decide to get to work on putting my own stamp on the apartment. I need to display some of my photos and change some of the furniture around, just to make it feel like it's mine now. After adding the final touches to my new abode, I'm feeling exhausted, and I literally collapse into my bed.

"How would you feel about trying my attempt at cooking tonight?" Jack asks.

"Oh, Jack, that sounds fantastic. Thank you." *What a keeper you are, Jack Morgan.* I lie there and can feel my eyes closing. When I wake, it's to a wonderful smell.

"Pasta carbonara OK for you?" he asks with a smile.

"Oh yum, delicious!" I say with enthusiasm. As he plates it up in front of me, I tuck into it with great gusto. *Yep, you definitely are a keeper, Jack.*

On Tuesday morning, I decide to treat myself. I've opted to go shopping and throw in a new hairdo en route. I head uptown, and the atmosphere is electric. I can't help but get caught up in the buzz that is filling the air. As I walk past Buddakan, I hear roars of laughter coming from inside; it sounds like a lunchtime party taking place. I think of Karen. I reach for my phone and key in her number. However, I never press the ring button, and I quickly place the phone back in my pocket.

I head for the hair salon. I need a bit of an overhaul, so I give the stylist a direct order not to cut my hair too short. I've never had it short before, and I'm not going to now. That is, I haven't had it cut short since I was nine years old, when the stylist made me look like a boy, and I prayed each night that my hair would grow at least five inches by morning.

The finished product is surprisingly nice as my hair is cut up to above my shoulders. It looks very stylish, and it suits me, thankfully! She'd be in trouble otherwise.

I carry on about my business, and when I return home, there are two missed calls on the phone. Both are Karen.

"Jen, Jen, it's me, Karen."

It sounds like she's slurring. When she bursts into tears on the message, I know she's drunk.

"I don't know what's wrong with me. I can't stop; I just can't stop. I need your help, yours and Aly's. I'm sorry for being such a terrible person."

The message finishes.

I can feel the tears building up. She had clearly not realised that it was my number she called. She sounds in a terrible state, and I'm worried in case she'll do something stupid. I decide to listen to the second message.

"Jen, it's me again. Why won't you answer? I suppose I don't blame you. I'm a shitty friend with a shitty problem and a shitty life. You and Aly both hate me now, and I can only blame myself. I'm a horrible person. Please forgive me?"

That's the last straw; the tears are flowing, and I just have to call around to see her. I ring Jen, as I know she'll be curious.

"Jen, it's me. Karen is in a state. She rang my phone thinking it was yours and left two messages. She sounded drunk but very apologetic. I'm heading over there now."

"OK, I'll meet you there."

"Are you sure? I didn't ring to put pressure on you. I know you've got far more to unpack than me, and it's stressful enough."

"No, it's fine. I'm on my way out the door now."

I hang up and start a jog in the direction of Karen's apartment. It's a good thirty-minute walk, but trying to get a taxi now is a nightmare. I seem to be a lot fitter than I thought as I reach her apartment in fifteen minutes jogging, which by my standards is very good. The buzzer shrieks loudly, and I wait patiently, praying that she hasn't done anything silly.

I press the buzzer and wait. No reply. She's hardly gone out. I hang around in the hope that someone will exit the building and let me in. I call Jen again.

"Jen, I don't suppose you thought to bring the spare keys to Karen's flat, did you?"

"Yep, no worries," she says. "I have them with me; why?"

"No answer here."

"OK, don't panic. I'll be there in ten minutes."

I hang up.

Once Jen arrives, we make our way upstairs and open the door.

"Karen?" Jens shouts. No reply.

I cover my mouth. "What's that smell?" I ask.

"Dirt and puke, by the looks of things," Jen replies.

"Christ, it's rank. Karen, are you here?"

Then I spot her, lying in a pool of vomit with an empty bottle in hand.

"Shit, Aly! Is she alive?" Jen exclaims.

"I don't know!" I start to panic. "Karen, Karen, can you hear me?" I shout as I prod her. I feel for a pulse, and thankfully, there is one. However, it's very weak. "She's alive, but call an ambulance, Jen."

Within ten minutes, the ambulance arrives. Jen is shaking as she watches them remove Karen from the apartment on a stretcher.

"OK, who wants to come along for the ride?" the paramedic asks, trying to lighten the mood.

"I'll go," Jen says. Before she leaves, I grab her arm.

"See you there. I'll just clear up some of this mess first." She nods with a look of sadness.

Before I leave the apartment, I need to know exactly how much drink Karen has been consuming. The apartment looks like it hasn't been cleaned in weeks. There's rubbish everywhere and a ridiculous number of empty bottles lying around. I decide I'll return another day to clean up properly, but for now, I'll clean all the vomit up before it makes the place smell any worse.

Once the floors are somewhat clean again, I make my way to the hospital.

"Jen, what's going on?" I ask.

"She's lucky to be alive, Aly. Ten more milliletres of alcohol, and she'd be gone."

"Sweetest Jesus. Thank God we got there when we did."

"God, Aly, this isn't fair. Have we been bad friends for what we said to her?"

"No, chick. Look, we tried. Maybe this was meant to happen for her to see what she's doing to herself. She's in good hands at least, now."

Pangs of guilt wash over me. *Did we do this to her?*

Within hours, Jack and Tommy appear.

"Hey, how are our beautiful girls doing?" Tommy says.

Jack approaches me, and it only takes a glance before my eyes well up and I cry. "We almost lost her, Jack."

"It's OK, sweetheart; she's in good hands. She'll be fine," he says as he hugs me tight.

"You girls have to go home and get some rest," the doctor says as she approaches with a smile. "She's going to be fine. We've given her a glucose drip to snap her out of it. We'll do some tests tomorrow, though. We need to check for liver damage."

"OK," I say as I look at the others. "I guess we can go home, then. Thank you, doctor."

"No problem. Actually, we'll need someone to take care of her for a while when we discharge her, so can one of you do the honours, or do you know of anyone? Her family?"

"She can stay at ours!" Jen pipes up.

"I've only got a couch, unfortunately, but am happy to give her my bed," I say.

"Aly, it's fine. She'll have a room at ours; and to be fair to you, you need the space you have."

I smile. "Thanks, Jen."

We leave the hospital, everyone looking despondent.

"Let's all go home and relax for the night. At least we know Karen's in good hands, and tomorrow is a new day. You girls need some sleep," Jack says.

"You're right, Jack; I'm exhausted," Jen replies.

The next day I'm up early. I was so exhausted that I fell asleep the minute I hit the pillow.

"Jack, Jack?" I say as I head for the door.

"Hey, sweetie, where are you off to?" he asks.

"I'm going to head to Karen's. I need to clean it up as it looks like a tip still."

"Want me to come with you?"

"No, love, you're grand. Jen and I want to sort it out ourselves."

"OK, sweetie, I'll drop by later."

We arrive at Karen's apartment thirty minutes later.

"We'll be here all day, judging by the condition of this place," Jen says.

"Right, less of the chatting. I'm going to gather some of Karen's things," I say as I beckon at Jen to follow me into the bedroom.

"Jen, we'll have to clean this place up a bit. Check all possible areas where she has drink hidden."

"OK, how about I start clearing up, and you carry on packing her stuff?"

"Suits me. I'm so used to packing and unpacking the last few days, I'll have it done in twenty minutes or less."

"Good woman," she says.

We check every crevice and find only two bottles of vodka and gin.

"Didn't know she was hitting the hard stuff," I remark.

"No, neither did I. Seems this is a lot worse than what we thought, Aly."

"Maybe we should check every room. I don't believe this is all she has, Jen."

I walk back to the bedroom and check her massive walk-in wardrobe. I spot the collection of knee-high boots Karen has, and I go through them to find another eight bottles: a mixture of wine and spirits. I then proceed to where her handbags are and find another four bottles of champagne stashed in oversized bags. My heart is sinking as I now know the big secret my dear friend has been trying to keep from us for so long. I'm giving up now; I don't want to search anywhere else as I feel I've invaded her privacy enough for one day. I'll have to return another day with Jen to clear the rest of the place out, though, just in case of another hidden stash.

"Look what I found," I say to Jen.

"Oh my God! That's a ridiculous amount of drink!"

"I know it is, Jen, but we're looking for signs of an alcoholic, and now we've found them. How about we have a look at these brochures Jack got me? Not for me, of course, but for Karen. Jack said all of these clinics are equally as good as each other."

"Good idea. We need to get her into one as soon as possible."

We both sit and study the brochures carefully and finally decide on one which might suit Karen's needs. I decide to ring them immediately and explain how we need urgent assistance. The staff are full of empathy and suggests we bring Karen to the clinic once she is feeling up to it.

"Time for you to go home, hon," I say. "Thanks for all your help, but I don't want you to have to put up with more nonsense from the people you work with tomorrow."

"Well, that's another story, Aly. I was going to tell you tonight but thought it wasn't really appropriate with all that's been going on. I've left. I contacted my old company yesterday, and they only got a temp replacement while I was gone. In fact, they've gone through a few, but none of them matches up to me, apparently," Jen says with a smile.

"That's fantastic! So does that mean it's your job again?" I exclaim.

"Yep! I'm so happy. I met with them yesterday afternoon, and they were upset to hear what I had gone through. They told me they'll support me in every way possible to get me back to full health, and they're delighted to have me back on board. You know, I have to admit, I really missed them. Not to mention all the freebies I used to get there."

"Oh, Jen, that's the best news I've heard all day. I hear what you're saying about the freebies! Are you starting tomorrow?"

"Not until next week," she says. "I rang my current employer—well, ex-employer now—and told them yesterday that I wasn't coming back. I actually did it before I rang my old boss. I couldn't be putting up with their crap any longer, and to be honest, they didn't even care, I'd say."

"Well, their loss. You're going to be so spoilt when you return to your old job. They love you there, and who can blame them?"

"Yeah, I think this whole therapy thing has helped me greatly, and I feel I'm starting to gain a little confidence again. Have you thought anymore about going, or do you need to now?"

"Well, since Jack visited last weekend, I've been feeling really good, actually, so I might leave it for now—unless he dumps me, that is."

"Aly, he won't! I could see how much he loves you when you both came to visit that day. He was watching every expression and move you made. Not in a psycho way but in a loving way. There's no way he's dumping you. Besides, he's hung around through all of this business with Karen to be here for you. He's a keeper, Aly, and you are, too, so stop putting yourself down."

"Well, if what the tarot cards say is true, then I won't get dumped!" I say with a smile. I give her a huge hug, and she leaves. I'm exhausted too and head for home.

The following day, we go visit Karen in the hospital. I call the doctor to one side. "We've been talking about admitting Karen to rehab. We have some brochures. How do you think she'll react to it if we suggest it to her?"

"Well, she knows already she has to go. She's gone cold turkey here already. She knows she's not getting any drink and has no way of getting it. I think she got a fright from this episode, so she may be willing to go. There's no harm in mentioning it to her. Give her the brochures, and I'm sure she'll tell you straight away if she doesn't want to go. Now, if you'll excuse me, I've got an emergency case on the way in," she says with a smile.

"Of course; thank you for all of your help. We really appreciate it."

"I know you do."

"She's smiley, isn't she?" Jack pipes up.

"Yeah, I like her. She's a good 'un, Jack. Oh, I'm dreading this, but I might as well get it over with now."

I walk towards Karen's room and knock on the door. "Hey, you, how are you feeling?"

"Aly, come in, please," she says. "I'm not great, but that's to be expected."

"Karen, love, I've spoken to the doctor, and she says it's OK to show you these."

"What are they?"

"Rehab brochures."

"Oh yeah, she said I'd probably have to go there."

Karen seems remarkably calm. "Aly, I really don't think it's necessary to go there. I'm feeling much better than what I was."

"Sweetie, I know you are, but you could relapse at any time. We're all worried about you. Take a look at least?"

She grabs the brochure from my hand and throws me a withering look. She sighs as she flicks through the pages and then utters the words, "Hmm, there's a pool."

I glance at Jen and Tommy, who smile back. Karen always had a thing for swimming, and the fact that there's a pool there must appeal to her.

She's now crying like a baby. "I don't want to go! I don't want to go! I don't want to go!" she sobs as she hugs the cushion. "I can't afford this," she squeals. "I've lost my job. I'm way behind on rent payments, and I've been threatened with eviction."

We all look at each other. I stand up, lean over her bed, and hug her tightly.

"Oh, Karen, when did all of this happen?"

"Three months ago. I've been trying to hide it from you all, but I knew the money would run out eventually. I even started selling my designer shoes and jewellery on eBay as a means to living."

"Karen, don't worry about paying for the clinic. We'll take care of that," Tommy announces.

"But I can't pay you back, Tommy, I can't pay you back!" she roars and breaks down in hysterics again.

"It's OK, sweetie; it's OK. We just want you better. You don't need to worry about paying anyone back," Tommy says as he approaches her and takes her in his arms. "There, there, we can't have you crying like that. You're ruining that pretty face of yours," he says to calm her. I spot Jen looking at him dreamily.

Jen approaches her. "Karen, it's for your own good. Please think about it. You will have your life back. Remember the good old days when you got up early with a smiley face and had a normal day at work without any alcohol? Remember the days when we used to go shopping and never touch a drop, and we'd spend the whole day laughing? Well, it could be like that again."

"I hate myself right now," Karen squeals.

"I know you do, honey, but if you go here, it will help you to improve; and you can have the old you back. How does that sound?" I say.

Karen wipes her face with the sleeve of her pyjamas and gives a weak smile. "OK."

"OK?" Jen asks.

"OK, I'll go."

She appears from her room forty-five minutes later. We're all lounging around, drinking coffee. I need it.

"Can we get this over and done with, please, before I change my mind again?" Karen asks.

We grab our coats and usher her out.

Following a two-hour drive, we arrive at the rehab centre. Karen's hands are shaking, and she is sweating like I've never seen before.

"What's happening to me—why am I sweating so much? Look at my hands."

"It's OK; they'll make that stop in the clinic," I say to reassure her. Tommy puts his arm around her to help support her on the way in, and Jen and I comfort each other. I have no idea what exactly is in store for her, but it seems like the only way for her to get past where she is right now.

When we enter, I'm pleasantly surprised, as it looks quite homely. The rooms are large, and there are quite a few young people hanging around. I'm reassured by the nurse that she will have a massive support system, and we'll have nothing to worry about. I promise Karen I will ring on a regular basis to see how she is doing.

Karen looks upset. I really want to stay and help her through it, but I know this is something she will have to do alone. Jen, Tommy, and I leave feeling drained, sad, and hungry. We all sit in silence as Tommy starts the engine and drives down the long, winding road to reach the small town. I can't take the silence any longer.

"I'm feckin' starving. Let's get a big mother of a breakfast somewhere."

Jen and Tommy both laugh.

"We're with you there, Aly," Tommy says.

"Sorry, did that sound bad? I'm just trying to lighten the mood. She's in the best place now, and in no time we'll have our sober buddy back with us."

"Aly, it's fine. I don't think any of us knew what to say, but that broke the ice nicely. I know I'm feeling the hunger pangs now too," Jen says.

It's not very often I hear Jen say things like that these days, and I'm certainly not complaining. Tommy parks the car, and we make ourselves comfortable in a beautiful little café overlooking a river. We order a giant helping of blueberry pancakes as we admire the scenery and soak up the sound of the gushing water from the nearby river. Everything seems so peaceful in this town; it's the perfect escape from New York.

Chapter 27

Oh, Jack, why did you have to go back to LA? I miss you.

"Are you sleeping there, or what? Did you hear me at all, Aly?"

"What? Oh sorry, Jeremy, what did you say?"

"I said I need you to work late the next few nights. There's a lot on with Christmas approaching."

"Jeremy, I can't tonight. I'm off to see Karen."

"Cancel it well!" he roars as he turns his back and walks out of my office.

I can't believe this! *That fecking asshole. Do I have to leave this company completely? I've gone from one asshole boss to another. I really can't take this for much longer.*

"Jeremy, hold up one minute," I shout as I run after him. "I'm done with you speaking to me like this. I will not cancel any appointment I have to go see my friend. She's ill, and she damn well needs me more than you do."

"So you're refusing to work? I could fire you right now, Aly."

"Jeremy, I don't know what the hell is wrong with you, but you need to understand this is a working relationship. You need to get over the fact that we are no longer involved romantically."

"Excuse me, Ms. Confident? I think it's you who needs to get over herself. Although there is one way of you getting out of not working tonight..." he says with a smirk. I'm waiting patiently for what will follow. "I got new blackout blinds fitted in the office yesterday as you saw. We can try them out and see if they work?" he says confidently.

"You make me puke, Jeremy. I wouldn't—" I turn as I hear a rustling sound to my left and spot Debs hiding by the bookshelf. I take my chances and continue, "—sleep with you again if you were the last man left with three legs. To threaten me with my job if I don't is just so wrong on every level."

"Hahaha, oh, Aly, you think you run everything, bar the world. You listen to me. I run this show, lady, and you have a choice: miss your chance to see Karen or sleep with me now. If you choose neither, your head might just roll, darling."

"Fuck you, Jeremy," I say. "I'll work late this once, but you can forget about harassing me again."

I turn and look at Debs out of the corner of my eye. She looks upset, and I actually feel sorry for her. I ring Karen and explain I won't make it, but I'll spend Saturday with her instead. Thankfully, she's fine about it all.

It's midnight before I reach home. I don't know what to do. I can't carry on being harassed like this. Debs's face pops into my head. *I wonder if she's mentioned anything to Jeremy.*

The following Friday, I'm sitting in my office. My phone rings.

"Hi, Aly, it's Sabrina from HR. How're you doing?"

Oh my God! I'm going to be fired. That little bastard!

"I'm OK, Sabrina, thanks. How're you?" I ask cautiously.

"I'm good, thanks, sweetie. Could you come downstairs, please? We need to talk to you."

What's this "we" business?

"Sure, I'll come right down." I hang up, straighten my skirt, fix my hair, and make my way down the stairs. *Deep breaths, deep breaths.* I knock weakly on the door.

"Hi, Sabrina."

"Hi, honey, come on in. Take a seat. I'm gonna cut to the chase, sweetie. Jeremy Sullivan was fired yesterday evening."

I can feel my eyes grow larger. "Erm, why?" I ask.

"We've been reliably informed that he was harassing you on a regular basis, Aly. We take job threats seriously here. He did threaten you, didn't he?"

"Well…he…" I stammer.

"It's OK, you can tell us. He also admitted it."

"Yes. Yes, it's true, but I'd hate for anyone to be fired because of me."

"Aly, if it wasn't you, it would be someone else," she says.

"Who told you?"

"We can't tell you that. We'll fill his position quickly, though, as there's high demand out there, but right now our main concern is you. Are you OK?"

I cry and cry. My nightmare is finally over after months, and the only one I could think of to thank was Debs. As I poured my heart out, Sabrina took notes and listened to every word.

"There, there, honey, it's over now. You need a strong cup of coffee, I think."

"Thank you; I think you're right."

I sit and chat with Sabrina for another hour or so.

"You know, you should take the rest of the day off, Aly. You need a break now. Go home or go treat yourself, but you need to get out of here, I think."

"I think you might be right," I say. I leave the office and make my way upstairs again in a bid to get my things and leave for the day. The first person I pass as I leave is Debs. I look at her and utter the words, "Thank you." She smiles and touches my arm. It is the first time I see her in this light and realise she's just human like the rest of us as she, too, was hurt and caught up in this situation. One thing is for sure: I'll never forget her for what she did.

I rush home, and once I gather my thoughts on the couch, I pick up the phone and call Jen.

"Jen, I need to talk to you urgently," I sob down the phone.

"Jesus, Aly, what's happened? I've never heard you this upset. Where are you?"

"At home. Oh, Jen, I feel so guilty. Jeremy's been fired, and it's my fault."

"What? Hang on. I'll see if I can leave early, and I'll call over to you. I've never heard you like this before."

"OK, thanks," I sob. I hang up.

Thankfully, within the hour my doorbell rings. "Hi, come in."

"Aly, how long have you been crying? You're eyes are all puffed up and swollen, love. Tell me what's happened." I unfold the story to Jen. "And while I thought Debs overhearing might go against me, she did the right thing and reported him. I never wanted anyone to get fired because of me, though."

"Oh, pet, he's the creep here and the last person you should worry about. You know, I'm sure Tommy and Jack will have something to say about this."

"No, no! I just want to forget about it all now. I'm not even sure I want to tell Jack. He'll freak out."

"Well, I don't blame him," she exclaims. "That gobshite has even made me mad, and I don't get angry too easily."

"Yeah, and you never use the term 'gobshite,' either."

"No wonder! He could have done anything to you in that office, Aly."

"I honestly don't think he's capable of that. I think he just wanted to scare me. It would be completely out of character for him, at least what I know of him. I think it was all words, dented pride more than anything, because I knocked him back that day. Oh, it's such a relief to get it off my chest."

"OK, I'm staying here tonight. We can go see Karen if you're up to it tomorrow or over the weekend."

"Sure, let's see. Although I should, really, as he already made me cancel on her once this week."

"If she knew the reason, she'd be more than understanding, Aly. I think you need to get some rest now. Go on, off to bed. I'll make you dinner and call you when it's ready."

"Thanks, Jen; you're a true pal."

She smiles and rubs my arm as I make my way to the bedroom.

Chapter 28

September 2013

"Hello?" I say into my phone.

"Hey, trouble, how are you?" Jack replies.

"Hiya, I'm almost there. I'm good, thanks. I'm assuming you've landed if you're ringing?"

"Yep, I'm just waiting for my luggage."

"OK, pulling into the airport now." I hang up quickly. Once I get to the airport, I park at arrivals, as I know Jack won't be long. Tommy was kind enough to let me borrow his car to collect him. Jack arrives within ten minutes, and I greet him with the biggest hug.

"I'm so happy you're here," I say.

"Me too," he says. "Is that new perfume? You smell great."

"As opposed to how I normally smell, you mean? How was the flight?"

"Great. Very smooth and slept for most of it, so I'm in flying form and ready for this party."

"She'll be so thrilled to finally meet you properly."

"Me too. Do you think I should take my shoes off?"

"I'd say you'll be safe enough this time, Jack."

We drive back to my apartment where Jen and Tommy have been preparing the place with party banners, and only soft drinks will be displayed on the countertop.

"Wow, is this for me?" Jack asks with a large grin across his face as he opens the door.

"Sorry, not this time, Jack, but you're very welcome back to New York!" Jen says with great fervour.

"You guys have made a great job of this. It looks awesome. I'm sure Karen will be delighted. Thank you, Jen."

She walks towards him and gives him a hug.

"Jack, my man, good to see you," Tommy says as he shakes his hand firmly and then hugs him.

"OK, listen," I say. "I'm going to go now and pick Karen up. Tommy, are you sure I can take the car again?"

"Absolutely. You and Jen go. She'll be thrilled to see you both, I'm sure of it. Us guys can hang out here and eat!"

"Well, you're both very good at that!" I snigger.

"See you later," Jen shouts as she bolts down the stairs.

I quickly give Jack a peck on the lips and leave.

It's a long drive to the clinic, but it's been weeks since we've seen Karen and well worth the trip. It's great to see her walk towards us rather than stagger. She looks fantastic, like the Karen who left Ireland all those years ago to live in New York. Her skin looks fresh, and she has perfectly applied make-up. She's standing tall and has lost weight.

"Ladies, how are we?" she asks. We throw our arms around her, and she starts crying.

"Oh, please tell me those are tears of joy!"

"They are, Aly, don't worry. I'm so sorry for everything I've put you all through. You're the best pals anyone could ask for."

"Stop with the apologies already! We're just happy to have you back," I say.

"Welcome back, Karen. Now, we've a long drive ahead of us so let's get going," Jen says.

"OK. We can chat on the way."

The drive back isn't so bad, probably because we know Karen is feeling and looking good. She informs us of a programme she's going to join. It will keep her on track, and she seems happy to do it.

We arrive back at my apartment in the early evening. I send Jack a text so he knows we are outside. Once we get upstairs, I open the door and let Karen walk in ahead of me. All I can hear is "Surprise!" Her old work mates have also turned up, and there are at least twenty people in the apartment.

"Oh my God! Did you do this for me?" she quizzes.

"Course we did!" I say.

The tears are flowing. I've never seen her so emotional before. It's a side of her that I like, though, and I hope it's here to stay.

"Thanks so much, everyone," Karen utters. She then turns to me and asks, "Is that your Jack near the kitchen?"

"Yes, it is. Go say hello. He's been dying to meet you properly."

"I can't. Remember what happened the last time?"

"Karen, it's forgotten. Go."

She's striding across the floor like a model. The old Karen is definitely back. I join her.

"Jack?"

"Hi, Karen, nice to see you again. How are you feeling?"

"Oh, I'm good, thanks. I want to apologise for the first and last time I saw you. Your shoes were ruined."

"Karen, please forget about it. I did take my shoes off today, though, just in case," he says with a glint in his eye and a smile.

"Jack, what are you saying to the poor girl?" I exclaim.

"It's OK, Aly; she can take a joke," he says.

"Aly, he's right. I can, even though I did look down to see if you were in fact without shoes. Seriously, Aly, please don't feel the need to tiptoe around me. I'm fine, and I need you to act normally around me, please?"

"OK. Sorry—and sorry, Jack."

Jack pulls me close and tousles my hair with his hand. I look at him disapprovingly and just laugh.

Karen carries on working the room like someone famous. I'd imagine even Jack can't work a room as well as she does. Jen and

Tommy are relaxing on the couch, and I can see Jen is nodding off to sleep. I'm envious right now as it's what I want to do myself, but being the hostess, I have to stay alert and attend to everybody's needs.

I'm hanging with exhaustion. Everyone helps me clear up once Karen's ex-work mates have left. Jen is still sleeping on the couch, and none of us wants to wake her as she had an early start to get here this morning. Tommy and Jack are a great help and are more than happy to stack up the dishwasher while I clear away what's left in the lounge. Karen wants to help, too, but it was her party, so I usher her off to relax on the couch with Jen and Tommy. I'm happy to see it's been an enjoyable day for all. I'm finally finished cleaning, and now it's time for me to retire to the couch and kick off my shoes.

Tommy gently pats Jen on the head to wake her up. "Sleepyhead, time to go home."

"Oh, what time is it?" she asks.

"It's getting late, honey. Come on; let's hit the road. Karen, sweetie, are you ready?" he asks with a smile.

"Sure, whenever you guys are," she says.

It's taking poor Jen ages to wake up for the journey to the car, not to mention the journey home.

Karen says her goodbyes and leaves in what seems to be a very happy mood. I'm feeling quite happy myself and incredibly lucky to have Jack all to myself for a week. I'm looking forward to every minute of it.

"You know, Aly, I was thinking that you don't get a break from here too often, except maybe when you go home for Christmas. Why don't you come to LA with me next weekend when I head back?"

"Seriously?"

"Yeah, of course."

"I'd love to! Thanks. I've never been to LA before. I always wondered what it was like. I won't be hounded by paparazzi, now, will I?"

"I can't say. I'll try to keep you low-profile. I'm sure you'll be OK. They don't bother me too much. The only time they camped outside my door was when Nicole used to cause trouble. I haven't seen them around for a long time."

"Oh, good, because I really can't be dealing with my make-up-free face being sprawled across a trashy mag with it stating how ugly Jack Morgan's new girlfriend is."

"Aly, stop it. Jeez, I've told you already; you're gorgeous to me. You look good without make-up, and you shouldn't care what people think."

"OK," I say. "Did you just get narky with me?"

"Yes, I did. Now stop because I'm beat, and I don't want an argument."

"All right." I smile to myself. I know that he isn't so perfect after all, and I like it.

"Are you sulking?" he asks.

"I am not! What made you think that?"

"You just looked a little off with me."

"Well, you did shout at me, but no, I'm not. I'm fine."

"OK, let's go to bed. I'm exhausted."

"That sounds like a great idea."

We head for the bedroom. A little romance would be nice, but there's no chance of that as Jack is snoring before I even manage to turn the light out.

I'm tossing and turning as I'm finding it difficult to drift off to sleep. I think I'm overtired.

When I look at the clock and it's 10:30 a.m., I'm happy to see I drifted off at some stage last night. I hear the doorbell and get up to see Karen standing there.

"Anyone for pancakes?" she asks.

"You're up early!"

"Yep. I'm so used to it at the clinic that the habit has stuck. Hope you don't mind, but I've taken the liberty of making you both breakfast."

"Of course I don't, and it's great to see you up and about at this time, bursting with energy. Blueberry pancakes, no less. Where did you learn to make them?" I ask.

"Rehab. I've learned so much there, and the people are amazing. At the start, I didn't think so, but they helped me to a great extent. Thanks to you guys, I have a fresh start."

"That's so great. I'm thrilled to see you like this, Karen."

"Actually, Aly, I want to talk to you about something. I was thinking about moving back into my old place. It's just not fair on Jen and Tommy, and I don't want to cramp their style. I'm just not sure how to tell them."

"You know you're not. You're welcome to stay with them as long as you need."

"I know I am, but I think I'd feel better in my own surroundings."

"OK, but…"

"But what? I can tell by your face. Don't worry, Aly, I'm not going to drink. I've met my sponsor, and he's very helpful. If I feel the urge for a drink, I'll just call him, and he'll talk me out of it. Speaking of which, I don't know if you have checked my apartment, but I had drink stashed everywhere there. I really should get someone to clear it out before I move back."

"Well, we kind of did that already. Sorry, I feel like we've invaded your privacy."

"Great! Don't be sorry, Aly. This is what I have to do now. I need to avoid it at all costs and be strong, say no to it. You've helped greatly by doing a sweep of the place."

"OK, so when do you want to move back?" I ask.

"I was thinking today? It's fine, really. I'd like to get back into routine as quickly as possible."

"Well, if you feel good about it, then I don't see why not. When are you going to tell Jen?"

"I'll go there once we polish off this lot," she says. "I just wanted to run it by you first and see what you thought. Where's Jack?"

"Snoring. I'm sure he'll get up soon."

"OK. I'd like to have you all over for dinner before Jack heads back to LA. Don't worry; it will be drink-free."

"That's really sweet, and I'm sure everyone will be there. I know Jack will be thrilled. He really liked chatting to you last night. We're both very proud of you, Karen."

"Thanks; that means a lot. Right, try this lot and try not to choke, puke, or bounce them on the floor."

I stuff a pancake into my mouth and smile at her as I do. She's looking at me like she's waiting for me to spit it out, but it tastes amazing. When I give her the thumbs up, a look of contentment appears on her face.

"Oh, Karen, I'm so happy you're back! I've missed you so much."

Chapter 29

I can't believe how fast this week has gone. Jack and I are eating, drinking, and generally just making big pigs of ourselves while he takes a deserved rest from work and LA life. I'm enjoying our time immensely as I, too, really need a break after everything that has happened in the past few months.

We had dined at Karen's on Wednesday evening, and she put on the most amazing spread for all of us. It was like old times, except with a sober Karen who still managed to keep her sense of humour, thankfully.

I'm just back after an afternoon of shopping and need to finish my packing.

"Honey, I'm getting a little impatient now. I've been waiting for over five hours for you to pack your things in between your shopping escapade. You're coming for a week, not a month!"

"I know; I'm sorry. Nearly ready, Jack."

"Please, can't you do it later? It would be nice to go for a romantic stroll after dinner to see the sights at night, as it could be another month before I'm back here."

"OK, I'll leave these and sort them later."

I change into something a little more respectable and pin my hair up. I already have a tiny flourish of make-up on my face from earlier in the day, and it still looks reasonably OK. A quick lash of mascara, and I'm ready.

"See, I can do it in five minutes when I need to."

"Is that right? Shame you didn't have that attitude when it came to your oversized bag there, Hughes! Still, I know you by now, especially after seeing the bag you took to the Hamptons the first time we went away together. I'll have to give you brownie points for this one, though. It's slightly smaller."

"Oh, Jack, your humour makes me die laughing. You're so, so funny. You just crack me up."

He sniggers. "I'll never be as sarcastic as you, will I?"

"Probably not," I say with a cheeky grin. I turn to walk out the door, and he slaps me on the arse. "Oh, cheeky. Not in the corridor, Jack."

"You'd like that, wouldn't you, Hughes?"

"Not really. Not with pervy Marvin living there. He gives me the creeps."

"Why? He seems like a nice guy."

"He does while you're here!" I exclaim. "You have never opened the door to leave the apartment as he just happens to be reaching for his paper in his dirty old underpants."

"Aly, it happened once, and I'm sure it was a coincidence. The poor guy."

"Twice, twice it happened, and I'm not even in the apartment a month. Do you realise that could amount to twenty-four times per year or more, Jack? That's just not good for the health. I wouldn't mind if he were fit, but he's got forty muffin tops hanging out over that underpants!" I grin as Jack starts laughing out loud.

"Aly, you can be so cruel sometimes," he says.

"Ah, you know I'm kidding around. I don't mean it. He only has thirty muffin tops," I say as I run for the elevator in case of said pervert exiting in underpants.

We are walking aimlessly, and as dark falls, the buildings light up the evening sky. Jack has a grin across his face every time I glance at him. He loves New York so much. It's getting late, though, and we have an early start in the morning. We return to my apartment.

The minute I'm inside the door, I head straight for my luggage with the weighing scales.

"What are you doing?"

"I'm weighing my bags, as I'm not going to get caught tomorrow. I refuse to fork out extra money, and I just need to double-check I'm within the twenty-kilo limit. Ah, there ya go. I'm three kilos under. I'm sorted."

I'm feeling contented, so I head to the kitchen to make a cup of tea. As I'm doing so, it feels like Jack is staring at me. When I turn around, he's standing there wearing nothing but a big smile across his face.

"You're certainly one for surprises, aren't you?" I say.

"Yeah, I do like to surprise you from time to time. Are you telling me you don't like the surprise?"

"Ah, 'tis grand," I say with a smile.

Jack walks towards me and squeezes me close to him.

"It's our last night here for a while. Let's make it an early one," he says.

"I have no problem in doing that, Jack Morgan," I say, and before I know it, he's whisking me up in his arms and into the bedroom.

It's Friday morning, and I'm incredibly excited. I'm finally off to LA with my sexy man. He's just as excited, and everything is running smoothly until we reach the airport.

"Ma'am, your luggage is overweight. I'll have to ask you to remove something, or we'll have to charge you."

"What? It can't be. I weighed it myself last night."

"It's overweight."

"Aly, either take something out of it, or we'll pay for it—I'll pay for it, whatever—just please don't cause a scene."

"I'm not causing a scene. I weighed my bag last night, and it was well under the specified weight. I'm not going to be ripped off by some ground stewardess who's probably pocketing the money!" I whisper to him.

I turn back to the desk. "Now, as I said, I weighed it last night, and it was well under the weight limit. Are you telling me the weight restrictions have changed since then?"

"No, ma'am, I'm not, but according to these scales, you're over."

"OK, I'd like to see a supervisor, please?" I demand.

"Oh, Aly, please, just pay and let's go. This is getting embarrassing," Jack whispers.

"Jack, I'm not moving until this gets sorted. It's not about throwing money about. It's the principle."

"Right, I'll wait over here," he says. "I can see you're going into one of your stubborn modes."

"Good man, you do that."

I can feel my face reddening. It feels like it's going to explode as the supervisor approaches me.

"I hear there's a little problem with your bag?"

"Yes. It's more than a little problem, though. This lady is saying my bag is overweight, and it's not. I refuse to pay. Last night I weighed it, and it was just over seventeen kilos. Today it's showing up as twenty-one kilos! Now, how can it increase by four kilos overnight unless it got peckish and raided the cookie jar? Even then, it wouldn't weigh an extra four kilos."

"OK, let's place it back on the scales. It says seventeen kilos. Lorraine, honey, did you have something resting on the side while you were weighing the bag?"

"Not that I was aware of! I apologise for the mistake, Here's your ticket, and have a safe flight," she says with a dirty look and an air of contempt.

"Thanks." I snap the ticket out of her hand, which admittedly is very impolite, but I have a sneaking suspicion Lorraine was doing a little extra work on the side by charging customers. I wander over to where Jack is, and he doesn't look impressed with me. "You OK? You look like you're about to shout at me or something."

"No, I'm not going to bring any more attention to myself, thanks. What happened?"

"What's wrong with you? I didn't bring any attention to you. She was accusing me of having an extra four kilos in my bag, which I didn't have, and she wanted to charge me thirty dollars per kilo! Why should I fork out an extra one hundred and twenty dollars into Lorraine's hand?"

"Are you serious?" he asks. "The bag wasn't overweight?"

"No, it wasn't. I knew she was wrong, and I hope she's getting a good bollocking now. She was trying to cheat me out of my money—the damn cheek of her."

"OK. Sorry for getting snappy with you. I'm just trying to avoid any attention. I've had enough paparazzi around me in the past giving me bad publicity, honey. I don't want it again."

"Oh, Jack, I'd forgotten. To me you're just you—Jack. I never really think about the fact you're so well-known here. Sorry. I'll bear it in mind when the next person tries to rip me off. I'll send you off on an errand or something," I say in jest.

At least he's smiling now.

I grab his hand, and we stroll to the gate.

We land in LA in the early afternoon, and the sun is bursting out of the sky. Jack has a car waiting to pick us up, and we're going directly to his house.

"Another mansion, no less?" I ask.

"Yeah, it's big, I guess, but I'm used to seeing it," he says. "It's just home to me. Go ahead, Aly—my home is your home. Enjoy it."

I'm amazed at the big stone mansion that stands in front of me. The door is unlocked, and I open it to see a small lady standing there, waiting to take my coat.

"Thank you," I say. "I'm Aly. It's nice to meet you."

She smiles. "Lovely to meet you. I'm Sally, Jack's housekeeper. I like to help him out when he has guests in the house. I do a little cooking and baking for him. I like to make sure he's well looked after."

"Wow, you sound like a gem to have around. I'll look forward to catching up with you properly later, Sally. Thank you for taking my coat."

Directly in front of me are two large glass doors. I open them, and inside there is a cinema for ten people. I turn around as I can feel Jack's presence behind me. "Jack! You never told me you had a cinema in this house! I'm in heaven!"

"I thought you'd like it. At least now you can bring the girls up whenever you want for girlie weekends, and if you fancy watching a movie, you've got your own cinema."

"I love it. What's over here?" I quiz as I move on to the next room. I open the door to a lounge, which is probably the size of my entire apartment. After I take in what I've seen, I proceed up the stairs.

"Is this another seven-bedroom house?"

"No, this one has six," he says. "However, the rooms are much larger than the ones in the Hamptons. I think you might want to veer into the one on the right. That's our bedroom. I've had something special fitted in there for you, as I knew you'd be bound to come visit me at some point."

"Jesus, I worry what that might be," I say with a smile.

"Ha! It's something you'll like, don't worry."

I gaze around the corner and see the biggest bedroom I've ever seen in my life. It is bigger than any hotel bedroom or suite I've ever stayed in. I see a few extra doors at the far end of the room and have to investigate, but not before looking back at Jack for his approval.

"Go on, go on!" he urges me.

I open one door to see a massive en-suite bathroom, almost the same size as the bedroom. It has a Jacuzzi bath, his and hers sinks, a large power shower, and an exit leading onto a decked patio.

"This is amazing. I'm just speechless."

"Oh, this—yeah, this is great, but you haven't seen your surprise yet."

"What is it?"

"Well, go check the other doors!"

I run back from the patio and into the bedroom. I open one door, and the one next to it opens itself, as if by magic. I walk in to see something I'd always dreamt of: a huge walk-in closet with dressing room attached. There's an area for shoes, an area for bags, space for hanging clothes—actually, there are four separate large hanging areas and shelving.

"I can't believe you did this for me!"

"Of course. I had to make space for all that stuff you bring with you every time you travel," he says as he plays with my hair.

"I don't know what to say, Jack. No one has ever done anything like this for me before. I feel really spoiled when I'm with you."

"Well, I don't just do it for anyone, you know. Now, how about we change and have a swim?"

"You're on! It's damn hot here. Big difference in temperature."

"Yeah, you'll find that it's far warmer here."

We sit by the pool for the afternoon, and Sally makes us some snacks to keep us going until dinner. We return indoors later and get spruced up as Jack tells me that Sally has set up the dining room to make it more romantic for us. Candles are lit, and she has laid out a huge spread for us.

"Sally, I can't believe you did all of this by yourself!" I tell her.

"Oh, honey, I love working here. Jack is such a good boy, and it's a pleasure for me to cook and clean for him. He's like one of my own. He's told me so much about you, too, far more than what he's ever mentioned about any of his past girlfriends. I shouldn't say this, but between you and me, honey, I think you'll be the one."

"The one what?"

"You know, the one," she says with a wink.

My heart flutters. The thought of being Mrs. Jack Morgan is something I haven't even considered yet. Sure, I wish it might happen one day, but I never really thought about it properly.

"Oh, thanks, Sally. It would be nice if that were the case, but no pressure on him. We aren't even together a year yet, and it's long-distance. It might be a bit too soon for him, especially after the past problems he's had."

"Tell me about it. That gal caused him so much pain and suffering for nothing. She was only after his money, but you, you're different. You're what I call a homely girl. Someone who's got true roots and knows right from wrong."

"Sally, that's very sweet of you. I hope Jack thinks that though," I say in jest.

"You hope Jack thinks what?" comes his voice.

"Oh, you weren't supposed to hear that, Jack. I hope you think I'm a homely girl who's not after your money."

"Of course I think that. I know you're not after my money."

It seems he's told her everything about us, which is sweet to a certain degree. He looks upon Sally as a mother figure, and she treats him like a son.

"Come on you two, take a seat," she says. "Dinner is about to be served."

We both sit down, and romance is definitely in the air. Jack plays some of his eighties vinyl after the meal. Mainly slow music to suit the mood: Frankie Goes to Hollywood, The Police, U2, and Foreigner, to name but a few.

"Dance with me, Aly," he says.

I feel a little silly as we're the only two here, and it's his front room. The last time we did this was on the steps of my old apartment on our first proper date—but without music, unless you can count Jack's rendition of "Lady in Red." Maybe I'm just not used to being treated so well, being wined and dined, and being wooed properly.

"I will if you promise not to sing 'Lady in Red.'"

He laughs out loud. "I'll try not to, but you have to admit, you loved it that night."

"Hmmm, OK, I did. Not the song, but I suppose I've grown to like it slightly after you serenaded me."

"I knew you would."

He holds me close, and I feel the connection between us is stronger than I've ever felt it in our relationship. We continue to dance to a few tracks and then decide to retire for the night. I can hear Sally cleaning in the kitchen. I go to help her, but she insists on me going to bed.

"You go. You've a handsome young man waiting for you upstairs. I'm happy to clear up here alone. Besides, there's not much to do. Thank you, Aly; you're a lovely girl. Oh, and let me know when to buy the hat." She giggles.

I say nothing; I just smile.

Chapter 30

December 2013

I'm at the airport with Jack. It's five days before Christmas, and it's chaotic. Feeling both nervous and apprehensive about what will happen at home, I'm not in a very talkative mood.

"What's wrong? You're not your usual chatty self today. Just having a quiet day?" Jack enquires.

"Yeah something like that," I say.

"Jeez, Aly, come on. Have I done something wrong? I normally pick up on it if I do, but this time I can't figure out what's up with you."

"No, love, you haven't. I suppose I'm just a bit nervous about you meeting my family, especially my parents. It's a bit of a big step, isn't it?"

"It's bigger for me. Remember, they have expectations. I'm just going with the flow, but it's their daughter who's dating me."

"True, I suppose. OK, I'll try to cheer up, but I think I should warn you, my father will do his best to embarrass you. He does it to everyone. You just have to learn to deal with it."

"Well, I'll look forward to meeting him, then. He sounds like such a character, Aly. I can't wait. Your entire family sounds like such fun to be around."

"They are, but I worry in case you think we're a bunch of freaks or something."

"I won't. Now you need to calm down, and I'm thinking the best way of doing that is to get you a cup of tea. I'll be back in five minutes, if the line isn't too long."

Jack heads in the direction of the restaurants. I sit there watching him walk away. He's so lovely; I hope my family doesn't cock it all up for me, though.

Seven hours later, we arrive at Cork airport. I'm cringing as I walk through the arrivals door and try to keep a straight face. However, when I see the damn banners they have made to disgrace me and welcome me home (in that order), and of course to welcome Jack, a grin escapes. They are hideous-looking banners. Not only have my parents turned up but so have my sisters and brother, which I'm thrilled by, and their boyfriends and girlfriend as well; and there are a few children thrown in for good measure. I've no idea who they belong to, though.

"Oh, Jesus, brace yourself, Jack."

"Ha! Don't tell me that's them with the banners. How amusing! Your face has turned so red right now, Aly."

"Yeah, that's them, and thanks for stating that. I can feel my face burning up; you didn't have to point it out to me. Oh, this just sucks."

I'm walking towards them, and my father and mother run towards me with open arms.

"Welcome home, pet. We're delighted to have you back for Christmas." They both have tears in their eyes, and I become overwhelmed by it all and burst into tears myself. Jack is next to me, and I introduce them. I can tell they like him straight away, and judging by the handshake he and my father share, he'll be flavour of the month—or even the year. My mother gives him a hug that nearly squashes him. My sisters are gawping at him like they've never seen a man before. I open my eyes wide and beckon them over to meet him. My brother and his girlfriend follow. I have no idea who she is; she must be a new one.

"We didn't realise that's who he is!" one of my sisters exclaims.

"What? Are you telling me you know him?" I exclaim.

"Ah, yes! He's only the hottest actor to hit Irish TV screens in the past month. Dr Evans, that's his name. We do have TV here, you know."

"Yeah, I know that, but that's his new show. I've only seen him in that myself recently. I wasn't expecting you to have that series over here just yet, as he's not really known in Europe. That's all."

"Aly, you've done us proud now," Sarah says as she walks away to call her friend.

Vicky approaches. "Sis, good to see you. Welcome home." She throws her arms half-heartedly around me to give me a loose hug. Dad must have warned her to behave.

"Vicky, thanks. This is Jack. Jack, my sister Vicky." I leave them to chat while I have a small moment to myself and watch as everyone swarms around Jack to welcome him and to satiate their boundless curiosity. He's still being bombarded by my mother's questions but looks contented. I feel a bit more relaxed knowing that my family isn't going to be in any way cold to him. I did worry that because he isn't Irish, they might not warm to him as much. My father always told me to marry my own, as only an Irish man would get my sarcastic sense of humour and be able to handle me. I'm glad I can now prove him wrong in those assumptions.

We arrive home, and the house looks amazing. They've decorated the tree beautifully, and my mother and sisters have invested in some pretty Christmas garlands to place along the fireplaces. It looks so festive.

"Wow, I'm loving your family already, Aly," says Jack. "They're so welcoming!"

"Yeah, they're great. They're super excited to meet you finally, and would you believe my sister informed me that she's seen you in your new TV series over here?"

"Really? Ah, great, finally some recognition in Europe then. I'm not going to get paparazzi here, am I?"

"The only paparazzi you'll have to deal with here are our nosey neighbours, Jack," I say. "Trust me, they'll have stories nationwide before any paper will."

"OK, I can handle that, I think."

He looks so at ease, and I have to admit, I too am feeling very happy right now.

A little later, we all sit down to dinner. There are so many of us today that we've had to extend the table. This is a rare occurrence.

"Jack, as the guest, I'd like you to sit here at the head of the table, and we'll put you here, Aly."

"Oh no, I couldn't, Patrick," says Jack. "That's your seat."

"Ah, Dad, that's so good of you. What are you looking for?" I ask with a smirk.

"Aly, don't talk to your father like that," says Jack.

"I'm well used to her and her sarcasm, Jack. I'm not looking for anything for now, Aly. Jack, come and take a seat. I insist."

Jack sits down, looking very uncomfortable.

"Jack, it's OK," I say. "Seriously, we're just joking. We're always like this. He always lets the guests sit at the head of the table. He feels good when he does that, so just accept the gesture and enjoy it."

"Oh, OK. Thanks, Patrick."

My mother has prepared a massive feed for us, and we tuck into it with great gusto. There are about four different conversations going on at once, and I manage to contribute to each one. Jack looks mesmerised.

"How do you know what everyone is talking about? I can only manage to talk to whoever I'm near, but you seem to be contributing to every conversation. It's like chaos."

"Welcome to the Hughes household, Jack," I tell him. "Don't ask me how I do it. Years of practice, I'd say."

He sits back and just observes. He seems to be enjoying it and looks a bit more relaxed. We're all pretty relaxed after a few drinks, and the banter at the table is great. Then my father starts.

"So, Jack, how many hectares of land do you own?" he asks.

"Ahem, excuse me, sir?" says Jack.

"Land, do you own land?"

"Jesus, Dad, shut up, for feck sake. You'll disgrace me."

"No, it's fine, Aly. I'll answer his question. I own two houses: one in LA and one in the Hamptons. Both are fine houses with land attached."

"Jack, seriously, you don't have to answer his questions. He's—" I begin.

"Aly, it's fine, really," he interrupts me. "He just wants to know that I'm secure and that I can look after you."

I start laughing. Jack has no idea, and seeing as he's cut me off when I was going to warn him not to say anything, I decide I'll let him be. He can answer any more questions my father plans to ask him.

"So, Jack, I'd say that means you've a fairly hefty bank balance. Would I be right in thinking that?" my father asks.

Jack looks slightly taken aback by his question, and I can tell he's not sure what to say. We all sit in silence looking at him, but as I glance around the table, I can see my entire family is choking back their laughter.

"Well, Patrick, I think it's fair to say that I—"

My father bursts into laughter. "Jack, I don't expect you to answer that at all. I'm only pulling your leg, young fella. Relax; don't answer. I'm a joker, Jack. I do this to any prospective long-term man who enters any of my daughters' lives. These poor feckers went through it too," he says, gesturing at my sisters' boyfriends.

I finally feel relieved as I laugh out loud. I do feel sorry for Jack, but he should have heeded my warning rather than cut me off. He finally realises what jokers my family can be, and he sits back, shakes his head, and smiles.

"You got me, Patrick. You got me good," he says.

My mother is fretting around the place, embarrassed by my father's antics. "For God's sake, Patrick, what are you like?"

We retire to the lounge, where my father starts nodding off by the blazing fire, and Jack and I huddle up on the couch.

"I've never experienced a proper, roaring, open fire like this before. It's beautiful," he says.

"Yeah, it is nice, isn't it? I miss it as I don't have one in New York."

"And I never had any need for one as I'm never in one place long enough. I'm really enjoying myself here already, Aly, and I've only been here a few hours. Your dad is some character."

"I knew he'd do that to you. That's part of what I was worrying about earlier in the day. I wasn't sure how you'd react to him, and I was worried in case you'd think we're a pack of nutters."

"No way. You've a real family here. You're blessed, so enjoy it."

"Thanks. Well, you're fitting right in, love, and I can tell they adore you already. Oh look! It's starting to snow. How Christmassy is that!" I say.

"It's stunning and very romantic. Aly, thank you for letting me share this Christmas with you and your family. I know it's one I'll never forget."

"Oh, you definitely won't, Jack, and as I said before, you'll not want to leave when the time comes."

He hugs me tight, and it feels lovely to have the burning heat of the fire keeping us warm while the freezing snow is falling outside. Sarah and Jessie are outside building snowmen with their boyfriends. My brother and his girlfriend are chatting with my mother in the kitchen, and Vicky and her boyfriend, Tony, have already left, social as ever. Jack and I decide to venture outside to join the others in the snow. After all, nobody knows when it will snow this heavily again in Cork for Christmas. The others are pelting each other with snowballs, and I lie down to etch an angel in the snow. Even at this age, the snow brings out my inner child. I will definitely remember this Christmas forever, and I hope it will be the first of many in Jack's company.

Chapter 31

Mid-May 2014

$\mathcal{I}$'m busy cleaning my apartment when I hear what sounds like a knock on the door. It gets louder as I walk to the door. It's Jen, and she looks to be in a state of panic.

"Hey, you OK?" I ask. "You look like something's happened to you."

"Something has."

"Come in. Here, take a seat." *Oh, please don't say she and Tommy have split. I'll cry!*

Jen starts waving her hands frantically in front of me, and then she bursts into laughter. "You're a bit slow to catch on, aren't you?" she quizzes.

"What are you talking about? You've been ranting about nothing for the past few minutes, and I've no idea what exactly you're trying to say."

"OK, maybe I've been a bit too much on the acting front. I'm in great form, Aly. I've never been better."

"Well, why the long face when you came in?" I demand.

"Look at my hand. I had to pretend I was upset, but I'm actually ecstatic!"

"Oh, my God! Come here and give me a hug. Oh, congratulations, Jen. I'm so happy for you both!"

I'm staring at the massive rock on her left hand. It's stunning. *Lucky girl. I hope Jack will present something similar to me one day.* It won't need to be massive, either. Just the thought of him propos-ing sends shivers through me—nice shivers.

"This is the best news I've heard in weeks. Wait until I tell Jack! He'll be so delighted. He loves you guys. He thinks you are great together, as do I. Must buy some bubbles to celebrate!"

"I already brought it with me. I'd like to celebrate it with a little tipple, but I can't really do that in front of Karen. We can have a drink-free girlie celebration at Buddakan with Karen, and we can have a drop of champers now. What do you think? I've taken the liberty of booking the table already. Hope you don't mind."

"That sounds great, and I'm free as a bird today, girl. I'm ex-pecting Jack to call, but I'm free after that. Have you actually told Karen yet?"

"No, as I haven't seen her. I was going to tell both of you over lunch but then thought it would be nice to tell you as I'd see you first anyway, and we could have a little glass of bubbly. Besides, I probably wouldn't be able to keep it to myself until we saw Karen."

"I actually think she's OK with people drinking in front of her now. She's doing really well," I say.

"I'll wait and see what she says later," Jen says.

"Yeah, fair enough. She'll be pleased you thought of her when it came to the drink, though. That's very thoughtful of you to spare her."

"Woohoooooooo!" Jen yells as she pops the cork on the bottle.

"Hang on, I must get the glasses. Don't let it go to waste, what-ever you do. Put your mouth over the bottle or something," I say, laughing.

I run to the kitchen as quickly as possible and grab two cham-pagne flutes. We quickly fill them, and I make a toast to her and Tommy. I can't take my eyes off her flashy ring as I do so.

"Please let me try it on," I plead.

"Sure, here. Don't forget to make a wish! Turn it three times towards your heart. I think that's it."

"Something like that. I'll try it and make a wish, anyway."

"So how're things with you and Jack these days?" she asks.

"Great. It's just a shame he's working so much in LA. I really wish he could be closer, you know?"

"I know. He's great though, Aly. I definitely think there'll be a ring there someday soon."

"You think? I don't know. I mean, yeah, we're together a year, but he has a lot of commitments in LA that I don't think he can give up that easily."

"Well, you don't really have that many here, bar your job. Why don't you move there?" she suggests.

"We'll see. I'm not suggesting it, though, as he might think I'm trying to crowd him or something. Besides that, I like my job now, and I don't know how easy it would be to get into the same market in LA. I could start my own business, I suppose."

"I'd say he'd be more than delighted if you did. When's he due to come to New York again—or are you going there?"

"He's coming next week," I tell her. "Just for three days, but three days is better than nothing. I'm thinking I might take a trip to LA when he's flying back again, but I'll have to see what his schedule is like."

"I think you two are definitely coming to a point where something else will have to happen with you. I bet he'll propose soon."

"Oh, don't say that, please? I'd love that, but don't put the idea into my head because I'll expect it then and it might not happen."

"OK, I won't mention it again. Oh, I'm so excited!" she exclaims.

We drink our champagne and chat about wedding dresses and honeymoons and all the things that are associated with a wedding. I wonder if she will choose Karen and I as bridesmaids or if she will choose someone from Tommy's side.

My phone rings.

"Hello, my sweetheart, how are you today?" comes Jack's voice.

"Oh, Jack, I'm great, thanks. I've some very exciting news for you."

"Sounds like it! What is it?"

"Well, Jen and Tommy got engaged!" I squeal.

"Wow, that's fantastic. They are an awesome couple. I'm very happy for them."

"Hang on two seconds; Jen is here. I'll put you onto her."

I pass the phone to Jen for a few minutes, and I can hear her shrieking down the phone to Jack with the excitement of it all. I love seeing her so happy. She deserves it, and with them just after moving into their new house, I'm pretty sure this will seal the whole deal nicely for her. She passes the phone back to me and wanders into the kitchen.

"Are you guys drunk?" he asks.

"Merry, I'd say. Jen brought a bottle of champers over with her. She's so excited. She's in the kitchen, so we can have a proper chat now if you want. You know Jen; she'd like to give us some privacy."

"Yeah, she's great. I'm really pleased for them."

"So, oh great love of my life, how's life been treating you these days? You're working hard, I take it?" I ask.

"Aren't I always? I'm a little ill, actually. Flu, I think."

"Ah, don't you mean man flu? Is every drip from your nose causing you excruciating pain?"

"I know what man flu is, and you exaggerate," he says. "It's not quite that bad. I've had an iffy stomach the last few days, but it's all OK now. The cold side of it I can handle. I don't get man flu; I don't need to man up in any way, baby."

"Oh, I know you don't, Jack. I just wish you were here to prove it to me now."

"Well, we'll see each other soon, love. I know it's difficult for you, but bear with me as I might have news for you shortly."

"News about what?"

"Like I said, bear with me," he says. I can hear him giving a slight chuckle down the phone, but I don't know why.

"Jack Morgan, are you up to something?" I ask.

"Not really. You'll know soon enough, Hughes."

We continue chatting for over thirty minutes. I feel the need to close the conversation now, as I know Jen is waiting in the kitchen for me. We need to get moving if we want to make our table reservation at the restaurant.

We get to the restaurant in good time, and Karen is waiting for us when we get there. It's unusual for her to be punctual.

"Jen, is this Karen's first outing since she left the clinic?" I whisper before we approach the table.

"I'm not sure, to be honest, hon, but we better not chat too much about it, to be fair. She's seen us now, so let's drop the subject."

"Sure."

"Hey, gorgeous! How are you?" I ask.

Karen stands up and greets both of us with a hug.

"Oh, this is so great that we can do this again," Jen squeals. "Sorry, girls, but I need the ladies', and badly, so excuse me for two minutes." We laugh as she totters off to the ladies' room.

"So, Aly, it's been a while since we've come here," Karen says with a massive smile.

"It is! Are you OK with this, Karen?" I ask.

"Sure! Honestly, I've been braving so much more of late. A couple of nights back, I went to a club with some work friends. I'll be honest, it did bother me a little that I couldn't drink, but not greatly. I felt really good afterwards for staying so strong and having willpower. I think the last time I did that was back when I was fifteen! Then last night, there were drinks at work, and I sat there drinking a soda while everyone else was getting rat-arsed. I felt very pleased with myself. I also saw the state of some of them at the end of the evening, and it was embarrassing. It made me realise what I was doing all along."

"Well, to be fair, we're all guilty of doing embarrassing things after a few drinks, not just you, Karen. I'm so proud of you. You're doing really well. But please be sure and let us know if you feel the need to leave at any stage today, OK?"

"I will, don't worry. Thanks, Aly."

"So what are you two gabbing about?" Jen asks when she returns.

"I was just telling Karen how proud I am of her. She's doing really well."

"You are," agrees Jen. "I'm very proud of you too, and to be honest, it hadn't even entered my head today that this place might be tempting for you. I'm sorry if it is, but we can leave at any time, OK?"

"That's what Aly just said. It's fine, girls. Let's enjoy our lunch— and please, feel free to drink in front of me if you wish to. It's not a problem."

"No, we did that already in Aly's this morning. I didn't want to drink in front of you."

"This morning? I thought I was the one with the drink problem."

"Well, I've got news, Karen."

"You're preggers?"

"Nope! Hardly, if I was drinking this morning," Jen says as she starts waving her hands frantically again. Karen is a bit sharper than I was and spots the ring.

"You're getting married?" she exclaims.

"Yep. You like it?"

"Oh, Jen, come here. I want to hug you, girl. I'm so happy for you. Tommy is a great guy, and you make a fantastic couple. Let's go hat shopping later!"

"Well, that's something I wanted to mention to both of you together. You won't need hats, as I'd like you both to be my bridesmaids."

It feels like we are spending the entire lunch hugging, but this is a good reason to. For once, I'll look forward to being a bridesmaid. As we are having our group hug around the table, our waiter approaches. Unfortunately, it's the one whose bum Karen pinched all that time ago. I know it's something that she won't remember, so I say nothing and hope he won't say anything, either.

"Good afternoon. I'm your waiter, Michael. Can I take your order, please, ladies?"

"Can you give us five minutes, please? We're just having a bit of a girlie moment here. We're so excited, we forgot about looking at the menu," Karen says with a smile.

"Of course. Celebrating something?" he asks.

"I'm getting married!" Jen squeals.

"Congratulations to you," he says. "I'll return in five minutes."

Jen nudges me when he leaves. "Do you remember him?"

"I certainly do. I wasn't going to mention him, but the question is, Karen, do you remember him?"

"Me? No, should I? I didn't, you know, *do* anything with him, did I?"

"Not quite," I say. "You would have liked to, though. Sadly, on that night it didn't work out as planned."

"I'd like to now!" she says as she erupts into laughter.

"Some things never change, do they?" I say with a grin.

"What happened for you to say it didn't work out?" she asks.

Jen and I both respond in unison, "You pinched his arse!"

"I didn't, did I? I'm mortified. Oh, how can I sit here knowing that?" she exclaims.

"You're fine; just pretend nothing happened," I say. "I don't think he even recognised you."

"OK, it takes a lot for my face to flush, Aly, but knowing that I accosted the poor guy has been enough to embarrass me."

"Ladies, compliments of the manager: Laurent Perrier," says the waiter. "I hope it's to your taste."

We all look at each other. I feel so bad for Karen as she loves that champagne. Maybe I should get up and tell the waiter that we can't take it, but Karen doesn't seem to mind.

"That's lovely, thank you," she says. "The girls will enjoy it, but I don't drink."

"Well, I'll see if I can organise a fruit cocktail or two for you then, madam. We can't have you not being spoiled also."

"Thank you, very kind of you."

"Woooooo! You worked that well, Karen. He seemed to take a shine to you today," I say.

"Well, let's hope he thinks that part of me is actually ladylike. I can't believe I did that to him. He is very hot, though, in fairness!"

"He is," says Jen. "Shhh now, here he is again to take the order."

"Now, ready to order?" asks Michael.

"Ready!" we all exclaim in unison.

Once he's finished scribbling on his notebook, he turns to leave the table but then pauses and returns. "Sorry, madam, your fruit cocktail is being made right now. Oh, and I hope you're not in a butt-pinching mood today," he says as he winks and walks away.

Jen and I laugh so hard, and Karen's face lights up like a Christmas tree.

"Please tell me he really didn't say that. Did I imagine it?" she asks.

"Nope! I was certain he didn't recognise you. That's so funny," I giggle.

"No, it's not! I won't be able to eat anything now as I'll be so self-conscious."

"You will, and it was funny, Karen. It was more your face when he said it than anything. Your facial expressions are so funny sometimes," Jen says.

"Cringe, cringe, cringe," Karen mumbles.

"Ah, come on. You'll be fine. Let's forget about it now and just enjoy our meal," I say.

We all agree to forget it, and although the whole episode keeps popping up in conversation unintentionally while we eat, by the time we finish, Karen is treating it as a joke also. She is happily sipping on her second fruit cocktail when Michael approaches again.

"Everything to your satisfaction, ladies?"

"Wonderful, thank you," Karen says. It sounds like she wants him to rush off again, but he stays there for a moment, clearing the dessert plates and looking at Karen every few seconds. When he finally catches her eye, he smiles at her in a very flirtatious manner.

"OK, now if that wasn't flirting with you, I don't know what was," Jen shrieks.

Karen just smiles. It's lovely to see her behaving in such a shy manner. I remember the last time I saw her like that was when she was around fifteen or sixteen, just before she started drinking. It's quite endearing. I know she won't ask Michael out herself, so I decide to butt in and give her a helping hand.

"I'm off to the ladies'. Back in a few minutes," I say.

"OK, see you then."

I walk at a brisk pace towards the ladies' but know I'll have to take a detour up the stairs to find Michael. I don't want the girls to see me and so have to do some ducking and diving on the way. Eventually, I find him. "Hi, Michael is it?"

"Yep, that's me. Is everything OK?"

"Yeah, everything is fine. Listen, Michael, I couldn't help but notice that you took a bit of a shine to my friend earlier."

"Oh, the one who pinched my ass that night? Yeah. She's hot, but she was very drunk that night, and I'm not big on drunken women."

"Well, she doesn't drink anymore, as she said earlier, and she's quite embarrassed about that night. In fact, she didn't even remember it until we told her at the table. So I just came over to tell you that I'm sure she wouldn't mind if you were to ask her out on a date or for a drink—soda, of course, or fruit cocktail!"

"OK, thanks for letting me know. I wasn't sure if I was getting the right vibes from her or not, but I was going to ask her anyway. I'll catch her on the way out. Thanks, um…"

"Oh, Aly. My name is Aly, and she's Karen."

"Cool, thanks, Aly."

I return to the table as quickly as I can.

"You OK? You've been gone a while, Aly."

"Yes, all's great, thanks. I was just fixing my make-up."

We pay the bill and make our way to the exit. I make sure Karen is the last of us to reach the door so that Michael can talk to her. Jen and I are waiting outside for a good ten minutes. Finally, Karen makes an appearance.

"Where were you?" I ask.

"Well, I can't believe this, but it looks like Michael must not have minded me pinching that fine arse of his after all. He's asked me on a date!"

Karen's face is glowing. It's the first date she'll go on since her stint at rehab, and I've a feeling that it will be a proper date for a change. Michael seems like a decent guy.

"Hon, that's fantastic news. I could see him staring at you, trying to catch your eye at the table," Jen says.

"I spotted that, too," I chime in. "Good woman—see, you haven't lost it, and you have no drink in you!"

"Come on, ladies, let's grab a cab and head home," I say. My thoughts on the taxi journey home turn to Jack. I'll call him once I get home as I think our conversation was cut a little short this morning. I miss him terribly, and I hope that one day soon, my life will be as plain-sailing as my best friends' lives are turning out to be.

Chapter 32

*J*ack is arriving from LA today. I'm organising Jen and Tommy's engagement party, which is happening at the weekend, and on top of that, I'm trying to organise a summer party for the work crew. It's stressful, but it's also fun.

Once Jack arrives, I don't want to let him out of my sight as I've missed him so much this time around. I try my best not to be too clingy, though, as I know he likes his space—something we have in common.

It's Thursday afternoon, and we're both lounging around, enjoying each other's company. My phones rings, and it's Jen.

"Aly, how're the party plans going? Sorry for being a stress head, but I just remembered there are four other people who need to be invited."

"No problem, Jen. It's all under control—so much so that I'm having a chill-out day today with Jack. Another four people won't be a problem. I think it will be better to phone them rather than send the invite at this short notice, though. Can you email me the numbers, and I'll call them, please?"

"Maybe I should do it myself. I don't want to cut into your time, hon. It's not often enough that you get to see Jack, so I can do it."

"No, no, listen, I swore to you that I was going to organise this party for you, and that includes late invites also. Email me the numbers. Otherwise, I'll have to call around when you're home later, and I'll dump everything on your shoulders for the party. I really don't think you'd enjoy that somehow."

"OK, OK. I don't particularly want the entire thing to look after; it's your baby after all, even if it is my party. Thanks, Aly; you're the best. I can't believe you are happy to actually organise all of this."

"You know me; I love organising events. Maybe I should change careers. Even though I'm happy enough in my current job, party planning would certainly be something that I'd enjoy. Why has that never occurred to me until now?"

"Why not? Sounds like a great idea, and I'm pretty certain you'll pull out all the stops for us!" she replies.

"I'm certainly doing my best, Jen. See you later, and stop panicking!"

"Will do, thanks, Aly. I'll pop the email through to you now. See you later. Bye."

I hang up, head straight to the computer, and switch it on. This is something I could do without having to think about on my chill-out day, but it's for Jen after all, and it will only take twenty minutes. I walk from the kitchen into the lounge. Jack is looking extremely happy with himself, just sitting there in his sweatpants and bare chest. He's looking hot, if truth be told, but I'm not in the mood for complimenting him as he'll probably end up leading me to the bedroom for some sort of shenanigans, which I don't have time for now, so I keep my mouth shut.

"How does this grab you?" he says.

"What?" I ask as I laugh. I have no idea what he's talking about. The word "grab" has caught my attention though.

"I'm thinking, how about we get dressed up and then go to Central Park for a nice long romantic stroll, maybe take in a bit of dinner on the way home? It's a beautiful day. A little hot right now, but later, when it cools down, there's nothing nicer than a romantic stroll in Central Park. I don't really want to just lounge around here all day, as we have limited time together this time."

"Good call. I don't want to stay in all day either. I just thought you were happy to stay here as you've been working so hard. It's like a treat for you to lounge around these days."

"Yeah, but there's a limit to lounging, and I'm about to reach it now, I think. I'd prefer to be out with you enjoying what this amazing city has to offer."

"Great. Start getting ready, and then I'll sort myself out. I've to ring a few people for Jen's engagement party. Last-minute invites she had forgotten about. They probably won't turn up at this short notice, but no harm in contacting them anyway."

"Oh, honey, it's not a long list, I hope, is it?"

"Nope, four people. Will take a maximum of twenty minutes, I'd say."

"OK, I don't mind at all," he says. "I just know you were enjoying having the day off and doing nothing."

"No problem. You go get ready."

I watch him stroll off towards the bathroom. His sweatpants are just lying at the top of his arse, and I'm unable to take my eyes off him. His upper torso is so tanned from the LA sun, and his fair hair has turned a very light blond. He turns around suddenly and smiles at me as if he can feel me staring at him. I walk to the computer. I can't let him distract me now or I'll never call those guests, and Jen will be frantic.

Finally, I'm ready to leave the apartment. I've tried calling the numbers Jen gave me, but some of them didn't answer, so I had to keep trying until I managed to catch them. I rush out of the apartment as soon as I'm ready.

We stroll into the heart of Manhattan. We saunter past the shops of Fifth Avenue to soak up a bit of atmosphere, and as we pass one shop on a side street, Jack points to a sign on a doorway.

"Look, it's a sign," he says.

"Ah, you're joking. Is it really?" I reply.

"Smart ass, you know what I mean. Read what it says."

"Aly's Parties," I read. "All the help you need with your children's party. Magicians and clowns provided at no extra cost."

"Maybe Jen was right about you," he says. "This could all be a sign."

"Jack, I wouldn't say anything until after you attend the engagement party. It might be dreadful, and people might ridicule me," I say.

"Come on, even if it's crap, nobody is going to say it," he says with a smile.

I throw him a withering glance, jokingly. "Seriously, event planning is something I might look into—but definitely not children's parties. Good on her for coming up with that idea, but I couldn't see myself dealing with auditioning clowns and magicians. Clowns freak me out!"

"Well, I wasn't implying that you become a children's party planner, but why not general parties for offices or even a wedding planner?"

"Now that is something I'd love to be: a wedding planner. It all sounds so romantic, but damn stressful on the day, I'd say. As I said, let's see how the party goes first—and did I tell you I'm organising the summer party for the office also?"

"No, you didn't," he says. "Why aren't you stressed out? You seem so calm about everything, yet you used to stress over the slightest thing to do with meeting up with me before we got serious."

"I know, but that was in case I'd mess things up with you. So you see us as serious?" I ask.

"Uh, yeah, don't you?"

"Yes, but I was just checking. How serious?"

"Very. Aly, remember I mentioned to you that I had something I wanted to talk to you about?"

"Yes."

Oh my God! Are you going to propose to me, Jack Morgan? Please do, please!

"Well, yesterday it was confirmed that we'll be filming in another location for at least six months. It's not in LA, though."

I can feel my heart sink. I'm stupid for thinking he was going to propose. I could chastise Jen for putting the whole idea in my head!

"Where is it?" I ask. I'm hoping he's not going to tell me it's some town that time forgot, where the only style of car that exists is a Lada and there's no such thing as phones or washing machines.

"It's here. New York," he says with a smile.

"Are you serious?"

"Naaawwww. I just said I'd say it for the craic, Aly. Of course I'm serious."

"Jack, are you picking up my Irish sayings and my sarcasm?" I ask.

"Ha, maybe I am! So what do you think?" he asks as he squeezes me tightly.

"Oh, Jack, you've just made my year," I say with a squeal of delight.

We've just entered Central Park, and dark is falling. The sky is a dark-blue shade with a red hue where the sun is setting. It feels really romantic. I still wish he had proposed, but having Jack to myself for six months or more is the next best thing.

Late in the evening, we take in a show. It's great, but I can't concentrate properly as I'm so excited at the thought that in four weeks, I'll have Jack all to myself with no more toing-and-froing between LA and New York for at least six months.

On Saturday morning, Jen calls to the door.

"Sorry to be a pain calling over at this hour, love. I just need to know that everything is in order."

"No problem. Eight thirty is a little early for a Saturday. However, all is under control, my dear. The caterers will be at your house in approximately one hour."

"Oh, caterers? Lovely!" she exclaims. "Aly, you little genius. I thought we'd be making a few sandwiches and cakes ourselves!"

"I do hope you're joking. I'm organising a party, not a cake sale! I'll be over in an hour or so. Is that OK?"

"Perfect. How's Jack?"

"Great, perfect. I love him. He's just amazing," I say with a grin and start swinging out of the door like some loved-up teenager.

"Wow, a good night last night?" she asks.

"The past two days have been good. And, the best news of all is that—are you ready for this?"

"Yes, what is it? Come on, tell me!"

"He's going to be working in New York for six months. It won't come fast enough for me. I'm so happy, Jen."

"Aly, that's fantastic news! This means he won't miss the wedding, either. Although, I'm sure he wouldn't anyway, but I'm so pleased for you."

"I've been grinning from ear to ear since he told me. Look, we'll talk more later. I know you have to go get your hair done and all that. I'll be at yours in an hour or slightly after."

"Thanks, Aly; you're a true pal. I'm so thrilled Jack is here for a while with you. I'm telling you, it's getting more serious, Aly. The proposal is on the way."

"Oh, I don't know about that, Jen. I don't think he's thinking like that. I'm happy to just have him here with me."

"I know, I know, and I don't want to be putting those thoughts in your head again, as I know if it doesn't happen it will be disappointing for you. Sorry; I'll zip my mouth in the future. See you later, girl, and thanks again."

Jen waves at me as she leaves the building. I know she doesn't want to plant any seeds in my head, but I think it's too late for that as I really hope I will be Mrs. Jack Morgan one day.

I run inside and get myself ready to face what I hope will be a well-organised party. I kiss Jack goodbye and walk to the end of the street to Jen's new abode. It's a jaw-droppingly beautiful house. Jen has it decorated to perfection and had all the old floorboards sanded down and varnished. It must have cost them an incredible amount of money to finish it, but I'm certain it's worth every penny.

Tommy lets me in and leaves me to get on with things. I've ordered certain artefacts to place at various points throughout the house. They give it a Roman effect, which Jen has expressed an interest in. Thankfully, the caterers are bang on schedule and get to work immediately. To make things a little less expensive on them, I'm doing the flower arranging myself. I bought the flowers in bulk yesterday, and they were delivered to the house this morning.

I've just started an arrangement, and as I reach for another flower, I feel a hand pulling my hair back and lips kissing my neck.

"Hello. I wasn't aware you did flower arranging. Isn't that something old women do?"

He's lucky he's hot as it's making the temptation to give him a little playful slap wane. "I'll have you know, this is a form of art, and any age group can do it," I say. "For that comment, there'll be no canoodling tonight, and it's your last night here."

"Canoodling? What kind of a word is that for a modern-day woman to use? Wow, between flower arranging and canoodling, I think I'll be better off," Jack says with a laugh.

I actually agree with him, but I'm not going to admit that to him! "Flower arranging isn't something I do on a regular basis. It's something I learned at school many years back. Not that there is anything wrong with it! Oh, I hate when you make it difficult for me not to laugh, Jack," I say with a grin.

"I'm only kidding around. They look awesome. Jen is going to be thrilled. I was just talking to Tommy out back. He's very excited about the wedding. They are thinking three months' time."

"Oh, that soon? Jen didn't mention anything the other day or this morning. Although she did mention that you'd be here for it when I told her you're going to be working here for six months. Maybe they plan on announcing it today," I say.

"Yeah, maybe. Maybe there's a baby on the way?" Jack suggests.

"I hadn't thought of that. Maybe, Jack! Wouldn't that be exciting? Or it could just be that they don't want to hang around."

"Sure, actually on that note…" Jack slides his arms around my waist. "You never mentioned kids before. Are you interested in them?"

My heart is thumping. *Are you asking me if I want to have your babies?*

"I am, yes. Why? Are you planning on giving me one?" I say.

"Ahhhhh, and she's off on her sarcastic trail again. I knew I wouldn't be able to have a serious conversation with you about this."

"OK, I'll be serious. Yes, I'd like a baby, or maybe even two if it happens. I take it you'd like one yourself if you are bringing this up."

"I'd love babies; maybe even more than two. Aly, picture it—can you see our kids? They'd be pretty good-looking kids," he says with a broad smile.

"That'll be thanks to my beautiful genes," I say with a smirk.

"But of course!"

"One thing, though. Remember, I'd be the one pushing them out, so we'll see about more than two," I say and turn my attention back to the flowers.

I wasn't expecting Jack to come out with something like the baby question. It definitely makes me realise that he is very serious about me, and maybe Jen is right. He might pop the question soon.

I glance back to Jack, and he looks happy. I know he'll make a fantastic dad one day, and I hope it will be to my children.

The day progresses nicely. Jack mingles with the guests, and I run from point A to point B like a lunatic for the day. I don't want to let Jen down, and it means a great deal to me to ensure everyone is happy and that my party planning works out well.

Tommy asks everyone to gather around. "I've got a little announcement here, if I could just get Jen up here as well, please? Lovely, my future wife has run off already."

Everyone laughs.

"I'm here, sorry!" Jen squeezes through the congregation and makes her way to the centre of the room.

"I'd just like to thank our best friend, Aly, for organising this party today. I think you'll all agree it's been a great event."

I'm puce. I hate when people place the attention on me. They all clap politely and smile. It's a very upper-class party, and the people are very reserved—a little too reserved for me and definitely for Karen. I glance in her direction, and she smiles and holds her glass of orange juice up as if to say "cheers."

"Also, I want to say how beautiful my future wife looks today, and above all, we wanted to share with you that we have set the date for the wedding already. It's going to be a little over three months' time, and invites will be issued six weeks beforehand. I'm sure and hope most of you will be able to make it, and it should be a wonderful day. Anything to add, Jen?"

"Not much, Tommy. I just want to say a big thank you also to Aly for planning today. I told you, you should set up your own party planning business! Also a big thank you—"

I hear the doorbell ring. I go to answer it, as I need fresh air after being the focus of everybody's attention for a few minutes. When I open the door, a very handsome man is standing in front of me. He's carrying a bottle of Laurent Perrier champagne and a few bottles of various fruit juices. He looks familiar.

"Hello!" I utter.

"Hi, Aly. How are you?" he says.

"I'm fine, thanks; and you?"

"Great, thanks. I can tell by your face, you're not sure who I am. I look a little different when I'm not in my waiter's uniform. Michael...from Buddakan?"

"Oh, Michael, I'm so sorry. You do look different. It's probably because Karen's hand isn't glued to your arse. I jest. Come in, Karen is over there," I say, pointing in her direction.

"Can I use the restroom, please, Aly? I've had a long walk here."

"Of course; it's just over here."

Once I usher him into the bathroom, I run to Karen.

"Lady, you never told me Michael was coming! I haven't seen you all week. Did you go on your date already?"

"We did. In fact, Aly, we've been on two dates since. He's different."

"Different in what way?"

"I honestly don't know. It could be in the sense that he actually cares about what I say and think. He listens to me. That's a first. I'm used to going out with gobshites. Well, you know what kind of guys I used to see before."

"That's great news, Karen. Yeah, I remember those guys. Not the nicest, if I recall. Still, that was the old days. He's certainly a chivalrous sort. Look at the ridiculous amount of stuff he brought with him!"

"I know, and he remembered you both like the Laurent Perrier."

"Well, that's for Tommy and Jen. I won't be touching it. He's lovely, Karen. Are you in this one for the long haul, then?"

"Bit early to say that, Aly. Two dates?" she says, laughing. "I will say, though, I've never been interested in a guy as much as I am him."

Michael returns and walks towards us, smiling.

"I'll let you two chat. Michael, delighted you came today. It's great to see you again."

"I'm delighted to be here, Aly. It's good to see you, and I'm sure we'll chat more later."

I can't see Jack anywhere, so I go search for him. It's starting to get a little darker outside, and I have a feeling my man is probably sitting out the back, watching the sunset.

"I thought you'd be out here," I say. "You OK?"

"I'm fine, Aly. I'm just thinking about things."

"Baby things?"

"No," he says. "Well, yeah, sort of. I'm just summing up the whole picture in my head. Meeting you, how we got together, how we've stayed so strong through the distance. It's so nice when I'm here with you or you're in LA with me. I shouldn't really declare this to you as you'll take it as an opportunity to mock me."

"No I won't. What is it?"

"Well, lately I haven't been myself. I've really missed you terribly when you're not around me. I don't know; we need to fix that."

I pull a puppy-dog face.

"I'm not going to mock. I just feel the urge to give you a massive bear hug now—one that you won't forget."

"Well, luckily I won't have to remember the bear hug in four weeks. I can get them on tap then. This is the right thing for me to do, Aly. It's the next step for us. Are you happy with that?" he asks.

"Jack, I couldn't be happier. I just wish it was tomorrow and not another month away."

"I'm just glad to know that. It'll be six months of us together every day. I hope I don't crowd you too much," he says.

"I'll kick you out if you do; don't worry. I mean, I love you but not that much," I say with a smile.

"Hmm, is that right? Should I move into my own apartment if that's the case?" he asks teasingly.

"OK, if that's what you want."

"No, wait—Aly, I was joking."

"I know. So was I, ya big eejit," I say light-heartedly.

"Well, come here, ya big eejit, and let me kiss ya," Jack jests in a very fake Irish accent. It's bad, but it does make me laugh.

We walk back into the main area where people are still linger-ing, but the crowd is starting to dwindle. Jen looks very elegant in the new dress she's bought, and Tommy is incredibly tall and hand-some next to her. They make a perfect couple. I study the room and see Karen and Michael getting closer at the other side. He's exactly what she needs to get back on track, and they both seem just as eager to get to know one another. I take Jack's hand and lead him to the front door. "Time for us to slip away, Mr. Morgan."

"Won't they miss us?" he asks.

"No. They know you're going back tomorrow, and we need our time alone."

"Suits me!"

It's so romantic at night-time on Charles Street. The old-style lamps that light the pavement add great charm to the street. I always get a nice feeling in the pit of my stomach walking here. We decide to take a detour and pass by the old building where I used to live. I always smile when I see it as it reminds me of my first kiss with Jack. Sadly, the scaffolding that surrounds it distorts my memory slightly. We're walking past the building when Jack stalls for a moment, looks up at the steps and smiles. Then he grabs my hand and keeps walking.

I wonder what he's thinking about.

$\mathcal{A}$fter two successful events, I've decided to conduct some research into costs of setting up on my own. The office summer party went down a treat with everyone, and I'm very pleased
with myself.

The weeks are passing by quickly, and Jack calls every night or
vice versa. Both of us are waiting for the day when we can actually
live together as a couple rather than just every second or third
week or weekend.

It's Thursday afternoon, and I'm extremely busy in the office.
David, my new boss, keeps passing more client accounts my way
as we're getting more and more new customers each week. The
workload is heavy, but I don't complain. He has just as much on
his plate—at least that's how he makes it look. There's a knock on
the door, and I look up to see David standing there.

"Sorry, didn't see you there. You haven't been waiting there
long I hope?" I say.

"No, Aly, don't worry. Just a few minutes. Thought it would be
fun to see how long it would take you to spot me, though. I've an
idea I want to run by you."

"OK, fire away. What is it?"

"You did a magnificent job of the office party, and everyone's
been commenting on it," he says.

"Oh, thanks very much. I have to admit, I'm quite proud of myself of late as I organised my friend Jen's engagement party, too, which was far more refined and reserved than the office party."

"Yes, well, to be fair, they are very different events. You really surpassed yourself, though, and I've mentioned to the big guns if they'd be interested in having a corporate event planner in the company, as we must be the only company out there that doesn't have one. Even the Cork office has one."

"I agree. I was a little shocked to discover that position doesn't exist here."

"They thought it was an excellent idea. So if you're interested, there's a promotion on the cards for you. I know you're pretty swamped dealing with our new clients right now, and to be fair, you've been dealing with most of the problems the team has on top of some creative duties you've taken on. However, I suggested to them that we could take on one or two extra team members to offload the freelance verse decision making to them and some of the new design decisions. What do you think?"

"I'm speechless!" I exclaim.

"Really? That's a first for you. You normally give us a pain in our brains from talking," he says with a grin.

"Not really, but I am in shock, and thanks. I won't talk anymore if that's the case."

"You know I'm kidding."

"I know. It does make sense to have an event planner. Would it mean dropping a huge amount of my current workload and job? I don't want to lose what I'm doing now, either, as I really enjoy it. Dealing with our big clients is a good experience for me."

"I've taken all of that into consideration, and we had quite a lengthy discussion about the event planning. I don't think there would be massive demand on you just yet, but when it gets to the stage that you need assistance, we'll get someone in to help you out. I think it would be a great opportunity for you, particularly as you've expressed an interest in becoming self-employed one day in that line of work."

"True. OK, can I think it over and let you know tomorrow, please? Is that OK?"

"Sure, of course it is," he says. "I wasn't expecting you to give me an answer right now, but I definitely think you'd be the right person for the job. By the way, you'd be getting a considerable raise, too."

"OK, now you've caught my attention," I say. "It certainly sounds great—and you're right, it would be a great opportunity for me. I'll sleep on it, and I'll want to discuss it with Jack also to get his input."

"When are we going to meet this famous Jack, by the way?"

"Maybe at the next office event!"

David smiles and leaves my office. I'm so excited, I have to call Jack immediately and tell him.

Later that day, I meet Jen. She's happy as the wedding plans are coming together nicely.

"I hope you're not offended that I didn't get you to organise the wedding," she says.

"Please tell me you're kidding me. Jen, I've no experience of organising something as grand as a wedding. The engagement party was fine. Smaller crowd, and to be honest, you didn't have any massive expectations, but a wedding? If you had asked me, I would have probably had to say no anyway, hon. I just wouldn't have the confidence to do something so large-scale."

"I'm relieved to know that. However, I can see you doing larger-scale events someday."

"Well, on that note. I've been offered a promotion at work. They want me to take on the role of event planner, as they don't have one. They'll take some of my current duties off my hands to accommodate me. I'll be on a salary similar to what Karen used to earn!"

"Nice! I assume you'll take it?" she asks.

"Yeah, but I want to have a think about it," I say. "I'll let them know tomorrow. I'll chat to Jack first."

"I'm so thrilled Jack is coming to New York for six months. It's so great for you, Aly. You're really good for each other."

"Yeah, we are a good combination. I'm curious as to how we'll get on, though, as we're not used to being around each other so much."

"I'm sure it will be fantastic, Aly. It's like when Tommy and I moved in together. We had the odd spat at the start, but then we realised what got on each other's nerves and what not to do or say. It's great when you get to know the person that well."

"That's the part I'm looking forward to—knowing him inside out. I think we know each other pretty well already, but it will make all the difference having him here."

Time passes a little too quickly as we are both really enjoying our chat, and before we know it, it's time to return to work.

"Thanks for the lunch, Aly. I'll see you Saturday for your dress fitting!" she says.

"See you, Jen. I'll be there on time! I'm looking forward to this. You haven't told us what colour we're wearing yet!" I say.

"I know. It's a surprise. You'll both like it, though. Bye!"

We both go our separate ways, and I think again about my prospective new job as I stroll back to the office. It's definitely the right decision to take the challenge and gain the experience I need to set up on my own.

Friday morning, I wake with a grin etched across my face. In one week, Jack will be in New York, and I'm ecstatic. It's very early for me to wake, but I can't sleep anymore, so I decide to be healthy and walk to work. I really enjoy New York at this hour when there aren't many people around yet. The rush hour is a while away yet, and I can think properly when it's like this, without horns blowing and people shouting.

There aren't many people in the office yet. It's too early, but I spy my boss sitting at his desk.

"Hey, good morning, boss!" I say with a smile. "Can I have a word, please?"

"Sure, Aly, come on in. Have you come to a decision?"

"I have indeed, and I'd love to accept the offer."

"Wonderful, Aly; we'll get the paperwork sorted as soon as possible. I think you've made a really sound decision here. Well done, and congratulations."

"Oh, thanks, David. I feel I've made a sound decision, too. I'm really excited about it all. On that note, I've loads on my desk that needs to be dealt with. I really just wanted to drop in and let you know as soon as I got in."

"Sure, I appreciate you not making me chase you for an answer. Thanks, Aly. I'll speak with HR now about your contract."

"Thanks, David. Speak to you later," I say as I leave the office. I feel elated. For the first time in a long time, I feel happy in the workplace again.

The day passes very quickly as there are stacks of verses that need correcting and submitting for printing, and when I finally get home, I kick my shoes off and relax in a nice hot bubble bath.

The next morning, I'm up early to get myself ready for the dress fitting. I still have no idea what colour dress Jen has picked for us. I'm guessing it isn't yellow, as I'd never forgive her if she put me in a yellow dress.

I pass by my old apartment on the way and decide to call in on Mr. DeAngelo. It's been a while since I've seen him, and I miss him. I ring all the bells in the building.

"Ha! I knew it was you, ya crazy kid. Come on in!"

I make my way inside and give Mr. DeAngelo a great big hug.

"Mr. De, it's great to see you. Is everything good with you? I haven't heard from you in a while. I was worried and missing you."

"Ah, Aly, I know you're busy. I didn't want to disturb you. How's that nice fella of yours? You must bring him around. The building will be finished soon, so the place will look more respectable then."

"Oh, I will. You'll love Jack. He's a New Yorker by birth."

"Well, you can't go wrong with him then. Is he in the card business, like you?"

"No, he's an actor. You might know him. Jack Morgan is his name."

"Holy moly, you're datin' Jack Morgan? He's famous, Aly! Jeez, you got a good one there, honey. Plenty of notes in the bank. You won't starve," he says with a chuckle.

I laugh out loud. "I certainly won't. He is a good guy and treats me well. I'm a lucky lady."

"You certainly are a lady, and it's all you deserve. I think he's the lucky one. I definitely want to meet him. Maybe he can give me a few acting lessons, and I'll start a new career for myself. You're never too old, not even at seventy-eight."

"Ah, Mr. De, you're not seventy-eight, surely? I thought you were only thirty-eight."

"Oh, you charmin' Irish lass. I dated an Irish girl once. She was hot, but we didn't last long. I was, ya know, sowing my wild oats as they say. I had no interest in anyone for too long. I regretted it afterwards. She married that Pete Cusamano. That made me sick. Anyway, enough of my waffle. Where are you off to today?"

"You know Jen? She's getting married. I'm a bridesmaid, so I have a dress fitting now. In fact, I'm sorry, but I'll have to go, or I'll be late. I promise I'll bring Jack over soon, though, as he's moving to New York for six months. Once the building work is completed here, we'll pop over, OK?"

"You go, honey, and enjoy life. Marry that man of yours, and if he tries to let ya go, tell him he's a fool. He could end up like me, regretting it for the rest of his life," he says with a smile.

I give him a hug and carry on in the direction of the dress shop.

I reach the boutique before anyone else, and I wait inside. The assistant is very friendly, and I can't help trying to obtain some information from her.

"So what style of dress did Jen pick again? She mentioned it to me during the week, but I can't visualise it."

"I don't think she did. She told me it was a surprise for you when you both get here. I'm not saying anything."

"Just please tell me it's not big, flouncy, and yellow. Please tell me that at least?"

"No, it's not. It's really beautiful. I'd imagine it will be amazing on you."

"OK. Hmmm, I'm intrigued now."

Jen and Karen arrive within one minute of each other. After plenty of air kisses, it's down to business. We wait patiently for the assistant to bring the dresses to the front of the shop.

"Oh, Jen, I'm excited. I was trying to squeeze some information out of her before you got here. She wasn't budging, though. Although, I did manage to get her to tell me that it's not big, flouncy, or yellow."

"As if I'd put you in a yellow dress!" exclaims Jen.

"I know. That's what I was thinking, but I had to double-check. Oh, here she comes!"

"Ladies, these are your bridesmaid dresses," says the assistant. "I hope you like them." She peels back the dress bag covering them to reveal a beautiful royal-blue shade. It's stunning. The dress itself is straight with a cowl neck effect at the front and a button-up back. I'm so happy.

"Jesus, that's stunning," Karen says.

"It is. Come on, let's try them on," I shriek with joy.

Jen looks pleased with her choice and at our reaction.

Thankfully, they fit reasonably well but might need one or two alterations. We proceed to the front of the shop again where Jen is sitting patiently, and we perform like models on the runway for her.

"Girls, you look so beautiful. Aly, the dress is perfect with your eyes. It really makes them sparkle. Gorgeous! Karen, I always love that colour on you. You look so gorgeous, both of you do. I'm really pleased. Do you like them?"

"We love them!" we both exclaim.

Everyone is happy with the dresses, and the shop assistant gets to work placing pins in the areas where the alterations need to be made.

"I've no boobs at all in this dress. I should really be wearing a padded bra," I say.

"We can give you chicken fillets now and perhaps wear them on the day also?" the assistant suggests.

"Oh, no chicken fillets, thanks. I'll stick with au natural," I utter.

"Good for you, Aly," says Jen. "You look beautiful, girl. I don't want you being uncomfortable, either, on the day. Chicken fillets are a pain in the arse."

"OK, I go as myself then. Karen, are you happy with yours?"

"I love it, girls. Sorry if I'm a little quiet. It's been a long time since I've worn something as beautiful as this. I'm really looking forward to the wedding, particularly as I'll remember every minute of it."

Jen smiles as she heads for the changing room to try on her dress.

I look at Karen's stunning face, which is smiling effortlessly. She has come so far, and her progress is incredible. It's a pleasure to see her smiling and looking good again.

"Karen, you look a picture of prettiness in that dress. We'll all have such a great day. Oh, and by the way, I'm assuming Michael is going as your date?"

"Yes, he is. I asked him the other day, and he was thrilled. He thinks you're all so lovely and couldn't believe you're going out with Jack. He thought he was so cool and friendly on the day of the party. He loved the fact that he was seeing someone who is so down to earth."

"I still don't see him as being famous, though. Michael is a sweet guy, Karen. I'm really happy for you."

"Thanks, Aly. It means a lot to me that you like him."

Jen approaches looking like a princess. Her dress is ivory and floor length with a small train at the back. It isn't very fussy—some beading and crystals in the bodice and along the edge of the train. She looks like every bride should: beautiful.

"Well?" she asks.

I look at Karen and Karen looks at me. Both of our eyes fill with tears.

"We don't have words, Jen; you look so beautiful."

"That dress. If I ever get married, that's the kind of dress I'd like," Karen says.

Jen glances at herself in the mirror, and I can see a few tears form in her eyes also. Eventually, we calm down, and our tears of joy turn to laughter.

The assistant pins Jen's dress. She's had to go up one size, but it's a little too big on her. It's great she's gaining weight, and she will look the picture of health for her big day.

"What will we do now? We're all so happy," Jen asks.

"I can suggest something which one of you will cringe at and the other will probably agree with," I say.

"What's that?" Karen says, sounding sceptical.

"Well, we've all been very busy of late, and we haven't had as many girlie days out. So why don't we head back to mine and grab some DVDs? I'll cook dinner, and we'll throw a bit of a Bon Jovi and eighties party into the mix. I haven't heard music in so long. I've just not had time to listen to any."

"Sounds great, bar the Bon Jovi side of it," Karen snarls with a grin.

"I'm good for that. Let's do it. Come on, Karen, we know you secretly like them," Jen says.

"Oh, they're OK. Just not something I'd listen to on a regular basis. Then again, anytime I ever heard them I was drunk, so maybe I'll find I do like them now I'm sober."

We all laugh.

"OK, let's go girls," I say.

We walk out of the shop and into the noise of Fifth Avenue. It doesn't bother us as we're all feeling so happy, and the best is yet to come: quality time with each other, something we haven't had in a long, long time.

Chapter 34

"Honey, I'm home," the voice coming from the lounge says. I run out to see Jack standing there, arms wide open, waiting for a hug.

"What are you doing here? I was meant to collect you from the airport."

"I know. I thought it would be nice to surprise you here instead, in what I can now call *our* home."

"It was lucky I wasn't out then, wasn't it? Glad I gave you that key. You would have had to either pester Jen and Tommy or else sit on the steps outside until I reached you."

"Well, that was the whole point of me doing this. I wouldn't have just arrived here unless I had a key. Admittedly, I took a chance on you being here, but then again, haven't I taken many chances on you so far, Hughes?"

I smile and hug him tightly. It's no longer my home but our home, and it sounds and feels so right.

After sharing a nice, relaxing weekend together, it's all go today for Jack as he starts his new job. My day just seems to be dragging. I'm dying to get home to hear all about it. I'm out the door like a bolt of lightning before the workday officially ends.

I reach home, and there's no sign of him yet, so I decide to cook a nice romantic meal for us. I'm making a lovely steak-and-Guinness pie, which he loves. I leave it simmering on the hob while

I quickly go to buy a bottle of wine. There are horns blowing and people shouting in all directions when I get outside.

I reach the corner and ask a lady who is standing there, observing, "Sorry, do you know what's going on?"

"There was a major accident, honey. It's causing chaos with the traffic. The taxi drivers are going ballistic."

"I can see. I hope no one got hurt."

"Not sure. There were a few ambulances on the scene, though."

"OK, thanks for the information."

"Sure, doll, it's no problem."

I carry on walking to the shop and buy my wine. I realise I'll have to rush back as soon as I can, as the pie will be ruined and the apartment on fire if I stall too long.

I return home within five minutes and go straight to the kitchen. I check the food and then call Jack's mobile. It's ringing out, as I expected. I leave a message asking him to call me back.

It's getting late in the evening, and there's still no news from Jack. I start to worry as he always calls when I leave a message for him. I dial his number again. It rings a few times and diverts me to voicemail again.

Half an hour later, there's a knock on my door. I run to open it, as it must be Jack after forgetting his key.

"Hi, ma'am. Are you Aly Hughes?" asks the uniformed man at the door.

"Yes, I am."

"My name is Officer Delaney from NYPD."

Jesus! Why are the police here? Am I in trouble?

"OK. How can I help you?" I ask.

"Ma'am, I'm afraid I've got some bad news. Do you know Jack Morgan?"

I think my heart is going to explode! My hands are trembling, and my eyes are full of tears. I swallow the large lump which has formed in my throat and manage to say, "Y...yes, I do. Has something happened to him?"

"Ma'am, he was in an accident today not too far from here. There was a three-car pileup, and unfortunately, he got the brunt of the damage."

"Oh, my God, is he, is he de—"

"No! Ma'am, no, don't think like that. Thank God, he's alive, but he's been badly injured. I'm sorry, are you OK?"

I try to choke back the tears, but they have already started falling. The relief that he's alive makes me want to cry even more.

"What hospital is he in? Can I go see him? Will he know who I am?"

"He's in bad shape, but you never know, he might be able to recognise you. They are doing various tests on him still. However, I think it would be good if you go to see him. I'm assuming you're related to him. There have been a number of missed calls from you on his cell phone, which is why we're here."

"I'm his partner," I tell him. "He's only just come to live in New York. I can't believe this has happened. It was his first day on a new show today."

"I thought it might be that Jack Morgan. I wasn't on the scene myself. Do you need a lift to the hospital?"

"Yes, please, if it's not too much trouble."

"No trouble at all. I'll wait outside until you're ready. Take your time. I know this has been a shock for you."

"Thank you, Officer Delaney."

I ignore his advice in relation to taking my time. I grab my coat and rush outside. Thankfully, as I'm closing the door, I remember the pie ingredients are still cooking on the hob, and I return to switch it off.

Ten minutes later, I'm in the hospital. I head straight for the emergency room, and when I reach it, I catch a glimpse of myself in a mirror. I have streaks of black running down my face, my make-up is blotchy, and I really look a sight. However, it doesn't matter. All that matters to me right now is Jack, and I really want to see him.

The nurses and doctors are running from one room to another, and it seems like they have experienced more than one accident in their emergency room today. It's all a bit chaotic to me. I am feeling tired and weak and need someone to help me. The whole strain and worry of what has happened to Jack has left me in a mess, and as I stand in the middle of the room with people rushing about me, I start crying. I cry so hard and crouch down against the nearest wall I can find to support me. I'm feeling so lonely. Right now I'm alone in a big city, and the only person I have ever truly loved is here somewhere in this hospital in pain, and I don't know where he is.

A nurse approaches me. "Honey, are you OK? Here, dry your eyes. What's happened?"

"I'm looking for Jack." The words stumble from my mouth. I don't even know if I'm making sense. I'm in a daze.

"It's OK. Are you talking about Jack Morgan?"

"Yes, he's my partner."

"OK, I don't want to sound rude, but I need a name from you and your ID if you have it, please. We don't have big stars like him around here too often, and we need to protect him in case of any fans finding out he's here. I'm sure you understand."

"Yes, that's fine. Here's my ID. I'm Aly."

I'm only now realising how big a star in the United States Jack actually is. I've always seen him as Jack Morgan, my man. However, now I know what comes with his career: the security, the fan base, the psychos!

The nurse takes my hand.

"Let's get you cleaned up before you go see your handsome man. You're such a pretty woman; you want to give him something to smile about when he sees you, don't you?"

I nod my head. My hands are shaking, and I just want to get washing my face over and done with. All I care about is seeing Jack, and I know he won't give a damn about whether I have streaks of mascara running down my face or not.

"Now, honey, I need to prepare you," she says.

"For what?" I ask.

"Jack's been injured pretty badly. He's just back from having some head scans, and the doctor should be around shortly to discuss them with him. I'm sure if the doctor gives it the all clear, you can stay with him. He was in shock and didn't know what happened when they brought him in, but he's been muttering your name, so that's good. He's badly bruised and has some broken bones. You need to be prepared, OK?"

"OK."

We walk towards the room, and I start shaking again. There's a police officer sitting outside. "What's he doing here?" I quiz.

"He's security, honey. As I said, Jack's a high-profile client. We have to keep the overzealous fans at bay."

"OK, I'm his partner though, not a fan. Well, I am obviously, but you know what I mean."

She gives a chuckle. "I know what you mean."

I turn the handle on the door and enter the room. I can't believe my eyes. My handsome man is purple from head to toe. His face is swollen, his eyes almost closed. Both of his legs and one of his arms are in plaster.

"Jack, love, it's me, Aly."

He turns his head slightly and lets out a sigh. His right arm edges towards me. I hold his hand gently so as not to hurt him.

"I...I can't. I can't speak very well. It hurts," he whispers.

"It's OK; you don't need to. We can sit here in silence, or if you want, I can talk the arse off you, and you'll wish I never turned up," I say in a bid to lighten the mood.

He smirks as best he can, but he's also wincing in pain.

"Sorry, love, I don't want to cause you anymore pain," I say. "I was just trying to cheer you up a bit."

"I know. You have. Thanks," he says.

"I won't stay too long. You need to rest. The doctor should be here shortly with your scan results. I'd like to stay for that, if you don't mind?"

He nods his head in agreement.

"OK, Dr Jackson is here with the scan results. Are you staying, honey?" the nurse asks.

"Yes, please," I reply.

"Hi, I'm Dr Jackson. You must be Aly?"

"Yes, that's me."

"Jack is a very lucky man, Aly," he says with a smile. "Well, Jack, I have good news. You've escaped any brain damage."

"Oh thank God!" I yelp.

"However, you have got a concussion and obviously the various broken bones, which you know about already, and you've got a punctured lung. We'll be keeping you in intensive care unit for observation for the next few days. It's just a precaution, and then we'll move you to a private room."

Jack nods.

"Thank you, Dr Jackson. Can I have a quick word outside?" I ask.

"Of course."

We edge our way outside the door.

"What damage has been done exactly?" I ask. "I can see he has broken bones, but internally, how much damage has been done?"

"He suffered a punctured lung, Aly, so it's difficult for him to talk. So please don't try to force any talking out of him. In addition, he has two broken legs, a fractured left arm, multiple bruising throughout his body, and a broken nose and cheekbone. Bad as it sounds, he'll be back to himself in a few weeks. It will take time, but a lot of TLC from you will put him back on his feet quickly."

"I didn't realise it was so bad. He has a punctured lung, too? Can you fix that?"

"Yes, we've worked on it already. However, right now he needs to keep the oxygen mask on."

"I'll make sure he does. Thank you, Dr Jackson."

I return to the room and smile at Jack. I wonder if he can see the worry on my face. I hope not. I sit here with him for the rest of the night. I really want to leave him in peace and get some rest. However, he's holding my hand, and if I give the slightest inkling that I'm leaving the room, he looks upset.

The following morning, I have no idea where I am when I wake. My head is stuck to the blanket—I wish I didn't drool so much in my sleep—and Jack is awake and staring at me. I can see the little twinkle in his eye and know he is smiling—probably even laughing at me over the drool-stained blanket. I don't mind. If it brings a smile to his face, I'm happy.

"How are you feeling today, my love?" I ask. "Actually, don't answer. It could hurt, so just squeeze my hand if you're feeling a little bit better. A smidgen will do."

I feel a light squeeze. He probably did it just to make me feel better as he looks like he must be in terrible pain.

"Love, I'm going to go to the ladies' and then to ring the girls, OK? They have no idea that this has happened and will worry if they've tried to call me and can't get through. My mobile is switched off."

He squeezes my hand again.

Walking out into the fresh air is just what I need. I take a few deep breaths. Looking at my reflection in the glass door, I look like something from *Night of the Living Dead*. However, my appearance is not the issue right now. I dial Jen and Karen's numbers. Jen is practically in the car on her way already. Karen says she'll call around to the apartment and gather a few things for me in case I want to stay at the hospital. I gave both girls a spare key in case of any emergencies ever happening.

Jen arrives and cries the minute she sees Jack.

"Please, Jen, try not to cry," I tell her. "He gets really upset."

"Sorry, Aly. Look, I'll come back as he's not up for us crying into his face. I just can't get over this happening to poor Jack. Look, I'll call in later again with Tommy. Aly, I'm so sorry. Are you coping OK? If you need anything, you call me immediately, OK?"

"Sure, thanks. I'm doing OK. I was worse yesterday, but I've had a little sleep at least. Thanks. I appreciate you coming here."

"I feel I should stay," she says.

"No, you go, Jen. You'll only be hanging around in the waiting room, as he can't have many visitors. Maybe when he's feeling a little better in a few days, we can try and cheer him up then."

"OK. I'll still call this evening with Tommy, though."

"Thanks, Jen," I say with a smile as she squeezes my arm.

She leaves, and as she does, I see Karen trotting down the corridor in her seven-inch heels. Thankfully, she's a little more thick-skinned than Jen and manages to keep the tears at bay until she leaves the room.

I walk the corridor with her.

"Oh, Aly, I'm so sorry," she says. "I didn't realise it was so bad. He's so lovely; he doesn't deserve this."

"I know he doesn't, Karen, but we have to look towards him improving now and getting back on his feet. I need him to think positive thoughts."

"You're right. I'm so upset to see him like this. I'll stay out here for a while. I can't go home knowing you're here on your own."

"Honestly, it's fine. I'm happy once I'm here with Jack, and it's going to be boring for you sitting around a waiting room. Really, Karen, go home or do something with your day, pet. I appreciate you wanting to stay, but it wouldn't be fair to you."

"OK. Make sure you call if you need anything else from the apartment or anywhere," she says.

"Thanks, I will, Karen."

Later that night, I decide to go home to get some proper rest. The nurse suggested that I go as Jack is sleeping soundly. They have sedated him for the pain, and I know there's nothing I can do for him.

The following day, I don't manage to wake until midday. I've been sleeping for over fourteen hours. I rush to get myself organised and head back to the hospital. When I get there, Karen, Jen, and Tommy are sitting in the waiting room.

"Hi," I say with a smile.

"Hey, you. You OK? We were worried when you weren't here. Jack's out for the count," Jen says.

"Oh, thankfully. I went home last night as the nurse suggested I should get some rest. He was sleeping soundly when I left."

"Seems like he's still in snoozy land," Karen says, smiling.

"I hope he's OK. I mean, that's a lot of sleep."

"Aly, he's sedated. He'll drift in and out of sleep all the time. He won't even realise you're there half the time. It's probably better for him, though. He's on morphine too, I'd imagine, for the pain," Karen says.

"Yeah, a high dose of it, I believe. Well, good. Wouldn't it be fantastic if he woke up and felt great?" I say in a hopeful voice.

They all look at each other. I know in my heart that it won't be the case. He will be in pain for some time yet, but I will help him get through it.

Six weeks pass, and after many sleepless nights by his side, Jack is finally allowed to go home. I feel elated at the thought of actually having him back with me, even if it will be difficult for both of us. The bruising on his face has gone down considerably, and he's starting to look like the Jack Morgan I first met. The plaster from his arm and legs has been removed, and it will only be another week or so before he can start to work properly on strengthening his legs. He's been through a week of physiotherapy already. We arrive home. Jack is smiling and seems happy until he has to be taken upstairs via stretcher.

"What's with the long face, Morgan?" I ask.

"Why can't I attempt to walk up? I've been flat on my back for long enough!"

"Grumpy drawers, these men are here to help you. You would probably have to drag your body up, as you've no muscle built up in your legs. How many flights of stairs do you think this building has, one?"

"OK, OK," he says. "I'm not being grumpy, just a bit annoyed."

"Same difference," I say.

Once I get him settled, Jen, Tommy, Karen, and Michael arrive to see him. He's pleased to see everyone and to be able to relax around them finally. He always felt uncomfortable in the hospital. I can sense he feels better in his own surroundings. Now that he's home, he'll manage to get around easily enough as the hospital has provided him with a wheelchair.

Another four weeks pass, and Jack has worked extremely hard at getting himself back in shape. The wedding is one week away, and he's determined to be up and about for that. It's Friday evening, and I've just arrived home from work to find him lounging on the couch, looking very pleased with himself.

"Hi, babe, did you have a good day?" he says with a massive grin spread across his face. "I've something to show you. You know while you were out and about a lot the last few weeks?"

"Yeah," I say.

"I've been practicing getting back on my feet properly. Watch this."

He's lifting himself up from the couch and straightening his back. He looks great. He's walking across the room with a tall, proud stride.

"How did you manage that? You were practically limping yesterday!"

"No, I wasn't. I was pretending. I knew you'd like to have me in good shape for next week, so I've spent plenty of time strengthening my legs for the big wedding."

"Jack! That's amazing!" I exclaim. "I'm so proud of you. Well done."

"Doctors told me I've made excellent progress and that I should be very proud of myself. However, they told me I may need to take a wheelchair to the wedding as I may not handle the pace for too long."

"That's fine. I was expecting you'd need to, anyway. How do you think you're managing with stairs?"

"Good. I walked up and down the building stairs for the last three days. It's great. In fact, Aly, I'd love to go for a walk. I really need fresh air. When they collected me to take me for physio the other day, they informed me then that I should practice on the stairs. I wanted to surprise you."

I rush across the room to kiss him.

"Jack Morgan, you're the best. If you want to go for a walk, let's do it."

"How about we go for dinner?" he suggests. "We can take the chair if you're worried I can't go too far."

"OK, sounds like a plan. Are you sure? I don't want you regretting saying that when we get as far as the restaurant."

"It's only around the corner. Sure, let's do it, Aly. It's been so long, and while I know it's local, we should get dressed up."

"Good call. It's been a while since I got myself dolled up for a night out," I say with a smile.

I watch him stroll to the bedroom. He looks in great form, and I can see he's getting his humorous spirit back again. I'm trying to figure out what to wear when I come across my red dress, the one I wore on our first date, and I think it's appropriate for the occasion. I haven't worn it since then, and it still looks beautiful. I pin my hair up and put a little make-up on. I haven't felt so glamorous in months. It's a nice feeling.

"Wow! You know I love that dress on you. Very appropriate; it's like our first date again."

"I know. I saw it peeping out from the rail and thought it was a sign that I should wear it."

"You look beautiful, Aly."

He holds the door open for me and is holding my gaze as I look at him. It takes time for him to get down all of the stairs, but that's to be expected. When we reach the door, he feels very pleased with himself and breathes in a deep breath when I open it.

"Maybe you should take it easy now, and I'll push you around the block. What do you think?"

"As the lady wishes."

He sits in the chair, and I push him at a slow pace around the block to the restaurant. It's lovely to have a night out together again. We chat and sip a nice bottle of wine followed by a glass of champagne to celebrate Jack's ability to walk again. I'm glad I brought the chair, as one of us will definitely need it after the alcohol consumption.

When we leave the restaurant, Jack wants to "go for a spin around the block."

"Let's go past your old apartment on our way home and see how it looks without scaffolding," he suggests. "Would you like us to move back there? Maybe there's a bigger one available."

"Hmmm, I don't know. I hadn't really thought about it. Let's go see, anyway."

As I push the chair onto Charles Street, it's lovely to see that all the scaffolding has finally been removed, and the building looks immaculate. I can see into my old apartment, and it looks newly painted. I gaze up at the steps and remember our first date and that first kiss. I turn to look at Jack. He has a goofy-looking grin on his face, and I can only assume he's thinking the same.

"Let's go up the steps and enjoy that moment again, Aly."

He removes himself from the chair and takes my hand. He leads me to the top of the steps, albeit slowly, and holds me tight. We start to dance. I giggle as he bursts into song.

"Jack! OK, I don't mind the whole renewing of the kiss side of it, but 'Lady in Red' again?"

"OK, I'll stop, but only if you say yes."

"Say yes to what?"

I spot Mr. DeAngelo peeking out of his door and grinning, rubbing his hands together. I smile at him, wave, and turn my attention back to Jack.

I gaze at Jack as he bends down on one knee. He wobbles slightly, and I really want him to get up because if he falls, we'll be back to square one.

"Aly Hughes, I, Jack Morgan, love you with all my heart and with every achy bone in my body. Will you marry me?"

I look at him in shock for a moment and finally find words.

"Oh, my God, Jack! I wasn't expecting that. Oh, yes, Jack, yes, I'll marry you, most definitely!"

I can't believe it. It's the most romantic moment of my life. I have my gorgeous man nearly back to full health, and each day I spend with him makes me love him more.

It's the perfect ending to our night. There's one thing I am certain of: I'm glad I found my new life in New York and above all my future husband, Jack Morgan, my star…

The End

Elaine Cremin is a native of Cork, Ireland. She's lived in London for the past eleven years, and it would be her dream to follow her fictional heroine, Aly Hughes, to the Big Apple. She makes a living as a PA, but for the past four years she's been honing her craft as a writer. She plans to write more novels and eventually tackle a screenplay. *Waiting for a Star to Fall* is her debut novel.

Connect with Elaine at
www.facebook.com/pages/Elaine-Cremin or
www.twitter.com/ElaineCremin

CPSIA information can be obtained at www.ICGtesting.com
Printed in the USA
LVOW07s1605181115

463168LV00019B/1467/P